Doc

Claire Post studied English Literature at the University of Dundee. She holds a Phd in Literature. Her research subject was the medieval Franco-Italian writer, Christine de Pizan. She is currently News Editor for *Jane Austen's Regency World* magazine. *Doctor Abbot* is her first novel. Claire lives in Edinburgh.

clairepost.com

Cover Art: Laboratory Still Life 01

Don Shank is an artist currently working at Pixar Animation Studios. He has done design and art direction for TV and feature animation including *Up*, *Inside Out*, *Finding Dory* & *The Incredibles*. Don lives in California with his beautiful wife and daughters, and a funny dog.

DonShank.com

Doctor Abbot

CLAIRE POST

After The Light Press

First Edition 2018

Copyright © Claire Post
2018

Claire Post asserts the moral right to be identified as the author of this work

A catalogue record for this book is available from the British Library

ISBN: 978-1-9999495-0-1

This novel is entirely a work of fiction. The names, characters and
incidents portrayed in it are the work of the author's imagination.
With obvious exceptions, any resemblance to actual persons,
living or dead, events or localities is entirely coincidental.

Typeset in Andrade

Printed and bound in Great Britain by Clays Ltd, Elcograf S.p.A.

All rights reserved. No part of this publication may be reproduced,
stored in a retrieval system, or transmitted, in any form or by
any means, electronic, mechanical, photocopying, recording or
otherwise, without the prior permission of the publisher.

For IH. And for J and A – my brilliant boys.

Acknowledgements

Thank you to all those who have helped me on my journey towards publication.

My husband, Ien Hien, and my sister, Rachel, were the first to read *Doctor Abbot*. Happily they enjoyed it!

I am grateful to Don Shank for generously allowing me to use his painting, *Laboratory Still Life 01*, for my cover. His trust, from the outset, meant a lot.

Lauren Harms, my designer, was always patient and attentive. She helped me turn a fantastic painting into a wonderful front cover.

Many thanks to my super editor, Rachel Small. Her attention to detail and kind words were always much appreciated.

Raina Schnider's proofreading was just as it should be - helpful, thorough and precise.

My typesetter, Andrew Tennant, was ever-ready to expertly guide me through the final stages of production.

The last words are for my sons. Yes, Mummy's book is finally out there now.

But unto us she hath a spell beyond
Her name in story . . .

(Lord Byron, *Childe Harold's Pilgrimage*: Canto IV)

1.

The Scientist

Presently she would kill herself. The predictable effects left by a suicide littered the bed. Letters mostly. There was one for her brother, another for her parents, and one for Adam, the man she had loved and lost. Methodical and organised, there were also legal documents such as her will, and instructions or requests, whatever you like, for her funeral.

One final check on the dosage of her medicine, a quick tightening of the tubes and wires attached to the Renaissance machine (her own invention, though, quite stupidly, she recalled, not yet patented); the electrodes were smeared with lotion and fixed to her temples. She was almost ready. The dial on the machine was set for thirty minutes and the default needles were positioned to inject life-giving fluid into her veins and, effectively, switch her back on if the machine failed to do its bit. Was the coolant mechanism that would help delay the onset of muscle stiffening charged and ready? Yes, it was.

She sat back in her chair and thought again about her reasons for doing this. As a scientist, she understood it was not a question of why but when. This was her work's purpose, and if she was correct, as she believed with her whole being that she was, then she had made a discovery of the most momentous significance. If she was wrong, and she really died, well, science would still be the winner because she knew she was on the right track, and all of her notes and instructions on using the machine were neatly filed and available by her bed. Science could still make use of her research even if she was gone. Either way, this would surely be the making of her name. If *she* didn't do this, then others would doubtless make her discovery and use it themselves, and they'd use it to help answer the most fundamental questions concerning human existence. This was, she reasoned for the hundredth time, her shot at, well, an immortality of sorts, why should she deny herself this? Indeed, perhaps she had no right to *not* do what she was about to. Every year people were brought back from the brink of annihilation through medical progress and science. How many more people could soon be given a second chance at life?

New knowledge, through her, was now in humanity's care. And she firmly believed that knowledge, rather like the bacteria with which she was working in her humdrum job at the laboratory, must multiply and be given the opportunity to evolve. After all, one could only learn from and counter the bacteria if one fully understood it.

Well, she had no intention of properly dying—just for thirty minutes. In those moments, she hoped to confront what no other human being had ever faced for such a protracted period of time, and importantly, returned from: death.

Adam was gone. She could afford to take chances with her own destiny since it no longer personally affected anyone else's. Should she even bother leaving a letter for him? She lifted the letter and thought about putting it into her shredding machine. But, no, he had been part of her life for too long. He deserved a final goodbye and an explanation. She placed it back into the pretty lacquered box with the chinoiserie top that her grandmother had bequeathed to her when she died, seven years ago. Two intertwined letters were engraved in the top-right corner: G and A. With her finger she traced the A, and a sudden image of Adam tore at her heart; young and fresh, her hero and idol, as well as all her hope. But that was a long time ago now and he had failed her badly and was gone. The box had not been engraved for her and Adam but for her grandparents, Grace and Alexander.

Gracie was named after her grandmother who had always been Grace while Gracie had always been Gracie. She'd never really questioned why she had to forever be known by the bastardised, rather childish form of her own name just because the full version had belonged to her grandmother. Now, however, at this of all moments, she did just that.

Couldn't we both have been Grace? she thought. *One makes all sorts of assumptions about people before meeting them, often based entirely on their names.*

Didn't Grace and Gracie conjure up completely different images? Grace was a grown-up's name, classic and complete. The name Gracie, like many diminutive names, gave the idea of being unfinished; it suggested youth and fun. The owner of such a name was an extrovert whose personality could not be contained within the confines of its more sedate form. It sprawled out; it gained another letter, not being satisfied with its lot. Its bearer was impulsive, naughty even, a breaker of convention.

The name did not suit her.

This was very clear, she ruminated, as she punched into her machine the number of electrical volts necessary to activate her heart. How unfair it was that so many associations should follow her simply by her parents' decision to name her after her grandmother.

God, it's so important to name a child correctly! So many judgements ride on a name that you had better hope that your child and those judgements will agree. Or maybe they just grow to fit in some cases. Anyway, Gracie realised for the first time ever just how much she detested her name and all its girlish qualities. She should have been Grace—how much might have been different if she had been allowed this? Or if she'd the foresight and courage to just assume her right to it? Would she be sitting here now, in this contraption? Oh, it was all so complicated. But if she ever had children, a possibility that seemed distinctly remote, she would be sure to name them for themselves, whatever that might mean.

Every name has a literal meaning and a thousand previous bearers and connotations, she thought. *Maybe the trick is to never name someone after a family member.*

Gracie struggled to make sense of this concept as she stirred some sedative into a tumbler of water. *In a family, two individuals who have the same first name are, in many ways, identified together, as if a special bond exists between them, as if one is an extension of the other.*

Of course, she mused, good things could emanate from this, such as a sense of belonging and history. But bad things could too. If you felt that you compared unfavourably with your elder namesake, as Gracie most certainly did, then feelings of low self-esteem and shame could also result. Gracie knew she wasn't the sort of person who should be carrying her grandmother's name onward.

Her grandmother was famous—oh yes, the most famous actress of her generation. She'd received every award and plaudit there was to be won. She was legendary and adored and idolised and would certainly be remembered forever. Gracie was well aware of how many people still loved her dead grandmother with a passion that perhaps bordered on the pathological. She often put her own name into the search engine of her computer and all kinds of tributes to her grandmother's beauty and talent would appear on the screen as soon as she hit Enter. She would examine the fine contours of Grace's spectacular face and strain to recognise some sign that they were related. Why should she expect to look like her grandmother, given that she, Gracie Abbot, possessed all sorts of other genetic material that had no origin in the stock of Grace Abbot? Gracie didn't think this would bother her in the same way if she hadn't been the one to share the "special bond".

Her cousin Johanna was the one who deserved to be named after their grandmother. Johanna was an aspiring actress and really quite good. She would have been, in every way, the successful inheritor of all the glamour attached to the name. Gracie had the double misfortune of not only failing to live up to other people's ideas of her name, but also of being, so she felt, a plain face in a family which contained the incomparable Grace, recently named one of the most beautiful women of all time. And she'd accepted all of this for years, and despite the ramblings of her mind now, it had never bothered her before.

At least she'd never thought that it did.

What was wrong with her? Why go over such old rot now when she had so many other things to think about? And why couldn't she shake this damn feeling that someone was in the room with her, watching her, waiting, even?

Am I becoming hysterical?

Her pulse was racing and her palms were sweating. She was hot.

Would love a glass of water. Well, too bad, can't have one, must have an empty stomach. Am I getting ill?

If she was, she couldn't safely carry out the procedure and would have to postpone until another day.

Better take my temperature. A little under 37 degrees, fine. Gracie put it down to nervous energy and kicked her shoes off.

Any metal on me? No.

She looked at the clock before her. It was 2:20 pm. The time was deliberate. Gracie was an afternoon person and all of her best ideas came to her during these hours. She licked her lips, picked up the polystyrene cup that contained her first mixture, and drank. There was no going back now. 2:21 pm. Panic set in.

Do I need to use the toilet? Should I ring someone and let them know what I'm doing? Should I ring the police, the hospital, a madhouse? Calm down, Gracie . . . Grace. Lean forward and start the process. That's right, push the button, sit back and relax. It's in God's control now.

Why did she just think that? She didn't believe in God and this was no time to start. Or perhaps it was? Perhaps there was no better time to start believing in Him because she was in His hands now. Who was she to think that she could control her life to the extent where she could pause it for half an hour? Would God be furious with her for being so impudent? Should she say a prayer, just in case? No time to worry about that now—maybe there was no God, no nothing. Then *why* was she doing this? 2:23 pm.

Relax, relax, take it easy and fix the wiring to your chest. That's it, nice and gently.

Gracie often spoke soothingly to herself in this manner when she was feeling anxious and she was now, her hands shook uncontrollably, at fever pitch. 2:25 pm.

Take the second mixture quickly, close your eyes, slide your arms into the restraints, let yourself slip away.

The drugs would take some minutes to reach full effect. In the meantime, her body would just shut down, bit by bit. As far as she'd been able to judge, there wouldn't be any pain involved in this process, just the desire to go to sleep. She opened her eyes for what might be the last time and saw that it was 2:28 pm. Life was ebbing away from her; she could feel it. Her limbs felt so heavy, and she was having trouble keeping her head upright. Her legs and arms were secured to her chair so that the default injections wouldn't miss their targets if they were needed. The strapping was uncomfortable and the cord felt as though it were eating through her flesh. She wanted nothing more than to break free and escape, to no longer be bound to this weary body and this hurtful world. Now she sounded as though she wanted to die. She didn't, of course, but she was so tired.

Her eyes caught a snapshot of Adam on her pinboard. It had been taken on his birthday a few years ago. They'd still been together then. *Oh Adam, why did you let it come to this, to me sitting here dying in a room alone? I loved you so . . . Mustn't cry; relax.*

Was someone in this room with her? No, of course not. She looked around at her walls and fixed her gaze on a movie poster promoting one of her grandmother's classic films, a period drama, and then closed her eyes.

It was definitely working. Her mind started racing once more and she let it. She thought of her grandmother and how some of the completist-fan tributes on the Internet contained information on the star's family. Such sites had frequently hurt her. Shocked and disturbed, Gracie had read information about her father, who was Grace's eldest son, about her aunts and uncles, and even about herself sometimes. Family photos would also appear on the screen, like the one where her father was proudly placing a Union Jack flag atop a sandcastle on a California beach. Her grandmother's face had shone out of dozens of images taken with her family. There were photos of Gracie on some of these sites, such as the one showing the night she attended a benefit her grandmother had hosted. Gracie looked shy and stunned in that photo, sixteen and clinging to her brother's arm. That photo haunted her. She almost felt she had never . . . could never move beyond it. Perhaps she'd been trying to counter the unworthiness she'd felt that night every day since. Had it brought her here? If she'd felt better about herself, would Adam really have had the power to hurt her so?

Her heart, it had almost stopped beating, and she felt calmer. *Can one's heart ache if it no longer beats?*

Was it the desire to stop the pain caused by Adam that had brought her here? Her mouth was so dry but it didn't matter.

She thought again about the websites. Gracie had once been described by a fat housewife from Oklahoma, who claimed to be Grace's number one fan, as plain yet highly intelligent—a scientist who took after Alexander, Grace's second husband.

How dare that fat housewife . . .

My God, what's happening?
My head . . . my body . . .

If Gracie had been able to, she would have recorded her time of death as being 2:33 pm, on Saturday, 21st May, 2005.

2.

Death

Gracie was still somewhere. She could feel that. She hadn't ceased to exist and she was capable of thought. She opened her eyes and saw that she was in total darkness, but her bedroom never got as dark as this.

Mustn't panic, must stay calm and rational and think this through.

Now, what had happened? Was she dead? Was she hallucinating? Was this cold darkness that enveloped her the result of serious illness? Had she already died and woken up?

First things first. My body, how does it feel?

The only word to describe how Gracie felt when she realised that her body no longer seemed to be there was *wretched*. She had assumed that she was still sitting down but when she tried to move her feet, clench her hands, she could not. They simply were no longer there. What was she then? Was she thoughts ... or a head floating in the air? She couldn't tell, of course, whether she even had a head because she had no hands to touch it. She gasped aloud at the thought. What living human had ever had to think such a thing?

She was truly dead.

Where was God then? Where were the other dead people? Why all this darkness? Where was the white light? Was she in

Hell? Did she have to stay like this forever, with so many questions unanswered? Would she remain a lone voice crying in the dark?

Gracie opened her mouth, stuck out her tongue and forced it down to touch her chin. At least, it felt as if she were doing this. She was aware that she might be only imagining what it would feel like to have a mouth and to stick out her tongue. And she quickly, and sickeningly, realised that this was indeed what she had been doing.

I have no mouth, no tongue, no lips.

As soon as she thought this she became more aware of it than ever. But her thoughts and emotions remained because she was terrified and profoundly lonely. She still had some sensory feeling because she would swear that she felt coldness around where her body should have been.

That could be my imagination too though.

She could also still create noise, and as she screamed, her voice sounded broken and desperate and weak—but it was her voice, wherever it was coming from. For some reason, she was also aware that her spirit was low and distressed. This strange thought disturbed her. Gracie had never really thought of herself in a three-tiered way before. She had her physical and mental aspects, of course, but she'd never devoted much time to any thoughts on her spirituality. Now the spiritual aspect seemed to be as real and important as the other two. The physical had vanished but she still seemed to have the full command of her mental resources. Yes, the spiritual, whatever it was exactly, seemed to be worth hanging onto.

How on earth was she going to get out of this? How long had she been "sitting" here? When would those injections or the

Renaissance rouse her from this nightmare? That's what this felt like—a bad dream. The mother of all bad dreams.

She was dead, doubtless, and really, she should try to make the most of these hallucinations and work out what they might mean. She was well aware of research that claimed that the brain, even after it shut down entirely, was still capable of some sort of neural activity for a limited time. This debate was complicated by many issues though, such as whether an individual was clinically or biologically dead. Gracie was no expert on the subject, but she had believed it was possible that even after her biological death, the billions of nerve cells in her brain could still effectively be stirred up and act rather like the way a blown electric bulb does—before it cools forever, it continues to be hot and capable of causing pain. Similarly, her brain, although dead, could perhaps still produce flashes of thought or memory that would decrease and stop eventually. This was the theory, but as with all matters concerning death, it wasn't proven. The limited number of people who had died for brief spells and reported mind activity could simply be recalling dreams that had occurred when they were still alive.

When Gracie woke up she knew she would discover whether there had been any brain activity while she was dead. The wires fixed to her temples were attached to the part of the Renaissance that held the EEG and blood flow recorder, and their monitoring charts would reveal what had been going on during her death.

How did her mind feel now? Still sharp, remarkable. Gracie felt as lucid as she did when she was fully awake and alert. This was so much more than the white flashing lights and blurred images that neuroscientists believed the brain might be capable of after death. She still possessed full consciousness, but consciousness was, from moment to moment, directly caused by the brain. How could this degree of consciousness be possible when any doctor examining her, including herself, would have pronounced her dead? This knowledge and her memories of the autopsies she had attended as a medical student made her feel suddenly nauseous.

Please, please, I need to go back—I want to wake up now.

She knew that such pleading could have no effect. She was stuck with the half hour if she was to wake up at all. But still she cried out desperately, begging to be released from this awful *nothingness*. Any degree of pain or sorrow was preferable to this blind and useless fear.

While Gracie's eyes cried what she believed were pointless and imaginary tears, a different set of eyes scanned the space. And if Gracie had been able to see those eyes in the darkness, she might have longed to be as alone as she believed she was.

As her tears stopped and her sobbing became whimpers, she had a sudden sense that she wasn't alone. She froze and the pair of glowing eyes so close to her immediately sensed that she was at last aware of their existence.

'I'm really dead, aren't I?'

Gracie had spoken the words before she'd even realised she was about to. Still, she was shocked when she heard a cool, calm voice answer.

'Yes and no. You are a gifted scientist and your invention is capable of prevailing. You have now been dead for eleven minutes. You can awaken and be back in your bedroom soon, if you choose.'

Gracie was stunned yet unspeakably relieved to hear this.

'I am not the voice of your mind, Mistress Rational, nor am I attached to you physically in any way. Oh, I am also not God.'

'Who, who are you then?' Gracie whispered. 'Not the . . .'

'No, I am not the Devil. You need have no fear of me. You know well who I am. At least you begin to know my name. Think now.'

'Your name, I don't know, really, I don't . . .'

Gracie frantically tried to find an answer but was stupefied.

'Think. Think not as you usually do but as you must now. Clear your mind and focus upon only the question at hand. My name will come to you. You have always known it. Somewhere you always have.'

As quick as a lightning bolt Gracie realised that she was talking to Cianna. Before she could say the name aloud, the voice in the dark answered.

'Correct. Cianna is my name, and despite everything, I am perfectly happy with it. I do not have the feelings towards my name that you do towards yours.'

'You were there? Just before I died?'

'I have always been there.'

'In my head? I was only thinking about my name.'

'I told you, Lady Scientist. I am not connected to you, but I feel you. I know exactly what you shall do, say and think. Though occasionally you surprise me.'

'Are you dead too then? Are you a spirit or are . . . are you my guardian . . .'

'Angel? No. I am not an angel.'

'What are you then? Are you alone or were you with others when you were with me?'

'I was alone.'

'Please. Please, maybe I'm too stupid to come up with the right questions, but you have to tell me what you are and what's going on. I beg you, please.'

'Certainly. The best way your mind can understand what I am is if I tell you that I am not of your order. I am rather like the elements. They are me and I am them. You may also say that I have abilities that you would term "godly". I believe that I have some part of me that is human, although others have disagreed with this. It all seems rather irrelevant now. However, I say it because I think it might be of comfort to you.'

'Thank you,' said Gracie lamely. She felt strangely calm. And very young.

'Listen to me, Gracie. I am not about to tell you everything that I could. You would not understand even if I did. It would take you years of experience to even begin to appreciate what I know. You just have to take my word for that. I know you will find it difficult because the human mind, not least yours, is adapted to be always looking for concise and rational answers. You want to know everything now and if you cannot then you want to invent ways that will speed up the process. I will also hold back information from you if you are going to return to your world. Are you going to return, Gracie?'

'I, well, yes, I shall. I don't want to be dead. Are you suggesting that there is another alternative?'

'Perhaps. Do you want your body back?'

'My body? Can you do that? Do you mean now or when I'm alive again?'

'Now, while we talk. You would perhaps find it less distressing if things were more familiar.'

Gracie was beyond thinking about things being familiar, but in a flash, light flooded in. Rather than just surrounding her, this light felt as if it were a part of her. It seemed drawn to where her body should have been. In seconds, Gracie felt the light flowing out of her, and her body was back. It was so unspeakably good to possess it once more that she cried out with excitement and gratitude. Her surroundings remained lit. She was sitting on a wooden chair in a room that was not unlike her own bedroom but larger and grander in scale and design. In fact, it was just the sort of bedroom she would like to have if space and time were in ready supply. She was wearing her own clothes, even her own old slippers, and there was a window in the corner that seemed to look out over her own street. And wasn't that the sound of the neighbourhood children playing on the lawn?

Yet for all the familiarity, this was not her room, and it was disconcerting to be confronted with what she knew so well while facing the absolute unknown. Her senses seemed more alive than ever, and she was sure she could smell violets, her favourite scent. Cianna really had done her best to make her feel relaxed and comfortable. Cianna. Now how did she know—

'Yes, how do you think you knew my name?'

'I really have no idea,' said Gracie. 'I swear I've never heard of you before. I don't think I've even been aware of your name; it's so unusual.'

Gracie leaned her head towards where Cianna's voice seemed to be coming from.

'Are you always invisible?'

'To you, yes. You know me because you, all humans, in fact, have many different capabilities of which you remain unaware. You use very little of your brain, although someone as intelligent as you spends her time designing ways to kill it! With death comes an awareness of some things that you have always had the potential to realise but do not. That is how you know my name now.'

'I see. And you've always been with me, at every moment of my life?'

'Every one.'

Gracie could feel her cheeks burning with shame. This being had been witness to every one of her moments. All of her private and ridiculous moments. Cianna evidently felt her discomfort.

'At such a moment as this, only a human could take the trouble to feel ashamed to have been seen singing at home alone, making love, bathing. I have also seen you cry many, many times. Especially recently.'

'Can I see you now?'

Gracie felt at such a disadvantage that she wanted to face this elemental force, person, whatever, no matter how scary or strange it might appear.

'Yes. Are you ready?'

'Okay. Where are you then?'

'I am right by the window.'

Gracie turned and saw a woman, an ordinary woman, standing and smiling at her. She was, like everything else recently, both familiar and unfamiliar at the same time. It was all very strange.

On looking more closely, Gracie saw she'd been foolish to think that the lady in the room with her was ordinary—she was far from that. The most beautiful women in her world, her own grandmother perhaps, were an overcast and dismal night in comparison to this woman, who was the exquisite array of stars and lights in one of Gracie's favourite paintings by Van Gogh. This woman simply glittered. Her hair was long and dark and luxuriant, and she was pale with deep and sparkling blue eyes. She was neither fat nor thin and wore a long dress of yellow material. Gracie couldn't draw her eyes away from Cianna. Looking at her felt like a blessing. Finally, Cianna spoke again.

'I have always been here, and I mean to help you. It has been painful to watch you over the last year. You have been so sad. Now, your thirty minutes will end soon, so we must think and talk fast. What would you think if I offered you an alternative to your two present options of either death or returning to your usual life? Are you interested or are you keen to continue as the scientist Gracie Abbot?'

Gasping, Gracie pushed her hands against either side of her head.

'But I *am* Gracie Abbot. I can't be anyone else. Do you mean something like reincarnation? I really don't think I want to be born again and go through, well, go through the whole business of life again. I mean, getting to this point again. I just couldn't! I found it difficult enough the first time. Anyway, I've invented this machine, the Renaissance. I suppose I don't need to explain it to you. I have to go back and let other people use it. Give them another chance at life.'

'Very strange. You are tired and jaded at the thought of life yourself, yet you talk now of "letting" other people have a chance at life. Do you think they will always thank you for that?'

Gracie bit her lip. She felt challenged by Cianna's last question.

'Who are you? You say you have always been with me and you know all of my thoughts yet you are not connected to me and you are not God. Are you the voice of my conscience? When I wake up will you be remembered as nothing more than a dream?'

'I am not the voice of your conscience.'

'Why are you here then, making offers that I can't understand?'

'Forgive me. I can see that I shall have to explain some more things to you. Are you ready, Gracie?'

'Yes. I think.'

'Then let me begin.'

3.

Cianna

Gracie smoothed down the material of her skirt and sat alert and ready.

'Before I begin,' said Cianna, 'you should be aware that your thirty minutes will end in the next few moments. You will need to be without life for longer.'

'I suppose you can do that, can you?' asked Gracie. 'My machine is only capable of resuscitation within thirty minutes of death. That's its limit at present. Will I be okay when I wake up?'

'Gracie, you will be fine. I can take care of that matter easily.'

Cianna moved away from the window and came to sit in a floral armchair in front of Gracie. The chintz design looked entirely inappropriate for her. And Gracie was sure it hadn't been there before.

'Precisely now. Your thirty minutes are over. Finished. I am very aware of time, you see.'

Cianna gazed directly at Gracie, as though asking how she felt about this news.

'I feel no different,' Gracie said. 'Just scared, anxious. There are so many things I want to know but I don't know where to begin. I'm afraid that you're only going to allow me a certain number of questions so I want to be sure that I'm asking the right ones.'

'Let simplicity be your guide then. Here, you are shivering.'

Cianna quickly rose and went towards the bed, where she picked up a brightly patterned quilted duvet. She returned and dropped the heavy blanket over Gracie's body, ensuring her shoulders were well covered. It felt nice to be looked after in this way, and Gracie looked up to smile her gratitude. Cianna looked suddenly embarrassed and awkwardly stumbled back towards her seat. Gracie didn't quite know what to make of this behaviour and put Cianna's discomposure down to the possibility that she was unused to doing things like that for people. But it had felt nice to be mothered by Cianna . . . and now she could easily drift off to sleep . . .

'Gracie, let us talk now.'

The stern voice snapped Gracie back to full alertness. Cianna had gathered herself and was as cool and intimidating as before.

'Sorry,' Gracie stammered. 'Okay, firstly I want to know where I am. Also, am I dead or alive right now?'

'I shall answer your second question first. You are neither dead nor alive. It is rare for a human to occupy this position, but you are not the first to do so and will doubtless not be the last. You are, in a sense, at a crossroads between life and death. You certainly could not remain indefinitely in this state, but you will be fine for the present. Now, as to where you are, let me say that you are in what was an empty space. I have appropriated this space for us and filled it with things intended to make you feel comfortable. Does that make sense to you?'

'I, well, yes I suppose so, but what do you mean by "space" exactly?'

'Just that. Space. It was empty and now it is filled. Is that not enough for you to know?'

'No, not really, to be honest.'

Gracie faced Cianna squarely and prepared herself for her disdain. Even in such a short spell of acquaintanceship, she could tell Cianna was trying to disguise her impatience.

'There is infinite space. I can command this small amount for us. Do you see?'

Gracie nodded and waited for Cianna to continue. But she didn't. Now Gracie was the one struggling to contain her impatience.

'I sense this isn't going to be a no-holds-barred discussion. You're obviously not about to reveal all about the universe and its creation. I can see that.'

'No. I shall only tell you what you need to know and a little more besides. We require purpose. I could spend an unspecified time discussing issues relating to one question from you. Each new sentence I uttered on the subject would elicit a thousand new questions from your lips.'

'I'm hardly stupid—'

'Yes, you are,' said Cianna flatly. 'The questions which you will ask, you see, which you believe are the most complex, are to do with what is most simple to me. It would take an age to make you see things as clearly as I do. Frankly, I doubt it could be done.'

Stung, Gracie looked down at her feet.

'Thanks very much for your confidence in me.'

'I have confidence in you, or to put it more accurately, I have confidence in what will be. You must also remember that because you have not yet died in the true sense, you have no right to be given a full explanation of anything. That, or anything like it, can only be attained following absolute death. This law can never be trifled with, even by one as arrogant and demanding as Gracie Abbot.'

Gracie raised her gaze from her slippers at this, and was met by an amused expression. Why, Cianna was laughing at her!

'Yes, you're perfectly right, I am arrogant. It's gotten me into all kinds of trouble over the years.'

'I'm quite aware of that. Rest assured, my way is best. Let us not be combative. Discussion is so much more preferable to interrogation. We can learn a great deal from each other. Yes, that is true. I greatly enjoy talking to you. I have been your silent observer for so long that it feels quite strange to now be actively participating in your life. But learning from you is part of my purpose. Now, I have just been very honest with you in so openly declaring my feelings. Do we share friendship?'

'Yes,' Gracie said. 'We do.'

'Good. Now I have a question to ask you.'

Cianna leaned forward and smoothed the silk of her dress.

'Why did you do what you did? Why did you kill yourself?'

'Well, I'm a scientist and I felt it was my duty to—'

'Yes, I know all of those reasons. I want you to talk more about the other ones.'

Gracie knew that there was little point in trying to be anything other than absolutely honest.

'I thought that until Adam . . .'

Gracie sighed deeply. It was never easy talking about him.

'Until he did what he did,' she continued, 'I thought that I was happy. Yes, really quite happy. Looking back now, I can see that I've been miserable for years. All this stuff went through my head while I was getting the Renaissance ready—stuff about my family, my name. I realised that I've always been insecure. I think that's why Adam left me reeling so much. He knew how much potential he had to hurt me and yet he still chose that path. He never loved me, that's clear.'

'Do you believe that?'

Strange. Cianna seemed to really want to know the answer to this.

'I suppose he did, but not the way I loved him.'

'Ah, yes,' said Cianna slowly. 'I understand. And your family?'

Gracie winced on being asked about her family.

'To be truthful, they're not much good either. Except for Kenneth. He's the best brother—you know how dear he is. My parents though each make it clear that I've been a terrible disappointment to them. My father has issues he's never sorted out to do with his crazy childhood, and my mother, she's just so dried up and bitter. I can't remember her being any different. The way we're talking now, really talking, I've never had a conversation like this with either of them. There's too much baggage. I mean, they carry too much baggage.'

'Does not everyone?'

'Yes, I suppose, but they've given their baggage to me.'

'Is that not usually the case?'

'Cianna, if you are trying to make me think that my parents aren't so bad, it's never going to work. I have no sympathy for them.'

'No, I agree with you. They are dreadful parents.'

Gracie wondered whether Cianna was trying to be facetious, or ironic. But her opinions were always given so drily and matter-of-factly, indeed she was blunt to the point of rudeness, that it seemed clear that she was simply offering her honest opinion.

'It's odd that you agree with me then. Anytime I've opened up to anyone about my family, I get a lecture on how I should make the most of them while they're here, on how I'm ungrateful, oh, and on how I'm so lucky to belong to the Abbot family. People really do believe that you should love your family no matter what. Do you think that one should?'

'No. True love can only come with respect, and parents have to earn the respect of their children if they wish to be loved.'

Gracie brightened.

'That makes perfect sense, but most people seem to think that there's some sort of biological, I don't know, *something* within us that dictates we must have some feeling for our parents, however irrational or undeserved that love might be.'

'Well, do you concur with that, Gracie?'

'I don't know. I just don't know. If I suddenly had new and better parents would I feel more for them than I do for my natural parents? I wonder. It would certainly make sense if I did.'

'Yes, it would.'

Gracie suddenly realised that she'd spent some of her precious time with Cianna talking about her family and being asked questions!

'Yes,' Cianna said in response to her thought, 'we are supposed to be making sense of things.'

'What can you tell me about who you are?'

Gracie pushed on herself before Cianna had the opportunity to ask anything else.

'I can tell you that it is my task to prepare you for whatever it is you decide to do.'

'And are you dead or alive?'

'Alive.'

Amidst all of the strange things that she had encountered of late, Gracie was still relieved to discover that Cianna was alive.

'But in a way that I have always been. It is different from your alive,' Cianna added.

'And you've always been with me?'

'Yes.'

'Have you ever thought that I was picking up on your being there?'

'Yes. Several times.'

Gracie nodded. 'I think I remember some of those times. Once, when I was at primary school, I was standing in the playground quite alone and sad because nobody wanted to play with me. I was very young, about six, but I remember the feeling of shame very clearly. Anyway, a girl, Linda something, I can't remember her name—'

'Walker.'

'That's it, exactly. Well, she was shouting things at me and I cried, and when I was alone again I wished so hard inside me for a friend. I felt that someone touched my cheek then. I've never forgotten that moment. It made me feel much better. I went and ran after Linda whatsherface and gave her a good thumping. You did touch my cheek then? Someone really was there?'

'I was.'

Gracie smiled at Cianna with affection, and Cianna returned the smile.

'Does everyone have someone like you watching out for them, waiting until they die?'

'Certainly not. There are not many like me.'

'Why are you with me then? Are you suggesting that I'm special?'

'What you have done could be described as special. It was known that you would reach this point, and I was here to see you to it.'

'It was preordained then? That sounds like we have no free will.'

'Lack of free will is the opposite of what you have. Humans have absolute free will, but an order higher than you knows everything that will happen. Each individual will play her part and exercise her free will and each one of you, no matter how modest the life, shall leave an imprint of her existence on the world.'

'Okay, so where do people like you fit into this? What do you bring to the world?'

'Balance.'

Gracie sat quietly for a moment and tried to puzzle through all of what Cianna had just related to her. Balance. What did she mean by that exactly?

'Cianna, before we talk anymore about me, tell me about yourself. So far, I understand that you are not connected to me but you know my mind and what I will do. You are not God, or the Devil or an angel. Yet you've always been with me. I'm going to break the habit of a lifetime now and stop asking questions. Please, just talk. You know everything about me, and if we're really friends, I want to know something of you.'

Cianna spoke quietly. 'For almost the first time in a very long life, I find myself at a loss for words. Few have ever wanted to know anything about me. Their questions are usually related to figuring out their own place in the universe. Everything is really about them. I can always see that.'

She smiled wryly before continuing. 'I am old, Gracie, very old indeed. Yes, I know I look young and beautiful, but I am old. I have always looked like this. I, my people, many peoples actually, share your image. We are beautiful and supremely intelligent. No order even approaches us with regard to the gifts with which we have been endowed. We are truly peerless. I am a relatively young member of my people. Even the most aged of my order has no recollection of how our society originated. We no longer question our superiority but accept it and know our purpose. There are many names for my order. Some have called us the Benedetto, for others we are the Libero. We refer to ourselves as the Pondera, or, in older days, the Libramen. There have also been other names accorded to us, such as Perfectus, the Sine Sodalitas and the Solitario. I know you think carefully about the importance of names, and I think it would be effective if I used these various names to enlighten you about my kind.'

Gracie nodded encouragingly, wanting Cianna to continue.

'Firstly, I will talk to you about the names other people have given us. It is understandable why we are known to some as the Benedetto; the blessed. We have the unique power of immortality. Indeed we have many powers. We can be as light as air, burn with the hottest fire, ride the fiercest waves and be at home on the highest mountain or in the driest desert. We are the best of all things. We know everything; we are incomparably lovely. My people can manipulate that which humans would term an impossibility.

'We were created, as all things are. We have been around much longer than you humans and are the oldest surviving beings. We know that there is a force which controls and governs us all—yes, even my people—and we are in tune with it, but truly, the wonder of this is that even those as gifted as we do not fully understand this force. We do, however, know far more than your kind. We know that we can receive deeper understanding when we die, and many of us do eventually choose to die. That is our right. I choose to live. The thought of no longer being able to scale the heights of the stars and swim at the very bottom of the deepest lagoon fills me with unassailable sadness.

'In the beginning, we did just these things. We knew everything, so there was nothing to learn. There were never any surprises. No ups, no downs. We were all equally intelligent and equally beautiful. We often did not breed with our own kind because we did not feel anything special for other members of our group. We could not fall in love with one another. Many of us began to grow angry that we had been created in such a perfect state.'

Gracie saw in Cianna's face a look she had not seen before and it made her recoil. Cianna sensed this immediately and quickly continued.

'So we began travelling alone. We made discoveries and found an infinite variety of other people. Some chose to forsake immortality and live amongst these new beings, usually for reasons connected to love. Our way of life slowly started disappearing.

'One day I sat by a lake near my home thinking of our predicament when one of my countrymen came to tell me that he knew of a new civilisation—he had seen it. It was your world, Gracie, just in its infancy. I visited it myself and knew that it would eventually be as full of the variety and promise that we lacked. These qualities, you see, are greatly attractive to us. We gathered together, my people and I, and concluded that this new world, as well as some others, would be our destiny. You gave us purpose. It was clear that we could not live together as a society, for we could find no stimulation and no cause. That is our burden, and that is why we have been called the Solitario, the lonely, as well as the Sine Sodalitas—those without fellowship.

'Can you imagine being unable to find contentment, passion or interest in any of your own kind? When you are all flawless and complete—Perfectus, another of our names—it is very difficult to find real joy. And so we decided to use our skills to try to bring balance to the universe. We became the Libramen and then the Pondera, both words meaning "balance" and "equilibrium". Formerly we were a nameless people. We knew that the creative force, which I shall call the Origin, wanted us to do this. To it, we are the Libero. That word has many meanings, including "liberate", "raise" and "deliver". This pleases us greatly, but it is only for the Origin to call us by this name.

'We work in the following way: we sit alone and our next task is transmitted to us through our thoughts. It is as basic as that! This is what happened to me thirty-one years ago, when you were about to be born. I knew that I should be with you and that you would reach this point. I must give you the opportunity to choose your own destiny. I do not know what you shall do or where you shall go, and I do not know why it is of importance. And that is a delight to me. I do know, from experience, that there will come a time when it shall be revealed to both of us why you were given the opportunity to make this choice. So, my dear friend, that is my story. That is who I am.'

4.
The Glass Bell

There had been silence in the room for some moments. Gracie had avoided making eye contact with Cianna for most of the time that she had been talking. It felt disrespectful to gaze upon such latent pain. Cianna stood by the window again. There was darkness outside now and all was silent. Cianna stared out at the stars that shone in the clear night sky. Gracie was at a loss for what to do, or say, next. Finally, Cianna returned and sat down to face Gracie again.

'Why so sad, my friend? I have told you my story, and now you know that I take great pleasure in assisting you.'

Cianna's eyes were blazing and Gracie felt overwhelming respect for her.

'I am sad for many reasons. Firstly, I don't think that you intended to tell me so much of your life story. You did so because you knew I wanted to know about you primarily for reasons of friendship. Thank you for your trust in me. Before talking to you, I would have thought it an anomaly for anyone to be angry about being perfect. I realise my gross ignorance now, and I hope that I'm worthy of the time you've already invested in me. I'm also sad for you because I sense that you've withheld the part of your story which gives you most pain of all.'

Cianna took hold of Gracie's hands.

'You grow very wise, my friend. I think you shall be worthy of whatever it is you have to do. And now, we must proceed with haste. My dear, these are your choices: you may return to your old life, or you can begin an entirely new existence in either the future or the past. The decision is wholly yours, and if you speak from your instincts and your heart, your choice will be the correct one. You need have no fear there. In your position, you have the right to be given this opportunity.'

Gracie's eyebrows raised on hearing this, but Cianna's continued discourse halted her from speaking.

'Now, some essential points. You will remain in your own world; you are not permitted to divulge the information you now possess to anyone else; and you will be provided, should you decide upon a new life, with all the details necessary to ensure that you are both comfortable in and knowledgeable about your new home and surroundings, as well, of course, with the new people in your life. I can continue to speak but perhaps you desire to ask questions? Gracie, what will it be?'

Gracie's mind raced. Go forwards or backwards in time? Cianna's fantastic offer sat so much at odds with its cool delivery that Gracie felt an uncanny chill take hold of her. Yes, chill, that was the word. She tried and failed to speak and instead merely looked at Cianna, her mouth open, her hands clasped tightly between her knees. She could find nothing to say. Her brain started processing all it knew about wormholes and superstring theory and relativity . . .

'Dr Abbot, we have no need for any of that. Simplicity, as ever, is best. Time, both forwards and backwards, is not a straight and unalterable line. Try to think of it this way: we may be finished with the past, but the past is not finished with us.'

The weight of centuries and their possibilities strangled Gracie's voice to the extent that she could physically feel it. With supreme effort, she gained mastery of herself and stood. Stumbling, she made for the sink in the corner of the room and filled a beaker with cold water, which her dry throat thirstily received. Cianna watched her silently but offered no assistance.

Gracie smoothed her hair in front of the mirror that hung above the sink. A postcard of the Eiffel Tower, from Kenneth, was taped to one of its corners. She'd stuck an old payslip which showed an error in her wages to another corner so she wouldn't forget to query its contents. She'd forgotten anyway. An invitation to an engagement party, a university reunion letter and a cinema ticket also papered the mirror. To leave all of this behind? How gladly she could. There was so little to regret leaving. Even her dear Kenneth had his family, his own life; he'd be okay without her. Her face in the mirror looked resolved and strangely serene. It was almost as if she were gazing at someone else, that the old Gracie had already begun to fragment and disappear and an altogether new apparition faced her in the mirror. Could she accept this? Or would the loss of her physical identity be too difficult?

As ever, Cianna was in tune with her thoughts.

'Experience shapes and moulds us, on the outside as well as the inside, but past, present or future, you will essentially remain the same Gracie that you have always been. You can be given a different name, a different life, but you will still be the same person with the same face and body. I have no power to alter that.'

'I see. And if I do choose a new life, how will you get me out of my old one? Will I die, or will I disappear or . . .'

'My dear, it will be as if you never existed. Life will be as it would have been if you had never been born. Nobody will miss you because you will never have been there to be missed. Your brother, your parents, Adam: you will cease to exist for them. No sorrow, no pain, not for them at least.'

Strangely, Gracie had not foreseen this scenario. It had been too impossible, despite all of this unreality, to guess at how easily she could be erased. Cianna spoke as if it were the simplest thing in the world. What was it all for? Love. Her brother's love for her gone in the blink of an eye. Along with all the pain and sorrow that had eaten at her heart for so long now.

'Cianna, I want to begin again. I've no interest in the future. I want the past. Let me live an entirely new life. No, wait, am I able to return to my own real life if I hate where I end up? Or am I stuck there until I die?'

'A highly pertinent question. You will one day be given the chance to either return as Gracie Abbot and continue exactly where you were, or you will be able to continue your new life with absolutely no possibility of leaving it. I cannot tell when this moment of decision will arise. We will simply have to wait and see. If you leave your new life behind, you will be erased from that one too. It will be just as if you had never been there.'

'Will I be able to recognise this make-or-break moment that you speak of? Or will I be presented with my choice entirely out of the blue?'

Cianna smiled, and then almost laughed. 'My dear Gracie, that is also a shrewd question. But one I will not answer. Come, sit back down again and let me tell you more of what you need to know. Do you need anything? Another drink? No? Then come here.'

Gracie obediently returned to her seat, and Cianna explained that for her new family, friends and anybody else, it would be as if she had always been there. They would have a wealth of memories of Gracie and she would have all of these memories too. After all, it would all really have happened to her.

'So, let me get this straight,' Gracie interjected. 'I'm not returning as a baby with all of my new life before me? I'm going to, I don't know, be slotted into my new surroundings, and everyone's memories will be altered accordingly?'

'Forgive me, Gracie, I have misled you. You can certainly return as a child if you wish, and experience the whole of your new life. I made an assumption from my own knowledge of you. I thought you would wish to remain an adult. Please do not let my assumption influence you.'

'No, it's okay, you're right,' said Gracie. 'I really wouldn't want to go through babyhood and childhood again somewhere else. I feel I'd have no chance of holding on to what I am now, or what I know.'

'You are correct. If you choose to be a baby again, you will have no knowledge of your life now, or of me. I will have to tell you everything afresh.'

'And when my moment of decision came, I'd have no recollection of what I'd be returning to. With babyhood goes everything of Gracie Abbot today. I certainly have no wish to be so ignorant. So, the only way to keep my memories alive is to remain an adult?'

'True.'

'An adult I'll be then. But do I have to be quite so adult as I am now? I'd like to be a little younger.'

'You can be as young as sixteen or seventeen if you choose.'

Adolescence again, Gracie quickly thought. But to do justice to this experiment, she ought to be, within reason, young and fresh enough to appreciate all of the new experiences that awaited her. And, really, to be given the chance to be sixteen again, how delightful it would be!

Gracie ran a hand through her hair and sighed. She shook her head as though trying hard to clarify her stream of racing thoughts. Pursing her mouth, she drew in her breath and continued.

'So, will I look sixteen on the outside but still be a thirty-one-year-old on the inside?'

'The answer to that question is one that you will only fully understand, no matter how I explain things, once you are living your new life. You have to accept that the knowledge and opinions of Gracie Abbot will remain alongside the knowledge and opinions of your new self. Your brain can easily cope with that. You will never confuse what you can discuss with what you need to withhold. You must simply trust me when I say that these issues present no problems. So yes, you will feel sixteen, but you will still be aware of your other, older identity.'

'How strange this all is! I was just thinking about whether other people have been given the chance to lead these double lives. I've every reason to think that of course they have. Perhaps I've even met one of these people. And I never knew it! Please, Cianna, tell me, are there many people who've been given this opportunity?'

'No.'

'But there are others?'

'Of course.'

'It's so unfair, really. Should I feel guilty about the chance I'm being given? I feel as if I should. We're not operating on a level playing field.'

'But life is never, can never, be a level playing field, as you call it. Some people are cleverer, more attractive, richer and so forth. It is what you make of your portion that counts. It is silly to spend time feeling guilty or embarrassed about your advantages, whatever they might be. In any case, the more you have, the greater your responsibility. If you feel you have been given an unfair amount, let that be the extra charge you carry and in that way, your account is cleared.'

'Yes, Cianna, what you say makes sense. I will have a family, I suppose. Will I feel love for them, or must I pretend to so as to not arouse anyone's suspicions? Am I able to choose a really nice family?'

'You will be placed with a family that has been selected for you. That is all. You choose the time, the location and some other practicalities, as we have discussed, but other than that I have no idea what your family will be like. Gracie, I do not know whether you will be happier in your new life. As to whether you will love your family, that depends on you and them, does it not? There will be no automatic or unconditional love, if that is what you mean.'

'I see. Well, I hope my family will be good people then. I'd very much like to know what it feels like to respect my parents. But I cannot imagine that they will feel like my parents!'

'Perhaps you will be an orphan and all of these worries will be in vain. Now, do you know when and where you want to go? That is, after all, our main concern, yet you have given no time or thought to its discussion!'

'Cianna, what is it you do exactly when you're waiting to learn about your next task?'

'I told you that I sit and think and the information comes to me.'

'I'm going to do the same. Excuse me for a few minutes.'

Gracie closed her eyes and breathed deeply. She did the best she could to stop random things she sensed were unimportant from cluttering her thoughts and instead tried to focus upon anything that seemed to have deeper meaning. Her instincts had long been blunted and relegated to the sidelines in preference of common sense and duty. Nonetheless, within a few minutes, Gracie knew without a shadow of a doubt where she would be going.

'My friend, I am not very surprised by your choice. But I could not have guessed at it beforehand.'

'Then I will be content with surprising you even a very little. Oh, Cianna, is it the right decision? Do you think I am suited to that sort of life?'

'Enough. It has been decided upon. Time grows impatient to have you settled. Now, do you have a precise year in mind? Or shall we wait to see exactly where you begin?'

Gracie thought for a few seconds and knew that she did indeed have a year selected for her new birth. Cianna, unblinking and impassive as ever, was nonetheless clearly impressed by the swift and precise nature of Gracie's decision-making. She nodded her head briefly.

'That year? Why, Gracie? Oh, because of that person?'

'I want to be an exact contemporary, Cianna.'

'So, we now have a location and a birth year. And I know that you wish to be sixteen. We can soon depart.'

'Oh, Cianna, I'm terrified! But I'll be okay with you by my side. Your being there will give me strength.'

'Gracie, I will not be with you. You will be alone.'

A sickening pain tore Gracie's left side. Cianna would not be there with her? How would she cope?

'My little scientist, you are a puzzle to me! You did not know I was there with you for all these years but yet you coped. Now I am leaving, you feel you cannot function without me. Of course you can. There can be no further discussion. I shall not be with you.'

All the time Cianna had spoken, her steady gaze had made Gracie feel stronger and a little better. At some point, she had dropped to Cianna's feet, though she had no recollection of it, and Cianna had placed her head on her lap. She stroked Gracie's hair while continuing to speak.

'We will meet again, of course. I will come to you when your time to leave or stay beckons. And you can summon me at any time, you know. But only when you really need me. Here, I have something to give you. Raise your head a moment and look at this.'

Gracie, still on the floor, sat up and watched Cianna pull an object out of the folds of her dress. A little red box covered with silk.

Cianna handled the box as if it were rare crystal, covering its top and bottom with each of her hands. She seemed unsure and nervous—states of being that Gracie suspected were largely unusual for Cianna. Gracie watched intently as Cianna pulled out from the box a little glass object. Flushed with emotion, she placed the box carefully on the table behind her and held the glass object in her hands. For several moments Cianna simply gazed at the item. Finally, and with some reluctance, she handed it to Gracie.

'Here, take this. It is a bell, you see.'

Cianna passed the bell into Gracie's hand. The tinkling sound it produced reminded Gracie of water running from a stream or a fountain. It was beautiful. It also sounded strangely familiar.

'There is no sound in the world that could rouse me more forcibly! Ring the bell and I will come with the greatest possible speed. Keep it with you at all times and let nobody take it from you. Pretend that it is a little paperweight, or an ornament. I give it to you for as long as you need it.'

Gracie could tell that this was no small sacrifice for Cianna. Panic struck her. What if she broke or damaged it? It appeared incredibly delicate.

'Have no fear, Gracie. I have had the bell for a long time, and it has become such a part of me that indeed nobody could smash it. It has become an extension of me. It is immortal. Look.'

Cianna took the bell from Gracie and threw it to the ground. Gracie gasped and automatically covered her face with her hands, to protect it from the expected shards of glass. But, no, there were none. The bell remained perfect. Cianna bent and picked it up. Despite its unbrokenness, she checked it over, cradling it in her palm as if it were her own child. She held it to her lips and kissed it gently before she handed it back to Gracie. All the while, with every movement, the bell tinkled its pretty tune.

'I've heard that tune before,' said Gracie. 'I've fallen asleep to it many times. Always at the back of my mind, the limits of my hearing, but still, I've heard it. You've sat holding the bell while you've watched over me. Cianna, are you sure you want to be without it?'

Cianna's mouth took on the most peculiar shape, neither a smile nor a frown. She looked longingly at the bell, and Gracie was ready to give it back, expecting it would be gratefully received. Instead, Cianna handed her the silken box and said her mind was fixed upon Gracie's having it.

'To no one else would I give this precious thing, but you have touched my heart in a way that is strange to me. I want you to have it.'

Gracie did not know what to say. She decided to speak simply and honestly.

'Thank you, thank you, Cianna. I will protect it and keep it safe. I see what it means to you. It's also a very fine thing to know that we can still see each other sometimes.'

'Yes. Let me have the bell once more and then I want you to put it away. I am afraid I cannot be myself fully while it is in my sight.'

Cianna kissed and stroked the bell with a fervour and urgency that Gracie had never seen before. Then, with great effort, she placed it back into Gracie's hands. Seeing the tears that fell unchecked onto Cianna's smooth cheeks, Gracie hastily put the bell into its box and placed it out of view.

'You must find my behaviour very strange? I cherish and worship that bell you see, and I have never been parted from it since it became mine. It reminds me of both the sweetest and the most painful times of my long life.'

Gracie spoke quietly.

'I think that the sadness which I told you I felt for you earlier is connected to the bell. It is, Cianna, isn't it?'

'Yes. The memories I have . . . I recall its being given to me in perfect detail.'

Gracie could tell that Cianna longed to share her story. Was she so unaccustomed to expressing her feelings that she was shy to begin talking unbidden?

'Tell me about it. Tell me about the bell.'

'Sometimes I have no other task than to find my own pleasure in travelling and roaming the many worlds. I like to visit beautiful places and be amongst learned peoples. Your world has served me well for these things—and it did so especially long ago.'

Gracie placed her head back in Cianna's lap, thinking it might be easier for Cianna to tell her story if she wasn't looking at her.

'Several hundred years ago I was in Murano, which is near Venice. The first clear glass, called *cristallo*, was invented there, and I very much liked to watch the glassmakers and artisans go about their daily business. So much beauty and artistry in their creations. All the glassmakers of Venice had been banished to Murano many years previously—you know, due to the risk of fires.

'Now, the little place was an island of glass. A prison of glass, some might say, as the expertise of the Murano glassmakers was so considerable that they were unable to leave the island for fear of their secrets being discovered by rival glassmakers in other countries. To this most beautiful of fortresses I would sometimes journey. I used to walk about the square where the men worked, always with a dark cloak covering my face and body. I never wish to draw attention to myself. For many days, I found myself returning to one shop, one workspace in particular.

Here, the men seemed to produce the most extraordinarily beautiful objects. I would stand and gaze for as long as I thought it safe. I had little to fear though, for the men were so industrious that they paid me no mind. Besides, the square was always so busy that I attracted scant attention.

'My favourite shop employed four men. The owner was an old man who spent little time there, and he designated most of the responsibilities of its daily running to the youngest of the men. There was also a middle-aged man who was almost as skilled as the youngest. Lastly, there was the brother of the owner, and he was frequently drunk and quarrelsome. The young man was often out of patience with him but could do little against him, and the drunken man knew this. I was always happiest when he was absent from the shop and I could simply watch the men working without their having to stop for arguments or fear of their precious objects being carelessly broken. The young man was so strong that he could blow and manipulate the liquid into the most intricate shapes. I was always worried that the man, who I soon learned was named Antonio, although he was always called Nino, might hurt himself, but he never did.

'One day the drunken man stumbled in late, as usual. Nino had just hung a large mirror on the wall. It was to be collected by some fine visiting Venetian lady—something to adorn her home. Nino chided the drunken man and told him to mind what he was doing, for the mirror had taken a long time to mould and cool. He was met with ridicule, and a fight ensued. The other man who worked with Nino ran off to get assistance, so there was only Nino, the drunken man and I in the vicinity. The detestable creature then picked up a heavy candlestick and threw it, intending to either strike Nino or the glass mirror that had taken so much care and skill to create. Being so drunk, however, the man missed entirely and the candlestick flew towards me, positioned as I was several feet behind Nino. The man then fell on his back, unconscious, his violent efforts proving to be too much for one in his stupor.

'Instinctively I moved my head to one side to avoid being hit, although I knew well it could do me little harm. My quick movement made my hood fall back from my face, and Nino caught my reflection in the mirror. I will never forget his expression the first time he saw me. He moved towards me and our first look . . . to relive it again after all these years . . . Gracie, he was the most beautiful of your men. Tall and strong with thick wavy, no, curly brown hair. Time almost stopped for me. We simply gazed at one another for a few moments, and then . . .

'"*Signorina*, are you hurt or shaken? Please, forgive us. Take a seat."

'Nino took hold of my hand and pulled me into the warmth of his cluttered shop. I refused the seat that he offered and told him that I was unhurt and needed to go. I pulled my hood up over my face again, but he immediately took it down. He seemed surprised by his boldness.

'"*Signorina*, you are perhaps unhurt, but you are certainly shaken. See how you tremble? Can I fetch your husband?"

'"I have no husband."

'"Oh, well your father then?"

'"I assure you I am fine. I tend to myself."

'I turned to leave again and once more Nino stopped me. He pulled me towards him and reached into a basket on the floor. Then he placed an object in my hands. It felt so cool on the warmth of my skin.

'"It is a little bell which I finished making only yesterday. Listen to the noise it makes. Your voice reminded me of its sweet sound. You look like the kind of lady who ought to have her every request obeyed. I cannot imagine that anyone could refuse you anything if you rang this bell to demand it. Please accept this as a token of my sorrow that you had to witness such an ugly scene. It is lovely, is it not?"

'Before I could respond, some men ran into the shop and, at Nino's request, they dragged the sleeping drunk outside. Nino kept a tight hold of my arm the entire time he talked. The hold was hardly necessary though. I did not wish to leave.

'Once calm had again descended upon the shop, Nino told the good man with whom he worked to go off for his meal. The man did so, but shot many glances at me before he departed. Although I was aware of this, I confess that Nino and I had eyes for only one another.

'"Nino, I should leave you now. This cannot—"

'"Ah, you know my name! What is yours, my love?"

'"Cianna is my name."

'"It is almost as lovely a name as you deserve. Here, take off your cloak and sit down. We have much to plan."

'He opened my cloak then and started to take it from my shoulders. I wore a red silk dress that day, and he gathered together some of its material that brushed my knees in his hands and held it to his lips. Both of us were beyond speech. A lady then entered the shop, and I quickly understood that she was the owner of the lovely mirror that had been the cause of the earlier commotion. Nino swiftly moved towards her.

' "I apologise, *signora*, but due to unforeseen circumstances your mirror is not quite finished."

'The lady began to protest but Nino soothed her by saying that only the finest craftsmanship was suitable for her. He would not be swayed on this. The lady smiled then and enquired about the mirror that hung behind him on the wall.

' "Oh, that is to be delivered to another patron. Have no fear; your own mirror will be lovely. How can I produce anything but loveliness when I have such beauty now in my sights?"

'The poor lady blushed and left, and Nino rushed back and took me in his arms for the first time.

' "Why did you not give her the mirror, Nino?"

' "Because, my sweet Cianna, the only place that mirror shall hang is in our house when we are married."

'We left the shop then, hands clasped, and ran through the busy streets laughing and giggling at I know not what. Every day for many weeks after that, we were together. Nino had his own rooms and I lived by his side—I slept with him, ate with him, cooked and cleaned for him. I . . . we were deliriously happy. Of course, he wanted to know about me and where I came from, but he never pushed or forced me to talk. In any case, we were so content with the present as well as with planning for our future that the past interested us little. Still, I sometimes felt troubled by it. I knew that we would have to face it eventually.

'One day I went with Nino to visit his mother and some other members of his family. They were very kind to me and so welcoming that I cried with happiness as we returned to his rooms that evening. My future promised to be wonderful. I had been living an entirely human existence for some time now, and my thoughts were wholly bound up in Nino and our love. But as I was preparing for bed that night, combing my hair before Nino's little shaving mirror, I noticed a small bruise on my cheek. I recalled that I had knocked it against a cupboard door earlier that day. It was the first time I had ever had such a blemish on my skin. While I remain as I am I can never be marked or hurt, you see. I was beginning to become human. I examined the rest of my face in the cracked mirror and could see that I looked tired. Again, a first for me. Cold horror gripped my heart then. Old—I would become old and eventually I would die. I might face pain and suffering. Even worse, I might have to see Nino suffer and know that there was not a thing I could do about it. I would never soar above the clouds again. I would be grounded forever.

'Lost in my reverie, I had not seen Nino come to stand behind me and rest his head gently upon my own. I felt ashamed that he should see my bruised and puffy face in his chipped mirror. Surely he could not avoid contrasting it with the lovely face he had first seen in his beautiful mirror. I thought he might stop loving me once I became like other women, once I was no longer perfect.

'"Come to bed, my dearest."

'He could tell that I was upset, and he knelt before me and asked me to forgive him if he had done anything wrong. This sweetness only served to make me feel worse. To lose the absolute love and devotion of this man? I could not. I could not watch him slowly grow tired of me until he eventually despised me. I am ashamed to say that my own self-pity got the better of me that night, and we quarrelled, Nino and I, for the first time. Later that night, when I knew he was fast asleep, I crept into his room and kissed his dear face and pressed myself to his body. At that moment, I felt sure that I could never leave my dear Nino. And he would never stop loving me.

'Everything was happy again for a few days, though not as happy as before. Moods I was unaccustomed to began to take hold of me at times, and I did not like it at all. Three days following our quarrel, during a picnic by the water near his home, I felt it was the right time to tell him everything about me. Nino was the kindest and most intelligent of men, and I knew that he would understand, eventually, what I had to say. We were holding each other on the warm ground, and Nino's heart was beating against my ear. *Soon that heart will stop beating forever*, I thought, *and so will my own too*. Such dark thoughts were regularly beginning to sour my moments with Nino.

'I watched the birds overhead swoop and soar and could not bear to think of never again being able to join them. This place, so lovely to visit, would be my final home, for Nino would never be permitted to leave Murano. The fragile beauty of the glass now seemed restrictive and nauseating. Nino sensed my tension and kissed the tears which ran down my face.

'"My love, what is it? Tell me what has been troubling you these past days. Is it because we are not yet married? Let us marry as soon as we are able to, shall we? I cannot wait until I can show you off as my wife. We will have a large family, you and I, and I will adore you when every one of your beautiful dark hairs is snow white."

'The tenderness and clear truth of these last words broke my heart, and I sobbed into Nino's chest, telling my darling again and again how much I loved him. I did not deserve such a man. The truth was that I was apprehensive about giving up my old ways and powers for him. It had been dishonest of me to link Nino with my own fear and vanity. I did not trust that I could be happy merely being his wife. That was not a good enough fate for my Nino. He should have a wife who every day blessed her good fortune at being given the chance to share her life with such a man. I was resolved, then, and I knew what to do.

'We returned home and I prepared a lovely dinner for Nino. I did my best to forget what was to come, and we laughed and loved the whole evening through. As Nino lay asleep, I crept out of his arms and dressed. I kissed him goodbye and put my little glass bell into the folds of my gown. The night sky was dark, and there was little light to be seen from the stars. *So much the better for me*, I thought, and I flew upwards and upwards until the world below seemed a meaningless dot. *Somewhere down there my Nino sleeps. Perhaps he has awoken already and he is worried because he cannot find me. If he is pained he shall not be for long.*

'Though exhausted because my powers were weakening, I took the necessary steps to erase myself from Nino's mind. I visited again the time when Nino and I had not yet met, and I saw, from a safe distance, the drunken man begin to fight with Nino. This time the candlestick was flung out into the street. Nino and the men who soon arrived dragged the fool out into the road and returned to their work.

'I saw the woman arrive and purchase her mirror, our mirror. A servant took possession of it outside the shop and the woman went on about her business. I followed the servant for a little way, and as he stopped to talk to a friend I caught my reflection in the mirror again. I looked as fresh and beautiful as I had previously. My powers were fully restored.

'I had one last thing to do in Murano that day. My bell was gone, of course, because now Nino had never given it to me. So I returned to the shop and waited until Nino had left and it was quite safe to step inside and take possession of it once more. I left some money where it had lain, and I departed from the shop and my dear Nino.'

Gracie finally raised her head from Cianna's lap, fearful of what she might see. How could she best go about comforting her? But Cianna looked very much in control of herself once more, as though telling her story had been cathartic.

'You understand now why I feel such a connection with the bell,' Cianna said with a smile. 'I will always find you if you have it.'

'Thank you. You know I will take great care of it. But, you've never seen Nino again?'

'Oh, yes, I see him sometimes. I return and watch him occasionally. I know he married. I never choose to see him beyond his youth, though. It would be too painful to witness his infirmity, or death. To see him is enough for me. It is all I deserve— more than I deserve. Nino. Simply to say his name aloud to another person makes him exist for me once more, even though he has been dead for so many centuries. I could have been dead for centuries.'

Gracie shivered at the prospect. 'Do you . . . was it the right thing to do?'

'I ache for Nino every day of my life. The pain has never eased. I do not take the same pleasure anymore in the things I found too difficult to relinquish. As to whether I should have stayed with Nino, I find that question difficult to answer. It is these lonely years that have shown me beyond doubt that he cannot be forgotten. But I would have been left wondering, possibly even resentful, all those years with Nino, and that would have been unfair to him.'

'I understand.'

'Now, we are soon to depart. I must leave you for a spell to prepare for your journey. Can I leave you with a reminder of twenty-first-century life?'

'Oh, Cianna, yes!'

Seconds later, Gracie was surrounded by many of her favourite things: Chinese food, Champagne, Diet Coke, chocolate, cakes, roast beef and Yorkshire pudding with vegetables, and all manner of other tasty treats. The stereo was playing her favourite pop song of the moment, that had simply a woman's name as its title, and all of her CDs were piled before her, as were some of her books and DVDs.

'Make the most of these things, Gracie, for they will be gone from you before long,' Cianna said as she walked towards the window.

And then she was simply gone. Gracie listened to her music and tried to enjoy her feast but found it impossible to quell her nerves. She knew that she might soon long for each and every thing within this room, but what did that fact mean to her now? Why in Hell's name was she doing this? Earlier that very same day she'd been filled with thoughts of her own self-importance, filled with the hope of prolonging other people's lives. She'd been prepared to sacrifice her own life for this hope. Those other lives and the Renaissance machine had hardly influenced her most recent decision. Clearly, it all didn't mean as much to her as she'd thought. But it had led her here. Had it long been designed that she should reach this point?

* * *

It seemed only a short time had passed before Cianna then appeared again and laid her hands on Gracie's shoulders.

'Ready, my dear?'

'Yes, but I was just thinking about the fact that my mission to save lives didn't seem to be as important to me as I thought. All I've considered in reaching my decision to do this is myself.'

'Yes. But what is your main reason for doing this?'

'Main reason? Oh, I want to escape my sadness, learn new things, find a little happiness, a little beauty, some grace.'

'Back to your name again.'

'Oh yes, I suppose so.'

'Here, wear this.'

Gracie looked down and saw that she was dressed in the smartest outfit she possessed—an expensive dark suit usually reserved for interviews and funerals, in spite of the fact that it was really lovely. She had bought it for her grandmother's funeral, seven years ago. And now here she was.

'Take my hand, Gracie. It is time to depart.'

5.

Footsteps

Cianna led Gracie to what was her own bedroom door in another time and place. Gracie's grip on Cianna's hand tightened as her new friend opened the door to what lay beyond.

Darkness. Darkness lay beyond.

Gracie could see not a thing at first, but gradually she began to decipher outlines and shapes. A straight and narrow path stretched out before her, and high walls rose on either side of her—she had a sense of being hemmed in. Stimulated more forcibly than her sense of sight, however, were her senses of smell and hearing. The unmistakable aroma of old things surrounded her: books, clothes, houses? Gracie had never found this sort of mustiness unpleasant. Yet it was mingled most definitely with something else. What was it? Food? Paint? Smoke? Even blood?

'You are smelling all of those things, Gracie, and indeed, many other things too,' said Cianna. 'It is an assault upon your senses, is it not? Each time someone passes through here, certain aromas from wherever they are going reach in. As you can see, these smells have nowhere to escape to, so they stay here and mingle with the smells of other centuries. It is so strange for you because you, of course, do not associate the smell of gunpowder with steam engines, the smell of perfume with burning bodies.'

'No, indeed.'

Gracie suddenly felt as if she were inhaling lethal poison. The air now seemed thick and foul. Absolute silence and stillness permeated the space, but the very absence of noise produced a sound all on its own. And now, here *was* a noise. Quick and precise footsteps moving across a stone floor—and these footsteps appeared to be moving with some haste towards where Gracie and Cianna stood. Or were they? No matter how much she strained her eyes in the dimly lit corridor, Gracie could see nobody.

'Not yet, Gracie. A little more time yet.'

More light started coming into the walkway. Or at least, light was affecting what lay far beyond. Although Gracie was still essentially in darkness, little dots of light were appearing in the distance. They were spaced evenly and attached to the walls on either side of her. And these dots were growing ever closer, keeping a rhythm with the footsteps. Whoever was walking toward them was having their approach met with lights. Silently, Cianna and Gracie watched the procession of lights advance. Gracie noticed how dry her mouth was, and she wished that she'd had a larger glass of cola before they'd left. What a time to think of such things! But she could badly do with a drink now. Cianna's voice cut into her thoughts.

'Soon now. Look.'

Gracie looked ahead; the lights were growing very close. Their flickering suggested candlelight. She could see there were some objects on the left-hand side of the passageway, although the right was uncluttered. What the objects were though, she could not tell. The footsteps were now so loud and clear that she kept expecting a figure to appear before her at any moment. But still, nobody. How far a distance was this person travelling? And why did the walker not wish for more light? The candles lit up their walls but didn't have much effect on the centre. Who *was* this creature walking towards them in semi-darkness?

And then, apparently from nowhere, a small man was before her. The candles extended to where she and Cianna stood, and the footsteps stopped. The man, little more than five feet tall, was grinning impishly at Gracie and seemed in a highly excitable state. He waved his hand and more light appeared around the three of them. After bowing lowly to them both, he addressed Gracie.

'My dear Dr Abbot. Your good friend the Lady Cianna has explained to me where you wish to go. I shall escort you, and I am honoured to do so.'

Upon speaking, his mouth seemed to hang open. He drew the back of his hand across his mouth and wiped away the saliva that would otherwise have dropped onto the flagged-stone ground. He was certainly a strange-looking fellow. He spoke English with a strong Italian accent. His thick curly black hair was matted with grey, and he could have been any age from thirty-five to fifty. He was dressed in a white crumpled shirt and red trousers. Gracie noted that his shoes made rather a grand contrast to the rest of his apparel, for they were of a very pointed design and their shiny black leather looked expensive and new. He shifted his weight continuously from foot to foot and seemed impatient to be moving again. This boisterous and energetic little man had made quite the measured and precise entrance!

'Gracie,' said Cianna, 'it is my pleasure to present you to Angelus.'

Gracie smiled and nodded, and Angelus took hold of her shoulders and kissed her, rather ferociously, on each cheek. His beady eyes then appraised her from head to toe. Apparently satisfied with what he saw, he nodded and, placing his hand lightly on her elbow, he led Cianna towards the door she and Gracie had recently exited.

Nervous, wondering if Angelus was about to tell Cianna she had to leave, Gracie turned to them and saw, to her amazement, that the passageway extended as far behind her as it did in front. She had assumed that she was standing at its end. Countless doors, with objects laid outside, were situated, at regular intervals, along her original left-hand wall. Gracie also saw that her own bedroom door was just another of these huge, varnished doors. Some pictures of famous people were stuck to its frame, along with photos of people whom she did not recognise. What did this mean? She dropped her gaze to the objects at the foot of the door, some standing freely and some propped against it. There were newspapers with headlines detailing world-shattering events which Gracie knew all about. Then there were newspapers with front pages on which Gracie recognised nothing. One of them told of the death of an important person who had not yet died. The purpose of the objects meant little to Gracie—various books and a painting as well as an architect's model of a building. All of these things had not been there when Gracie stepped through her door. She surely would have stepped on or tripped over them if they had.

Cianna and Angelus were huddled close, engrossed in conversation, but Gracie couldn't hear them. Turning towards where she had originally faced, Gracie felt a strange sensation that she was at the centre of this corridor and that, even if she ran for miles and miles in either direction, she would never find her way out. And even if she did, what lay beyond?

The only way to escape was through one of these doors.

She was reminded of a friend's house she had visited not so long ago, a stately home that members of the public paid to see on certain days of the week. Gracie had been shown around parts of the house that were private, and she had especially enjoyed walking amongst the many cellars and walkways rooted at the base of the building. They would have been in regular use hundreds of years previously. The atmosphere of these dark and immense spaces had both excited and unnerved her. What might have taken place in them? *Who* might once have leaned against their walls? Sylvie, her friend, had teased her about her sense of the romantic and said that they'd probably been used as little more than storerooms for wines and corridors for servants and rats to scuttle along. No more and no less. But Gracie hadn't been convinced. She'd rested her head and hands against the cool of the stone walls and took pleasure in the sound her modern heeled shoes made against the old stone floors. Sad and broken though she'd been, something in those walls had supported her, had told her she wasn't alone, for she too had joined the company of ghosts who'd also heard their footsteps echo around them. She had felt keenly that day that she had a part to play. Now *she* had been in this underground maze, it would never be entirely the same again—it possessed her breath, her scent and the tiny specks of dirt and mud that she'd brought in on her shoes.

And now, she had a similar feeling. A feeling that she could not be here without contributing something. It was impossible to do otherwise.

Cianna and Angelus joined her again, and Gracie took comfort in the feel of Cianna's hand clasped within her own. Angelus now had a little lantern, and the centre path was clearer than before. It seemed to go on forever with no bends or curves. Indeed, its straightness was relentless. Gracie felt intimidated; even the slightest turn in the road ahead might have allayed some of her anxiety, though why exactly she couldn't tell. The next door lay several feet in front. Would she depart through it or perhaps one of the other doors? Angelus gestured for her to follow him, from the same direction he had arrived.

'Come now, Dr Abbot. It is time.'

Gracie and Cianna followed, side by side. Angelus seemed natural and happy to lead. In any case, the passage wasn't wide enough for the three of them to walk together. Silently, with Cianna on the left side and Gracie on the right, they set off.

As they passed by the nearest door, Gracie looked to see what images and objects lay with it. More faces that Gracie both did and did not recognise appeared. Some of the pictures were of famous people that Gracie hadn't seen or thought about for years. There were also newspapers, a few books, electrical and computer equipment—all whirled by in a flash. Gracie found the sound of their footsteps hypnotic. The combination of Angelus's firm leather with Gracie's heels and Cianna's satin shoes sounded almost musical. Although different, each step accorded with and complemented the others. Gracie let her thoughts drift away and focussed upon nothing more than the sound. Then Angelus suddenly stopped at the next door.

'Wait, my dears. This door is not as it ought to be.'

It looked perfectly fine to Gracie. The pictures at this door were of people Gracie hadn't seen on the news or the television for even longer than those on the previous door. Also, a Chinese newspaper with a photo of the aftermath of Tiananmen Square; a computer; a picture of the Berlin Wall. Other things that Gracie remembered from her childhood. All gathered together on this door. Upon straightening a picture, Angelus was ready to depart again. Gracie got the impression that this door had been opened fairly recently, for Angelus seemed so particular—surely he would have noticed if it had been disordered for a long time. But with all these doors, who could say?

As they advanced, the lights at their backs vanished. One, two, three, their steps passed on, and Gracie again became entranced by their sound. After some steps, another door, with even more distant but celebrated faces fixed upon it. Steps again. There were exactly ten steps between each door. Another door, this one with pictures of The Beatles, President Kennedy and Marilyn Monroe. Also, an American poster calling for army recruits for the war in Vietnam. All things strongly associated with the 1960s. Why, each door represented a decade. Did the decade lie beyond it? Why not, after all? Wasn't she being taken to the past? Moreover, mightn't each step they took represent one year? Ten steps, ten years in one decade.

Cianna whispered in the darkness. 'You are always good at working things out, Gracie. And so often correct.'

The door into the 1950s passed by. Rock and roll; James Dean; the Civil Rights Act; Soviet space programme. Gracie suddenly stopped. Angelus immediately halted and turned to see Gracie looking with some shock at a photo of her grandmother. The 1950s. Of course. The height of her fame.

'We continue now?'

Angelus was doing his best to curb his obvious impatience. Cianna nodded and Gracie walked on with her. She looked over her shoulder in time to see the light going out on Grace Abbot's face.

Gracie knew that the next door would show images of the Second World War. Yet it was still electrifying to realise that behind the door on which was displayed a picture of Hitler in full Nazi regalia lay the actual man himself. The next door, the Great Depression; Picasso's *Guernica*; *Gone with the Wind*. Clark Gable was beyond that door!

On and on they walked. Angelus frequently turned around to grin at Gracie, but nobody talked and nobody stopped. After some time, Gracie whispered to Cianna, 'All of those objects and people on the doors. They are the defining moments of each decade?'

'In some ways. Nothing is absolute, though. The pictures and objects can change as time changes.'

'You mean as the past is altered, some people might grow in importance and others might fade?'

'Yes, just so.'

This was a speed lesson in history but with no apparent rules.

Although she was curious to see who and what represented each decade, Gracie sometimes felt sick as the famous faces flashed by. Every step she took forward was really a step back, and this was no easy thing to accept.

She wondered about Angelus. Who was he? He certainly didn't seem to be one of Cianna's people, one of the Pondera. So, he wasn't like Cianna and he could not, living as he did, be an ordinary human. Cianna had said that many different peoples shared the same image, so the fact that he looked as human as she, or Cianna, told her little.

'He is very old,' Cianna whispered. 'Although young indeed in comparison with me. He *is* a human being though.'

'Oh,' Gracie said, trying to hide her surprise.

A portrait of the Brontë sisters sped past. Gracie was again finding it difficult to absorb what was going on. Concentrating on the sound of the footsteps calmed her somewhat. So many lights had switched off behind her now. She had travelled quite some distance. Surely few had travelled so far. Many of the portraits that she was passing now were of people she did not recognise, but she had no doubt they were famous. But who of her contemporaries could readily recognise Williams Wordsworth or Wilberforce? Perhaps there were people represented on these doors who, in their lifetimes, had had no portrait painted, and the only images that existed of them were to be seen by the minority who would pass this way. Had their images been painted by some unreal hand to adorn this most sophisticated of filing systems? A true marriage of the artistic with the scientific, but to what purpose?

Gracie knew that she would soon come to the end of her journey. She understood enough about history to determine that through one of the next doors she had to pass. And here it was. Angelus, who had controlled their pace past so many "years", stopped.

'Dear Doctor. Here you are. I cannot tell you what a pleasure it was to guide you.'

'Thank you, sir. Thank you, Angelus.'

'Well, Gracie, now we part,' said Cianna, placing her hands on Gracie's shoulders. 'Remember all I have told you and you will do well I am sure. You have learned so much already in the short time we have spoken, have you not?'

It was true. Gracie had learned more in her short time with Cianna than she had in her entire life. It made her original plan to control and conquer death seem hopelessly pathetic. She had known nothing.

'What will you do, Cianna? Will you look after someone else now?'

Gracie felt an unaccountable jealousy at the thought of Cianna, her Cianna, being a silent observer of anyone else.

'I shall travel for a spell. I cannot be with anyone else. I have not yet finished with you, of course.'

This made Gracie feel better. She smiled and then hugged Cianna.

'Goodbye. Goodbye, Angelus.'

He smiled at her genially, kissing her hand.

'Use the bell if you need me,' Cianna said. 'And if we do not meet before it, I shall come for you at the moment when you must decide whether to leave or stay behind. Do not worry. Everything will be clear to you when you pass through the door. You will possess a lifetime of new memories, but you will still also be Gracie Abbot. Learn well, my little scientist.'

'I'll do my best, Cianna. I promise.'

Angelus was about to open the door when a thought occurred to Gracie: how could she be sure that she would arrive in entirely the correct year? The door was closed upon a whole decade, after all.

'Angelus will take care of everything. See, his keys.'

Gracie looked at the enormous number of keys Angelus was sorting through. He carefully selected one, and Gracie guessed it was the only key that could lead her home. Home? How strange to use that word to describe a place she had never seen. Looking at her door, Gracie smiled at one of the portraits that hung upon it, and for whose sake she was about to experience this great adventure.

Angelus put the key into the lock, and it turned immediately. He pulled at the doorknob and daylight and air filtered into the passageway. After being in the dark for so long, Gracie welcomed the light; even Cianna gasped with delight. Angelus beckoned to Gracie, and she pulled it wide the remainder of the way. It was a warm day, and the scent of grass and the fresh outdoors surrounded them. A light breeze blew at their clothes. Gracie felt Cianna's hand stroke the back of her hair as she stepped through the doorway. She checked that the bell was still safely in its box and tucked into her jacket pocket. It was.

She had arrived.

Angelus closed the door behind Gracie and carefully locked it again. Both he and Cianna paused for a few moments before they moved and reflected upon the fact that now there was only two where there had once been three. Only two sets of footsteps working their way along the silent passageway.

6.
The Mountain

Cianna sat atop the highest mountain in the world of the Pondera. Deep snow lay all around, but that troubled her little. Indeed, she had taken off her shoes. With her chin resting upon her knees, she dug her bare feet into the snow, enjoying the crunching sound it made and the cold sensation that invigorated and cleared her senses. It felt good to be here again, at the top of her world.

She thought about Gracie, who had been in her new life for a few hours now. Cianna hoped that she would be happy. *If anything goes wrong, or if she needs me, she can call for me*, she reminded herself. She rested her hand against the pocket concealed within her gown and felt that it was empty. Her bell was gone, existing in another age, without her. If Nino had known when he was making the bell of all the places that it might see, of the person to whom it would mean so much, of its becoming a part of their life . . .

Darling Nino, where do you lie now, my dearest? If I might touch a piece of the earth where your body has rested.

Where should she go now? What might she do? Return to Gracie's world—Nino's world? Despite all of the sad associations she had there, if she went anywhere else, as she frequently did, she knew that she would long for that planet. *A strange state of affairs for one who comes from this, infinitely superior, world.* Cianna smiled ruefully. But this world had never known Nino. Nino's body was not part of the ground, the trees; it was only in his world that she might clench a handful of earth while kneeling beside the lake where they enjoyed their last picnic all those years ago. It still looked remarkably the same. Perhaps she could find a stone or a rock that still bore his imprint or touch, just as she did.

Restless, she shifted, and her hand fell back upon something that lay slightly under the snow. Turning to see what it was, she clapped her hands with joy as she spied dark green framed by pure white snow. The white head of the flower, simple and complete—as the most beautiful things always were—was just like three large drops of milk. *Impatient and pushy creatures.* Cianna smiled again. It was always something of a shock to note their arrival. *Only they can survive in this weather. Yet their drooping makes them look as if they desire to return to where they so lately left.* Cianna had always loved the Galanthus, or as Gracie would say, the "snowdrop", a prettier name. Moving some of the snow around this solitary bud, Cianna could feel that there were many others about to burst through the surface, probably within the next few hours. *This one has come to welcome me home though*, Cianna thought. *To cheer me, and I thank you.* Kneeling, she bent down to caress the little flower and then considered that it might care to leave its home and join her as her companion. *It has an adventurous and bold spirit, so we will do well together.* Cianna carefully removed the flower and kissed it. This ensured it would remain pure and fresh, and each of its three petals would stay safely together.

About to resume her seat, Cianna noticed a shape high in the sky and still quite far away. Putting the flower into the pocket that used to be the home of her bell, she shaded her eyes with her hand, but the sun was too bright to recognise anything with certainty. Running towards a large rock that lay less directly within the sun's glare, she rested one foot upon it. Seeing her good friend Theodore, she waved delightedly and called to him. Theodore was flying with some speed through the clear blue skies, and within minutes the two of them stood together on the mountain, warmly embracing. Like Cianna, Theodore's physical perfection was clear. Athletic and handsome, he smiled as he kissed his old friend lightly on each cheek.

'My sister, it has been a long time since we have met.'

'Yes, my Theo, I have been with my dear Gracie, and she is now occupied elsewhere. I do not know when she will need me. I am free again until she does.'

'I see. Well, I am about to attend the celebration tonight for our dear Manuel. He has been gone from us for a long time, and we are eager to see him again. I have missed him dearly, as I have missed you. How happy I am we can all be together once more.'

'Manuel. He has been gone since before I left to be with Gracie, has he not?'

'Indeed so. Come, Cianna, let us go. What a surprise. I shall bring our brothers and sisters!'

Cianna and Theodore flew from the mountain and made their way towards the place where the remaining Pondera lived together. As they travelled, they talked of all they had done and seen since their last meeting. They both greatly enjoyed the feeling of being with one who understood, and from whom there was nothing to hide. Theodore had lately been in love with a lady from a world that was different from Gracie's. He had left her, and she would believe that he had forsaken her for another. She knew nothing of what he was.

'I would rather she was angry with me for leaving her—I think that will make it easier for her to love again. Eventually she will hate me but, as we know, hate can prove to be strengthening, and I want her to survive without me.'

'But Theodore, why did you not let her forget you, as I did with my darling Nino?'

'I want to be remembered. That is all. If she forgets me then our time together will be in large part lost, and I do not want that. Instead, it will live on in both our minds.'

'But she will not have any contentment. Any peace.'

'Nor shall I. I thought about leaving you all, as I have done so many other times, but I could not extinguish all I am, all I have. This old Libraman will live on to face another love affair! Perhaps that one will prove my undoing.'

'Oh Theodore, you can always make me laugh. And there is home!'

Many beautiful and large houses were now clearly visible on the ground. They were positioned in a rather circular shape with the inside of the circle having the fewest number of houses and each subsequent circle having more and more, forever moving further away from the centre. Several of the houses were empty, as those who had occupied them had left to live, and die, elsewhere. An enormous trestle table had been erected in the space at the centre of the houses, and it was this space that served as a meeting place for the Pondera. Here they held parties and homecomings; this was the heart of the Pondera's world.

The table was laden with food and drinks, and all were happy and dressed in their best outfits to welcome home Manuel, who had achieved great things on his latest journey. Now Cianna would also take centre stage.

'Look, look who I bring!'

Everyone ran towards them, and the Pondera were overjoyed to see Cianna. She was happy to see so many of her old friends, who hugged and kissed her and made much of her.

'Run and change, dearest! We shall celebrate long tonight.'

Cianna's close friend, the Lady Agathe, rushed with Cianna to her house. Cianna had not been in her home for a long time, but it had been kept clean and tidy. It was the Pondera way to never let anything lovely and beautiful become dirty and degraded. Even the empty houses were maintained and kept fresh. They would rather knock the houses down and grow cherry trees in their stead than allow them to go to ruin. Cianna selected a beautiful white silken dress, in memory of her snow-drop, and a red robe. She attached her snowdrop to the front of her robe and departed for the party arm in arm with Agathe, who, in her emerald green gown, looked as breathtakingly beautiful as Cianna.

At such gatherings, the Pondera took note of who was no longer with them, and Cianna did this now. Rather than feel sad, the Pondera preferred to celebrate these friends and wish them happiness. Jadon, thought to be the oldest surviving member of the Pondera, clapped his hands and welcomed everyone. He usually led such gatherings. Everyone turned to look at the tall young man with the thick chestnut-brown hair. He was a striking figure in his inky blue shirt, which emphasised his tanned, muscled arms. He commanded them to eat and be merry. Several of the group played instruments so music, and then dancing, could also be enjoyed.

Cianna danced with Theodore and Jadon as well as many others. Everything was relaxed and carefree in a way that cannot usually be the case in such gatherings between the sexes. But, here, most of the Pondera had long ago resigned themselves to being unable to form attachments with another of their kind. Some of the Pondera had chosen partners amongst themselves, and although they were happy, this was not a fate that Cianna and most of the others could contemplate. They were family to each other and nothing more.

When they had eaten and laughed and danced themselves to a contented tiredness, Jadon stood in the centre and called for silence. He invited anyone who had something new to impart to share what he or she had learned. Manuel rose and told of his travels on a ship that had sailed from England many hundreds of years ago and arrived in the New World, so the people termed it. He had successfully saved the life of someone who had previously died but should have lived to become the father of a great and famous man. Now the world was a better place—this lost figure would achieve his rightful fate. Everyone applauded Manuel and felt proud that such a brave and good man should be one of them.

Cianna then shared with her people the story of Gracie and her Renaissance machine and her dream of enabling people to live longer. The Pondera were fascinated and said that Gracie sounded a remarkable member of her kind. But they didn't know why she had been called back to the past. Years of experience had taught them that there was little point in trying to guess the reasons for the work they undertook—despite all their wisdom, they invariably failed.

The sharing continued. Inara had comforted a woman who had lost her husband and child, Khalid had helped tend fields for a farmer who had become crippled and would have lost his lands and seen his family starve without this assistance, and Arin had done her best to prevent a fire from killing many people. The Pondera didn't know whether such things would have any particular or great impact in the time to follow, but they were sure that in their quest for balance, these things were nonetheless important. When it was time to retire, Cianna walked home with Agathe, who lived nearby.

'Will you stay for a while, Cianna?'

'I do not know. I will return here soon, but I think I will travel some days first.'

'Of course. Farewell until the morning, my friend.'

'Farewell, Agathe.'

Cianna knew that while she was free, it was her responsibility to stay here for at least a short spell. She had to help keep the Pondera world functioning. She would take her turn maintaining the houses and doing the many things necessary to ensure their world remained unique. This was vital for their way of life to continue. Yet she burned to see Nino. She stood in front of her long mirror and removed the snowdrop, still fresh, from her robe. Tomorrow she would return to Angelus. She would see Nino again before the passing of another day. With this thought, Cianna fell asleep with a happy smile on her lovely face.

7.
Life

A traveller approached a running stream. Jumping down from his horse, he led the beast towards the water. It would be thirsty. He certainly was.

What a warm day. The man fanned himself with his hat and bent to drink his fill, cupping the cool water with his hands and splashing his face and neck. When his thirst was quenched, he stood and stretched and surveyed his surroundings.

Certainly a pleasant-looking little town. It seemed prosperous enough—some shops, a nice church, people walking about dressed almost fashionably. *Almost.* He smiled. But this wasn't the city, and he'd seen quite enough pretentious villages and towns. No, it was the city for him. He was London bound and expected to arrive tomorrow.

He turned to see that his horse had wandered off.

'Here, boy,' he said, moving towards it. 'Come on, King, time to go now.'

Nibbling at the grass, the horse lazily inclined its head towards its master.

'Yes, boy, I know, we're both tired in this damned heat, but I promise you a good rub-down and as much hay and oats as you can manage before long. Now come on, lad. Another twenty or thirty miles and we'll stop for the day.'

He took hold of King's bridle and started to lead him back to the road. Then something white caught his eye. Across the stream, which was not at all wide—why, he could swim its width in a few minutes—was a lady lying on the grass. He hadn't noticed her before because she was mostly hidden from view by the greenery that shaded her.

A splendid spot to rest on such a day, he thought. She looked young. Her white dress was simple enough, no frills, little pattern. *A servant? No, not a chance. She'll be the daughter of some moderately rich farmer or tradesman. A fine prospect for some local lad.* Her dark hair flowed loosely over her shoulders. Not unbecoming at all. Her straw bonnet lay in her left hand, and its long pink ribbons stirred in the gentle breeze. Her profile appeared to be pretty and her figure well proportioned.

She must live nearby to lie there alone so contentedly and relaxed, he reasoned. Only near home could one be at such ease, and this was surely especially true for a young lady. She was not married—that was clear by her outfit. He assumed that she was probably not engaged either, for who would allow his betrothed to expose herself in such a public manner? He certainly wouldn't. She clearly had some spirit and a sense of adventure to be so self-sufficient when she might subject herself to possible censure or ridicule. So different from the London ladies of his acquaintance who cared greatly for form and protocol.

He stifled a yawn and felt King nuzzle his shoulder. His horse was tired. Might it not be best to stop here for the night? He'd passed an inn, had he not? The surrounding countryside looked sublime; he could hire some fishing rods, make a little holiday of it, perhaps get to know some of the locals, even that young lady across the stream . . .

But his aunt. She could not be put off. On he must travel. He climbed onto King's back and took one last wistful look at the lady. Yes, a fine-looking girl.

'Now, boy, come on.' King trotted off and within minutes the man had almost left the town behind already, the dust from his horse settling back upon the road.

The young lady's thoughts lay far away. She hadn't even noticed the stranger who had almost changed his plans because of her. Gracie Arundel, formerly Abbot, had been resting upon the grass for an hour, occasionally thinking about trying to read her book. It remained closed. The year was 1798. Gracie had been here, *really* been here, since 1791, when she was sixteen years old. Today was the seventh anniversary of that arrival, and she had come here every year except one in memory of that day. This lovely spot was where she had arrived. Those initial steps into her new life had taken place upon the grass she was lying on now. Every year she made a little event of visiting this area— alone, of course, for the date would mean nothing to anyone else—to think about all that she had discovered and felt with the passing of another year. It meant a lot to Gracie to do this, and in the year that she was not able to come, due to a holiday in Lyme Regis, she had still taken care to spend time alone.

Strange to consider that she had already been here for so long. The memory of that first day, that first moment, was still so vivid. She had stepped out into the sunshine, into a space so lush and green and quiet. Everything seemed to move in slow motion. She felt herself exactly suspended between the touch of Cianna's hand on her hair and the feel of the soft earth beneath her feet. The first living thing she saw was a bird, a moorhen with a bright red-and-yellow bill.

In the instant that her feet were firmly on the ground she knew all about her new self, just as Cianna had said. Gracie had looked around immediately to see if Cianna and Angelus were still there although she had known they would be gone. She was Gracie Arundel, daughter of a retired lawyer and resident in the town of Bourton-on-the-Water, in Gloucestershire. She knew about her new family and where to find her new home—everything. The strangest thing about it all was that, although she felt entirely natural as Grace Arundel, Gracie Abbot seemed no less real. The women coexisted for her, and in each skin, she was at ease.

Her first eighteenth-century steps had taken her towards the stream, and she had knelt and gazed at the reflection that confronted her. It was her face, as she'd known it as Gracie Abbot, although significantly younger. Her hair was pulled back in an intricate-looking knot at the nape of her neck, and loose tendrils fell onto her cheeks. She smiled at her reflection and reached out to touch it, causing the water to ripple and her face to disappear for a few moments. Soon it settled back into shape, and Gracie liked what she saw.

She had arrived not in Bourton-on-the-Water but in Northleach, a small town some four or five miles from her home. Her first walk from Northleach to Bourton was a wonderful concoction of discovery and recognition. Given all the places in England she might have ended up, she could have no complaints about her new home—it was truly breathtaking. To the eyes of a modern Londoner like Gracie, the rolling landscapes and thatched cottages on her route home, as well as the winding and bubbling River Windrush, which ran under the little bridges in Bourton, were enchanting. In her life as Gracie Abbot she had travelled through the Cotswolds once before, but she didn't really know the area. Yet now it was hers, and she *knew* this place. She had memories of playing and fishing here, of shopping there, of visiting that church every Sunday and of attending supper parties at the inn. Someone had even tipped his hat to her on that first walk home, a local man.

'Good day, young Gracie.'

'Hello, Mr Parker.'

She knew his name, and that she had taken drawing lessons with his daughter, Charlotte. And she didn't just know these "facts" either—she really knew the man.

Her path led to a large and, at first sight, rather plain-looking pale-bricked house. The Abbots had been a wealthy family, but to live in a house as grand as this in modern London would have taken the wealth of a millionaire many several times over. The house was wide and fully detached with its own substantial gardens to the front and rear. It had a flat triangular roof that housed chimneys neatly at its centre. From its front Gracie counted five windows on the upper floor and four on the ground floor. These were small, all the same size with a typical sash design, and positioned in neat rows. The door was grand and wide and stood at the top of ten white steps. Her new home was a traditional seventeenth-century manor house.

She walked through the gardens to find them well tended, but a modern visitor might reasonably have thought them rather unused as nothing much seemed to be growing. Gracie knew, however, that most of the fruits and vegetables consumed by the family originated here. They were of greater importance than flowers, though there *were* several rose bushes in both the front and back gardens. Unlike many of the other neighbouring families, the Arundels did not keep livestock as they were wealthy enough to buy all of their meat, although they did keep poultry for eggs—they would have appeared extravagantly wasteful otherwise. And they were regarded as eccentric and different enough already.

Her mother was the first family member Gracie had met. She was busy in the entrance hall telling the young maid how to properly stitch some curtains that needed mending when Gracie opened the door.

'Ah, Gracie, you're back! Sometimes I wonder where it is you find to disappear to. Sally, off you go now, and bring some tea and bread and butter in for Miss Gracie's luncheon. And some of the leftover ham from last night's dinner.'

Gracie, her heart thumping, had watched as her mother busied about with various little jobs and orders. *She really has no idea*, Gracie thought. Alicia Arundel was then in her early fifties, and Gracie could clearly detect the faint German intonation in her mother's voice, even though she had lived in England for most of her life. She took hold of Gracie's chin and examined her face.

'Mmmh, a few more freckles. Wear your bonnet next time you go for long rambles on such a sunny day. Oh, there you are, Sally. Go and eat, Gracie.'

Gracie and her mother followed the young maid into what was called the morning room, where the family generally ate their light midday meal. The simply decorated room was large with a low, bare ceiling. There were none of the rose and cornice decorations so beloved in Victorian dwellings. The sofa was uncomfortable and did not allow for its sitter to slouch.

'And why did you not take Polly with you?' her mother continued, standing before her. 'You know how she loves to follow you about.'

Polly. Polly Cecilia, her little sister. She'd been eleven years old that day. She met Polly for the first time upstairs, in her room. She had remembered Cianna's bell and was searching fervently for it on her person. She soon found it, still in its red box, in the deep pocket of her dress. Relieved that it was safe and with her, and thinking she was alone, she held it to her lips.

'What is that?'

The sharp little voice made Gracie start with surprise. Polly popped her head out from under the bed, where she was obviously hiding.

'I wanted to pay you back, for not taking me out with you,' Polly said, 'but I can see that you're more interested in your box. Where did you get it? I think young James gave it to you. You and he are in love, are you not?'

'Don't be silly, Polly.'

The young girl was skinny with black hair in long plaits and a very pale complexion. Every time Gracie recalled that first meeting with Polly, she felt it was apt that they had begun with cross words, for their relationship could be tense at times. The only times Gracie ever had reason to think that anyone from her new world suspected her were those when she caught Polly looking at her as if she recognised her for the interloper she was. Other times, though, they could get along very well, and it was clear to Gracie that her little sister looked up to her.

Their father, Ernest, had married later in life—when he was almost fifty—and he was now in his seventies. Ernest had worked in London as an attorney and had amassed a substantial fortune through saving and careful investments. Alicia was in her midthirties when she and Ernest married. This was positively middle-aged for her day, but the marriage had been happy and had produced their two girls. Alicia was not rich when they met. She had worked as a governess and companion for many years. Indeed, Ernest had met her as the companion of one of his elderly aunts. She had been born in Germany to a German father and an English mother and it was the slightly odd, foreign way that she had of seeing the world and doing things which had first attracted Ernest to her. Gracie had been born in London soon after their marriage, and Polly had been born in Gloucestershire; Ernest had retired there and bought Bourton Manor by the time she was born.

So this was now her family.

As Cianna had said, love had been neither automatic nor unconditional upon Gracie's meeting these people. But in due time, it *had* followed. Indeed, her mother was an extraordinarily easy person to love. She was completely unselfconscious and didn't feel the need to apologise for or explain her earlier, humbler way of living, despite others' doing their best to encourage a sense of "proper" shame in her. Their arrows failed to penetrate, and though some didn't entirely approve of her ways, Mrs Arundel had long been accepted in her community as an "original", and that certainly made life easier. She taught the children of the local labourers and the poor how to read and write, as well as some basic counting skills—free of charge, of course, and with no demands for gratitude. Rather, Mrs Arundel, comfortably well-off with two grown daughters as well as servants to carry out the menial and laborious tasks of running a home, felt that she owed her services to those who needed them. Teach she could, so this she would do. To her daughters she offered love and advice without suffocating them, and to her husband she gave devotion. These gifts were returned to her in equal measure.

When Gracie became very sick with scarlatina, or scarlet fever, a couple of years after her arrival, she began to feel that Alicia was really, in the truest sense, her mother. She had nursed Gracie through every moment of her illness, and once when Gracie, feverish, awoke in the middle of the night, she heard her mother praying that her daughter would be spared. Alicia's voice, typically calm, had broken with emotion. Gracie had called for her then, realising that she had been blessed in her new life, for Alicia was entirely the mother she had always privately wished for.

This episode of scarlet fever had also been the cause of Gracie's calling for Cianna too—the only time that she had done so. She had begun to feel unwell but was not bedridden yet, and on seeing the anxious faces of her parents and the doctor, she'd been terrified that she was about to die. That night, following a bad dream, she had awoken to see her father and mother and sister surrounding her bed.

'Hush now, child,' said her mother. 'No need to cry out like that. We are here for you. Dry your eyes and try to get some sleep. Ernest, she's burning up. I'm going to go downstairs and make a cold compress for her head. I think you had better write a note to be taken to the doctor.'

Her parents left the room, leaving her alone with Polly.

'Mother and Father didn't hear what you were shouting, but I did because I'm only next door and I got here first. Why were you calling for China?'

Gracie frowned. 'China? I don't know. I must have been dreaming, I suppose.'

'Or maybe it wasn't China. Perhaps you were shouting for someone called Cianna?'

'No, no . . . I don't know anyone by that name. I feel so weak . . . must have just been dreaming.'

Alicia entered the room again and Polly stepped aside. But she kept watching Gracie.

That moment had been unpleasant, but thankfully Polly had let it go and Cianna was never mentioned again. And who could prove anything, even if Polly *had* spoken about it? The words of a delirious woman could hardly be assumed to have deeper meaning.

The next night, when Gracie was quite ill and the household was asleep, she had slipped from her bed and moved slowly across the room to a loose floorboard by the window, where she'd hidden the key to her writing desk. She opened up the desk to find that the red box was safe. Gracie soon had the cool bell within her grasp. What should she do? Cianna had told her to ring it and she would come as soon as she could. But what reason did she have for calling Cianna? Would Cianna be annoyed at being bothered? Gracie didn't have the strength to work things through in her head. A sick and frightened eighteen-year-old girl, she just wanted someone she knew really cared for her to tell her she would be fine.

So she had rung the bell.

Three gentle tinkling noises issued forth. Gracie put the bell back into its box in the writing desk and deposited the key under the floorboard again. Nothing for her to do but wait. She crawled back into her bed.

Cianna arrived a short time later, when Gracie was between sleep and consciousness. She felt a cool hand touch her forehead and opened her eyes to see Cianna's face in the half-light.

'Oh Cianna, I'm so glad to see you.' Tears streamed down Gracie's face. 'I thought for a while that it was all a dream, that Gracie Abbot was a dream and that you never existed. I'm so glad to know you're real.'

'Yes, yes, dear Gracie,' Cianna replied softly. 'I am real, and I told you I would come if you needed me.'

They spoke quietly for many hours. Gracie felt better simply being around Cianna, who was living with her people now.

'But have you seen Nino again?'

Cianna smiled and said that she had, once.

'When I got sick, I thought that this might be my moment of decision. But then you never came to see me, so I assumed it wasn't. But still, I've been afraid to die.'

'You are not going to die yet, my Gracie. Are you happy in your new life?'

'Yes, I am. My family members love me, and I love them. It's funny—in spite of all the things that I *can't* do here, I feel so much freer in this life. Things are simpler. I feel that I'm appreciated for being Gracie Arundel in a way I never was as Gracie Abbot, despite all of my fantastic qualifications and the secondhand fame I had as the granddaughter of the great Grace. The small things I do here seem to mean more than the big things I did in the past—well, the future. I always felt that I had to do bigger and bigger things just to get any kind of respect.'

'Yes, but was that respect from others or from yourself?'

'Both, I suppose. But the same level of pressure just doesn't exist here.'

'How do you spend your days?'

'I read a lot, and play the piano and the harp. Oh, don't laugh! I also sew, of course, and help my mother with her little school. I like to prepare for balls by learning new dances and deciding what to wear and—'

'But what about your love of science? Your studies? Can this be the same impatient young woman with all those ambitions to change the world?'

'Those ambitions are pretty pointless now, aren't they? Now that I've met you and travelled here, my experiments with life and death seem little and meaningless. I'm simply a pawn to be shuffled about. I'm not a Pondera or anything like one. No, I take the view now that what will be will be. If I have a role to fulfil then I'm sure someone like you will let me know all about it.'

Cianna rose from the bed and moved away with her back turned. Gracie felt anxiety knot in her stomach. Had she disappointed Cianna?

'Are you angry?'

'No, no, my Gracie. I am not angry but I am a little sad. Your response is typical, you see. Often when humans are given the information you've been given, they react by saying that they have no real choice, or that effort and hard work is pointless. I cannot emphasise enough that your studies are as important here as they were in the future, your past. You have walked through the corridor of time. You have seen that the past is as changeable and open as the present and the future. Nothing is written. I am about balance, as you know. I was told to lead you here, and I trust that in doing so balance will somehow be brought to your world. I do not know how. If the balance is about your life personally, and that is all, then so be it. Be happy with your dancing and your music. You, as an individual, are important. But if you are suppressing what you know you ought to be doing then that is wrong. Are you doing that, Gracie?'

'I don't know, exactly. I suppose I do sometimes long for my old studies. Yes, I miss them. But do you suggest that I construct another Renaissance machine and carry on where I was? If so, I'll have to invent an awful lot of things because the technology just isn't here. I'll be wiping many very important people from Angelus's doors, and I'll be judged to be the greatest scientific phenomenon that ever lived. If I could only recall all those formulas, and who invented what—'

Cianna cut her off. 'I see something of the old spirit and drive of my Gracie. I like it. No, I am not suggesting that you build another Renaissance, but I do suggest that you listen to your instincts again. Trust them. They will tell you if you ought to start taking an interest in anything scientific. I, for one, would find it odd if one as gifted as you was not meant to pursue these interests.'

'Cianna, you do realise that I'm living in an age which still thinks it's a good idea to let leeches suck blood? It's going to be difficult to pursue scientific interests, knowing what I know, without stealing the thunder of someone from the future.'

'Little Dr Arrogant has returned,' Cianna said with a smirk. 'Well, Gracie, you do as you see fit, but remember that those leeches are still usefully applied at times in twenty-first-century hospitals. All I ask is that you listen to your instincts. Do not let them become rusty or suffocated under all that lace and all those bonnets! Remember, you were once very good at listening to your thoughts and decisively acting upon them. By the way, have you met the person who led you here in the first place?'

'No,' Gracie said with a laugh. 'I haven't met Jane Austen. What a strange thing to say! She's not famous yet—her novels haven't even been published at this moment. I don't feel that I should pursue her. I just loved her books and they've brought me here. Perhaps that's the only connection there will ever be between us.'

'I see.'

They talked a little while longer, and then Gracie grew tired. Cianna told her to close her eyes.

'I am going to take a look at my bell while you are asleep, but I will put it back safely before I go.'

Gracie snuggled under her covers, and Cianna kissed her and said goodbye.

Gracie smiled at the memory and sat up in the grass in Northleach. Dear Cianna, how she missed her at times, as well as Kenneth, and some friends . . . and Adam, of course.

After she'd recovered from her illness, she'd thought about the studies she could pursue. It was still science that enthralled her. She decided that she would learn everything there was to know about scientific method and procedure up to the present day. Perhaps then she'd realise if there was anything she could do with all that knowledge.

She applied herself to her studies with some gusto and raided her father's extensive library, for Ernest was a voracious reader. All of his reference books and scientific manuals would be useful for her research. Her mother was delighted with her newly discovered enthusiasm for science, but her father found it a little perplexing. Soon, however, impressed by her intellect, he began encouraging her, and ordered in all the latest books that he thought might be useful. They spent hours together in the library, and their mutual love of study brought them closer.

Now, Gracie loved to attend lectures and discussion groups with her father, and she took pleasure in his obvious pride in her abilities. Still, these abilities had made her something of a joke amongst many of the local families. Gracie had rejected a proposal of marriage from James Sharp a few years ago. This was much to the relief of his mother, who certainly did not want her precious boy married to that "unnatural Gracie Arundel". Ah well, James was now happily enough married to a lady who took no interest whatsoever in the current studies of Dr Edward Jenner.

Gracie followed Dr Jenner's career with great interest and enthusiasm, despite knowing how it would all turn out. She still vividly remembered being taught at secondary school, and later at university, about Jenner and the dairymaid who consulted him about her rash, which turned out to be cowpox. Jenner had then deliberately infected a little boy with some of the material from one of the dairymaid's pocks. The boy recovered and was better within the week, for cowpox was not a serious threat to people. Knowing that cowpox could pass from person to person as well as from cow to person, Jenner then tested whether cowpox would protect the boy from smallpox. Jenner variolated him and, no doubt to his great relief, the little boy did not develop smallpox, no matter how many times his immunity was tested.

This had all taken place in 1796, a couple of years ago, and in Gracie's current year, Jenner had published all of his research in the book that now lay by her side: *An Inquiry Into the Causes and Effects of the Variolae Vaccinae: A Disease Discovered in Some of the Western Counties of England, Particularly Gloucestershire, and Known by the Name of the Cow Pox.* Jenner lived in Berkeley, some thirty or forty miles away from Gracie, and it was exciting to be so close to the famous doctor, in both historical and literal terms. Jenner's method of protecting people from smallpox had not taken off due to a practical fact— cowpox was relatively rare and doctors who wanted to test the procedure had to obtain cowpox matter from Jenner—and a more mercenary reason—wealthy variolators using live smallpox didn't want to lose income due to the safer and more effective cowpox treatment. But Gracie knew that Jenner would be remembered as a medical genius, the man who rid the world of the scourge of the most hated and feared of diseases.

In terms of Gracie's scientific studies, Jenner's recent endeavours meant that the issue of vaccination was the exciting medical topic of her day. She had begun to apply herself to the study of diseases. For her recent birthday, her father had bought her a compound microscope, and she spent many hours examining bacteria under its lens, including samples from willing, sick neighbours. Her bedroom had begun to look like a laboratory, and it was small wonder that old Mrs Sharp thought her son had made a lucky escape. Gracie was happy though; she had never spent much of her spare time in her previous life in such studies, but the work was interesting.

She rose from the grass and brushed down her dress. It was three o'clock now; time to walk home and prepare for dinner.

Some friends were arriving tonight, as well as some of her father's relations from Kent. In fact, they might have arrived already. She really had better get home quickly. Having had only had a quick bite of bread and cheese for lunch, she was hungry. That would soon be rectified by the enormous dinner that her mother had organised for this evening! Georgian dinners were large anyway, with many, many dishes to choose from, but tonight there would be little chance of finishing all of the meats and puddings and pies her mother would proudly display on her best Wedgwood creamware.

I see things differently now than I used to as Gracie Abbot, she mused, as she walked down the well-known path home. *I know that I have made no great change to humanity here, but I can accept that. I value my own personal happiness more. That must be what Cianna meant when she talked about balance.*

8.

Destiny

A month later, Gracie sat in the carriage of her Kentish cousins admiring the changing landscape as they journeyed south. Her father's wealthy relation, Mr Dawson, and his wife had invited her and Polly to stay with them for a few months at their home in Littlebourne, a village just a few miles east of Canterbury. They had already been travelling for several hours and had taken breaks to rest the four horses that pulled the Dawsons' carriage. Shortly, they would stop at an inn for the night, but they were making the most of the long summer evening and trying to get as many miles between them and Gloucestershire as possible.

It was a long way from Bourton-on-the-Water to Littlebourne, over one hundred and fifty miles, and the Dawsons, being elderly, although still very active, preferred to travel on the better turnpike roads in the direction of London and from there take the relatively safe route home to Canterbury. Gracie was happy to be so close to London again, and she eagerly looked out for the signs on the road signalling which town or village they were approaching. She recognised many names from her motorway journeys around London, but how different the world looked now! She smiled at eighteen-year-old Polly, who had finally drifted off to sleep. She had been too excited to rest the previous night, and nervous energy had sustained her long into the journey. Polly had never travelled so far from home without her parents before, and Kent promised all kinds of wonderful things to a pretty young girl with the right connections. Gracie had to admit that she too was excited. For most of the day she had felt an apprehension in her stomach that was not unpleasant. She longed to see Canterbury in all its splendour as well as visit the seaside towns of Ramsgate and Margate. The days to follow promised fun and frivolity, and Gracie was not such a slave to her studies that she could not put aside her experiments for a while and enjoy herself as much as young Polly.

After several more days of tiring travel, Gracie and Polly strained to see from the window of their carriage the tall spires of Canterbury Cathedral outlined against the cloudless sky. This would be all they would see of the city for a few days, as Gracie knew that their relations would require a substantial rest before venturing anywhere in their carriage again. Although she and Polly could walk the few miles into town easily, she guessed the old people would take pleasure in showing them the sights. The Old Rectory house at Littlebourne, home to the Dawsons, soon came into view. It was indeed very grand, as her mother had told her it would be. A female servant at once issued forth from the house. As soon as the carriage came to a halt, Mrs Dawson tumbled out of its doors and into the servant's arms.

'Oh, Phyllis, what a journey! I could sleep for a week. Here are our young charges. Is everything settled for their visit? Oh, I have so much to tell you, and so much to organise . . .'

Phyllis, obviously accustomed to dealing with an overwrought Mrs Dawson, cut through her mistress's speech and manoeuvred her towards the house.

'Now, ma'am, you know right well that everything will be fine. When has your Phyllis ever let you down? I have your room all prepared as well as the rooms for the young ladies, and I'm going to have you settled down in bed in no time at all, but not before you have some of my warm vegetable broth.'

Apparently, this was all Mrs Dawson needed to hear, for she became as placid and pliable as a lamb.

Servants like Phyllis are worth their weight in gold, Gracie thought with amusement.

A manservant then helped her, Polly and her uncle from the carriage, and they all entered the house together. The interior of the house seemed to belong to an older generation—Gracie assumed this was due to the fact that, as the couple were childless, there had been no young people to introduce the latest fashions. Still, it was a comfortable and pleasant home, and everything was of the finest quality. Polly would be pleased that there was a piano in the corner of one of the rooms, and Gracie looked forward to exploring the contents of her uncle's rather-formal-looking library. Gracie and Polly were shown to bedrooms at either end of the landing on the second floor. They were large and airy and freshly decorated with white-and-lemon cotton-and-lace bedcovers and curtains.

'Lovely, just lovely,' Gracie assured the young maid who had been assigned the role of tending to her and Polly's needs. After they had changed out of their travelling clothes and into fresh dresses, Gracie and Polly joined their uncle downstairs for a lunch of salad, fish and game pie. Gracie was thirsty more than anything, and required several glasses of fruit cordial before she felt quite refreshed again. Her aunt had already retired but had promised the girls that she would be quite herself again after a day's rest and then they would tour the countryside together. Gracie had told her to rest easy—she and Polly would be perfectly content with exploring the village itself in the meantime.

After lunch, the sisters made their way down the lane to the village of Littlebourne. Their uncle had told them that the surrounding scenery and woodland was pretty, and he hadn't exaggerated. So close to Dover, the coast and therefore the warmer climate of France, this part of Kent had the appearance of being rather lush and exotic. Flowers that couldn't be cultivated in the rainier west of England bloomed here, and they found some trees with the most delicious cherries, surely Kentish Red. Polly filled her basket with some of these to take home for the cook to can or bottle or even prepare the Cherry Batter dish that her aunt had described on the journey. Their mouths watered at the prospect. They rambled further afield, delighted with all they saw. Polly found some apples on a tree which she didn't recognise.

She shouted to Gracie. 'They taste so nice though! I must take some of these too for my aunt and uncle. Oh, wouldn't it be wonderful if our mother and father were also here?'

Polly then spied a farmer ahead. She ran towards him to enquire about the apples and just as quickly made her way back to where Gracie waited.

'They are called Worcester Pearmain apples. Isn't that a nice name? That farmer did eye me queerly though. I could hardly understand what he said.'

Gracie laughed. 'Well, you are rather giving the impression that we in Gloucestershire have never seen a piece of fruit! Now, forget your appetite for a minute and come and see the church with me.'

They walked back towards the main road and soon arrived at the medieval Saint Vincent of Saragossa, a typical small country church surrounded by the rather obligatory fallen gravestones. It was terribly peaceful. Gracie read a notice outside that said the church was thought to have been founded by the monks of St Augustine's Abbey, and that it was thirteenth century.

'Thirteenth century,' Polly said, reading over Gracie's shoulder. 'Can you imagine anything as old as that? So many centuries ... Think of all the different people who have come to worship here every week. They died ever so long ago. Brrr, makes me shiver to think of such things.'

'Yes,' Gracie quietly agreed. 'I know what you mean. Let's go in.'

The building was in need of structural repairs inside, but it was still attractive. Gracie walked to the front pews and saw that one was reserved for her aunt and uncle.

'Look, Polly, this is where we'll sit each Sunday.'

Polly had wandered off and was gazing at a wall painting. Gracie joined her.

'It's St Christopher, Gracie—you know, the patron saint of travellers. We're travellers, so maybe seeing this painting here, on our first day, will bring us luck.'

'It's beautiful Polly. Yes, let's hope for luck.'

Travellers indeed, Gracie thought. *If only you knew quite how far I've travelled to be here in this spot on this bright and lovely day.* Gracie suddenly felt overwhelmingly sad. She loved Polly, but she couldn't tell her about her true self. There would always be this distance between them. There had to be. She remembered Cianna's words from what seemed an eternity ago now: 'Life is never, can never be, a level playing field ... It is what you make of your portion that counts . . . If you feel you have been given an unfair amount, let that be the extra charge you carry.' Yes, Gracie certainly felt pinched at times by that extra charge. She walked over and gave her sister, who was now reading the inscriptions on a family tablet, a hug.

'What was that for?'

'For nothing more than the fact that I am very happy to be here, just here, with you.'

'What about your smelly, awful bacteria things? Can you get by without them?' Polly teased.

Gracie laughed. 'Oh, yes, I can do without them very well.'

A few days later, their aunt was fully recovered and ready to take Gracie and Polly to visit Canterbury. They spent a wonderful and busy day shopping and walking and, of course, visiting the glorious Norman and Gothic cathedral. As they left the cathedral, Polly spied a little jeweller's shop with an eye-catching window display.

'What's Polly looking at? Oh, let me see.'

Aunt Dawson moved towards the shop and Gracie followed. Polly was greatly taken by a topaz cross suspended on a fine gold chain. It was quite costly, but Polly had her own money and was resolved to purchase it. Inside the shop, Aunt Dawson greeted the owner and said that she would like to buy *two* topaz crosses on chains. Gracie and Polly tried to intervene, but Aunt Dawson was adamant—she would buy the girls one each as a gift. The shopman said that he had two crosses to sell but that they were slightly different from one another.

'Even better, my good man. Then they will always be able to tell them apart.'

Gracie's cross was slightly larger than Polly's but in every way as lovely. As they left the shop, Gracie kissed her aunt for her generosity and said that she would always treasure her necklace. At that moment, an elderly lady stopped before them.

'My dear Harriet Dawson! And when did you get back from Gloucestershire?'

'Why, Mary! My dears, this is my very good friend Mrs Mary Chesterton. Mary, these are the daughters of my husband's cousin. Mrs Chesterton lives here in Canterbury.'

The women all smiled and shook hands, and it was agreed that they would return to Mrs Chesterton's for some afternoon tea.

'And now, my dears,' said Mrs Chesterton, when they were all settled upon the two sofas that faced each other in her receiving room, 'you have not been here long yet but I would imagine that you are very anxious to get yourselves all dressed up for a ball. Look, look at young Polly blush! She knows what I am talking about. I would wager that your trunks were filled with pretty dresses when you packed to leave your home. Ah, I have not always been old. I remember very well the delights of youth.'

Gracie immediately warmed towards Mrs Chesterton. *She and my aunt are on very good terms and, rather like everyone we have met here thus far, she seems to be extremely wealthy.*

'Harriet,' Mrs Chesterton continued, 'do you plan to take the girls to the Ashford Assembly ball?'

'Well, Mary, you know there are near twenty miles between Ashford and Littlebourne. A long way to travel for a ball.'

'Yes, I had not thought. Still, it would be a great shame for them not to see an Ashford ball while they are in the neighbourhood. No, they simply must go. Why not travel from my house?

I am fourteen miles away but you know it is a much better road the whole way, so it seems less. Come and stay with me, Harriet, you and the girls, and we'll all go to the ball together. I'm here by myself, you know, and I have plenty of room. It will be a rare treat for me to be out in society amongst dancing and courting couples. Yes, let's settle it now. We'll leave from here and return here in my coach.'

If Mrs Dawson had had a mind to argue, her effort would have been to no avail. In any case, Mrs Dawson was happy to acquiesce, and all was decided upon. They would go to Ashford a week from Saturday.

'We're too old to need chaperoning ourselves, aren't we, Harriet?' Mrs Chesterton joked. 'But don't you two forget that your aunt and I were a most delightful couple of girls once upon a time. And won't Mr Dawson be glad that he does not have to go to the ball!'

Mr Dawson did indeed seem to be glad when he was told all about their plans that evening at dinner.

'Although it is true that I do not enjoy a ball, I would be happy to escort you both to a day in Ramsgate or Margate. Does that sound nice?'

The girls were delighted at the prospect of a trip to the seaside. The weather had been so unusually hot lately that it would be heavenly, Polly declared, to feel the cool sea breeze against one's cheek.

And so, on a blistering hot day later that week, Gracie and Polly and their aunt and uncle climbed into the carriage together again and set off for the coastline, intending to also explore the town of Ramsgate. Gracie wore a light muslin gown, but all of the material that covered her legs still made her very warm. At times like this she thought longingly of twenty-first-century outfits. She would also have to shade herself underneath her parasol, as a suntan was the last thing anyone wanted here. There were also bags strapped onto the carriage that contained her and Polly's bathing outfits. Seabathing was quite an ordeal, what with having to go into a bathing machine, change in the dark and then wait to be rolled out into the sea. Still, it was so nice to exit the machine and be in the water that Gracie took advantage of every opportunity. Her aunt had said that the bathing machines at Ramsgate were very well set up and organised in such a way that no one had to wait long to be taken into the water or rolled back out.

A few hours after their departure, Gracie stood on the sand and looked out towards the sea, thinking about France, which lay just beyond it. The Egyptian campaign was taking place—Nelson and Napoleon were fighting it out on the Nile. Would it all work out in the same way? Since she had been here, all the important events had turned out exactly as she recalled. But would that last? She turned back to where her aunt, her uncle and Polly were seated on their sun chairs and smiled. They looked settled for the day—well, maybe not Polly, but certainly the old couple. In fact, was her uncle not already fast asleep? She poked the end of her parasol into the sand and drew little circles. She and Adam had walked up and down this beach before, so long ago. That day, noisy drunken teenagers had shouted rude things at them and flung tin cans—yes, she was sure that's what had happened. Everything looked very different here today. She felt very sad suddenly and, as a force of habit, immediately started thinking about her studies to blot out the bad feelings. Piles of shells of assorted shapes and sizes lay at her feet, and she bent to examine them more closely. Some had the most lovely and distinctive patterns and colours. Incredibly intricate. What would they look like under her microscope? She sorted the most interesting ones into a neat little pile to take home with her. Gracie had no idea how long she was absorbed in her rifling—she guessed later that it was probably quite some time. While lost in her shells, another one landed gently before her on the sand, knocking her neat pile into some disarray.

Gracie raised her head and turned to the right, shading her eyes from the sun. A tall, smiling young man stood a short distance away. He bowed.

'A pretty shell for you, miss, with my compliments. I saw you digging around and choosing your shells so carefully that I thought you really must have that one, surely the best the beach has to offer. I've stood here for some time to wait for you to rise but you didn't, so I'm afraid I decided to boldly gain your attention. Forgive me for my impertinence.'

Gracie had risen while he was speaking, and she bowed in return. Was he simple? What would people make of her talking to a strange young man on the beach? He was dressed very nicely, clearly he was a gentleman, and he looked around her age. Gracie felt nervous meeting his gaze although she scarcely knew why. He was handsome, though not in a terribly obvious way, and his blondish-brown hair was wet. He had clearly recently been in the water.

'Thank you, sir,' Gracie replied, making a point of brushing the sand from her dress so she wouldn't have to look at him. She picked up his shell—it was prettier than the others but not one she would have selected to examine under the microscope. Still, there was no point in telling him that, was there? She opened her little bag to find a handkerchief in which she could tie up her shells, but discovered she had forgotten to bring one. What could she do, then? She didn't want to get her violet drawstring purse dirty. Perhaps her aunt would have something . . .

'Here, let me, please.'

As if reading her thoughts, the man scooped up her shells in his hands and walked the short distance into the sea with them. Bending, he washed them in the water, then brought them back to her, drying them on his trousers.

'All clean now. If you will allow me to wrap them—'

He stopped speaking and bowed at Polly, who had just arrived. Gracie could tell that her sister was burning with curiosity.

'I have been assisting your friend with her shells,' he explained. 'They will make very pretty adornments to a box, or perhaps a screen.'

'Ha! Gracie is my sister, and if you think that these shells will be used for anything so frivolous then you are very much mistaken,' Polly replied mockingly. 'Show some respect—my sister is a scientist and she will, doubtless, have some clever way of proving this or that by them. I am Polly Arundel, by the way. What is your name, sir?'

The man was clearly amused by Polly's frankness. People were generally either entertained by her or offended.

'My name is Thomas—Tom—Blake, miss. I am very pleased to make the acquaintance of you both.'

'Polly'—Gracie turned towards her talkative sister—'do you have a handkerchief for my shells?'

'Yes, of course. Here you are. Anyway, I just ran over to let you know that our aunt and uncle are safely sleeping so you need have no fears. Farewell, sir!'

Polly bowed again, this time with a flourish, and skipped back to her seat.

'Honestly!' Gracie held a hand to her forehead. 'My sister is very young sir.'

'Yes, and quite charming, though I must confess, also quite terrifying. Do you ever know what she might or might not say?'

'Sometimes.' Gracie laughed. 'But not often, indeed.'

'Would you care to take a short stroll along the beach?'

'Well, yes, why not?'

As they walked, Gracie and Tom talked about why they were in Ramsgate. Tom explained that he was visiting with a good friend and his family. They were staying nearby. They halted for a moment to let some frolicking children pass by. A governess followed behind, tutting as she bent to retrieve their discarded clothing. Diverted dogs ran everywhere. The pair smiled at the happy, noisy scene before Tom resumed talking.

'I've actually just completed my studies, at Cambridge.'

'Oh, and what do you intend to do now?' Gracie asked.

'That is a difficult question to answer. The truth is, I don't know. I'm a younger son, you see. My father owns quite a large estate in Devon. My older brother will inherit that so his future is all settled. Mine is less clear. Indeed, it is positively poised between one thing and another at the moment. My father wants me to enter the law profession, but that does not appeal to me, I am afraid. I wish to please him, for he is the very best of men, but my heart is simply not in it. Still, I believe I shall be a lawyer.'

'What do you want to do?'

'Science, would you believe? I would like to spend my time in research and experimentation. I am interested in various fields, and am enthralled by the recent work of Dr Jenner—perhaps you know about him?'

Gracie's eyebrows shot up, and she replied enthusiastically. 'Yes! He lives relatively close to me, in Gloucestershire, although we do not know him. I have read all his pamphlets.'

'You have? How idiotic my remarks about decorating boxes must have seemed. I'm so sorry.'

'Please, forget it. But cannot you pursue your scientific studies?'

'Can I be frank?'

Gracie nodded.

'Well, I have no real money with which to support myself if I choose that path. I need a sound career. I have not trained to be a doctor, and I confess I have little relish for the idea of doing so. Setting broken collarbones and prescribing visits to the waters at Bath may put bread on the table, but I want to spend my days studying something bigger. Do you know what I mean?'

'Certainly.'

Tom continued. 'I have the opportunity to live for a few years with a very eminent scientist, in Germany. I met him while I was at university. The training and study I could receive there . . . But it is such an unstable life. If I wished to marry, well, I'm a pampered young man, you see. I've too long been used to the best ways of living. Could I be poor? I don't know. Still, every fibre in me tells me I should go to Germany and pursue my studies.'

They had stopped walking, and Gracie raised her face and looked into Tom's eyes. Something told her that this was exactly what Tom should do, even though she knew nothing about him.

'I think you know what you ought to do. Despite all of the money and comfort you might have in your legal profession, you will always wonder about what might have been. You should go to Germany. If you decide afterward to begin your career as your father desires, then what, really, has been lost? Does every instinct that you possess tell you that you are a scientist, not a lawyer?'

Tom appeared to consider her words carefully, as if his whole destiny depended on them.

'Yes, it does.'

'Then be what you were born to be. You only have one life, after all.'

How strange of me to stand here and tell someone that, she thought incredulously. *If only he knew.* The two young scientists gazed at one another for a long moment before reverting to small talk, embarrassed by the sudden intensity. Tom told Gracie that he knew parts of Gloucestershire fairly well. He had some family in Somerset, not too far away. Had she been to many entertainments since her arrival in Kent?

Gracie told Tom about the ball in Ashford the following Saturday.

'Ashford? And you are definitely going there?'

'Yes, most definitely.'

'Ah, your sister approaches us again. I shall take my leave of you now. I have taken enough of your time. I intend to visit Ashford too, so I will see you there. Perhaps you will be most kind to dance with me, if you are not otherwise engaged, of course.'

'I have no engagement.'

'I see.'

They shook hands rather awkwardly.

'I will never forget this day, Miss Gracie Arundel. I have agonised over something that you have made appear so simple. I will go to Germany.'

Tom bowed to both Gracie and Polly, who had now reached them, and walked back to find his party.

'A handsome man,' Polly said. 'Is he rich?'

'Not at all,' Gracie answered.

'What a shame.' Polly sighed. 'Now my aunt is awake and looks for you. Come, she wants to take us to bathe.'

Back in her bedroom at the Dawson house later that day, Gracie thought about her encounter on the beach. They had spoken to each other so openly. And about science, of all things. It had been so out of the ordinary, their meeting and subsequent conversation, that Gracie wondered if it meant something. Did she have some role to play in encouraging Tom to be a scientist? Was she about to, even in some small way, help change the shape of the past? Tom had said that he would most likely be a lawyer, after all, and now he would go to Germany and study and, if what he said was true, it was due to her. Thoughts like these unnerved her.

She checked to see if her bedroom door was locked and then pulled out the red box with the glass bell that was concealed within her dresser. She would never travel any distance without it. Should she ask Cianna about Tom? Gracie considered this option for a few minutes but decided against it. Much as she would love to see and talk to Cianna, and listen to her interpretation of the day's events, she didn't think that in calling Cianna she would be sticking to the conditions. Really, it probably all meant nothing. *Someone else might well have talked Tom into going to Germany in his other past, or he might still not go*, she thought. And even if he did dedicate his life to science this time, it didn't by any stretch mean that he would alter the world in any way.

But Gracie couldn't shake the memory of their conversation, or of him. She had never, she finally admitted to herself, felt that kind of attraction towards any man but Adam, either in this life or Gracie Abbot's. The fact that she *could* feel this way about another man shocked her. Oh, she'd had her flirtations with James Sharp and some others, but they had meant nothing. Had Tom liked her too? He had been most decided about ensuring that she would be at the Ashford ball, and he had already claimed a dance with her, and made sure to check whether she was engaged. *Yes*. Gracie smiled. *He likes me.*

On arriving at Ashford with Polly, Aunt Dawson and Mrs Chesterton, Gracie immediately scanned the reception room for Tom. She was finding it difficult to quell her nerves. She felt ridiculous, and she didn't want to think about how disappointed she would be if she arrived home without having seen him. She had taken a great deal of care over her appearance, and she knew she looked her best. Polly had told her so several times, and teased her that she would capture the heart of every single man. *I am not so greedy*, Gracie had thought.

She took off her cloak and smoothed her lilac silk dress. She was wearing her new topaz necklace, and she hoped it would bring her luck—after all, she had first learned of this ball the day she received it.

'Come, Gracie,' Mrs Chesterton called to her, an amused look on her face.

She thinks I'm an excited young girl who's eager to be danced with and admired, Gracie thought. *And I suppose she's correct.*

The four ladies entered the spacious and elegant ballroom, and a waiter quickly presented them with glasses of punch. They found some seats in a conspicuous spot and watched the dancers. Polly, who was a great lover of music, told them that the playing was of a very high standard and the dances fashionable. This seemed to please the proud Kentish ladies a great deal. Before long, a young man came towards them, bowed and asked Polly if he might dance with her. She accepted, and the other three commented upon the excellence and politeness of Polly's partner, as well as on how pleasingly they danced together. Still there was no Tom. A middle-aged man asked Gracie to dance. She tried to get out of it, but her aunt insisted that she accept.

'Let us sit and admire how well you dance. Enjoy yourself.'

Gracie and her partner joined the end of a group of couples, and the contredanse began. She smiled at her partner and tried to look polite. The sequence of this dance was so complex that she needed to keep her thoughts on her next step. As a result, she didn't notice Tom enter the ballroom. Accepting a glass of punch, he surveyed the crowd. *It was a warm night*, he considered, *but was Gracie here?* He noticed Polly first. Their eyes locked as she danced nearby. He smiled and bowed and she waved in return. *How happy Gracie would be now*, Polly thought, as she took her partner's hands again.

At the end of her dance, Gracie returned to her seat to see her aunt and Mrs Chesterton talking to a small group of ladies and gentlemen.

'Ah, Gracie,' said Mrs Chesterton as she spotted her. 'You are a delightful dancer. And may I introduce to you the squire of Godmersham Park, Mr Edward Austen, and his sister, Miss Jane Austen. You two young ladies are around the same age I think.'

Gracie tried her very best to remain calm—her red cheeks could be blamed on her recent dancing—as she extended her hand to her idol. It was received by a cool little hand that belonged to a slim lady of above average height with shiny chestnut-brown hair and bright, very bright, hazel eyes. She looked sensible and intelligent, although there was nothing extraordinary about her appearance. However, the more probing observer could not fail to notice the challenging glare in her eyes as well as her supreme self-confidence. This woman clearly knew herself, and others. The older members of the group resumed their discussion, leaving the two younger ladies together. Jane looked Gracie squarely in the eyes and enquired whether she was enjoying her stay in Kent. Gracie said that indeed she was, in spite of the heat that had been quite overpowering of late.

'Yes, you can expect at least one lady to faint in here tonight from it. And do you care to dance, Miss Arundel? Are you fond of music?'

'To listen to music, yes. I like to dance very much too, but I am afraid I cannot play very well.'

Gracie knew she must be coming across as nervous, and it irked her that she was making such little use of this momentous opportunity. This woman was the reason she was here, for Heaven's sake! Jane Austen looked little like the well-known drawing that existed of her. She was prettier in real life. Gracie noticed that she was looking quite intently at the cross she wore around her neck.

'Your necklace is lovely.'

'Thank you—my aunt bought it for me in Canterbury. My sister has one too, although it is slightly different.'

'I like it very much.'

It was time to be bold and test the waters.

'And how do you like to spend your time, Miss Austen? Do you ride, or play, or, well, how do you most happily occupy yourself?'

As if dealing with a question she was well practised at answering, Jane said that she liked to play the piano, and that she was also a proficient needlewoman.

'But then, isn't every woman?' She laughed. 'And what about you?'

Gracie responded directly and without hesitation. 'I dabble in science. I conduct all sorts of experiments in my bedroom. And I am an avid reader.'

Jane looked keenly at Gracie. It seemed she had not expected this answer. Gracie saw the flickering of thoughts passing behind Jane's eyes and knew that she was considering whether to be more honest.

'How unusual,' she said. 'You must be very intelligent. I also love to read all sorts of books, mostly novels.'

She hesitated, and then quietly continued. 'I also enjoy composition. Oh, nothing of any consequence, but it gives me a great deal of pleasure, I confess.'

Gracie could have kissed the hem of Jane's dress on hearing these words. Jane Austen had just confided in her that she liked to write! The two young women smiled at each other—really smiled at each other—then. They were equals and they knew it. Polly joined them at that moment. After Gracie introduced the two women, Jane admired her necklace too.

When a gentleman approached them and asked for the pleasure of a dance with Miss Austen, Polly whispered to Gracie, 'He is here. I saw him. He was looking for you. Oh, he looked so handsome!'

This night was almost too much to endure! But how did Polly know about her feelings for Tom? She hadn't even spoken of him. She also noticed that Jane had heard every word of Polly's attempted whisper, and she was eyeing Gracie with some interest. Flustered, Gracie opened her mouth to talk, and then closed it again. Tom was coming swiftly towards her.

'Good evening, Miss Arundel, Miss Polly Arundel . . .'

After Tom was introduced to the whole of their party, including Jane Austen, Gracie accepted his invitation to dance. They walked to the dance floor, awkward but happy, while Jane, escorted by her dancing partner, watched them intently.

There was little conversation at first. Indeed, Gracie could barely make eye contact with him.

Finally she asked, 'And do you still intend to go to Germany, sir?'

'I do. It is all arranged. You must believe me when I tell you that it is your doing entirely, Miss Arundel. I lacked the resolve to commit to the more daring decision without the steadying hand of an obviously wiser person.'

'You give me too much praise, Mr Blake. And when do you leave?'

'In a few days.'

'I see.'

They were silent again for a while, and when the dance had ended, Tom asked if he could fetch her some refreshment. She said yes, and he led her to an area away from her friends, as if he wanted to keep her to himself for a while yet. Gracie sipped her punch and Tom sat down beside her.

'Miss Arundel, let me recapture some of the frankness of our earlier conversation. I feel so comfortable talking to you. Talking to you is indeed unlike talking to anyone else I have met. There is something so fresh and direct in your speech. Meeting you has changed my life. You came to me at a moment when I sorely needed you. If you could know how I have looked forward to this evening. I dreaded your not being here. I, well, you could not guess . . .'

Gracie's raised eyes told him, without need of words, that she could indeed guess.

'Let us dance again,' Tom said. 'If we have both looked forward to this evening so much we ought to ensure we enjoy it.'

They danced together most of the evening, and while they danced they discussed their scientific interests. Tom also spent time talking to Mrs Chesterton and Aunt Dawson. Soon it was the last dance of the night and Tom, once more, chose Gracie as his partner.

'In Germany, I will keep myself informed, of course, with all of Dr Jenner's research. I will think of you in all I read. You know, I almost dread going now. I have no prospects but . . . well, perhaps we will meet again when I return?'

Gracie's heart felt as though it would break. Of course they wouldn't see each other again. He would forget her and she, well, she might not even be here by the time he returned to England. Was it unfair of her to give him any false hope?

'Perhaps we will, Mr Blake.'

Jane Austen was preparing to leave, she could see. She had been aware of Jane throughout the night, but a moment to talk again hadn't arisen. She had discussed science with Tom while the greatest of all writers, to her mind, was within a few feet!

'You will continue with your studies too, Miss Arundel?'

'I will indeed. And,' she said jokingly, 'if I hear one day that you have become a famous scientist, I will be very glad and will tell everyone proudly that you once picked the prettiest shell off the beach just for me.'

'If I become a famous scientist then I hope you will take all the credit for it because it all lies with you.'

There was nothing for it now. The night was over. Gracie and Tom said their farewells, and he left with his party, which he had ignored all evening. Gracie caught a glimpse of his leaving the ballroom, his friend's hand on his shoulder. As soon as the music stopped playing, Gracie became aware of the sound of heavy rain lashing against the roof.

'A summer storm,' Aunt Dawson commented. 'Let us hurry into our carriage and be gone.'

Their carriage came to the front steps and, trying not to get too soaked, the ladies piled into the interior.

'What a downpour,' said Mrs Chesterton. 'It is really quite savage.'

The coachman drove back to Canterbury very slowly that evening. As a result, the ladies had time to discuss all that had passed.

'I thought at first that you might strike up a friendship with Miss Austen, Gracie,' Mrs Chesterton said. 'But she stood little chance when young Mr Blake appeared.'

Polly laughed at Gracie's blushes.

Mrs Chesterton continued. 'Yes, nice girl, Miss Austen, but penniless, of course. Perhaps brother Edward will do something for her, but with his growing family that might prove difficult.'

Polly began to doze, and Mrs Chesterton and Aunt Dawson talked on and on while Gracie stared out of the dark and rain-spattered window, thinking all the while that the devastating weather suited the aching of her heart.

9.

The Storm

As Gracie and Tom journeyed home from the Ashford ball, one hundred and fifty miles away, in Banbury, Oxfordshire, Benjamin Lockhart, a local farmer, stared out at the miserable, rain-soaked night and decided to stay in the warmth of his local tavern for a little while longer. It wasn't just raining outside—it was a positive storm. Walking the few miles home would be dangerous; he wouldn't be able to see a thing. He could not afford to take any foolhardy chances with his health, or life.

'Have another drink, Ben. She will be fine. Tucked up cosy and warm in your sturdy house. Why, I'll wager she'll be sleeping sound at this very moment.'

Ben nodded and accepted the beer he was offered from the tavern keeper and wandered to the window. Yes, Marian would be safe, but with her being pregnant, well, a man just worried. He'd felt unsure enough about leaving her tonight, but she had insisted. That was just like her; she was a good wife. Today had seen the end of a long and tiring week of clearing the fields. And what with the recent weather, it had been an exceptionally good crop. Ben traditionally celebrated the yield each year by taking his workers out for a good drink—they deserved it.

Marian was eight months pregnant with their first child and in good health, although the heat had recently taken it out of her. She'd looked particularly tired today, and he'd offered to put off the drinking and stay at home with her. But she would not hear of it.

'No. Ben, don't be silly. You know I'll be well tended to here with Martha by my side. She'll stay with me until you get home, won't you, Martha?'

'I will indeed, Mrs Lockhart. My Jason will come and get me at my usual time of 10:30 in the evening. Will that suit you, Mr Lockhart?'

'Yes, lass, it will. I'll be back by then though, so you can skip off home yourself as soon as I get in.'

Martha was a good girl, and sensible. She wouldn't leave Marian alone before he got home. Yes, all would be well. What a change in the weather though. It had been blazing sunshine when he'd waved goodbye to Marian and walked off down the lane into town at around five o'clock that afternoon. And now this! It was approaching midnight. Would Marian have guessed that he'd decided to stay put in the tavern until the weather cleared? Of course, she wasn't stupid, and she wouldn't want him setting off for home on a night like this. Only he, the keeper and another man, a stranger to these parts, were left in the tavern. The weather had grown very bad just before ten. If he'd left at ten he would have made it home just before the weather really took a turn for the worse. But he'd been cosy with his drink, and the stranger, a heartily entertaining man, had been regaling him with tales of London life and politics—and Ben did like to talk politics.

His men were long gone, but they all lived nearby. His drinking companion was staying at the inn just a few streets away, but he had nothing to rush off for and was happy to remain in the

THE STORM

tavern for however long it remained open. And Ben had stayed with him, enjoying the sound of his own voice, until realising it was really too late to leave. He walked back to the table where his new friend sat and told himself for the hundredth time that all would be fine.

Earlier that evening, at around nine thirty, Marian had heard a sharp rap at the front door. Who could it be? Ben home early and forgotten his key? Probably. But it was Jason, Martha's intended. A few minutes later, Martha hurried into the parlour where Marian sat with her knitting.

'Please Mrs Lockhart, my mam's come down sick again. She's asking for me. The doctor says she might not last the night. Jason's come to fetch me home, but I've told him I can't leave you, not until Mr Lockhart gets back.'

'Oh Martha, no, I didn't know your mother was so ill. Off you go instantly. I'll be quite all right. My husband will be home with me in no time.'

Martha looked undecided, so Marian stood and shooed her off into the kitchen and bade her cover herself with her shawl as it was beginning to rain. She packed some buns into a basket and gave them to Martha to take with her. The girl's family were poor, and no doubt there would be a lot of relatives and friends around the old lady's bed.

After Martha left, Marian resumed her knitting. She was sure Ben would be back with her in less than an hour. She'd doze by the fire until then, and if she slept, he'd awaken her with a kiss, just as he always did.

When Marian awoke at ten thirty to the sound of rain lashing against the window, she immediately worried that something had happened to her husband. She made to rise, but an agonising pain ripped through her belly. The hurt, whatever it was, strangled her breath. She tried to regulate her breathing, but each time she felt she was getting somewhere, the searing pain began again. Something was wrong. It was too early for her baby to arrive.

'Come on, little one, give Mother a chance to catch her breath.'

Marian's voice sounded weak and small in the utter silence of the room. Even the regular ticking of the pendulum clock seemed to boom inside her head. She thought she could hear Ben, and somehow, she made her way to the window. The barn door had blown open, and it was banging against itself. Marian turned to resume her seat and stopped, horrified. A thick trail of blood led back to her chair. Was all that blood from her? She touched her belly. Was she feeling the birth pains that meant the baby was ready to be pushed out? No. Marian screamed aloud as another pain gripped her. She fell to her knees, sweating. These fresh pains were much more intense than those she'd experienced just a few minutes earlier. She was completely immobilised. All she could do was lie on the ground, try to remain calm and pray. The local doctor would be nearby tending Martha's mother, but she couldn't go out to seek him. The clock said it was a quarter to eleven. Ben would be here soon.

By eleven thirty, Marian knew that Ben must have decided to stay at the tavern under the assumption she would be here safe with Martha and Jason, who normally would not have left her. The pains were relentless in their extremity and regularity. The carpet was saturated with blood—it poured out of her like water from a jug. She was so weak that she was beginning to lose consciousness.

'Ben, Ben, my love, please come home to me,' she whispered.

There was still no urge to push. She'd tried to anyway, but that had only made the blood come thicker and faster; a strange pain had settled around her abdomen. She put her hands on her belly and instinctively knew that her baby was still alive. But for how much longer? The rain was not abating in the least. Ben might not come home until morning. She thought wryly of how confident and safe she always presented herself as being in front of Ben. He would believe she would be fine, but she needed him to worry about her now and come home. An active farmer's wife, Marian knew enough about animals in labour to know that if the baby did not arrive soon, or if the blood loss could not be stopped by some means, then she, and thus the baby, would perish before long. She'd assisted Ben many times in the barn during the lambing and foaling seasons. A sickening thought suddenly entered her feverish mind. Would it come to that? Could she do it without harming her child? Marian writhed on the floor as another pain took hold of her, and she prayed once more that Ben would arrive soon to save his family.

At 12:30 am, Marian crawled to the cupboard in the hallway, where her husband kept his bag of medical instruments. It was no good—she was dying, but her baby still lived. The little mite would only have a chance if she got him out of her and into the world as quickly as she could. The bag was heavy. With the last remaining drops of strength that she possessed, Marian slung the bag around her neck and managed to make her way back to the weak fire she'd started in the parlour. The baby had to be kept warm at all costs. Her accounts-keeping book lay by her chair, and she scrawled a short note for Ben, no more than a few scratched lines, which explained why she was about to take this course of action. Her pen ran dry before she could tell him of her love once more but, no matter—he knew how she adored him.

Lying flat upon her back, Marian opened the front of her dress and exposed her swollen belly. The flickering flames cast shadows across its bulk. With as much will as she could muster, she found the tool she was looking for in Ben's bag and raised it high above her stomach, examining its condition. It was like Ben to keep his instruments in such good order, to be ready for use whenever necessary. Marian licked her parched lips and tasted salt water. Whether tears or sweat, she no longer knew. She'd seen Ben bring animals by the knife on a few occasions. Clearing her mind as best as she was able, she eyed her stomach and thought where best to cut. She held the knife to her belly but hesitated when she felt the cool steel blade against her skin. How could she do this? She thought of her unborn baby. Her faintly beating heart swelled with love for the little being she hadn't even seen yet. This was for her darling's survival, for the future. She was now the past. She held the knife firmly but lightly, as she had seen Ben do, and cut into her skin as forcibly and gently as she could. Her screams echoed in the empty house, frightening the horses in the yard so much that they kicked and whinnied.

Ben buttoned up his coat and stepped outside into the wind and rain. Unable to rest easy any longer, Ben had decided to make his way home at all costs. His companion was also about to make the short walk up the road to his inn.

'Well, goodbye then, Ben. It's been a rare pleasure talking to you.'

'You too, Josiah. If we don't meet again, take care on your travels.'

'Many thanks. Give my best wishes to your wife.'

The two men shook hands and set off on their separate routes into the treacherous night. It was close to two in the morning. Ben found his usual path and stuck to it grimly. Each time he slipped or fell on the wet and muddy ground, he picked himself up at once and ensured he didn't let himself get turned around. Luckily it was more or less a straight path. At last he saw the lights of his house. The trip home had taken twice as long as it normally did. As he drew closer, he noticed that there was no light upstairs—only in the downstairs parlour. He felt sick to his stomach to think that poor Marian had waited up for him. And Martha and Jason too? Shamed, for he knew he smelled of drink, Ben ran the rest of the way home. And when he reached his front door, he didn't even notice that the barn had blown open.

Although Josiah had had a far shorter journey to make than Ben, not knowing the town and being the worse for drink, he'd lost his way not long after Ben's departure. *Yes*, he marvelled, *that farmer could certainly hold his drink.*

Josiah was now utterly lost in the dark night. *Will this accursed morning never arrive?* He fell over heavily several times and thought, foolishly, about lying in the dirt until daylight. *Aye, and a fine man you'll look for that when the local women see you in the morning.* No, he'd move on and try to find his dwelling place. Suddenly he heard hooves running steadily towards him. It was clearly a horse, but how to avoid it? Where was it? Josiah spun wildly about. He thought to shout out to the person on the horse so that the rider could attempt to avoid him.

But the horse had no passenger. It was running free as a result of a stable blown to the ground by the winds. Josiah was now doomed. He knocked his head against the road as the horse charged into him, her back legs trampling his body. The stranger to town, who had arrived only that morning, died instantly.

Numb with shock, Ben gazed at his beloved wife lying amidst a vast pool of blood in the parlour. Her eyes were wide open, and he knew that she was cold dead. The knife, and her belly—what had she done? He forced his clenched fist into his mouth to stop himself from screaming. And at that moment he heard the faint cry of a baby—so faint he thought he was imagining it. But, no, there it was again. He moved like a walking corpse towards his wife and picked up the tiny baby boy that lay by her side. *She had held him at least.* Kissing his wife tenderly, Ben cradled his son to his chest. He sat down on a chair by the one which still held Marian's knitting. *My fault, all my fault! May I burn in Hell for this!* He viewed longingly the woman he had worshipped, whose face remained serene, even smiling.

Later that same morning, as Polly gazed out the window and admired the brightly coloured rainbow as they breakfasted, Mrs Chesterton reported on exactly how dramatic the previous night's weather had been. Trees had been torn out of their roots, houses blown to pieces. Indeed, it was even said that some lives had been lost.

For the residents of Banbury, two funerals would take place within the next few days—one for a long-time resident and one for a stranger.

Martha's old mother would live to see the passing of another year.

10.

Falling in Love

At the turn of the century, Alessandro Volta announced his invention of the electric battery, Frederick William Herschel discovered infrared light and Edward Jenner's friend, Humphry Davy, suggested that the gas nitrous oxide could be used to relieve pain during surgery, although anaesthetics were not used routinely until the 1840s. Jenner was continuing his work as a family doctor, and Gracie Arundel was still spending her time reading and absorbing all she could about the various branches of science. Although the term wasn't coined until 1902 in the world Gracie Abbot had known, Gracie Arundel's research focus lay firmly with immunology.

It was a crisp October day in 1800 and Gracie was sitting on a bench in the rear garden of her home, a black woollen shawl drawn tightly about her shoulders. Open on her lap was Herschel's *Investigation of the Powers of Prismatic Colours to Heat and Illuminate Objects*—in her opinion, currently the most interesting development in science. The fascinating thing for Gracie about Herschel's experiment was that it perfectly illustrated the idea that there were things that could not be seen with the eye: types of light, for example. She had seen many things that others would neither believe nor imagine, and although nobody could know her thoughts on the subject, such a discovery validated her existence.

She sighed and dropped her book onto the grass. She had been feeling anxious and moody of late. She rose and decided to walk around the vast garden briskly—maybe that would warm her bones and stop her from feeling so cold. She was lonely, too. Polly was staying with a newly married friend near London. Her weekly letters were filled with tales of balls and escapades and lovers threatening to duel over her favours—all very Polly-ish. Gracie smiled. She'd had the opportunity to visit an old friend, Charlotte Parker, near Basingstoke this month but had declined the invitation. Charlotte had recently had a baby, and although Gracie liked babies very much, she couldn't bear the implication from others that perhaps she should put aside her studies in favour of having one herself.

In that respect, she wryly thought, *things had not changed a huge deal from now to the twenty-first century.* Twenty-five years old, Gracie was still considered fairly young. But she no longer felt young. She had realised some time ago that her youth had reached its height and come to an end at precisely the same time—the occasion of her holiday with the Dawsons in Kent over two years ago now. She had set off on that holiday feeling all the promise of a new spring day but had returned feeling as bleak and desolate as the autumn winds which even now blew about her skirts. Since her meeting with Tom Blake, Gracie had felt restless and unfulfilled.

It wasn't as if she thought of Tom every moment, not even every day. She would hardly say she was in love with him. She frequently remonstrated with herself—*how can I be in love with someone I've met twice, and so long ago?* There had been no contact, of course, between Gracie and Tom during these years. She guessed he might have returned to England from Germany by now, but who could say? Would he even remember her? Perhaps, perhaps not.

Alicia watched her daughter parade up and down the garden and sighed. What ailed her? Alicia had long ago accepted the fact that her daughter was a gifted young woman, special, and this made her proud. But she was also wise enough to realise that with greatness came an added burden. With whom could Gracie converse? No one of her age or gender. Where would all these experiments lead her? Gracie was viewed in Bourton-on-the-Water as being rather like her mother—original, different, slightly foreign. However, whereas Alicia, a wife and mother, spent her time in the traditionally female occupations of teaching the young and visiting the sick, Gracie involved herself in more masculine pursuits and interests. It was not, the villagers often said, that she was a plain young woman, or that she lacked any social graces. Indeed, she was attractive, seemed to enjoy parties and always dressed fashionably and with taste. Why then, they declared, did she have to be so different? Alicia knew, from Polly, about the young man Gracie had met on the beach. A scientist too. She'd seen how withdrawn Gracie had been on her return from Kent, although she'd done her best to be in good cheer. Often Alicia forgot that there might be something troubling Gracie; perhaps Gracie did too. For now, she would take out this cup of tea to her daughter and tell her about the friends she had met in the town that day.

* * *

Gracie received her tea and gave her dear mother a kiss on the cheek.

'Ah, Mother, and did you get the lace you needed?'

'I did. And it was less expensive than I expected.'

'Oh, but we all know that Mr Fortescu is in love with you. He would gladly give you anything in the shop for free, so long as Mrs Fortescu was upstairs asleep, which she usually is, of course.'

'Oh, Gracie,' her mother said with a laugh, 'you could hear her snores all over the shop today! I hardly knew whether to remark upon it!'

The women laughed heartily, and Gracie rested her head on her mother's shoulder. These were the times she liked best, when she and Alicia could sit and chat and laugh together, friends as well as mother and daughter. As usual, her mother smelled of violet perfume, one of Gracie Abbot's favourite scents. Gracie often thought it strange that they should like the same smell so much.

'And what else did you do in town, Mother? Had Father's newspaper arrived?'

'It had, and he reads it happily now. But I ran into Sophy and her brother and mother.'

'Sophy! So they are home now? I must go and visit her soon.'

'Yes, I said you would go and see her. She was anxious to see you too, it seemed.'

'I feel quite guilty. She wrote several letters to me when she was away at Bath but I don't think I answered them all. Did she write to me to tell me she was returning, I wonder?'

'No, I shouldn't think so. Her father wanted to get back to his business. I think they would have stayed longer if it had not been for that. She seemed quite pleased by the prospect of travelling again. Her mother talked of sending her to stay with a cousin, in Bridgwater, I think.'

'And Sophy is getting to that "difficult" age, after all,' Gracie could not help but add. 'There are no eligible bachelors for her here in Bourton, so other areas must be considered, and Sophy must be seen in as many places as possible in the hope that someone will decide that she would make an excellent wife. Poor girl!'

'Now Gracie, consider, Sophy does not have a large portion by any means, and she is not very pretty, it is true. Her mother does right to try and get her settled with as eminent a man as possible.'

'I trust that her warmth and intelligence will help her in her quest to matrimony then. I would like to see Sophy happily married too, if only to stop her mother's presenting her at every party within a fifty-mile radius as if she were a prize cow!'

Alicia swatted Gracie's leg playfully, and Gracie smiled sweetly.

'I'll go and visit Sophy and her family tomorrow morning.'

On her walk to the Myerses' house the next day, Gracie stopped to look in shop windows and drank in the fresh morning air. The weather was more pleasant than it had been yesterday, and she was looking forward to seeing her friend again. After Charlotte married and moved away, Gracie had begun spending a lot more time with Sophy Myers, who had lived in Bourton-on-the-Water all her life. Her father was the local attorney and her mother the arbiter of all that was right and proper in the town's proceedings—a nice woman, but someone with whom Gracie could find little to speak about. The family dwelled in a good-sized house just off the main street. It was slightly before eleven in the morning as Gracie knocked on the front door. The maid led her into the front parlour. Mr Myers and his son were at work, but Mrs Myers and Sophy were busily unpacking some fripperies and knickknacks they had purchased in Bath, worthless things but pretty nonetheless.

Sophy and her mother greeted Gracie warmly and led her to a chair by the fire.

'Look at what we have been buying,' said Mrs Myers. 'Won't these napkin rings look wonderful with my green table linen? Do you remember my green linen?'

Gracie racked her brains but had no recollection of Mrs Myers's green tablecloth. As usual in these situations, she wondered whether to nod or tell the truth. She opted for the latter, and the good woman ran off to rectify that omission straightaway.

'Oh, Gracie, it is good to see you again,' said Sophy. 'I bought you some lace gloves. Here.'

Gracie admired how well they fit her hands. 'Did you enjoy Bath?'

'Yes. Although I think Mother was disappointed that I could not make more of an impression. But tell me, what else could I do? I went to as many parties as I could, tried to look my best at all times and smiled and nodded appropriately during every tedious story any man cared to relate to me. I dare say if I were prettier or younger or richer I could have broken a few hearts, but I do my best with the material I have been given. Now, if I had your looks or Polly's spirits or

Charlotte's way of making every man relaxed and talkative, well, I would be happy. But I know I'm shy and plain, despite my mother's best efforts.'

'Sophy, you run yourself down so much. You always have. Perhaps that is your problem. You are far more than you give yourself credit for. There is no woman in Bourton with whom I would rather converse.'

'Ah, but unfortunately, dear Gracie, I cannot expect you to make me an offer of marriage, can I?'

As the women laughed, the maid entered with some refreshments, followed by Mrs Myers and her green cloth, which was very much admired over the course of their tea and scones.

'And is your mother at the school this afternoon, Gracie?'

'She is, Mrs Myers.'

'Then I think I will go and see her. I brought back patterns for some new curtains for the classroom and I would like to show them to her.'

Gracie smiled but thought of how her mother would hardly relish the prospect of spending what would easily be an hour or more discussing colour schemes with Mrs Myers. Still, she meant well and they would brighten up the place.

'And did your mother tell you of Sophy's plans to visit Bridgwater in Somersetshire? I have a cousin who resides there. I had not seen her for some years— indeed, we had quite lost touch, although we were once very good friends. She is now a widow and we met again in Bath. She was taking the waters for her gout, you see.'

Gracie smiled and nodded as Mrs Myers talked on and on.

'And so she offered to take Sophy for a month or more to stay with her. She is rich and by all accounts has a very grand style of living. But, oh, the social life in Bridgwater, many good prospects. My cousin tells me that if Sophy did not have an offer within a week she would be surprised. Rich merchants and men of business, all for the asking by the sounds of it.'

Mrs Myers finally stopped herself, perhaps fearing she had gone too far. Gracie tactfully resumed the discussion.

'I have never been to Bridgwater, but of course it is a well-known trading centre. And it is always delightful to be near water.'

'Yes, Bridgwater Bay is nearby,' Sophy interjected.

'And, oh, I recall now why its name was familiar to me when I first heard mention of it. Bridgwater was the first town in Britain to petition the government to ban slavery, in 1797, was it not? I read about it in the newspapers.'

Although interested in the issue of mankind in Bridgwater, Gracie's remark only served to make Mrs Myers nod blankly. 'Now, my dears, I shall leave you and go off to see Mrs Arundel.'

Sophy smiled at Gracie as her mother busied about the room and then, finally, left.

'Mother speaks of Bridgwater as if it were another Eden.'

'Is she going with you?'

'No, I think she has had enough of travel for a while. She trusts me to be on my best behaviour. It is true that my mother's cousin is very rich. Mrs Wyndham is a nice woman who, I feel, is a little lonely. It is as much for her benefit as mine that she asks me to stay. I have thought about it and I would very much like it if you could come with me to stay there. I would need to write and ask for her permission, but I am sure Mrs Wyndham would say yes. If all is agreed, would you like to come along?'

Gracie thought for a few moments. A change of scenery would be very welcome. And Bridgwater certainly seemed to be an interesting place to visit. Her mother would encourage her to go, she knew. And, why not? A month, that was all.

'Let me think about it, Sophy. I'll give you an answer by tomorrow.'

'Of course. But where is Mrs Wyndham's address, in any case . . . Ah, here it is.'

Sophy pulled a sheet of paper from a book and laid it on the table before Gracie. Gracie glanced idly down at the paper and her eyes were drawn to one word that stood out from all the others. Mrs Wyndham resided at Blake Street.

'Actually, Sophy, I will go with you.'

As Gracie walked home later that afternoon, she felt silly that she had made up her mind to go with Sophy merely as a result of the name of a street. Ridiculous, that's what it was. She pulled a long branch from a tree she passed and beat it against the path as she walked. *This man, you fool, will have forgotten you. Do you think he would visit somewhere because it was called Arundel Place? Hah!* She stopped and took a breath before resuming her walk.

There was no harm done, really. She had been half inclined to go before she discovered the street name. Mrs Myers had talked of a varied and energetic social life. Good. That would be fun. Certainly she would enjoy taking her nicest dresses, and maybe she would buy some new things to take with her. She would assist Sophy wholeheartedly in her mission to find love or at least a husband. *Assist, but Heaven knows, I certainly will not follow that path myself.*

* * *

On the day of her departure, Gracie checked over the contents of her trunk one last time. Buried at the bottom was her glass bell. She had used it only the one time, although she often yearned to see Cianna with some urgency. It had been so long since they met. She wondered if Cianna missed her too, but she had the impression that the passing of time was very different for Cianna than it was for her.

Bridgwater was ninety miles away, a long journey, but Sophy was an excellent companion and the countryside was reputed to be lovely. The weather was fair and Gracie rather enjoyed travelling, despite the frequent stops and changes and bumpy roads. Her parents and the Myerses came to wave off the stagecoach. Both families were apprehensive about letting their daughters travel alone on it.

'Father, we will be fine.' Gracie kissed Ernest on the head. 'It is not as if we are young, foolish girls. And think how much extra trouble it would be for us to take our own coach and stop to hire horses along the way.'

'Well, but if in any doubt, do not get on another coach unless you have checked first that it is the correct one for your journey. And Mrs Wyndham will have her own coach meet you near Bridgwater?'

'She will. I will write to you and Mother as soon as I arrive, so you will have a letter letting you know of my safe arrival very shortly.'

The girls were about to climb into the stagecoach, and Gracie was surprised to see William, the Arundel family's manservant, standing close by. 'William, and have you come to wave me off too? How nice!'

William looked embarrassed and lowered his head. 'No, miss, I am travelling with you for the first twenty miles or so.'

'Father! And why did you not—'

Ernest cut Gracie off before she could protest any further. 'You may be older than Polly, but you are still my little daughter and I want William with you both for the first stage. Now, I want to see some colour in your cheeks when you return. Ensure that you breathe in those west winds blowing in from the Bristol Channel.'

Gracie felt tears sting the back of her eyes. She hugged her father goodbye again and clambered back into the coach. Alicia and Ernest stood arm in arm as they waved.

On the other side of the coach, Mrs Myers whispered to her husband, 'I do feel it sorely that Gracie is going with our daughter. I fear she will attract the best of the men away from Sophy. I can only take comfort in the fact that Gracie is so clever. What man would want her, after all?'

To Gracie, used to the rural and picturesque Bourton-on-the-Water, Bridgwater was every inch the maritime town, where everything from wine and fish to coal and timber was traded and imported. Exports were the usual agricultural products, along with wool, bricks and even cement and plaster of Paris. It was noisy and populous and its sense of its self-importance was tangible. It could not fail to provoke some reaction from its visitors, and Gracie liked it. Mrs Wyndham was relieved that her young guests felt this way about her town as she had seen Bridgwater dismissed as a miniature Liverpool or Bristol, less important in all respects and lacking in everything other than commerce. Gracie assured Mrs Wyndham that it was a pleasure to have so many well-stocked shops at hand, and the fact that the surrounding countryside was beautiful could hardly be argued. Lying in the valley of the tidal River Parrett, with the Mendip Hills stretched out before it, Bridgwater was a lovely place in which to wander and ramble. Gracie and Sophy would walk for miles along the coastline admiring the flat landscape and watching the twice daily tidal phenomenon, which the locals told them was called "the bore".

After only her first full day in Bridgwater, Gracie found it impossible not to notice how many references to the name Blake there were in town. Keeping her face as nonchalant as possible, Gracie asked Mrs Wyndham about it.

'Why, it's because of Admiral Blake, you know. He was born here. I'm afraid I don't remember much of the particulars, never could recall historical facts, but here, I have a book.'

Mrs Wyndham handed Gracie a book from one of the limited and rather empty bookshelves, and Gracie found the entry concerning Robert Blake, 1598–1657. She read aloud that he was a supremely important military commander of the Commonwealth of England, elected as Member of Parliament for Bridgwater in 1640, and thought of as the father of the British Navy. *Yes, perhaps*, Gracie thought, *but soon your name will be fatally eclipsed by Admiral Horatio Nelson.*

'You see,' said Mrs Wyndham, 'just as I said. Our famous Admiral Blake.'

Mrs Wyndham was rather a prematurely old woman, only in her fifties but set in her ways and often worried about her health, although Gracie could detect nothing very much wrong with her. Still, she was kindly, wealthy and generous, and she very much wanted her guests to have a good time.

'There will be a dance on Saturday—all of the best people will be there. We shall go too, of course. I can promise you that you will both be asked to dance several times. Many of my friends who have sons have already asked about your visit and about yourselves.'

Gracie was always uncomfortable during these sorts of discussions, but Sophy was alert and, as if her future depended on it, listening to everything Mrs Wyndham related.

While they were all out buying little necessaries for the forthcoming ball, Gracie noticed a crowd of passers-by creating a lot of noise. She moved towards the shop window and saw three or four gentlemen outside laughing loudly, very much in high spirits. Gracie smiled inwardly and thought that they had perhaps been drinking rather a little too much. They appeared to be of varying ages, between her own to perhaps around forty, and they clearly didn't work either with the ships or in trade. They would be lawyers, or doctors, or perhaps were without profession. *They might be at the ball on Saturday.* Should she call Sophy and let her take a peep?

Suddenly, the man who had been shaded most from her view fell back from the group and bent to retrieve a glove he had dropped. He picked it up and dusted it down on his trousers, and something about this action made Gracie catch her breath. The man, in that instant, looked towards where Gracie stood behind her window, and he too gained some colour as he recognised the woman who had rarely been far from his thoughts throughout the last two years.

For more than a few moments, Gracie and Tom did nothing more than stare at each other in disbelief. Recovering then from their confusion, they moved towards each other and met outside of the shop.

Tom took Gracie's outstretched hand and held it while he gazed at her. 'My dear Miss Arundel. That is, are you still Miss Arundel? Or do I have the pleasure of addressing—'

'I am still Miss Arundel. Hello, Mr Blake. I confess I am very surprised to see you again.'

'Yes, I am staying here with some family. I have been celebrating with my cousins and friends. One of them is engaged to be married.'

He pointed to the men, who had stopped and were waiting for him at the end of the street. They bowed clumsily to Gracie and she smiled back at them. Tom apologised for their condition.

'We have had, well, it is clear—we are a little louder than we usually are. Please forgive me.'

'There is nothing to forgive, I assure you. Are you staying in Bridgwater long?'

'Another week or so. And what about yourself?'

'Oh, around another month. I have lately arrived here with a friend from Bourton-on-the-Water. We are staying with her kin, a Mrs Wyndham.'

'I see.' Tom seemed to be struggling to gather his thoughts. 'Do you walk often?'

'I do.'

The desperation on his face made it clear to Gracie that he was trying to discover a place that they might meet again.

'I like to walk in the town in the early morning,' she said with a small smile, 'before the shops open and before breakfast. I usually take this walk alone.'

'Then perhaps I shall see you on your next walk.' He smiled at her delightedly. 'Oh, my dear Miss Gracie Arundel, I have so much to relate to you. But what ails you?' Tom had clearly noticed Gracie's embarrassed confusion. She had just had a sickening thought that perhaps Tom was now married or betrothed; how could she tell?

'Oh, it is nothing, sir. But, tell me, are you visiting Somersetshire by yourself? I mean, have you left all of your family at home? In Devon, I presume? And are they all quite well?'

'My family? Yes, they are all in Devon. And they are all well, I thank you.' A look of recognition suddenly lit his face, and he touched Gracie's shoulder gently, sending a shiver of pleasure coursing through her body.

'I, too, remain unmarried.'

At that moment, the door behind Gracie opened and its bell tinkled out into the street. Mrs Wyndham and Sophy looked curiously at the tall bearded man. Gracie introduced them to Tom, and Mrs Wyndham declared that it was a coincidence, his name, given that her young guest had only yesterday been quizzing her on the appearance of the name Blake so often in the neighbourhood. Gracie could only blush as the innocent woman talked so candidly of her earlier interest.

'I told her all about our admiral. Do you know of him, sir?'

'Yes, he is actually an ancestor of my father's. It is his relations whom I am visiting in Bridgwater.'

'Oh, Gracie, do you hear?'

But Gracie's thoughts were now spinning wildly over the fact that she had made up her mind to visit Bridgwater on learning that Mrs Wyndham resided at Blake Street. What did it all mean? A pure coincidence? Or was there a deeper meaning? At this moment though, Gracie could only feel happiness that she was again in contact with Tom, however it might all have arisen.

When Tom departed, Mrs Wyndham turned to Gracie. 'And what is his profession?'

'I cannot tell you, ma'am. I think he may be a scientist.'

Gracie swung between feelings of bliss and despair that evening. Sophy hardly knew what to make of her friend's behaviour but suspected it had something to do with the bearded, foreign-looking young man whom they had met earlier that day. Gracie excused herself shortly after dinner and retired to her room.

It must mean something, it must! Was it part of her purpose to meet him? After all, what were the chances of their meeting again? But then, coincidences *did* happen. They had happened to Gracie Abbot all the time; they happened to everyone. Although she possessed more knowledge than other people in her time, she did not, could not, know everything. Hadn't Cianna told her that the past could change? So, really, she was in the same position as everyone else here in 1800, in the dark about what was around the corner. Then again, that wasn't entirely true. So far, at least on a famous historical basis, everything had turned out as she had expected it would.

Balance. How did her and Tom's meeting bring balance to the world? Gracie couldn't even begin to guess.

Gracie had been walking toward the main street in town for only a few minutes when she heard brisk footsteps behind her. Her pulse quickened.

'Miss Arundel, good morning.'

'Why, Mr Blake, hello.' She couldn't resist adding, 'What a surprise to see you here today.'

They laughed together, both caught out.

'Well you know, Miss Arundel, I enjoy my morning stroll as much as any man, and I think I am especially in need of it today given my indulgences of yesterday. I hope I did not make too much of a fool of myself.'

'No, of course not.'

They were the only people on the street who seemed to have no particular place to go. Everyone else was hurrying about.

'Mr Blake, I must enquire whether you went to Germany?'

'I did go. I have been back in England only for a few months. The trip was everything I could have hoped it would be. It was entirely the right decision. I learned so much there, and the professor I stayed with, well, the man is a genius in my eyes.'

They walked on, and for many minutes Tom talked of his studies. He seemed to be interested in many of the same things that intrigued Gracie.

'But, have you also continued with your reading?' he asked.

'Yes, only last week I finished reading Herschel's book. I study anything and everything but, like you appear to be, I am most interested in disease and its cure and prevention.'

'Really? How fascinating! And I presume you have continued to follow the progress of our Dr Jenner?'

'Of course. Did your professor in Berlin correspond with the doctor?'

'Yes, they had met before in England, and Professor Bauer sends Jenner any articles or pamphlets he has recently written. Jenner is esteemed highly in Germany.'

'And do you intend to visit Dr Jenner yourself, Mr Blake?'

Tom thought for a few moments before answering. 'I have no plans to meet Jenner. I think there is a danger in meeting your idol.'

Gracie couldn't help but laugh. Tom looked confused, but as if her laughter were contagious, he began to laugh too, and they carried on along the street, oblivious to the fact that they were becoming something of a public spectacle.

Tom told Gracie that he was now employed by his old college in Cambridge and was teaching. He also hoped to be elected as a Fellow of the Royal Society, and he had recently met the society's president, Sir Joseph Banks. It all seemed very impressive and Gracie told him so.

'And is your father now resigned to the idea of your vocation?'

'Vocation? Yes, I suppose it is. It certainly occupies more of my time than my lawyer and architect friends spend thinking about their work. My father supports me fully in my endeavours. Indeed, I think he is proud of the independence I have shown in my choice of career. If only he knew it was as a result of a young woman I met on a beach one day in Kent! He was never much interested in the study of natural philosophy himself—indeed none of my family are—but he grows to become quite an expert on the planets.'

'Really!' Gracie laughed. 'How helpful! Well, I had better return home now, Mr Blake. Mrs Wyndham will be wondering where I have gotten to.'

'Of course. May I see you again soon, Miss Arundel?'

'I am attending the ball in town on Saturday, Mr Blake. Perhaps we shall meet each other there?'

'We shall.'

Tom offered to walk Gracie back to Mrs Wyndham's, and as they neared her home, he asked teasingly, 'So you were asking about Blake Street, were you?'

Tom stood underneath the street sign and grinned at Gracie's discomposure. Gracie regretted the fact that it was improper for a lady to stick her tongue out during this period. But both of them knew they would likely see each other again before the ball.

For the rest of the week, Gracie and Tom spent a good part of each day together. They met every morning before breakfast, and once, Tom accompanied the three ladies on an excursion into the countryside. Sophy confided to Gracie that Mrs Wyndham assumed they were engaged. Gracie's face coloured at this news, and she told Sophy that they were nothing of the sort. Several times, it was true, Gracie had thought that Tom was about to declare his feelings for her, which were obvious, but Gracie had steered him away from doing so. She could not resign herself to feeling that it was right to encourage or accept any offer of marriage from Tom, however her heart might long to do so. He would soon return to Cambridge and his teaching.

The night before he was due to leave, Gracie passed a troubled and mostly sleepless night. When she eventually fell asleep she dreamed of Adam. She could see only his back, his dark form moving away from her until he receded into oblivion. Tom then appeared and she reached for him, but failed to hold him. Cianna entered into the dream and smiled soothingly, her words soft and full of wisdom.

'Gracie, my Gracie, why did you not call for me? I sensed your sorrow. Did I not tell you that nothing is written? You are free to choose your own destiny. You will do no wrong if you follow your instincts. What will be, will be. I do not know how things will turn out, but it is not yet time for you to make your decision. I will be there with you when that time arrives. Remember that I am here for you, my dear child. This is no dream. I am here with you. Awaken now, and goodbye.'

Gracie woke with a start and sat up in bed. Cianna—was she here? Gracie called out her name. Though she received no response, Gracie had no doubt that Cianna had indeed been close. An unmistakable smell permeated her bedroom, pure and floral, lovelier than any perfume. It lingered gently. Gracie lay back upon her pillows.

Tom. Did she love him? She knew that she did, but enough to give up any chance of seeing her old life again?

The next day, Gracie didn't go to the spot where she and Tom usually met. And when Mrs Wyndham and Sophy went visiting some new acquaintance, Gracie told them she had a headache and stayed home. Tom would be leaving later that day, and he would think that she didn't wish to see him again. Well, so be it. Gracie couldn't commit to him; she simply didn't think it was fair given her remarkable situation. As the afternoon wore on, she decided to go for a walk in the nearby dense woodland. Within ten minutes she was strolling through greenery, lifting branches out of her way as she picked her route through the undergrowth. It was a breezy but fine day, and her spirits lifted as she got farther and farther away from the town and any houses. She had no umbrella with her, and when it began to rain quite heavily, she cursed herself for having left the house so hastily. She spied a large and desolate-looking barn not far off and made her way towards it speedily. The rain was so heavy that by the time she'd walked the short distance, she was soaked quite through.

'Damn, damn, damn!' she screamed.

There was nobody to hear her. She kicked the wall with some force and leaned against it, miserable and exhausted. Then she cried with all the force she had left. A few minutes later, Gracie felt a firm hand on her shoulder—someone was touching her hair and pulling it back gently from her face. She tensed and spun around to see Tom staring inquisitively into her face.

'What is wrong? I am leaving soon, so I trust your tears are nothing to do with me.'

He was angry with her. Of course he would be.

'I was caught out in the rain. I felt stupid to have walked so far and now I am all wet. What are you doing here?'

'The same. Caught out just like you. I actually arrived here only a few minutes before you did. I sought refuge on that upturned barrel over there.'

She had not noticed it, but he had seen and heard everything. This made her feel even more ridiculous, and she began crying uncontrollably again.

Tom's voice was soothing as he told her that he would see her home safely, that she would be fine. She looked into his eyes and saw how kind and gentle he was, how clever too. He had shaved his beard quite off. Instinctively, and impulsively, she reached out and stroked his soft cheek. He caught her hand then and kissed it passionately.

'I love you,' he said. 'I have always loved you. My family knows how I feel about you. You have met some members of them here, my cousins. I conceal nothing from them. I would not expect you to discontinue your studies; rather, I encourage them. You are as intelligent as you are beautiful, and it should be no other way. We could work together, you and I—we are interested in the same things anyway. Is it because I am not very rich, my sweet? If it is I will work harder, I will earn more money for us. I would prefer us to wait a while anyway, until I had more to offer.'

Gracie stopped his words by kissing him on the mouth. It was no good; she loved him too much. Let what would happen come and she would meet it. They would meet it together. They held each other close, and Gracie longed to be closer yet to him, but Tom made them both sit down on a bench and asked if he could come to Bourton soon and meet with her family.

'Yes, you may. Oh Tom, are we really doing the right thing?'

'Yes, my sweet, I know we are. Don't you know we belong together?'

Gracie buried her face in his warm coat, and neither of them spoke for a long time. They were content to simply hold this perfect moment for as long as they could.

'Look,' she said, when she finally raised her head.

A large and bright rainbow straddled the landscape before them. Tom kissed the top of her head, thinking only of how good she smelled.

'Yes,' he said absentmindedly. 'Do you know that rainbows have a little-known meaning? After a storm they can be interpreted as a symbol of doom.'

Gracie sat upright then and faced him. 'You are not serious?'

He laughed at her. 'I did not know you were so superstitious. Well, let us recall then that they have a happier, hopeful association too. We will choose to follow that meaning.'

As they made their way back to Bridgwater hand in hand, Gracie turned back every so often, checking to see whether the rainbow was still there.

11.

Unhappy Boy

Depending on the point of view, it was in either Gracie's future or her past that Sam Lockhart, son of Ben and Marian, reached his thirteenth birthday in the summer of 1811. No celebration would accompany this significant moment in the youth's life. He had long ago accepted that every day was just the same as the one before: lonely, monotonous and wretched. His uncle Caleb reminded him each birthday that this day was a scandal—he had no right to live while his dearly departed mother lay buried. He should be lying in the grave with her, or should never have existed, for only misery and destruction existed in his midst. In surviving his birth, he had shown a strange and unnatural tendency. Everyone hated him. Everyone. His uncle did, and so did the boys he went to school with; they bullied him daily. Even his own father had hated him. Uncle Caleb told Sam often that his father died cursing the day his son was born. Sam was only five years old when his father died, but he remembered him still, always drunk and always asking that the boy be removed from his sight.

'Take him away, Martha!' he would bawl. 'Can't you put him in another room?'

The shouting frightened the little boy, who just wanted to show his father a butterfly he had caught or a smooth pebble in his pocket. Martha, the only person who had ever shown him any compassion or care, would hurry into the room and pick him up, and he would cling to her.

'Now, Sam, what have you got there? Would you like to help me hang out the washing? Come and play with Mary.'

Sam would then run out into the garden to play with Martha's toddling daughter. Martha would bake them cakes with smiling faces on top and read them stories. Sometimes she would tell Sam the story of his mother, who had gone to Heaven.

'Your mother, Sam, was the kindest and most beautiful lady. She was so brave, and she loved you this much.'

Martha would hold her arms wide, and Sam and Mary would mimic the movement, shouting in their childish tongues, 'This much? This much?' These were his happy memories, the only ones he had, and they had come to an end when his father finally drank himself to death. Sam remembered feeling quite happy that day. Now there would be nobody to bawl at him or look at him and cry. His father had always smelled nasty, of the stuff he carried everywhere with him in a bottle. What was there for the bewildered five-year-old to mourn? Martha had cried though, and had told Sam that, once, his father had been a wonderful man, kind and fair. He had loved his wife so much that he could not get over her going away from him, and it made him very sad. He only wanted to be with her, and now he was; they should not be sad but happy. This idea had pleased Sam—it made him feel better about not being very troubled as he stood beside his father's grave.

A man called Uncle arrived that day, and he stared at Sam coldly and unblinkingly while they all stood around the grave and the earth was piled onto Ben Lockhart's coffin.

Sam remembered that Martha had wanted to keep him, to bring him up as her own son, but his uncle had said no and told her to get out of the house and not return. Sam never saw her again. The next day Uncle Caleb took him to his home in the city of Oxford without telling Martha or any of his father's family. Even if any of them had wished to argue Caleb's right to take full possession of his sister's son, they would have had little chance of successfully contradicting Caleb Finlayson, tutor in Latin at Oxford University. These people were simple, largely uneducated and, more importantly, poor.

His uncle soon made Sam feel that he was not only a person of little importance, but also a bad person. 'You are the very image of your father,' his uncle would tell him. 'Indeed, that is one of the reasons Ben could not stand to look at you. Marian, his dear wife, died as a result of you.' Sam was made to feel ashamed of his face, as Uncle Caleb often told him that to resemble his father so forcibly was a sin in itself. Caleb had hated Ben and told Sam that he was a cruel and thoughtless husband. The very day his wife had died, he had been in the tavern drinking—yes, drinking— and he never stopped afterward. Everyone knew that Marian could have survived with medical assistance in the early stages of her distress. She should never have died.

Sam tried everything he could think of to win his uncle's love, but to no avail. He debased himself, tried being scholarly and well behaved, and when that failed, he became rebellious and quarrelsome. Everything he did merely heaped more scorn upon his head and showed further, as if his uncle needed any other proof, that he was damned.

Now, on his birthday, he was polishing his school shoes, buffing the leather until he could see his reflection in them, though he knew that when he presented the shoes for inspection to his uncle, he would be ordered to do the job all over again. He hated his uncle with a passion that he did his best to conceal. Sam had a plan, and it was this plan that kept him going through the long and bitter days. He would make something of himself. Not just a little thing but a big thing—the biggest. He didn't quite know how yet, but he trusted that it would all work out to his interest eventually. This ambition had nothing to do with winning the love or respect of his uncle. Rather, he wanted to make his uncle fear him, tremble before him, as well as all the boys at school who teased and mocked him for his shyness and lack of family. He would be much more important than anyone else in Oxford, and he would be rich. He had already begun to hoard away, even steal, anything remotely valuable he could get his hands on. Like a magpie he jealously guarded his stash and allowed himself to inspect it every so often. He would turn over the objects in his hands and dream of when he might trade them in for money. Sam knew that money was the only sure protection against insults and disgrace. His uncle was unkind to everyone, but he was also very rich, so everyone bowed before him and did his bidding. That was power.

Sam had no reason to think that his plan was unfeasible. He was a clever boy and he knew it. He scored top marks again and again at school without much effort. It was partly due to this that the other boys hated him. When he was younger he pretended that he was less bright, had even let them copy his answers, but he was finished with all that. Now, he gloried in his good marks and uncomplainingly took the beatings he consequently received. His uncle despised him, but because it made him feel superior and righteous to do so, Caleb sent his nephew to a good school and supplied him with the finest masters. As such, Sam had every reason to think that a successful and rich future awaited him. He dreamed whole evenings away planning what he would do and what he would say once he had his enemies in his control. He sustained himself upon his hatred as a starving dog feeds upon a leg of meat, graceless and unstoppable.

By the time Sam reached manhood, he had decided it was not enough to become wealthier than his peers. Money was common enough; even fools could become rich. He would still like to be wealthy, of course, but he could wait. He did not want to waste these precious years earning money. To really make people sit up and take notice, Sam knew he had to do something that would change the world, change how people thought about things forever. And as they did so, they could not fail to remember his name, the origin of all their new wonder.

Relations between him and his uncle had changed in recent years. He no longer feared Caleb, and he faced him eye to eye whenever they spoke. Sam remained small and weedy; he appeared years younger than his actual age, so it wasn't due to his nephew's physical strength that Caleb was growing increasingly intimidated by Sam's behaviour around him. Rather, and Sam realised this, Caleb had begun to recognise the monstrous qualities within his charge, although he didn't stop to consider who had created the monster. As Caleb grew older and more infirm, Sam took over much of the running of his uncle's household. He gained this control without being asked to do so, and without having to resort to arguing, or even speech. There was power enough in a mere look, if done correctly.

When it grew time for Sam to go to university, people, his uncle included, naturally expected him to go to Oxford—his uncle had taught there for years, after all. But Sam said no, he was for Cambridge and there was no point in disputing the matter. Caleb knew that his nephew was implicitly criticising him, and he was not brought so low that he could not demand an explanation.

'Why, Uncle,' Sam answered, keeping his tone deceptively simple, as if he were talking to a child, 'your university spends too much time debating religion. High Church, Low Church, Broad Church, what does it all matter? Eventually there will come a time when such talk will be seen as worthless. Man will become master of his own destiny, subject to new laws. We will cease to have any need for God.'

Sam laughed as his strictly Calvinist uncle shook with fear and impotent rage. Like many devout followers of that faith, Caleb firmly believed he was one of those elected to be saved; and he believed just as firmly that Sam was a hopeless case. Sam had been reared on this notion, and he used it now to his advantage.

'Yes, Uncle, you may do as you like and still be saved but I, damned though I am, will live without fear of further punishment. After all, I am Hell bound whether I lead a good and obedient life or not. Thank you for ensuring that I understand this point.'

Sam laughed again, making it clear that he believed none of it. Religion had become merely a tool to him with which he could frighten and insult his uncle.

'You worthless sinner,' Caleb spat. 'God's grace cannot be turned aside! I have such faith, and justification by grace is through faith alone. You have no faith. I will see you damned!'

'Hush, Uncle,' Sam said soothingly. 'Do not tire yourself. Whatever you say, of course, must be true.'

Then he left the room and his violently coughing uncle, who was shaking as a result of his anger and, Sam fervently hoped, fear.

Sam's decision to go to Cambridge was based almost entirely upon his desire to irritate his uncle. He had frequently heard Caleb criticise Cambridge for a part of its history involving a group of mid-seventeenth-century divines—the Cambridge Platonists. Caleb called the men in this society "devils", and this had been enough to encourage the young Sam to find out more about them. On doing so, he learned that the men had reacted against the dogmatic and irrational tendencies of the Puritans and Calvinists. They had also condemned the materialist writings of Hobbes, the philosopher, feeling that his works denied the idealistic nature of the universe. Sam could hardly say why, but he detested the tenet espoused by materialist works that the only thing that could truly be said to exist is matter. In the part of his character that was still purely his own, Sam felt some kinship with these Platonists, and, like them, to a degree with the dualism of Descartes. And so the idea of going to Cambridge had in fact appealed to him at an early age, although he believed it was purely the result of his desire to annoy Caleb. Similarly, Sam believed it was as a result of his wish to upset his uncle, who detested all branches of natural philosophy, that he had decided to pursue scientific study at Cambridge. The truth was that Sam was drawn towards this path for his own reasons, and he had long been interested in the work of Newton, the great mathematician and physicist; indeed, Sam was also gifted in these disciplines.

In 1819, shortly after completing his degree, Sam returned to his uncle's house puzzling over his future. He was quite penniless in his own right. His father had died in debt, and his uncle was leaving all of his money to his church. Therefore, if he wanted to be rich, Sam would have to pursue an appropriate path. But he wished to continue his scientific studies. He felt that science held the key to his future greatness. As such, he did not wish to teach or share his scientific knowledge with anyone else but to hoard it until the time was right to impress everyone with his discovery. But how to live in the meantime? There was little money in science, and his work would take time and cost money.

Then Uncle Caleb became suddenly, and quite desperately, ill. He had been growing less robust for some time, but now, in his early sixties, he was obviously dying. There was nobody to tend to him, so the task, quite naturally, fell entirely upon Sam. His uncle relied upon him for everything, and at first Sam did what needed to be done while spending as much time as possible on his own. He was too caught up in his own plans and thoughts to garner much pleasure from tormenting the old heathen. Then an idea occurred to him, and it seemed so possible that he wondered why he had not thought of it before.

He spent his days and nights practising his uncle's handwriting. The thin, spidery script was not too difficult to recreate. After he had filled a sheet of paper, he would carefully burn the evidence. When he had perfected his new skill, he began to work upon his sick and feverish uncle. He would terrify the old man in his bed and tell him that the day of his reckoning was drawing near.

'You know I am damned, don't you, Uncle?'

'Of course.'

'But do you also know that I have been in communion with the Devil?'

This always provoked hysteria in his uncle to such an extent that Sam was forced to wait a while until he could continue.

'Yes, the Devil, Uncle. He tells me that he is not quite reconciled to the idea of your being one of the elect. He wants you for his own.'

'I have my faith! It is preordained that I will be saved!'

'Oh yes, Uncle, I told him, but he said you were mistaken. He said you had not signed yourself over to God and salvation. That's why he can still get you, I think.'

'No, no, you lie, you accursed boy.'

The doctor came to visit Caleb every few days, and the old man would ramble about what his nephew had told him. The doctor, like everyone, had little time for Caleb, so merely put it down to the ravings of a weak and degenerate mind. Sam had known the doctor would do this. And so it continued between Sam and Caleb until the old man began to show signs of actually believing what his nephew told him. It had taken four days to break his uncle, four days measured against decades of belief. Soon Caleb could not rest unless Sam was by his bedside.

'Will you see him again soon?' he asked one day. 'Will you see the Devil?'

'Yes, I may. Can I pass a message to him for you?'

'Yes, boy, tell him that God is for me. It would be too much trouble for him to have me. God will not allow it, I know. Tell him to forget me.'

'I will, Uncle. I will plead your case as eloquently as I can. But there is the fact of the document that you have not signed. I fear he will not rest until he sees you are most definitely one of the elect, and you are only a member of this group when you have signed the document.'

'But why, in my position, have I not seen this document?'

'Oh, Uncle—think, sir! Do you expect the elect to go around telling of these things?'

'But as one of the elect myself, I would have to know of this document too.'

'Yes, and so you are learning of it. The document only needs to be signed before your death. I know, Uncle, that you would have no problem understanding any of this if you were quite well. It is your sickness.'

'Yes, you may be right. I cannot understand, though, why the elect need to sign anything. It is predestined that we shall be saved no matter what we do on earth.'

'Sir, all I can repeat is what the Devil has told me. Will it really do any harm for you to sign the document? You will be saved anyway, in your belief. What harm can it do to provide extra security for yourself against the dark arts of Satan?'

This appeared to make some sense to the bewildered and failing old man, and he agreed to sign the document. Sam said he would go off to fetch it at once. Fit to burst with glee, he pulled the sheet of paper he had prepared out of his journal and took it to the dozing man.

'Here, Uncle. The Devil has prepared this.'

Sam knew that his uncle could read nothing without his spectacles, so he felt safe to hold it in front of Caleb's eyes. Caleb squinted and Sam told him to rest easy, he would read it out to him. He then dictated, as if he were reading, some nonsense about the soul of Caleb Finlayson being safe and untouchable if his signature appeared forthwith.

'It is so strange, but it looks like my handwriting, Sam. I cannot read what it says, but it appears to be in my hand. And I have never seen this!'

'We are dealing with the Devil here, sir. Did you think he would struggle to produce your writing on a page, even without your hand? I hope he is not offended by your suggestion.'

Caleb trembled.

'Here boy, give me the page. Where do I sign? . . . There you are.'

Sam licked his lips with suppressed glee as his uncle signed all of his considerable assets over to his only nephew.

'And how do you feel now, sir?'

'Better, better. I shall sleep now.'

Sam returned to his room and put the legal document in the drawer of his bureau. Now nobody could argue that his uncle hadn't meant to do this. The whole of the forged part looked as if Caleb had written it when he was fit and well and with a steady hand. Sam had thought that his uncle's fussy signature might have proven too difficult to believably recreate, and the fact that he now had it, a little shaken, just showed that it had been signed on a sickbed. He would be rich—rich to follow his dream of dedicating himself to science and greatness and with never any need to worry about money or position. That was now secured.

Only a little over a week later, Sam awoke in the middle of the night to the sound of his uncle feebly calling for him. Caleb had dropped his jug of water and glass, and needed something to drink; he was choking. Sam knew that he should go across the room to the bed and lift up the old man's head so that he would be able to breathe more easily. He stayed where he was by the door, however, and in a few short minutes it was all over.

'Where is your grace now?' Sam said mockingly.

The church that would have inherited Caleb's money put up some fight against Sam's inheritance, but they had no real case. The local attorney despised the Calvinist faith, and the suit was dropped before it had even begun. Sam, at twenty-two years old, was independent and rich. He had no need to seek employment and so, without any further hesitation, he launched himself into his studies in the autumn of 1820. He sold Caleb's house, packed up his few belongings and moved to Cambridge, where he procured small and intimate lodgings. He was finished with Oxford.

In a way very similar to Gracie, his methodology, in the beginning, was to read everything. He absorbed book upon book and confidently waited for an idea to come his way. But nothing did. He spent most of his time studying mathematics and the branch of natural philosophy that would later be called physics. The 1820s was a significant time indeed for such studies, and Sam shut himself away and read and thought and experimented until it became as natural for him to think in numbers and formulas as it did in words and sentences. Light, heat, electricity and magnetism, he pondered it all until his brain throbbed and he fell asleep on his books. All the while, other men achieved great things. André–Marie Ampère's publication in 1826 explaining the electrodynamic theory sent Sam to bed depressed for a week. A year later, when Georg Ohm published his complete mathematical theory of electricity, Sam was ready to give up. And so it continued. By the 1830s, he was spending more of his time studying the nature of light, as were many other scientists during the period. Was light a sequence of rapidly moving particles, or was it, as the wave theorists espoused, a transverse wave spread by the omnipresent ether? Sam spent days deconstructing rainbows until it became clear that the wave theorists indeed seemed to have it.

One day in 1832, Sam sat at his desk and tried to think of something to occupy his time. The room was silent and he felt alone and forgotten, as he always did. Was he simply wasting his time? He thought of his hero Newton, and how his major contribution to science, the theory of gravitation, had come to him at such an ordinary moment of his life, if the story was to be believed. No equipment, no books, no notes, just a great man sitting under a tree. Was he trying too hard? While he pondered Newton, Sam became aware of the ticking of the clock in his room, or clocks, for he had been emptying some old crates from his uncle's house recently and had found a rather grand one, which he'd placed in his study. So now he had two clocks nearby, and their noise created a soothing melody that pleased his anxious mind. They were slightly out of sync with each other. Sam smiled at the idiosyncratic idea of time itself being out of step, subject to change. Suddenly, he clasped his head in his hands. An alarming idea had just occurred to him. Might he not study the possibility of manipulating time?

This idea gathered momentum in Sam's head. Armed at last with what he felt was an original and truly inventive area of research, he attacked his studies with verve. Newton, once more, acted as his starting point. However, within a year, he found he could no longer agree with Newton over the fact that space was fixed, infinite and unmoving. Was there really a single absolute time that governed the universe?

By the passing of another few years, Sam had grown close to the relativity ideas that Einstein would discover less than a hundred years later. He conducted strange and wonderful experiments in his room, at first with inanimate objects, then with living creatures and, finally, with himself. These produced some positive results, and he frequently felt his heart could almost burst with excitement.

In 1838, he built himself a machine in which he hoped he might travel, significantly, through time. He had attempted experiments involving seconds and minutes, but with this machine he planned to push the boundaries far and wide. He chose his birthday as the day on which he would test his mission. Nervous but confident, he sat himself in his machine and set the dial on the counter before him. He was going to try to be in this room, this very room, one year from now. It had not even occurred to Sam to recapture the past. To his mind, his machine was one in which he would travel the future. The past was only mean and hopeless.

He was taking what he hoped was a last look around his room in 1838, when suddenly he had a strange sensation that he was no longer alone. He shook his head, put it down to nerves and closed the cabin door. He depressed the activation button, and within seconds, he lay by the foot of his bed, the smell of smoke and acrid burning permeating the room. He'd been flung out of his machine. It had all happened so quickly.

Had the experiment worked? He turned to look at his machine and saw that it was in tatters. It had not worked. The woman outside was still selling her flowers; he could hear her voice, along with all of the other familiar sounds of the area. He had failed, just as he always did.

Sam went back to his desk and sat down. Putting his head in his arms before him, he wept like a child—for his dead mother, for Martha, for himself. Behind him, a supremely handsome man stepped out of the shadows. Placing his hand gently over Sam's shoulder, the man waited until the startled scientist turned to face him. Sam would now, largely, undergo the same explanations and choices as Gracie, although the conditions of the latter would differ. His mind raced. Where would he go? Should he go anywhere at all?

Many hours later, the two men made their way to meet Angelus. Sam eyed Angelus apprehensively, and clung to his Pondera for reassurance. He felt a connection with this apparent stranger that was difficult to explain.

'Tell Angelus, Sam, what you have decided to do.'

'I would like to travel 150 years into the future. To 1988.'

Angelus licked his bottom lip and surveyed Sam from head to toe.

'The 1980s, eh? I think you have chosen the right age. I sense you will like it there.'

12.

The Workers

Christmas of 1800 passed by in a whirl for Gracie. That December, she acted as bridesmaid to her good friend Sophy. The trip to Bridgwater had proven successful for both young visitors as during that time, Sophy had met Matthew, a man who met all of the fervent Mrs Myers's expectations.

Now Sophy was an attorney's wife, just like her mother, and would soon depart Bourton-on-the-Water to return to Bridgwater. Matthew, a long-time resident of Bridgwater, had known Tom for several years, and spoke warmly of his friend to Gracie, telling her he trusted she would be happy in her life with him. Further, there would always be room for them to visit him and his wife in their smart new home in Bridgwater, a sentiment that Sophy concurred with readily.

'Oh, yes, Gracie. Do promise to come and visit us. You and Tom must put aside your potions and experiments for a little while and come and see your old friends!'

'Yes, Sophy, of course. But Tom and I are not married, and so you must be patient! I think it will be a few years yet before we shall be able to marry. Tom is so sensitive about being able to provide well and independently for us that I fear I shall be almost thirty by the time I exchange my name for that of Blake!'

Gracie always smiled and was suitably coy during any discussions of her engagement and forthcoming marriage. Privately, however, she was glad that Tom was not pressing her into a marriage as hasty as Sophy's. She was still frightened and apprehensive about marrying Tom, for she was anxious about his being hurt in the event that she might leave this life one day and return to the future as Gracie Abbot. But she always reminded herself that, if this indeed happened, then all memory of her would cease to exist in Tom's mind, just as had happened between Cianna and Nino. Such thoughts served only to feed her anguish. She didn't want Tom to forget her, but she knew absolutely that she would never be permitted to tell him about her journey here.

In the end, Gracie knew that when the moment for her decision finally arose, there was little chance she would return to her old life. Why should she, after all? She was happier here, much happier, and her life with Tom promised to be all she could hope for. The future, the old life, what did it offer? Well, she could return to the moment in which she "died" as a result of the Renaissance. The machine worked, and she could extend people's lives with it. Should she return for that reason if no other? She didn't like to think of herself as having an obligation to become Gracie Abbot again simply to aid other people. She felt selfish for these thoughts, but that was how it was. In any case, she frequently reasoned, some other scientist would create a similar device eventually. Einstein was only Einstein because he was the first to either get to a point or the first to publicly declare his findings, not because he was unique. In many ways, she wished that the decision would occur soon so that she could stop fearing its repercussions and get on peaceably with her new life. For now, she would continue trying to heed Cianna's advice that she simply follow her instincts; and her instincts told her that she loved Tom dearly and was right to have agreed to become his wife.

But still she worried—so much so that not long after her return to Bourton with Sophy in November, she had rung the glass bell and awaited Cianna's arrival.

Her father was visiting a friend in town, and her mother and Polly had business at the school. Gracie often stayed home alone during the mornings to read and study at her desk. There would certainly be nobody to disturb her today. She lifted the floorboard by the window and felt the silk-covered box in her hand. Taking a seat on the foot of her bed, Gracie rang the bell three times, swiftly and with purpose. She *needed* to talk to Cianna. A few minutes passed, and Gracie felt simultaneously nervous and excited waiting for her friend to arrive. Would Cianna simply appear before her or would she enter the room via the door or . . . well, who could say?

Instead, Gracie first *felt* that Cianna was close. Her unmistakable presence filled the surrounding space even though she could not be seen. The very light in the room seemed to be clearer, purified even. Gracie felt a light touch on her left shoulder and turned to see Cianna sitting behind her, looking every bit as young and fresh as she always did. They kissed and hugged warmly, and Gracie noticed that Cianna had a bright snowdrop pinned to the front of her dark green dress. She briefly wondered if Cianna had seasons in her world.

'Gracie, my dear. You did right to send for me. I sense you are still hesitant about Tom.'

'Cianna, I am. But you were with me in my dream last month, weren't you? While I was in Bridgwater? Your fragrance was in the room with me when I woke up.'

Cianna smiled and took Gracie's hands in her own.

'If you will not call for me then I must come to you! I see that you have chosen to be with Tom. If that choice follows from your heart and your instincts, then it is the correct path. Proceed without fear, child.'

'But it is so difficult to do that when I am every moment wondering about and waiting for the moment when I might be called away. I wish I could simply be done with any notion of choosing, and remain here forever.'

'If you have decided to remain as you are now then why are you so anxious about the decision? Why cannot you forget about it and live this life as you wish?'

'I don't know. The decision does matter in as much as it stops me from feeling that I fully belong here. Just knowing that I will have the ability one day to leave all of this behind stops my mind from feeling settled.'

'So you require to live without the spectre of departure in order to be at ease?'

'Yes, I do.'

'Gracie, even the most ordinary of human lives is lived in this way. Death hangs over you all. Every day might see your end, every moment might be the last you will share with a loved one.'

'Yes, I see what you mean but we, well I, don't focus on death like that. We would all drive ourselves mad, I suppose, if we did.'

'Can you not try to extend this type of thinking, then, to your special predicament now?'

'I shall have to. Yes, it is helpful to see things in that way. Thank you, Cianna. I knew you would be able to make things seem clearer.'

'Remember, whatever happens, you are the mistress of your own fate, Gracie. Whether you stay or return will be your choice entirely. I do not know what will happen, as you know, but we will understand things better one day.'

'But can I really have been given the opportunity to come back here just to meet Tom?'

'Are you not happy with him?'

'Yes, of course. I love him. But is my being in love really so important in the grand scale of things that it merits all of this?'

'You are the scientist, Gracie. If even a little part of the mixture in one of your experiments is not measured quite accurately, do you get the same results? The small details matter as much as the large, do they not?'

Gracie thought for a few moments and then smiled ruefully at her perfectly composed friend.

'I may be the clever scientist, but you make me feel rather basic sometimes! I resolve to wait with patience until the time comes for my decision. Yes, I shall be patient. I will lead this life as I want to and try not to dwell on anything else.'

Cianna nodded. 'That would be the best thing for you to do, Gracie. Now, talk to me about your plans.'

Gracie explained that Tom had written to her parents soon after his return to his teaching post at Cambridge. Her father had invited him to spend part of his next holiday visiting them in Bourton. Tom would stay with the Arundels for a spell after Christmas. Gracie was looking forward to presenting Tom to her family, and she was confident that they would like him. Tom's parents had also written to Gracie and told her of their pleasure at hearing of the engagement, and of their desire to see Gracie at their home in Dawlish, in Devon, as soon as possible. Polly thought it was all wildly romantic that they had met up again after so long, and that it was certainly written in the stars that they should be together.

'And how do I answer a comment like that?' Gracie playfully asked Cianna.

'It is easy,' Cianna responded immediately. 'You smile and say nothing and leave people to draw their own conclusions. It is all you can do, after all.'

Polly, now twenty-one years old, had been both happy and surprised to learn of her sister's betrothal. The thought of Gracie being someone's wife seemed strange to her somehow. She liked Tom though, and had instinctively felt that he was just the right sort of man to make Gracie happy.

Today, 30 December, she was helping her mother and Hetty, the maid, clean and prepare the parlour for his arrival. He would be here by five o'clock, and everyone was a little nervous. Gracie was still in her room, changing her dress for the second time that day. As Polly dusted, she thought that both her mother and father presented an air of calm, but it was clear to her that they were anxious to like Tom a great deal. Polly was confident that they would. If only his money situation was not so tediously difficult. Tom had little, of course, but Gracie had a good deal of money as a result of their father's careful and well-planned investments. Yes, neither she nor Gracie would ever occupy the shameful position of being women with nothing but their own charms to offer.

Gracie was certainly accustomed to a very comfortable life. Although Tom was born on a rather grand estate in Devon, everything would go to his brother, and it was doubtful whether he would ever be able to afford much in the way of luxury. Polly knew that she could only marry a very wealthy man. About this there was no question. She had never been as romantic as her sister in this respect.

Polly smiled. Gracie would balk at the idea of being termed *romantic*, but it was obvious to Polly that she was. Rather a lot about Gracie was obvious to Polly.

Well, I hope that everything can be settled soon and to my sister's advantage, she thought. Cambridge was quite a distance, of course, and if Gracie moved there after her marriage, being apart would be difficult and sad. But Polly had heard fine things about Devon, Dawlish even. How fun it would be if Gracie and Tom lived there. Imagine all of the grand balls she could attend at Tom's family's house when she travelled down to stay with Gracie. That could be wonderful. Perhaps Tom would have to abandon his scientific dreams in order to marry Gracie, settle down to a more acceptable profession—one that actually paid a good salary. Gracie would probably never agree to that though.

Polly's thoughts were paused as her mother ushered her out of the room and told her to go upstairs and get washed and changed.

'Mother, I shall. I will look lovely tonight, although I will take care to not outshine my sister,' she joked.

Polly ran up the stairs thinking how glad she was that Gracie was marrying Tom. Something about him made Polly trust him and feel that he would be a welcome addition to her family. And, of course, she would make the perfect bridesmaid . . .

Ernest had arranged to meet the stagecoach at its stop outside of town and travel back to Bourton alone with Tom in the family's carriage. As he waited outside of the inn, the coach came into view, ahead of schedule. *A good omen*, Ernest thought as he straightened his greatcoat and hat. He watched an intelligent-looking young man alight. Ernest knew at once that this was Tom, the man his darling daughter loved.

The two men bowed and shook hands, and Ernest showed him to his carriage; his servant, William, fetched Tom's heavy bags. Though he was a strong man, William nonetheless buckled under the weight of the luggage, and Tom explained that he had brought several books for Gracie to read.

'Ah! Your shared love of all things scientific continues,' said Ernest. 'Good, good. She will be pleased to read them. I have done my best over the years to keep pace and provide a companion for her in her interests, but I confess she overtook me many years ago to such an extent that this has now proven difficult.'

Tom surveyed Gracie's father and wondered whether he might not harbour a little resentment towards him, but Ernest was smiling good-naturedly and explaining that he hoped he was hungry as Gracie's mother had prepared such an excellent dinner.

'It would be a crime if we did not savour every delicious morsel.'

Tom and Ernest sat companionably during the journey to Bourton, and Ernest pointed out areas of local interest. There would be time enough to discuss money and financial settlements in the days to follow. Tom felt happier than his words could express at the thought that he would soon be with Gracie again. They had not seen each other since that fateful day in the barn outside Bridgwater, the day she had agreed to be his wife. He had written to her regularly, of course, and had received her letters eagerly in return. They spoke of their research and of their hopes and plans. Their love was transparent in every single line.

'And Polly, you remember her I presume?' Ernest asked.

'Yes, Miss Polly, I suspect that she is rarely forgotten.' Tom laughed. 'I look forward to seeing her again, as well as meeting your wife, of course.'

But, for the moment, Tom had thoughts and sight enough for only one person. As the carriage pulled up the drive towards the spacious and comfortable-looking house, Tom spotted Gracie at the entrance.

They greeted each other rather stiffly, formally even, but it would have been clear to even the most disinterested observer that Gracie and Tom were thrilled to see one another again. He took her hand in his and bowed, and she smiled at him, her eyes shining with delight. Mrs Arundel and Polly then appeared, and they all went into the house together.

Tom would be staying at the town's inn, only a few miles up the road, and Ernest would see him there safely after dinner. It would have been thought quite improper for the Arundels to put him up in their home. Although Bourton Manor was large, it was not quite large enough to make it impossible for Gracie and Tom to meet inappropriately.

Gracie sat next to Tom during dinner, and her heart raced as she felt him lightly touch her hand under the table. In fact, her heart felt fit to burst with love for him. She tried to recall whether she'd ever felt so strongly for Adam but felt sure she hadn't. Yet, she knew that if she and Adam had stayed together, she would have died thinking she had known real love in its fullest sense. Now she knew differently.

After dinner, Gracie and Tom took advantage of the cool and dark but clear winter's night and went for a walk. While they were visible from the house they didn't touch, but when they were safely shaded from its view, they held each other passionately and for a long time.

'I missed you so much,' Gracie said. 'I cannot believe you are really here—here, in a place I have walked so often, where I have read so many of your letters.'

'My sweet, it has been torturous for me too. Tutoring all those boys when all I wanted to do was be with you. The hundred miles may as well have been six hundred!'

They walked on and discussed how the first meeting with her parents had gone.

'They like me, I think,' Tom said. 'Am I correct? Or foolish to feel that?'

'You are right. I only hope your parents like me as well.'

'They will, don't worry. I told Mother that you could come for a visit in the springtime. Does that still suit you?'

'Yes. And do you really think Polly might come with me?'

'Of course—the invitation is extended to her as well.'

'She will be glad.'

Gracie then told Tom about Sophy's wedding, about how well the day had gone and how she already missed her friend who had gone to live in Bridgwater.

'I envy them,' Tom said. 'I wish we could be married so soon. I feel I should take a proper job. It is not too late, you know, for me to train as an attorney.'

'You have a proper job. Do you think that on the beach all that time ago I persuaded you to give up being a lawyer for nothing? Something will turn up, and if it does not then we shall be poor but happy. Do you think I fear not being rich? And anyway, we shall hardly starve. You know about my settlement.'

Tom kissed her head and told her to hush. It was his duty to ensure they had enough money, he explained. And however Gracie felt about this, she knew there was no point in arguing with him.

'Professor Bauer has written to me, you know,' Tom said. 'He says that he will come to our wedding if we give him plenty of notice.'

Gracie was pleased as she knew how much Tom esteemed the professor.

'And how are his studies progressing now?'

'Well, it seems. He is still looking into viable treatment for those who contract scarlatina. You remember that he lost two of his own children to the disease?'

Gracie nodded. She had been unlucky enough to suffer from scarlet fever in both this life and her last, and she knew that the professor was on something akin to a personal crusade to come up with a remedy that could kill off the disease in its sufferers before it became fatal. He was working in the same field as such men as Pasteur and Fleming would—men whose names would become forever synonymous with the word *antibiotic*. As she had never heard of Bauer before meeting Tom, she could only assume that his work would not result in any major findings. But of course, she had to keep this to herself. Although she didn't like to keep things from Tom, it was easier than she'd thought to withhold certain information. It simply would have felt wrong to say anything that would upset the balance of life. And so she'd never been seriously tempted to do so.

Tom continued: 'I find out in a few weeks whether I have been accepted as a Fellow of the Royal Society. I'm sure that it will happen, and then it will be much easier to find a patron—a nice rich patron who will fund my endeavours and who will little realise that he will be getting two scientists for the price of one.'

Gracie laughed. 'Keep my part in the plan to yourself. Few would give money if they knew that a woman had anything to do with her husband's proposed scientific investigations. I shall play the good housewife when they come to call and only don my lab outfit again when they have safely disappeared down the garden path!'

'That's probably a very good idea. Now, I think I had better return to your house and let your father take me to my inn for the night. I shall fall down from exhaustion if I do not, and I want to be at my best tomorrow so I can dance with you during the New Year Ball that Polly has talked of all evening!'

Gracie and Tom spent the last day of 1800 together happily. The weather was fine, and Gracie took pleasure in showing Tom the local places that she knew so well. After a light dinner at home, the Arundels and Tom departed for the ball. Alicia smiled as she saw Tom assist Gracie into the carriage, so assiduous in his concern that she be comfortable. *The boy is obviously smitten and that is as it should be*, she thought, as Ernest held her own elbow while she climbed into the carriage.

As the year became 1801, Gracie realised that she had now lived within four different centuries. And when Tom came to her side bearing a cup of punch, she knew that the only truly significant thing for her was that she had loved Tom through two centuries, a romantic idea that she couldn't resist sharing with him. He smiled delightedly as she whispered into his ear.

'At this moment, it is very difficult for me to keep my integrity and carry on with my humble job and poor income,' Tom said. 'I feel I could quite happily go off and become a banker, judge or politician, anything as long as I had you waiting for me when I got home each night. I want to marry you, Gracie. I don't want to wait for years and years.'

'We won't. Why don't we make a plan to marry in two years, even if things remain the same as they are now. We just won't wait any longer.'

'Do you really mean it? You know, up until this point I had an awful feeling that you weren't as eager to marry me as I was to marry you. I couldn't rid myself of these fears. But you really do want to be my wife, don't you?'

'You have no idea how much,' Gracie whispered as Tom pressed her hand to his mouth.

All too quickly it was time for Tom to return to Cambridge. Gracie and her family accompanied him to the place where the stagecoach had dropped him off. They arrived early, and the others discreetly moved a little away from Gracie and Tom so they could spend some moments alone together.

'Write to me as soon as you can,' said Gracie. 'Let me know you've arrived safely.'

'I will, my love. I have had such a happy time with you all. You have excellent parents.'

'I know. It has all gone very well, this first meeting.'

'It has. The only point of awkwardness was when your father offered to loan me money so that we could marry sooner.'

'Yes, but I confess I suspected he might do something of that nature.'

'And you do not condemn me for refusing his generous offer?'

'Absolutely not. I only ever want you to do what feels right for you. Ah, here is the coach.'

Gracie's gloved fingers then felt the slight pressure of Tom's own fingers before he turned and rather clumsily threw himself into the coach. They smiled sadly at one another as the driver, having dealt with the luggage, resumed his seat and picked up the reins. The Arundels stood together and waved Tom off until the coach was no more than a tiny dot receding into the distance.

'Now Gracie,' her mother said, 'before we go home I want you to come to that shop with me and help me choose some new bits and pieces for the school.'

Gracie let herself be bustled along, knowing fully that Alicia was merely trying to occupy her mind so that she couldn't dwell on her sorrow. And it helped, of course. She would see Tom again in the spring, in Devon, and in the meantime, she would simply have to make the best of things.

It was in early February that the fateful letter arrived. Gracie had been expecting a letter from Tom that day, and when it was duly placed into her hands, she smiled and ran up to her bedroom to devour its contents. He had certainly written a lot, but as usual, she would have to take her time over the letter as its "crossed" nature didn't make for easy reading.

She sat down at her desk and laughed again at the funny sketch, showing a grinning and slightly stunned looking Tom, that she'd pinned to the front of her pen box. Tom had sent it last week, when he'd written to let her know that he'd been made a Fellow. He'd also written that his father was very proud of him and had visited Cambridge last week with a Mr Franklyn, a long-time friend from his university days.

Tom now wrote:

My father has for some time been formulating a plan in his mind involving me and Mr Franklyn, although I have known nothing about it.

He explained that Mr Franklyn was an extremely wealthy man who owned substantial land and property. He was now in advanced age and had no wife or children—indeed, he appeared to have no family at all. Tom remembered him from his childhood as a good sort of man, though given to eccentricity and some strange habits and opinions. Mr Franklyn neither liked nor trusted women, for one. Yet there was no other way of describing him but as a philanthropist, and he gave vast amounts of his money to hospitals and charitable organisations. He approved of Tom's interest in science inasmuch as he concerned himself with disease and ways in which lives could be saved. However, he had no time at all for "vain fripperies", as he termed them—inventions designed to improve rather than save people's lives.

Mr Blake had thought it would be a very good idea to reintroduce Mr Franklyn into Tom's life in the hope that his friend might offer to become a patron to his son, who could then dedicate his time more fully to his investigations and research. And Mr Franklyn was indeed prepared to pay Tom a yearly amount as well as provide for travelling expenses and books so that Tom could spend his time wholly engaged in his studies.

Mr Franklyn wanted Tom to look into the nature of viruses and how they might be combatted. He did not want Tom to concentrate on the more obviously serious viruses such as smallpox or measles; they had their pioneers at the moment. Instead, Tom should examine the common cold, or the grippe—influenza. This arguably killed more people than anything else and, what was worse, it often developed into more serious illnesses such as pneumonia or it made weakened sufferers more susceptible to diseases like tuberculosis. And this was what Mr Franklyn would pay to have researched.

Gracie's scientific mind processed what she had just read. So, Tom's prospective patron was interested in viruses as opposed to diseases such as scarlatina and TB, which would eventually be treatable with antibiotics. Viruses were more difficult, even in the twenty-first century. They were, essentially, incurable. It was for this reason that AIDS was so feared in her old life and that Dr Jenner's vaccination against smallpox was so important today. In terms of her own interests and knowledge, Gracie thought spending her time studying all that she could about viruses seemed a good prospect. So much had still been unknown in her previous life that she wouldn't feel as hedged in or necessarily dumb as she would if she and Tom went down a similar path as Professor Bauer in his studies. But viruses were so small, and electron microscopes wouldn't be invented until the twentieth century!

I cannot think of such matters now, she thought, and concentrated once again on Tom's letter.

Mr Franklyn would pay Tom a better yearly salary than he received at present but not enough to enable him to save much or get married—for Mr Franklyn believed that as soon as a young man was too comfortable, all good enterprise swiftly departed. In any case, one of Mr Franklyn's provisos was that Tom remain a single man for the duration of his patronage. Women, the old man had said, would only distract him from his work, and on that point he wouldn't budge.

Gracie's heart sank as she read this. Such a fantastic offer, but to accept it would mean that they couldn't be together. Tom wanted Gracie's advice. He thought he might take up Mr Franklyn's offer for two whole years. If, at the end of that time, he had made significant progress and development then his name might be made and he could attract other patrons and other means of employment, with better pay. If at the end of the two years he had failed to produce any significant results then he would financially be in the same position as now—but with how much more scientific knowledge and experience? Professor Bauer had written to tell him there was a job for him in Berlin, at his own institute, when he wanted it, and this was something they could take up in two years, after they were married.

Tom felt that as a scientist, the opportunity to devote all of his time and industry to his field, and actually be paid for it, was too much of an opportunity to resist. Mr Franklyn had no other specifications to make regarding Tom's mode of living during the years of his patronage and, with Gracie's permission, Tom proposed that he come to live in Bourton. He could take rooms and turn one of them into a laboratory and workspace. This way, they could spend their days together, in research and analysis, full partners in all that they did.

Gracie sat back, stunned, her mind swimming with ideas and possibilities. What might they discover? After all, 1801 had never before existed with Gracie and Tom's dedicating all of their time together to the nature of the virus and its eradication. They might find a cure for the common cold! Was this why she was here? Would her work with Tom somehow bring balance? It was an excellent idea. She would write her thoughts to Tom at once. Aside from anything else, the thought that he might soon be positioned in the same village as her, every day, was too delightful for words. Her father would help them sort out all of the practical business, she was sure. Was there not an empty house in town that Tom might take? And it had plenty of space for them to work in, even a garden at the back, why, they could work outdoors when the weather was nice . . .

Gracie's mind raced ahead as she penned her return letter. That same afternoon, Gracie and her parents took a walk into town to look at the house, which was indeed still empty.

Tom arrived in Bourton in the spring, with as many of his possessions as he was able to carry. He and Gracie had christened his new home the Rainbow House, because of his mock fear that she would want the property decorated in her favourite bright colours. Although they wouldn't be living together, the couple very much felt that this would be a shared home, their first. For weeks Gracie had excitedly cleaned and prepared it.

The day following his arrival, Tom told Gracie more of Mr Franklyn as they strolled into Northleach. 'He is not nearly as curmudgeonly as he seems. Indeed, I think he is really quite soft underneath it all. He spoke to me, you know, of a tragic romance he once had in his youth. The lady died of a very virulent attack of influenza.'

'So that is why he is so determined to prevent others dying from it too! It is his own labour of love. And now he says he dislikes women. Nothing of that sort is ever so simple as it might appear.'

'No, my wise lady. Nothing to do with love ever is.'

Within another few days, Gracie and Tom, along with Polly, made the long journey to Dawlish. Alicia had kindly offered to maintain and order the house in Tom's absence. Gracie exceedingly liked her prospective in-laws, and was happy in Devon, finding it in every way as beautiful as she had been led to expect. After their six-week stay, Polly travelled on to London to stay with friends, and Gracie and Tom returned to Bourton. By necessity, they had to stop a few nights on their journey home, and they coped with the awkwardnesses and the probing looks of innkeepers and fellow travellers as best as they could.

'I long to be back at the Rainbow, alone, just the two of us,' said Gracie one evening as they dined. 'Even while we were with your family, and happy, I often thought of our work and how we would begin.'

'Yes. Mr Franklyn wants us to examine the nature of the virus, or especially influenza, so I propose that we spend some weeks studying what we know about viruses exactly. Why are they so successful, what makes them so aggressive, what features do different viruses share? I suppose there will be a lot of time simply spent reading and studying samples under our microscopes.'

'Hmmh,' Gracie murmured absentmindedly. 'Nothing very exciting.'

'Nothing exciting? Working together with a whole wealth of possibilities before us? What do you call exciting then?'

* * *

Their first proper day of working together at the Rainbow was indeed largely spent reading and note-taking. Gracie had resigned herself to the fact that they wouldn't be able to examine the structures of the viruses in anything close to the detail that would be possible in later years, but she was determined to remain optimistic. They would mostly examine the cells and samples of people that they knew to be ill—and to have a specific illness. She had worked in a lab before. Literally hundreds of anonymous samples had arrived every week, and she and the other scientists at the lab had been required to examine them all and determine exactly what was wrong, if anything. The technology they'd used wasn't yet available, but there was still much that she and Tom *could* do today.

Tom had recently ordered the finest microscope available to them—a gift from his father—from an eminent company in Edinburgh. He was also in contact with many scientists, professional and amateur, who were keen to share their latest findings and most interesting samples. Gracie knew this was in every way as vital a scientific period as the one she had previously known, and she felt a part of it all.

Even in these early days, Gracie and Tom put in long hours at the Rainbow, and they toiled happily and without complaint, despite all of the frustration and wrong turns. They felt they were making progress—and that was enough for the moment.

13.

Second Chance

The young man mentally willed his legs to keep moving up the last few flights of stairs. Why did the elevator have to be broken today of all days? This was his big moment to impress Mr Stanhope, and now he would appear before him a breathless idiot. The crisp shirt he had so carefully pressed that morning clung to his back wet with sweat.

Everything had been going so well. Nobody could deny that since he'd agreed to the terms set by Stanhope's agent, he'd done everything in his power to deliver the required information from within the rival company for which he worked. Not only a spy—a manipulator.

He was an influential force in the company he had once been so proud to work for, before Stanhope's man came calling. When the proposal was first made he'd been uncertain, frightened even. But though he'd never met the elusive Stanhope, his messages were immensely flattering and even sensible. He *had* been overlooked by his managers, taken for granted. And Stanhope hadn't liked that. 'Come work for me and I'll see you elevated to the position you deserve,' Stanhope's proposal had promised. And the cheque that had been placed into his hands made his eyes bulge.

And so the bargain had been sealed. He was now on Stanhope's private payroll, and his first task before he quit his old company was to cut and drain them as effectively as he could. Today was the first time he would meet Stanhope. He had attended a meeting earlier that morning at his firm, and he had vital documentation from it that Stanhope wanted immediately, delivered by the young man's own hands. Mr Stanhope had been so nice to him; he was determined not to let him down.

When he'd stepped out of his office building little more than an hour ago now, saying he had a dental appointment, the sun had been shining. A taxi halted for him almost immediately. Stanhope's building was a distance away, but he believed he would be there shortly. And then the taxi stopped. Some kind of emergency; the police weren't allowing any vehicles through. He drummed his fingers on his leather briefcase until he thought he would scream with rage: how could his day be disturbed in this way? The driver got out to speak with a police officer, and when he returned to his cab, the young man heard him say *Tragedy, people injured, dead*—but it all meant nothing to him. He jumped out of the car and ran and ran, not pausing to consider that if his journey had been a little more advanced, he wouldn't be running anywhere. All he could think of was pleasing Mr Stanhope.

Relief washed over him as he reached the fairly small and innocuous-looking building, and he made his way to the entrance as quickly as he could. Even running through the lobby, he noticed the atmosphere was much friendlier and less imposing than other company headquarters of its stature, including his own. The company name was everywhere, even upon the railing of the bannisters he dragged his hands along now.

He stopped to straighten his tie at the top of the steps and ran a hand through his hair. Nervous, he reminded himself that he was an "influential force"; that was what Mr Stanhope had called him. The young man often repeated this phrase to himself, along with other things Mr Stanhope had said. A smiling receptionist led him to a door with a highly polished brass plaque bearing the name of the man he had long imagined meeting. He knocked.

'Enter,' said a relaxed, smooth voice. The man wordlessly prayed that all would go well as he opened the door.

Half an hour later the young man could be seen on the pavement outside and he looked confident and proud, as could be seen by his gait. He was a marked contrast to the fearful and uncertain beings that surrounded him, still reeling from the news that was filtering through their city. Mr Sam Stanhope, previously Lockhart, moved away from his window and his perspective on the tiny people below, and resumed his seat at his desk. The information he now held in his hands would net him a fortune. The boy was entirely in his control. Even more since he had received such a warm and friendly reception. Sam chuckled. Everyone was always so eager to please him. And he rarely had to raise his voice in anger or aggravation. But when he did . . .

The year was 2007. Sam Stanhope was thirty-nine years old—positively young in this time—and his achievements combined with this youth had earned him enormous status, even fame. Gracie Abbot had certainly heard of him. She used one of the products bearing the name of his company, her computer, on a daily basis. Yet she would have struggled to tell anyone what he looked like. This was due to careful orchestration. Sam had no interest in being recognised everywhere he went. It didn't suit his purposes, but more than that, he had no desire to be famous in the way that celebrities were. It was enough that people knew his name and respected it. Indeed they trusted his company, admired the fact that he didn't care about showbiz parties or famous girlfriends. His enigma fed his success.

Sam had felt upbeat after the young man departed, but he quickly snapped back to his more usual state of melancholy. He rose and walked over to his favourite painting, Bernardino Luini's *The Christ Child Asleep*. The safe behind the painting contained documents that his enemies—and he did have enemies—would have given a lot to possess, for they told the secret story of his scandalous rise to power. Sam gazed at his painting until he felt a little better, and then he returned to his desk. Opening a drawer, he took out a heavy and old-looking coin and rubbed it eagerly in his hands. Despite his vast wealth, this coin meant more to Sam than anything, for it was through the coin that he could communicate with Magnus, his Pondera and only friend. It had been nineteen years since Sam walked through the door that Angelus had led him to and he had arrived in a world that was as different to his nineteenth-century eyes as if he had travelled back not just one century but several into the past—different but familiar.

He had spoken to Magnus several times over the intervening years. The greatest thing about Magnus was that he was a friend in the truest sense; Sam never felt judged. No matter what Sam did, Magnus looked at him with exactly the same eyes and seemed just as happy to see him. He was unshockable, and accepted Sam's behaviour as if it were natural and even exciting. Moreover, there existed between the two a sense that each rather admired the other's attributes. Sam loved Magnus's purity and Magnus appeared to be impressed by Sam's unnerving ability to capitalise on the bad things that happened to him, as well as by the decisive way he approached his endeavours. If Sam wanted to speak to Magnus, he had only to drop the coin onto the ground and the Pondera would come to him.

Sam wondered briefly whether he could reasonably do this now, but he shook his head and put the coin back into the drawer, slamming it with resolve. Over the years Magnus had told Sam much about his life and world and he now knew many of the same things as Gracie, some things a little more and some a little less. He returned to the window and saw there was far less traffic below than usual. A sudden idea occurred to him. He flicked on the Internet and brought up a news page that detailed the latest headlines. As he read, he considered the impact that all of this might have on his shares. Indeed, should he not sell or buy more of certain things now?

The mogul spent the rest of his day on the computer and telephone ensuring the whole of his empire would survive, even prosper, amidst the chaos much of the business world was facing. *Magnus would be proud of me.*

Finally, as light was substituted for dark, Sam stretched and decided to return home. He was exhausted. He had worked hard today, and had even set in motion the plan for the takeover of the rival company that employed the young man he'd seen earlier. All was well. He cheerfully picked up his telephone and called down to the man in reception that his car should be ready for him immediately. The building was deadly silent—everyone had gone home a long time ago, even the most obsequious of his lackeys. He switched everything off and put Magnus's coin, which went everywhere with him, in his pocket. Although the elevator had been fixed, he decided to take the stairs. Sam liked to keep fit and healthy. He jogged down the several flights of stairs to the door where his car and chauffeur would be waiting. It was true, as his visitor that morning had quickly realised, that the name of his company was everywhere. Nobody could ever forget it and Sam liked it that way. A recognisable and public name was everything.

Charlie, the driver, tipped his hat and opened the door of the shiny black Audi. Sam allowed himself to relax into the cool leather seat and invited conversation from his driver, who always waited to find out whether his boss wanted his company or not. Charlie chattered on about the events of the day and Sam questioned him and listened; sometimes commenting but rarely offering his own opinion, although Charlie never really noticed this.

Sam lived in a large and luxurious penthouse flat overlooking the Thames. He lived alone and always had done. Unlike other men of his stature, he had no servants, preferring to tend to his own needs. He lived simply but elegantly, and only very occasionally did anyone visit him. Business was business and should be conducted in a suitable environment—and as for any relationships, well, there were always other places for that. His home was his own. He poured a beer and prepared himself a meal of chicken and salad in his well-appointed kitchen, watching television as he chopped and mixed. He flicked the channels trying to find one that wasn't concentrating on the news; it was too depressing. He settled on an American comedy movie that was absurd but nonetheless crudely funny. Laughing, he sat down to his meal in the kitchen. Afterwards he took another beer into his living room and put on some music. He selected a book from his library and settled into the deep plush chair, kicking off his shoes and resting his feet upon the footstool. This was the time of day he liked best, when he could forget the day's events and relax. Tomorrow he would do it all again, but tonight, he could forget he was Sam Stanhope, director of a global company. In marked contrast to his workplace there was little evidence in his home of either his status or his business. No telephone notepads bearing the company name or logo could be found here. Sam had done it all himself and had no need to be reminded of his achievements or possessions. He closed his eyes and sipped his cold beer; yes, nobody could ever guess where he had come from.

Where had he come from? Who could tell that he had once dedicated most of his life to scientific pursuit, even built a time machine? Hah! How annoyed but gratified he'd been when he arrived here and discovered that a man so feted and praised, and rightly so, by the name of Einstein, had done little more than Sam Lockhart had come up with a century earlier. His sense of importance and superiority had swelled accordingly, and he'd decided that he no longer wished to pursue science— technology, yes, but not what he considered science.

He was only twenty years old when he arrived in 1988, the age he had requested, and found himself living alone in a bedsit in the final year of a business degree at a London university. Everything was a complete surprise to him, as Magnus had been unable to tell him anything of his new situation beforehand. Sam found he had a good head for business, and he enjoyed it too. It was strange talking to tutors who spoke to him of papers he had written last year: papers that he both could and could not remember writing. The strangeness of it all became less strange as time passed—indeed, strangeness just became his way of life and he accepted it.

As for family, he had none. He was an orphan who had grown up in a tough inner-city children's home. This fact merely added to the mystery and glamour of the man now, although it had hardly been glamorous at the time. Young Sam Stanhope also had very few friends and felt isolated and lonely in the same way he had in his previous existence. Hard work proved to be his saviour; his ambition knew no limits.

He beat out stiff competition from his double-barrelled-named peers, obtained a position at a top broker's firm and from that point on only advanced. His salary was good, plentiful, in those early days, but there were many opportunities to make more money. He lived frugally and used all of his capital to speculate, mostly in oil. The early 1990s was a difficult time financially for many people, and Sam, with all of his cash, bought up shares and interests in companies whose prices were flagging. The gamble was that they would come good eventually, and most of them did.

Although he made his first millions through oil, Sam quickly became interested in software. With the eyes of a true visionary, before most people even had home computers, Sam saw how things would turn out a decade later. Rather than doing anything creative or technical himself, he took over companies in which he was interested. Then he set up his own company, Mer, French for "sea", which manufactured computer components. This business continued for a few years with trusted and well-paid managers more or less running the company for him. Sam spent his time negotiating with specialists he poached from other companies. He would read their characters as much as their abilities, for he had plans for a select group of them.

In due time, the company then stepped up a gear and became Sea.co. Sam branched out into the fiercely competitive computer market, selling ready-to-use home and office computers rather than mere components. Nobody was too worried about or flustered by Sam, though. His company was far from one of the big-name nationals, and he kept a low profile. Indeed, most people, even his closest advisers, thought that Sam was a co-owner when in fact he owned it all. Sam presented himself as being interested in only a small part of the market, certainly not as a major competitor. And for reasons he could never guess, people believed him. Newspaper columns and articles reported that Sea.co was healthy for business. Soon it was recognised as the choice of the independent, trendy, even ethical purchaser, and Sam reinforced this idea by making a few public donations to charity. His company was loved as an underdog always is. Except this underdog had a real bite.

Sam was secretly at work on software that would counter the most aggressive and destructive computer virus yet known. He and his team had already created the virus. It had the ability to disable computers of all brands and programmes and, in these relatively unsophisticated days of computer technology, the ability to stop the business world dead in its tracks.

When the virus was unleashed the race was on to kill it. People and companies despaired that they would have to buy new computers. It was a disaster, and for many, it proved that wholesale trust should never be placed in machinery. People lost their faith in computers, and headlines screamed that they were being held to ransom by a computer virus. And then Sea.co stepped in with suitable software—the only software that could eradicate the virus from a computer so that there was no need to buy a new one. Businesses and individuals clamoured for the software, and Sam netted the biggest payday ever. Very few people realised that the company that had developed the antidote was also the origin of the virus, but Sam paid them enough to keep their mouths shut. If they didn't, Sam would sue them and win, and they knew it.

Sea.co restored the public's trust in computers, and the more discerning consumer would now select a computer bearing Sea.co's logo. People even drove around with Sea.co stickers on their bumpers. Newspapers confidently predicted that Sea.co was here to stay, and Sam was named as one of the elite super-rich. Suddenly everyone wanted to know more about him, and he struggled to maintain his anonymity. His appealing rags-to-riches story incited people's curiosity, and he was asked about the origins of his company's name. But this remained a mystery—he would never tell anyone, candidly stating that he wanted it to remain cryptic as he liked puzzling people. Nobody would ever know that the "Mer" of his original company was linked to the names of the women he viewed as angels: from the "Mar" of his mother, Marian, and his foster mother, Martha. He'd then toyed with a few variations, including MerSea, before settling upon Sea.co. And thus, a modern-day success story was born.

But Sam was not happy; he had never been happy. He had tasted two very different lives, had chased achievements in science and money and been successful in both, but still he yearned for what he'd never had.

He stood up and placed his unread book by his side. It was late and he should sleep. He was on the brink of pulling off another coup against a company that had been a rival for years, but he had no real heart for it. He had derived pleasure from this sort of thing in the past, there was no denying it, but recently its ability to lift his spirits had waned. Sam had been thinking about doing something soon, the thought of which made his stomach tingle with anticipation. Switching off all the lights, he walked through his silent home and wondered whether he would dream in the twenty-first or nineteenth century tonight. True, the modern dreams had long overtaken those of the past, but the ghosts of his Uncle Caleb, Martha and his father were still there, pulling him and calling his name.

Magnus arrived a few days later. It was a Sunday afternoon, and Sam needed to talk to his friend. He dropped the coin onto the ground and knew that Magnus would shortly appear in the quiet apartment. He busied himself in the meantime, plumping cushions on his sofa and tidying away magazines and papers. He sat down but then rose immediately and walked to the kitchen, where he retrieved two ice-cold bottles of beer. As he made his way back to the living room, he paused and then went back for some peanuts and a bowl. *Why not*, he thought, *Magnus liked the beer so why wouldn't he like the nuts too?*

Magnus was already waiting for him on his sofa when he returned, and the two men embraced before speaking of their most recent exploits. Magnus sipped his beer appreciatively and sampled a salted nut, which at first he did not like and then did. Sam laughed and told Magnus that he never entertained and only went to parties when it was really necessary; people might as well be serving pig swill for all he knew.

'Yes, you have never entirely fit in here, have you?' said Magnus. 'Where is your wife? Where are your children? Your friends? You were free to have as many of each as you liked.'

Sam felt his friend watching him keenly as he thought carefully about how to phrase his next words. 'No, I've always felt like a traveller here—a passenger, an interloper. Sometimes I feel everyone around me is as different from me as an animal. Their ignorance makes me feel nauseous at times. But then I hardly fitted well in my last life either, did I? Sitting in that room every day almost making myself go blind poring over those endless books with their tiny texts. How archaic all of that seems now.'

'Sam, what have you to say to me?'

Sam put his beer down and took Magnus's hand. He was shaking. 'You told me that day in my room, my last day in 1838, after my time machine failed me, that there were conditions to my coming here. We've never spoken of this again.'

'No, we haven't. But you remember what I told you?'

'Yes. You said that my life as Sam Lockhart would end there and then in that room. I would be found dead at forty and that would be that.'

'That is correct.'

'You also said that at any time, I could decide—and there would be only one chance to do this—to either stay in my future life until my natural death or return as Sam Lockhart with the opportunity to change one thing about my past life if I wished to do so. Is that all correct?'

'It is. And you wish to make your decision now?'

'Yes, Magnus. Yes.'

Sam's voice was firm and resolved, and Magnus again admired the swiftness of this man's decision-making.

'What do you want to do, Sam?'

'Sam Stanhope will cease to exist. I will return to being Sam Lockhart.'

'I see. You realise of course that it will be as if Stanhope had never been born? You will have no opportunity to resurrect him.'

Sam nodded.

'Do you wish to change anything about the life of Sam Lockhart?'

Sam had thought of all the things he could do. He could save Uncle Caleb's life, or at least prolong it and not take his money. He could become interested in something other than science, or he could alter history generally by declaring Einstein's theory before Einstein; he had been so close to it in any case. So many different possibilities and lifestyles glittered before him, but he swept them all away, looked Magnus straight in the eyes and made his announcement.

'I am going to save my mother's life, and she and my father will raise me.'

Magnus's face betrayed his shock. 'My dear Sam, it is difficult to surprise a Pondera, but you have done so today. You do realise that all of your memories will be gone if you do this. You will merely be an unformed baby and you will never have any knowledge of your prior lives and choices. You will remember nothing of me.'

'I realise all of that, Magnus. I have thought it through, and I guessed it would be so. But I will have a mother and father who love me. I will be a happy boy.'

Magnus embraced Sam then. To him, his friend was proposing to undertake the bravest of all actions, and one he knew he could never do himself.

'My friend, you will forget me, but I shall always remember you and love you. I have learned a great deal from our friendship.'

'Thank you, Magnus. Well, how do we go about pulling this off?'

'It is not straightforward. Your mother still has to go through her early labour and the complicated birth. That is her destiny and you cannot alter that.'

'I understand. But I can save her, can't I? I remember Martha and my father talking about the night my mother died. If there had been a doctor present, if she'd had assistance . . . Father always said that she needn't have died, and Uncle Caleb, for what it's worth, used to say the same. I know there was a storm that night and Father stayed too long in the tavern.'

'If there is to be any help given to save her, it has to be in keeping with what was available during the period.'

'Yes, Magnus. But even with that stipulation I feel sure that she can live—my mother can live!'

'I see the plan you have formed in your head.'

'And do you approve of it?'

'Sam, I hope it all works out for you, but you will never know either way because even if your mother does not survive again, you will be forced to remain there and live your childhood once more without her. You will never be any wiser.'

'No. But I'm prepared to take that chance.'

The first drops of rain began to fall at nine thirty. Heavy drops that promised a downpour. From his vantage point in a shed that faced the tavern, Sam prepared to approach his father. He could not unduly interfere with events—Ben had to be allowed to drink with his friends. Magnus had said that only when the rain started to fall could he begin to carry out his plan.

Sam was dressed in a long overcoat with the collar turned up over his face, and he also wore a hat that covered most of his head. His father would not, could not, recognise him of course, but it was best to be cautious. He'd watched Ben enter the tavern some hours ago now, and it had shocked him to see how young, strong and happy his father looked, so unlike the haggard drunk he recalled.

The tavern was small and smoky, and only men were present. At a table near the back his father sat with a large and boisterous group of men. Tankards of ale sat on the table, and Sam focussed on these as he made his way towards the men.

'I have a message for Mr Ben Lockhart. Who is he, please?'

Ben stood at once and surveyed the stranger before him. 'I am Ben Lockhart. And who are you, sir?'

'One who only means well. You must hurry home, sir, without delay, for your wife wants you.'

The other men stared at the stranger open-mouthed. They had all been called home from the tavern by their wives before but never by another man.

'My wife? Is she unwell? How do you know she wants me, sir?'

'I passed by your house not long ago and she called to me and requested that I fetch you from the tavern immediately. Seeing her condition, I have made my way here as quickly as possible.'

'Thank you, man, thank you. I shall go at once. Lads, I'm sorry but I must go.'

Ben tossed a few coins onto the table and scooped up his coat and hat.

'Don't be daft, Ben, go on,' said one of the men. 'And I hope Marian will be fine. We're all off ourselves soon.'

Another man rose and patted Ben on the back. 'My wife is available if needed.'

'Thanks, thanks, Jim.'

Then another man, one with a different accent from the others, rose and shook Ben's hand.

'It was nice to meet you, Ben. A rare pleasure to find someone who can talk politics all night. I hope we meet again. Your wife will deliver a fine child for you, I'll wager.'

'Thank you, Josiah. All the best with your travels.'

Ben stopped before Sam and placed his hand on his shoulder. Sam could feel the warmth of his father's hand through his coat, and he tried to steady himself as best as he could.

'And you, sir. My best thanks for passing on my wife's message. Did she seem very bad off?'

'I could not say, sir. But I would get home as swiftly as I could if I were you.'

'Aye, I will. Stay here and have a drink on me, will you?'

The other men shouted that he should do just that and pushed a chair towards him, but Sam said he had to go, and left the tavern only seconds after his father.

Ben arrived home at a quarter past ten to find his wife sleeping peacefully by the fire. Martha didn't seem to be around. He bent and kissed Marian on the forehead, and she woke with a smile.

'I knew you would waken me like that. But you're soaked through and covered in mud. What's happened to you?'

'It's pouring outside. I ran most of the way here, and just as well I did because it would have been harder to run through all that rain when it started to get so heavy.'

Marian glanced at the clock and saw that Ben was not late.

'Now, Marian love, how are you? The man came into the tavern and got me like you asked. You look tired.'

'The man? Ben, dear, I don't know what you're talking about.'

'He said you called to him and asked him to fetch me.'

'I've seen no one but Martha and Jason all night.'

'Yes, where is Martha?'

'Oh Ben, her mother's dying and Jason came to fetch her not long ago. She didn't want to go until you came back, but Jason said the doctor thought she might not last the night. It was likely Martha who asked this man to fetch you. She seemed very unwilling to leave me.'

'No, the man said it was you, my wife, who asked him to get me.'

'Well, all we can do is ask Martha about it next time we see her. Oh, I do hope her mother will be well.'

Marian made to stand up and Ben supported her only to flinch as his wife gasped with pain and fell down again.

'My love, what is it?'

Marian could only shake her head and grip Ben's hand. Ben stroked her hair and told her to rest until the pain subsided. There was a loud crash outside, and she jumped.

'It is only the barn door blown open, my love.'

Marian tried to stand again, and leaned on her husband's arm.

'I want to move about. Come on, little one, give Mother a chance to catch her breath.'

Marian walked a few steps before falling entirely into Ben's arms, and he carried her back to her chair. He saw the blood all over the floor and her dress, but he didn't want to let Marian know about it. He felt helpless in the face of such agony.

'Marian,' he whispered, 'I am going to run the quarter mile up the road to Martha's and bring the doctor back with me.'

'But the old woman, she needs the doctor too.'

'The doctor will just have to tend to two patients tonight. You must not worry about that.'

He kissed Marian and told her he would return before she knew it, and a moment later he ran off into the stormy night.

Marian moaned and writhed in her seat, rubbing her belly and trying to keep herself as calm as possible.

'My child, my child. Why hurt your mother in this way? Are you really so anxious to see me?'

Sam stood outside the window and gazed at the mother he had never known. If he had any doubts that he was doing the right thing, the sight of this woman and the sound of her kind voice dispelled them all. To have a mother like that! He gently closed the barn door and tiptoed back to the window to take one last look. His mother seemed more restful now. Her eyes were closed though her hands were still resting gently on her middle. They were resting on him. Sam blinked back the hot tears threatening to run down his cheeks when he felt a light touch on his left shoulder.

'Are you ready to be more than an observer of your life?'

'Yes, Magnus, I am.'

Sam and Magnus hugged each other fiercely and said their goodbyes. In a few minutes there was no trace of either of them. And in a few moments more, Ben returned with the doctor.

The next morning, the people of Banbury heard that Marian had delivered a healthy baby boy. There had been complications but she would be fine. Martha's mother, too, had pulled through the night and even showed signs of recovery. The doctor had been busy, but at least he was able to report good news. He received many claps on the back and offers of drinks and cakes.

A stranger to the town, Josiah, saddled his horse and listened to the gabble of the local women. He was glad that the wife of that nice Ben Lockhart was okay and they'd had their boy safely. That was good news indeed. This was certainly a lovely little place, very friendly. Despite all of the heavy rain, he had slept well the previous night. He'd retired not long after the party broke up in the tavern just before eleven. He rode out of Banbury refreshed and cheerful.

Marian lay with her newborn babe in her arms and smiled down at his sleeping face. 'You certainly gave your mother a fright last night, but you don't care, do you, darling?'

She kissed his forehead gently and smiled at Ben, who had entered the room with a cup of tea for his wife.

'I've spoken to Martha. She saw no man last night, so she couldn't have been the one who told the stranger to get me.'

'Well who then?'

'I don't know but, well, I don't want to think what might have happened if he hadn't come. I have to confess that I wasn't paying a great deal of attention to my watch. What if he hadn't come . . .?'

Ben held his face in his hands and wept. It had been a long and emotional night, and the thought of losing his beloved wife was too much to bear.

'My love, I am safe, and so is the baby. There is no point in torturing yourself with what might have happened. All turned out well. Perhaps we will never discover the mystery behind this man. I will think of him as our good angel.'

'Yes, that is one way to see it. There was something, I don't know, different about him. Something familiar.'

'Ben, I think we should call this little one Gabriel. After the angel Gabriel—you know, the messenger of God. And through this one's name we'll always remember the messenger who helped us.'

Ben thought for a few moments and then agreed that they really could do no better.

14.

Sickness

The door of the Rainbow House creaked as the battering wind blew it back and forth in its frame. It was bitterly cold. Gracie shivered as she wrote at her desk. Though she wore fingerless mittens, her fingers nonetheless remained numb and clumsy. She rubbed her hands together and squinted to read what she had just written. At only a little after 3:00 pm, the room was already growing dark. Soon it would be too dark to work at all unless they lit many candles, but even then, it would be difficult.

Gracie sat back and tried to calm herself. She was worried about Mr Franklyn's visit. He would arrive the following week. It would be his first visit in all the time he had been Tom's patron. Tom had travelled down to London to see him once, and they corresponded regularly, but Gracie was still an absent presence in Mr Franklyn's understanding of Tom's daily life and work. He knew that Tom was engaged, of course, but he hadn't taken the time to enquire about the young lady's whereabouts. He certainly would not have expected *her* to be a scientist too. They were deceiving Mr Franklyn, there was no getting away from it, but they had convinced themselves that he was benefiting from the situation in that he paid one salary but had two full-time researchers working for him. In truth, they had not spent much time thinking anything about Mr Franklyn, but now things could become very difficult.

Everything in this room told of two workers—two desks, two top-of-the-range but identical microscopes, notes written in two hands. They would have to come clean. And what then? Mr Franklyn might withdraw his patronage immediately. He could report Tom to the Royal Society, whose members would surely ridicule Tom for allowing a woman to even take a serious interest in his work. This whole way of life that they had loved so much might cease next week. Tom would have to take work elsewhere, or they would marry and go to Berlin and Tom could take the job with his Professor Bauer. But all of that would take them away from their current research.

Much as Gracie wanted to marry Tom, there was also a need within her to continue as they were, for it was only in this arrangement that she could give all of her time to her studies. Marriage meant running a home, and children. It called for an altogether different way of life. She recognised the conflict within her; she wanted to be a wife and a mother but also wanted wholeheartedly to continue with work that thrived on the selfish independence she enjoyed now. Despite Tom's assurances that she could have everything, she knew it was impossible. Gracie Abbot had never managed it and neither would Gracie Arundel. Something, even if it might seem only a little thing, would have to give, and Gracie knew that little things made all the difference. Thus for the moment, while she still could, she wanted only to advance with her work—but even the changing of the season seemingly wished to thwart her plans.

Gracie could hear Tom busy in his kitchen grating chocolate to make them hot drinks. It was early November 1802, and they had been working together at the Rainbow for a year and a half. Each day had been spent in largely the same fashion. Gracie would arrive at the Rainbow between nine and nine thirty, and then they would do examination and experimentation work to make the best possible use of the light. They would stop to eat something around one thirty. For the remainder of the day until dinnertime (which these Georgians still referred to as morning, something Gracie could not become accustomed to), they would write, read and discuss. It was, in many ways, an idyllic life, and they both realised this. They had nothing to worry about but their research and they were a spoiled, pampered pair. Even for their lunchtime meal, Nancy, the serving-girl from the nearby inn, would bring them pie or cold meat and cake and they would eat together either absent-mindedly or leisurely, depending on how their work was progressing. And they did so love to work together. Gracie would frequently raise her head from her microscope and gaze at the fair, bent head of Tom, so industrious and thorough. She respected him with her whole heart and prayed that nothing would ever occasion her to lose that feeling. In the evenings, Tom would often come to dinner at the Arundels, where he was welcomed. If the weather was fine, they would all take a walk together after their meal, or sometimes Gracie and Tom would walk alone, hand in hand, talking of what might fill the following day, or of when they might be married.

Tom placed Gracie's cup down in front of her and rubbed her aching shoulders. It was too dark and cold for anyone to be outside looking in, which people had often done when the pair began working together. Some had called the whole business scandalous, and had said so to Gracie's parents. An engaged man and woman shut away together all day! Why, it was just asking for trouble. But, in a short time, people had grown accustomed to their local "scandal" and the gossip had died down. It was really quite clear just how much reading and writing went on inside the Rainbow; the curtains were always open and the windows looked out onto the main street. Gracie had long been a different sort of a girl, queer, and that seemed to validate the respectability of their enterprise. Although Gracie had been exasperated, furious even, with the opinions of her neighbours, they had been right, of course. Gracie and Tom had resisted but ultimately succumbed to temptation. Now, between themselves, they felt no shame for this.

'Shall we stop for the day then, Gracie? I don't know about you, but I'm too tired and cold to work any longer. I'm hungry, too. I hope your mother has a big dinner waiting for us tonight.'

'She will do. But I feel I have to properly log those findings from earlier before I can happily stop. Just give me another fifteen minutes.'

'No, because it won't be fifteen minutes. Come on now, you're freezing cold. Let's take our drinks in front of the fire. You can write that down tomorrow morning.'

'But in the morning we need to make use of the light, and I want to see that sample we got last week from Oxford under the microscope.'

'Gracie, stop.'

Tom hauled her from her workbench and forced her to follow him to their chairs in front of the fire.

'Tom, we don't know how much longer we've got here. I just don't want to waste even a second.'

'Gracie, I'm as anxious as you are to discover something tangible, but you're feverish right now. We don't know what will happen with Mr Franklyn next week. We don't know we're losing our work. If we do then we'll set up again, somewhere else.'

'But it won't be here. It won't be at the Rainbow, like this.'

'We'll have a new Rainbow then. Now drink your chocolate and we'll go to your house.'

Gracie sipped her drink and pouted at Tom. He was right. Things could and would work themselves out. If she had learned one thing since she arrived here it was that there was little point in worrying about things over which you had no control. She reached out for Tom's hand, stroked her face against it and prayed again that nothing need ever change.

Alicia was waiting for them in the hall when they arrived.

'You're soaking wet, the both of you! Come into the parlour and dry yourself off, Tom. Gracie, go upstairs at once and change your dress.'

They happily allowed Alicia to order them about. As Gracie ascended the stairs she heard her mother tell the maid to bring tea. Yes, it was so nice to have other people take care of all those sorts of things. A few minutes later, Gracie sat on the end of her bed combing out her wet hair; Polly gave a quick tap on the door and poked her head into the room without waiting for a reply.

'Gracie, you're all wet.'

'Yes, funny that, given that it's pouring outside.'

'Is it? I hadn't noticed.'

'What have you been doing all day?'

'Oh, I've been with mother to the shops after breakfast and then I wrote a long letter just now.'

'A long letter! Who is so privileged to receive that?'

'Janey Scott in London. She's asked me to go and stay with her again. I think I might, after Christmas, obviously.'

'I shall miss you if you go away again.'

'No, you won't. You're so absorbed in your work and Tom that you won't even notice that I've gone. Don't deny it, Gracie.'

'That's not true Polly.'

Gracie slipped her feet into her house shoes and made a show of fixing the buckles shut, but she was really thinking over what Polly had just said. It was true that she often felt guilty over how much time she spent away from her family, especially Polly. She got up and went to her jewellery box, from which she pulled out a lovely red bracelet that she had bought in Devon.

'Put this on, Polly. It looks so well against your green dress.'

She fastened the bracelet on her sister's wrist knowing that Polly was perfectly aware that the bracelet was offered as a means to somewhat salve Gracie's conscience.

Both girls said nothing, however.

'See, doesn't that look really nice! In fact,' Gracie continued, 'come here and I'll do your hair for you.'

Polly's long black straight hair was tied into a loose knot at the nape of her neck. Gracie untied it and combed it out so that the brush could travel straight through without meeting any resistance. She then fished around in her comb-and-pin box. When she found what she was looking for, she tied Polly's hair up higher on her head in an elaborate knot.

'There, what do you think? It is very becoming. Lifting your hair up so high shows how slim your shoulders are. Wear it like that tonight, won't you?'

Throughout Gracie's proceedings, Polly had sat meekly before the mirror in silence. Now she tossed her head from side to side and smiled.

'Yes, I like it. Oh, Gracie, can I wear your little green stone earrings too?'

Polly was already rummaging. Gracie smiled and sat back on her bed. Polly was now a grown woman of twenty-two but, although she was far from stupid, she had retained a definite girlishness which many found charming. She had received many proposals of marriage from rich suitors but had refused every offer. Despite her protestations that she would rather marry for connections and wealth than love, Gracie had long suspected that Polly was far more romantic than she would have people believe.

'Have you seen Father since you've come home, Gracie?'

'Father? No, why?'

'We're to have company to dinner. Father's old judge friend who moved here last month has a sister and nephew to visit him. They arrived only this morning and they're to come here tonight. They're staying at the inn. You know that Judge Fairfax's rooms are quite small. Apparently sister Henrietta and son are too grand to squash themselves in amongst all of his books and naked ladies.'

'Polly!' Gracie laughed, pretending to be shocked.

Polly continued drily. 'Oh, yes, he's a lover of things classical, but it's all just naked ladies to me, and what a paunch!'

Gracie wiped away tears of laughter at this description of sober old Judge Fairfax. 'I thought it sounded like there was a new arrival at the inn today. There was a lot of commotion, and I heard a woman's rather shrill voice.'

'That would have been dame Henrietta. Mother and I met her and the judge today. That's how they all got invited to dinner.'

'So who exactly is coming then, aside from the old pair?'

'The nephew as well. We didn't meet him as he was away seeing about hiring a horse for the duration of his stay here.' Polly laughed. 'He's called Henry, after his mamma. Wonder if he'll have her double chin and half-shut eyes? Oh yes, Gracie, we're in for a treat tonight. Don't you and Tom dare go off together and leave me alone with them.'

Polly was still wagging her little finger at Gracie as they descended the stairs for tea.

A few hours later, Polly, usually so inquisitive about what people looked like, didn't even bother rising from her chair to take a peek as the carriage arrived outside. The nephew would be a hopeless case, she was sure.

Ernest soon entered the sitting room with his guests, and Tom and the Arundels stood to receive the judge, his stately sister and, a few steps behind, her son. Tom stifled a grin as he noticed that Polly, who had been slouching rather gracelessly, now stood to her full height and bowed as prettily as she could when it was clear that Henry Ford looked nothing like his mother. He nudged Gracie and stole a glance at her to see what she made of their guest. Gracie saw a tall young man in his midtwenties with thick black hair as dark as Polly's and a countenance that could only be described as very handsome. A slight frisson of tension crackled around the room now, the sort that is detectable when young people gather and there is the promise of all kinds of things to follow. The older people seemed unaware, but Gracie, Tom, Polly and Henry were perfectly sure of its existence.

Polly could never remain coy for long. After introductions and a polite chat, she asked Henry directly how long he would be staying in Bourton and what he did. Before he answered he looked at his mother. Seeing that she was absorbed in conversation with Alicia, he leaned forward conspiratorially and said that he preferred to be known by the name of Jack.

'After my middle name, John, you see. Mother will always call me Henry but she is the only one who does. So call me Jack, Miss Arundel. All of my friends do.'

Polly blushed a little but continued. 'I'll call you Mr Ford because we are not friends yet—perhaps we never shall be.'

Jack laughed and implored that Polly would never be so cruel.

Tom, a little distance away, leaned towards Gracie and whispered, 'I think we have the makings of a grand flirtation on our hands. Has Polly met her match at last?'

'Yes,' Gracie answered, 'Mr Ford is exactly the sort of man Polly usually admires, too. I'd wager that she no longer wishes for us to never leave her side all evening. She'll want Mr Ford to herself all night.'

'And what of that?' Tom teased, although it seemed not entirely in jest. 'You want no part in admiring him, do you?'

Gracie gazed at Tom and smiled. 'No, my love, my heart was won as I gathered shells on a beach some years ago now. It belongs as securely now to the rude young man who disturbed me as it did then.'

* * *

Polly was in raptures that evening after their visitors had said their farewells. Mr Jack Ford was everything a man ought to be and more. Gracie had certainly never seen her sister react in this way to anyone, and she said so to Polly.

Polly, standing in front of her sister's bed, rolled back on her heels and fell upon it as Gracie spoke, as if she were genuinely astonished.

'Why, you're right. But we could speak about anything, and so easily. Gracie, you know I can flirt—well, your laughter now tells me you know that I can—and I'm sure that Mr Ford is also practised in the art, but we went beyond that tonight. It was a sort of comfortable, warm teasing, but it was certainly more than flirting. He felt it too, Gracie, I know he did. Remember how long we spoke by the piano? The rest of you may as well not even have been in the room for all we cared. Oh, Gracie, how strange. I've met the man I'm going to marry.'

Gracie had been stitching the hem of a nightdress, but the seriousness of her sister's tone, as much as what she'd actually said, made her look up, her needle suspended in mid-air.

'Polly, are you serious?'

'Yes, I am. Jack and I shall marry shortly. I see how it all will be.'

Polly's voice sounded exultant, almost prophetic, shy. It sounded all of these things but also a little sad, and indeed, a tear dropped down onto one of her cheeks.

Mesmerised, Gracie rose and gave her sister a hug. 'My little Polly will be married! I'm so happy for you. But look at us. Mr Ford could surely scarcely guess that I am congratulating you at this moment on your forthcoming marriage!'

Polly thought for a few seconds and then answered seriously. 'He may be surprised but he will know the truth of it all. There are things about which I am never wrong.'

A few days later Jack Ford called to see Ernest and formally asked for his daughter's hand in marriage. Ernest was dumbfounded, but what could he say? The young man's credentials were good and everything promised a fair future, but the shortness of his and Polly's acquaintance naturally made him hesitate. Alicia felt the same way, as did Mrs Ford, but the young couple would not be swayed.

'Father, dear, we know what we want and nothing can prevent our marriage. You must all be happy for us and save your worries and protestations, for they will never be justified.'

Polly delivered this claim in such a determined but breezy manner that it was difficult to argue or even feel angry. Polly would win, as she so often did, and be married directly.

Jack was twenty-six years old and an only child. He had completed a degree at Oxford and had the good fortune of being independently rich and therefore in no need of a profession. Although this was the case, Jack was also something of a freelance architect, and he took commissions when interesting proposals came his way. Most recently, he had designed a house for a retired and wealthy sea captain who resided in Dorset, and the newspaper clippings Jack's mother showed the Arundels revealed that the house had been much admired as a handsome example of the "modern style". The Fords had a home on Dover Street in London, and the couple proposed that they marry in Bourton and then Polly would return with her husband and mother-in-law to London after Christmas.

There was no fault to find in all of their well-thought-out plans, and the Arundels, following Alicia's lead, soon became excited about the prospect of organising a family wedding in the next month. The only fly in the ointment seemed to be Mrs Ford, who sourly voiced her displeasure with everything. But as Gracie soon discovered, to her great amusement, Polly could smoothly and effectively deal with even the monumental task of appeasing a jealous and doting mother.

Arriving home from the Rainbow one day, Gracie was about to enter the morning room when she heard Polly and Mrs Ford having a serious conversation. Gracie drew back instinctively, but before she could retreat, Gracie saw Polly rise from the sofa and stand determinedly in front of her prospective mother-in-law.

'My dear Mrs Ford, now this will stop. Your son loves you, and I, for all our sakes, hope to esteem and love you too. However, despite your motherly ties, if you force Jack to choose between you and me, you will never win, I assure you. Now, be sensible. I am prepared to make your life as comfortable and easy as it ever was—indeed, I can make it more so. Work with me rather than against me and we will all be happier.'

Mrs Ford sat stunned. And then just as the woman opened her mouth to speak, Polly smiled, bent down and grasped her hand.

'My dear mother, I need your help and advice. I am reliant on you for so much. Help me please, won't you?'

Gracie caught the faintest discernible glimmer of resistance pass over Mrs Ford's face and then—wisdom prevailed. She smiled and embraced Polly. From that moment on, there existed nothing but the warmest relations between the two, and Gracie could feel only the keenest admiration for the diplomacy her remarkable sister had shown.

Amidst all of the wedding plans, Tom and Gracie also had to contend with the arrival of the curmudgeonly and singular Mr Franklyn. The old fellow had a private carriage, which Tom met outside the inn on a warm and sunny day. Gracie remained a discreet distance away and watched them enter the nearby pleasant and homely little tavern. They had arranged that she be at the Rainbow to meet them in an hour.

A few minutes before the appointed time, Tom spied her dark head flash past the window of the tavern.

'Sir, are you tired? I would really like you to come and see my dwelling place now. It is also where I carry out all of my work, as I have explained.'

'Tired? No boy. It would take more than a little journey to flatten me. Glad to see you are so keen to show me your work, my lad. I knew you would be a good and honest worker. Knew that any son of my old friend Blake would be a safe bet.'

Tom helped Mr Franklyn gather up his coat and stick, and showed him the way to his house across the street. Gracie felt flustered as she saw Tom and an old but sprightly enough looking man make their way towards her. She smoothed her hair down and straightened her dress. Within minutes they were all in the room together, and Tom introduced Gracie to the astonished old man.

'Your intended? Why, I am pleased to meet you, miss. Are you visiting too?'

'No, sir, I live in Bourton.'

'Ah, you do, do you?'

Mr Franklyn looked from Tom to Gracie and then to Tom again.

'And have you always lived in Bourton, Miss Arundel?'

'Yes, sir, I have.'

The penny, or the first one anyway, had dropped. Mr Franklyn rubbed his head and sat down on the end of the nearest workbench.

'Mr Franklyn,' Tom said, 'we have some explaining to do.'

Tom then related the whole story, and the look of disbelief on Mr Franklyn's face when Tom explained that Gracie was also a scientist, and his colleague to boot, was matched only by the shock he betrayed when he was shown some of Gracie's notes and she explained the latest work she had carried out. When all was told, Mr Franklyn stood and shook his head.

'I believed you had your reasons for living here, but after what I said to you about women, I did not think it would be because of a woman. Tom, I thought you dealt straighter than that.'

'Sir, I am so sorry, but I can assure you that we have achieved more together than I would have done alone.'

'Mmph, well of that I can have no proof. I need to spend some time alone with my thoughts now. Give me some of your latest notes to look through . . . Yes, yes, give me her notes as well. Now, I am going to retire to my room at the inn and I don't want to see either of you until ten o'clock tomorrow. Here.'

Mr Franklyn ignored the help Tom offered him with the door and hobbled off down the street. Tom and Gracie, feeling like chastened children, looked at each other. They could only wait.

The next morning, shortly before ten, Gracie carried a tray with some cups of tea into the living area. Mr Franklyn arrived promptly and settled himself down to face the still guilty-looking pair.

'I have thought over this business,' he said, 'and I am satisfied that this young lady is no incompetent amateur. I commend you on your talents, miss. I repeat that I am very disappointed to have been lied to by such a thoroughly decent young couple. However, much of my disappointment is aimed at myself for this. I had no right to tell you to not be married, and I was wrong in my opinion that a woman could be nothing other than a nuisance and a distraction when it comes to the serious business of science. I wanted you to study influenza for my own sake, my boy. I loved once, you know. Anna was her name, and she was the sweetest . . . Well, my old head is not up to the challenge of describing her with justice, but my memories, let me tell you, they are as real and perfect as ever. Anna died of the influenza; I think you knew that? I thought about Anna last night and how she would feel about a woman helping to find an answer for that wretched sickness and I knew it would please her. It seemed fitting that such a couple should do this for us. You were right to disobey me. Only death was able to part Anna and me. I want you to both continue, but no more secrets, no more lies. Everything must be above board and you'—Mr Franklyn pointed to Gracie—'you must begin to be paid the same salary as this young rascal.'

Gracie and Tom looked at each other in disbelief but Mr Franklyn continued.

'I think too much of this enterprise to wish for things to be carried out anything other than fairly. Miss Arundel, would you do me the honour of carrying on your work here?'

'Yes, sir, I think I can with all pleasure agree to that.'

'And, of course,' said Mr Franklyn with a smile, 'I raise no objections to your being married while you work for me.'

It all seemed too good to be true. Gracie and Tom made their way home as quickly as possible to tell the Arundels of their news. Polly immediately proposed a double wedding in December, but Tom shook his head ruefully and said that would not be possible.

'Gracie and I will marry here, of course, but I am afraid next month will not be enough notice for my parents and other family members to travel here. My mother has always set her heart on seeing me married, and I cannot disappoint her. Gracie, do you understand?'

'Of course I do.' Gracie smiled. 'We have waited this long, another few months can hardly make a difference. And anyway, Polly must be the star of this forthcoming wedding!'

And so, it was agreed that Tom and Gracie would marry in the late spring of 1803.

Polly and Jack's wedding passed wonderfully smoothly, and Gracie wept as she watched her little sister become Mrs Jack Ford. She thought of the first time she met Polly, and of all of their ups and downs. But most of all, she thought of the skinny little girl hiding under the bed demanding to know where Gracie had been. After the ceremony, when they were alone together in Polly's bedroom, Gracie realised how much she would truly miss having Polly close by.

'Well,' Polly said, breaking through Gracie's reverie, 'I said I would be leaving for London after Christmas and I really am, aren't I?'

'I'll miss you so much, Polly. You must write all of the time, and I'll write to you too.'

'Look after yourself, Gracie, and do everything that you have to do. May you and Tom be eternally happy amongst your bacteria and swabs! Thank Heaven you two found each other!'

Polly departed with her new family in due course, and life at the Arundel house settled to a new rhythm. Gracie made real efforts to spend more time with her parents, as much for her own reasons as for fear of their growing lonely. She would be a married woman and leaving them herself soon, and she wanted to savour life at home for as long as she could.

Gracie was now being paid for her hours at the Rainbow House, and although her parents could keep her more than comfortably, it was immensely satisfying to be independent, and to be recognised for doing the same work as Tom. Aside from missing Polly, Gracie felt as happy as she had ever been as the early weeks of 1803 progressed.

And then, without warning, an unaccountable sickness took hold of many residents of South West England.

It was not a particularly bad winter, but people nonetheless put their illness down to the cold or some other such seasonal ailment. It didn't seem a very serious malady for those who were hale and hearty. The newspapers took little notice of it and advised the sick to stay in bed, rest and "weather it through". Gracie and Tom requested that samples from those afflicted be sent to their laboratory, as much to add them to their catalogue as anything else. But before the samples arrived in Bourton, the newspapers reported that the sickness had taken a strange new turn. It seemed to have multiple phases. The first phase caused no more than the symptoms of a common cold—a patient might feel a little tired or off his food and would then appear to grow stronger. Then within a few days, he would become much worse. This time he would be reduced to lying in bed, unable to move, and breathing would be difficult. Again, the sufferer would rally a little, and it would seem as if he were growing better. However, there was a third phase to the illness, far worse than the previous two. People were beginning to die. A common factor of all three phases, strange in a climate in which scarlet fever and smallpox were so well known, was that there was no visual evidence to suggest that someone was affected by the illness, regardless of the phase.

As the epidemic spread, panic descended. With Bourton still free from the sickness, Tom read as much as he could gather on this new and perplexing virus. Gracie read everything too, but she wasn't as concerned as Tom or anyone else, as she trusted that it would eventually turn out to be of lesser importance than everyone feared. Her attitude puzzled Tom, but she had never heard of an epidemic in Britain in the early nineteenth century. As she would many more times over the coming weeks, Gracie wondered whether she should summon Cianna to talk to her about what was happening. But for some reason, Gracie feared doing this, and she continued to resist ringing the glass bell.

When the samples arrived, Gracie and Tom took the usual measures to protect themselves from contagion, ensuring that their hands and skin were covered and Gracie's hair was pulled tightly behind her ears. Looking under their microscopes they discovered, as was often the case, that the instruments were not powerful enough to detect the incredibly small structure of the virus. They then coated the samples with a special viscous mixture they had developed. Looking under the microscopes again, they could now gain a good idea of how the virus looked by the way that the visible particles in their mixture reacted to it—and it was like nothing they had seen. Gracie knew that the mixture was fairly reliable as she remembered, from her old life, what certain viruses looked like. She racked her mind but could not recall, at any time, learning about a virus with such an unusual shape.

By early February, many more hundreds of people were dead and scientists from far and wide were working around the clock trying to come up with a means to eradicate the disease. Every known medical treatment was given to the willing sufferers but every one of them failed. Despite Dr Jenner's recent achievements in vaccination through the means of inoculation, cure rather than prevention seemed to be the only channel available to fight this extraordinary new virus. Reports of the sickness spread to other parts of the country, and the idea of mass quarantine—forbidding people to leave their dwelling areas—was considered.

In spite of all of this, people carried on as normally as they could. The virus did not discriminate in terms of age or position, but some people, no matter how closely they came into contact with it, did not become ill. This fact provided momentary hope, but it was soon recognised that the mechanism of the virus was devastating in terms of it spreading around the country due to there being no visible signs of the condition and that the first phase was mild enough for many to work and interact in their communities as usual.

No record disputed the fact that the first phase always eventually resulted in the third. However, diagnosis through the usual means of examination alone was rendered impossible while a sufferer remained in the first phase as he or she could, in reality, have nothing more serious than a mild form of the common cold. The subsequent waiting to see whether the person would then succumb to the more obvious second phase of the virus was a terrifying ordeal, not only for the victims but for whole neighbourhoods. Also, one could never be entirely sure after recovery whether or not the suspected case had indeed been only a mild cold or, miraculously, an instance of the more dreaded disorder having been fought and beaten. For all of these reasons, it was difficult to consider any data even remotely authoritative.

Gracie and Tom, as expert in the field of virus studies as anyone else in the country, soon discovered that the new virus bore some things in common with influenza. However, a hopeful feature of the new virus, unlike influenza, was that it did not seem to mutate. As they attempted to find a counter for different forms of influenza, they attempted to do likewise for this new virus. They wrote to Mr Franklyn, asking his permission to undertake this further research and were dismayed to receive a letter from him, eventually, declaring that he too had succumbed to the illness. He gave his blessing for their plans. A few days later, Mr Franklyn's solicitor informed them by letter that their patron had died. Gracie and Tom were heartily grieved, and Gracie wept when she heard that Mr Franklyn had taken steps so that they would be able to continue their studies, at his expense, even after his death. That same day, many people suffering from the virus, now known as *ter* ("three times") syndrome, were forcibly removed from their houses and families and quarantined together.

Soon, the government sanctioned this type of action in the most heavily afflicted parts of the country and the military executed it. No foreigner did business in Britain, and no foreign country wished to receive anyone who had recently been there. In a very short time, the most trivial business of visiting a friend in a neighbouring village had become impossible for many people. Confinement and fear had become daily parts of life.

Gracie and Tom now concentrated wholly on the new virus. They had, in reserve and in note form, many different tried and tested counters for varying strains of influenza, and they intended to try all of these upon the new virus. Their attempts met with no success. By March, when the death toll had climbed to many thousands, Gracie and Tom had modified their original counters and were trying them all out again. It was a slow and laborious process, and they scarcely knew whether there was even any point to their efforts. However, as they learned more about this new virus, it became clear that without their intensive and recent work regarding influenza, they would have been in an even more inferior position.

Alone in her room at the end of March, Gracie read a letter from Polly which told of her sister's imminent return to Bourton with Jack and Mrs Ford. People were falling down daily in London at an alarming rate, and they would all feel safer in the healthier climate of Gloucestershire. Tom was worried about his parents and brother, but they seemed as safe in Devon for the moment as they would be in Bourton. Gracie held her aching head in her hands and wondered what more she could do. This illness had not existed in any history or science book she had read, and she had been quietly hoping it would simply disappear.

Her own wedding to Tom, which had been due to take place shortly, had obviously been forgotten. Aside from anything else, they were too busy to think of it.

Something had happened. Something had changed things.

Gracie, exhausted, lay down in bed, ideas for her work making it impossible for her brain to relax. Eventually she fell into a fitful sleep from which Cianna roused her.

15.

Precisely Now

The Englishman stood with his hands clenched deep in his pockets and stared out at the calm and sparkling blue water of the Jamaica Channel. It was clear and warm but as loathsome to him as if it were rank. How he longed to be home! How he hated this heat! How low he had fallen here when once there had been such promise.

Kicking the sand underneath his bare feet, he turned and made his way back up the beach towards the house. He'd never thought of it as his home, even though he'd lived in it for over three years.

Nothing's ever felt right, he thought. *I've had no real life for years. I've been in Hell.*

The man had no money, none whatsoever, but all he needed was his passage back to England. He could sort himself out once he arrived. Why, the way he felt now, even the prospect of begging on the dirty streets of London seemed like paradise. The latest ship from Africa would be docking at Kingston harbour soon, and on board would be the last of his assets, the slaves he had ordered when he was still part-owner of his sugar plantation. Those slaves were his ticket back to England, and freedom. Monterney had agreed to buy them and use them on the land that he had swindled from him. He hated the thought of seeing that smirking face again, but those in desperate circumstances could not afford to be choosy, even if it meant dealing with the Devil himself.

Arriving at the house, the man noticed again that his slaves and workers now looked at him with either less fear or less respect in their eyes. To them he was finished. Well, so he was. And as such, he would leave them to sweat and toil in the filth while he did something he had not done in years, not since he was a little boy and his mother put him to bed when he was sick. Although it was still relatively early in the afternoon, he went upstairs to his room and lay down. He was soon fast asleep.

The man had arrived in Jamaica in the early autumn of 1799 to take possession of a sugar plantation in Kingston with his business partner and friend. His friend, however, never made it to Jamaica and instead died of dysentery on the boat. Jointly they had purchased the plantation while in Britain, even though neither of them had travelled any further than France. Heartened by stories of ordinary working men like themselves getting rich and fat in the strange new world of wage-free workers and broiling sun, they'd decided to take the plunge. Of the two, only his partner, Heath, had had any family to leave behind, and he'd done so with the understanding that he would send money home regularly and that they would join him when all was settled and the lay of the land was known.

Some friends and family had raised objections to their plan and said it was wrong, evil, unchristian. An old Quaker woman told them it could only bring misery. But others, who had actually been to Jamaica and profited there, said that the slaves didn't really mind it at all. Indeed, they were better off than they had been in Africa, where most of them had been savage and heathen. In the European-owned plantations in America and the Caribbean, they were given food, care and a proper Christian way of life. The Negroes were merely children, even the oldest of them, and it was up to the white people to guide and protect them. Neither the man nor Heath had ever laid eyes on a black person and they, albeit uncomfortably, accepted the words of their wiser and better-off peers.

This would not be forever, they'd said—hopefully no longer than a decade. And then they could look forward to returning home happier and wealthier for their industry and experiences. They would not mistreat any of their slaves and would not ask any of them to work harder than they themselves would, on this they were agreed. But then poor Heath died and left his partner all alone in a foreign and unreal existence.

The man had done his best and adapted as quickly as he could. The plantation was comparatively small, but he made it pay well under the second year of his ownership and sent more money home to Heath's widow than he knew he needed to.

Upon his arrival, he'd been appalled by the condition of the blacks on his plantation, and he took some pains to improve their situation, but this resulted in problems. If he fed them better or gave them more rest time then he could not financially compete with his less-caring competitors. His overseer quit, saying it was a scandal that he was not allowed to run his slaves in the only way possible and the plantation had acquired a reputation for being troublesome and disorganised. A few of the male slaves, sensing the conflict, then organised an uprising that ended in misery and death for those slaves who had rebelled. So, ironically, although he had meant to help them, the man's efforts to improve the slaves' lives had actually produced the opposite. Following this, he never again tried to interfere unduly in the new overseer's handling of the slaves and turned a studiedly blind eye to all of the whippings and enforced breeding he knew took place. It was Hell on earth in many ways, but he'd tried to make the best of it.

Monterney had been after his plantation from the start, but the Englishman had refused to sell it to this odious and cruel man. The price he'd offered was nothing short of insulting, and, despite his horror of Jamaican plantation life, he felt he'd be damned if he'd come all the way out here only to return meekly to England with tattered dreams. He owed himself and Heath's family better than that.

Monterney owned plantations everywhere it seemed; he was certainly the most prominent businessman in Kingston. As a result, the Englishman did not have many dealings with him at first—Monterney spent a lot of time in Montego Bay and in Georgia, in North America. But everyone knew the stories about him, about how he had the strongest of his male slaves whipped for his own amusement, how he personally watched his slaves copulate (after forcing them to do so on pain of death) and how the better-looking of his slave girls, many of them very young, were forced to inhabit a personal brothel for himself and his degenerate friends—where they remained until they were superfluous to his needs—. This usually happened when they became pregnant, and Monterney was the father of God only knows how many mulatto children.

This monster had wanted the man's plantation and now he had it, and it had been wrested from him neither fairly nor honourably. When the next ship arrived in Kingston from West

Africa, carrying the man's slaves, he would see them safely deposited at his old plantation. From Kingston, he would then travel to Montego Bay to meet with Monterney, deal with the paperwork and receive his payment. From there, he would make his way home to Bristol on a British slave ship on the last leg of its triangular trade.

The man spent his remaining days in Kingston waiting for the arrival of his slaves with anticipation akin to that of a deprived alcoholic who knows that he will soon be offered a drink. He had long since abandoned troubling over such things as pride. When the longed-for day arrived, the Englishman stood alone on the docks, waiting for the approaching ship. He had none of his old workers with him. They paid him no heed now and were enjoying something of a semi-holiday until Monterney arrived next week. Their old employer thought nothing of this; they could run the place into the ground for all he now cared.

He'd stood on the dock calmly enough when he'd first spied the ship but grew anxious as it became obvious that something was wrong. The ship was not coming into the harbour. Instead, it remained docked some way out at sea, perhaps ten minutes away for a strong swimmer. Eventually a little boat was let down the ship's side, and several white men climbed into it. They rowed near where the man stood waiting, and he made his way to them to enquire what on earth was happening.

'And what business is it of yours, sir?'

'It is plenty my business, for some of those you have on board are my slaves. Here, I have the paperwork.'

'Your slaves, sir?'

Two of the men looked at each other, and this made the Englishman grow more uncomfortable still.

'Yes. My slaves. Are you telling me there is some kind of problem?'

'There is a major problem. Sit down here upon the sand, and let us tell you what has happened.'

One of the men then proceeded to explain that most of the hundreds of people who had been shipped from the pickup point in Africa were now either dead or dying. The ship was in the throes of some terrible and strange disease and nearly all its inhabitants, white and black, had succumbed. The seven men who now stood before the Englishman were all that was left of the white crew. They all, unaccountably, still felt fine, and they prayed that the sickness had spared them.

'And are there no blacks left alive?'

'Yes, around twenty or so are still alive, and they remain on the ship. Out of those twenty, around a quarter are close to death. The rest seem healthy, just like us.'

'Twenty? But I have already paid for one hundred!'

'Sorry, but that's for you to take up with the trader you dealt with.'

'His name was Brown.'

'Brown is dead. We threw his body overboard some days ago.'

The Englishman stared at the men, aghast. Without his money from Monterney for the slaves, he had no means to get home, at least not as soon as he wanted to. His money seemed lost to him.

'And what is this illness?'

'We don't know. It's like nothing we've encountered. There are so many strange and mucky diseases in Africa. This one is clean though, but deadly. It starts just like a cold. When the men thought they were recovering, the sickness took them down again and they could barely move or breathe. Then again, they seemed to grow stronger, until the disease took them down a final time. Most were dead within days. We were supposed to be on our way to Cuba after this, and then North America. But now we have no slaves to deliver.'

'Was this to be your only stop in Jamaica?'

'Yes. But this is where we'll have to stop for a while, at least until the next ship arrives.'

'What will happen to those sick on board?'

The men looked uncomfortably at each other. They clearly did not want to, or felt they were unable to, reveal anymore. But the dark cloud that'd fallen over the usually impassive face of their inquisitor, however, made them feel they'd little choice but to provide more information.

'The sick will soon be dead, and their bodies shall be destroyed and never brought ashore. The healthy, if they remain so, will be transported to Mandeville.'

'Mandeville? In Jamaica? But why? There is no slave hospital there.'

'It is where those slaves in these situations are taken. If they remain well, they will be brought back to Kingston and sold. If they don't, then they will die out of everyone's way. They won't pass the sickness on. We're talking more freely than we ought to because we're exhausted and have lived amongst the fear of death for weeks. All we have are our orders. We must now make our way to a house for white workers in our situation.'

'But who orders you to do this?'

The Englishman listened and grew ashamed at last as he learned that certain of his own countrymen were keeping the affair hushed up so as not to bring disrepute to the lucrative business of slave trading. This sort of thing had happened before, albeit rarely, but, if it was revealed, people would not want to work on the ships, might not want to risk trading slaves. Countries and empires relied heavily upon the work slaves carried out for free, so it was important that most people were left unaware of the fact that a deadly disease had been brought so close to their midst.

'The ship will be scrubbed clean once the Africans are cleared away. It will be fine to use again.'

'This is all kept quiet, is it?' the man asked. 'So even very important people do not know of this?' He was quickly formulating a plan.

'No, sir.'

'And people as far away as Montego Bay would not know either?'

'Certainly not.'

Could he not go to Montego Bay and pretend that the slaves had been delivered safely? The Bristol ship would leave soon after he met with Monterney. Yes, he might just get away with it. His reputation was unimpeachable in Jamaica. Monterney had even mocked him about it—he would never suspect that he was being deceived. By the time Monterney learned of the fact, the Englishman would be well on his way home. But he would require the documentation detailing the order and payment of the slaves, as well as their delivery. This was only given at the end of a trading transaction. Doubtless Monterney would ask to see it.

'I know the document regarding my purchase will not be given its final signature, as my transaction is incomplete, but can I have it anyway for my records?'

'Aye, you could have it, but all of that sort is still on the ship and we won't be going back on that. We'll tell the man who takes the slaves to Mandeville to go about his business, but nothing and no one would get us back on that boat amongst those sick Negroes—nothing.'

'Tell me where the documents are kept then, and I'll go aboard myself.'

'Don't be daft, man. You might come down with the illness and you'll die for sure if you do. And don't you care about spreading it amongst other folks? All for the sake of your records?'

The men sneered and spat in his direction, having instantly lost all respect and sympathy for his situation. They left him standing forlornly on the dock. He thought swiftly. It was still very early in the morning and there was nobody about. Indeed, as he'd been the only one in Kingston waiting for slaves from this ship, he was quite alone at the moment. And the men had left their little boat here. He could be on the ship and back within the hour, he was sure. How difficult would it be to find the document? He would just make his way to the ship's office. In any case, all the official stamps and seals would be there, and he could forge the dealer's signature. He was prepared to risk anything to get away from here. The slaves on board would be chained, as usual. He wouldn't go near them. He'd make himself safe. He looked around furtively, crept into the boat and rowed out towards the anchored ship.

It was deathly quiet as he climbed aboard, and he could see nobody as he stood on the deck. He spun wildly about and tried to guess where he should go first. Downstairs, of course—he needed to make his way down some stairs.

He saw a door in the middle of the ship and he knew there would be steps beyond it that would lead him to the captain's area and the office. As he found his way down the dank stairs, he became aware of a strong acrid smell. *The ship has probably not been soaked and scrubbed as it ought, due to all the illness,* he thought. But the ship smelled of something worse than mere bad housewifery. The air too was heavy and oppressive. He breathed a short sigh of relief when he discovered the office area straight ahead. He stepped in hastily and began rummaging, trying not to notice the various bags and piles of belongings scattered all over the floor and desk. They obviously belonged to those who had died, and were to be forwarded on to loved ones and dependants.

Within ten minutes he had all he needed. He made his way to the corridor again.

Damn.

There were steps and doors everywhere, and he couldn't recall which he'd just used. He'd barely slept the previous night and hadn't eaten properly for days. This coupled with the shock of the day's events and his horror at being aboard this nightmarish ship meant his poor head was not up to the task of remembering even recent details.

This door and these steps, yes, they look exactly the same as those I used before.

He began to climb and became forcibly aware of that smell again. Indeed, the smell alerted him to the fact that he'd selected the wrong steps. It was much stronger here. And now he could tell there were slightly more steps too. Should he return and begin again or keep going? These would likely lead him to the deck too. He kept climbing until he reached another door. Eagerly pushing open the door, he was entirely unprepared for what lay beyond it.

He was on the deck, but on a part of it that had been hidden from his view earlier. And all of the blacks were chained here. Some were slouched, their eyes closed. They looked dead. Others sat more upright with keen and alert eyes, though they looked wretched in any case. The chains had chafed and cut into their skin leaving raw red wounds. The contrast of the scarlet blood against the black skin seemed to him for a moment, bizarrely, almost beautiful. Attractive yet repulsive at the same time.

The Englishman and the slaves stared at one another for an intense few seconds, and it seemed as if they were inhabiting a strange new world in which things like race, colour and position meant nothing. They were all just men with the same desires and the same emotions. But these men were tied up and enslaved and he wasn't—well, not technically. He could feel, palpably, the weight of centuries of enforced belief. And he felt how hollow and fabricated it all was. Humanity was all that mattered in the end.

Then one of the slaves spoke to him, and the strangeness of the language created distance once more. He jumped back nervously, as if the words were brandished weapons. Although he didn't understand their language, it was obvious he was being asked for water. He looked from side to side and knew he appeared pathetic. He could see no water. What could he do for these men after all? Their lives, such as they had, were pitiful existences, and he alone could not change that. He had to get going.

His documents fluttered to the floor, and he bent quickly to retrieve them. As he stood he caught sight again of the face of the man who had spoken to him, and he knew that the dying slave understood what the papers meant. The slave shouted something at him with seemingly all of the bitterness and hatred he still possessed in his wasted and broken form. He then spat on the white man, full on the face. The stunned Englishman hurried away, wiping his face on his sleeve. The black man continued to chant the unknown phrase, and the Englishman could hear it, over and over, as he climbed off the ship and down the ladder into his waiting rowboat. What on earth did it mean? He repeated it in his head, phonetically, and knew that even if he never discovered what it meant he would remember its sound precisely for the rest of his days.

He began to row away but briefly stopped when he realised that the chanting had turned into weeping. Hopeless, terrified weeping. As he rowed into Kingston he knew he could never again hide behind that helpful guilt-chaser that the blacks were different. He wasn't leaving behind subhuman slaves but men—just ordinary men.

It was only when he arrived back at his house that he thought about the possible repercussions of a clearly ill man having spat on him. He scrubbed his face and then his whole person, and burned the clothes he had been wearing. What could he do? Go to Mandeville too? Of course not. There was no telling for sure that the slave was afflicted with this deadly disease, if such a thing existed. Perhaps they all had dysentery or something else of that sort, and he had nursed Heath through that and not caught it himself. He knew he had a hardy constitution. He would leave for Montego Bay today and try to not worry.

Dusty and tired from his long journey, when the Englishman arrived the following day, before he even procured lodgings for himself, he checked for news of the British slave ship and learned it would arrive in Montego Bay in four or five days if all was well. He turned to leave the dock when a naval officer stopped him and enquired whether he hailed from south Somersetshire in England.

'Yes, I do. From Sparkford, to be more precise, Captain.'

'I knew it! Sparkford is only a few miles from my home.'

The naval officer seemed delighted with this discovery and wanted to know all about his fellow Englishman. Immediately he suggested they share dinner, but his new acquaintance broke away embarrassedly. He hesitated and then confessed that he had no funds until he could sort out some unfinished business.

'Oh, don't worry man! If we ever meet in Sparkford you can return the favour and buy me a nice frothy glass of English beer.'

Then, suddenly realising how hungry he actually was, he allowed the kindly officer to lead him towards a nearby inn.

Over dinner, it was clear to the man that the fact that he and the officer came from the same part of a tiny faraway island seemed to count for a great deal. There was a sort of fellowship that would never have existed back home. He told the officer his troubles but withheld the details of the disease and the fact that he was selling Monterney long-dead slaves.

'Monterney? I've heard of him. That man has a devilish reputation.'

'Aye, and I have to go crawling to him on my belly or I cannot get home.'

'No, there is another way. I could arrange for you to board, as a guest of the British navy, on my ship, which leaves itself for Bristol tonight.'

The defeated old man smiled and gratefully accepted the kind offer. He knew he had been taken for much older than his fifty-odd years. After their meal, they walked back to the naval ship, where he was shown his lodgings for the journey. He then went back on deck and pulled out the papers from his pocket. After ripping them up into tiny pieces, he leaned over the ship and threw them into the shallow waters.

While taking one last stroll around Jamaica before he left it forever, he sat for a rest in the busy market square. A man who looked like some kind of British Baptist missionary joined him on the low wooden bench soon after. These missionary men were a common sight in Jamaica. Many of them had come from Birmingham to Christianise the enslaved in the Caribbean. Now that he knew he was on his way home, the Englishman was feeling a little bit more like his old self. He enjoyed chatting, so he invited conversation with the missionary. This man, he discovered, had been to many places in Africa and could even converse in some of its languages and dialects.

'Well, that is something.' He paused and then asked, 'And do you know what this means at all?'

He repeated as accurately as he could the sounds that the slave on the ship had shouted at him. The missionary listened carefully and then asked him to repeat it.

The missionary nodded. 'That is the Mandinka language of

upper West Africa, and what you have said means: "Shame on you, shame on you!"'

The naval ship sailed from Jamaica that evening, just as a heavy storm seemed about to begin. The old man woke early the following morning and spied a lovely and vivid rainbow from his small window as he lay in bed. Smiling happily, he fell back to sleep and dreamed of his old cottage in Sparkford.

A few weeks into his journey home, he began to feel poorly but didn't immediately connect his symptoms to the description of the disease. He always felt a little seasick, so he was unsurprised that he didn't want to eat at the outset of the voyage. But when he woke one morning to find that he could barely move his legs, he knew he was truly finished. He would be denied a last glimpse of his beloved home.

The naval men were shocked to discover his condition—they found him unable to move, talk or grasp with even the slightest pressure. And his mind was gone. The ship's doctor couldn't tell what ailed the man and put it down to a stroke.

The Englishman—called Josiah—died soon after, and his body was thrown overboard into the Atlantic Ocean following a short but dignified religious ceremony.

By the time the ship docked in Bristol Harbour, many more men on board had followed this same course. The ceremonies had become less formal when there were fewer able-bodied men left to carry them out. From the similarity of their symptoms, they realised they'd caught something from the old man, but what they could not say. As had happened on the slave ship, a select group did not seem affected by the illness at all, and these men related their horrific story to their naval superiors as soon as they arrived in England. The sick were taken off their ship and transported to a naval hospital before it was properly understood how contagious the sickness was. And so the virus was at large in the British community as the last weeks of 1802 dwindled away. The government and ruling authorities withheld the information that the illness had arrived in Britain from a country bound up in the business of working slaves. With the same reasoning as those in Jamaica who quietly sent their sick blacks to Mandeville, there was simply too much at stake for the British Empire if she lost her interests in the slave trade. In any case, it would all fizzle out soon enough, they were sure, so why unnecessarily upset the balance of commerce?

But it had not fizzled out and the government would shortly confirm, in early 1803, what many believed to be the case anyway that the disease was likely foreign and had gotten here as a result of the many British ships which traded overseas. For the sake of the country's pride, no mention would be made of the naval ship.

When Cianna finished relating the story, Gracie opened her eyes. It seemed as if she had really been there. She could smell the sweat and reeking corpses aboard the slave ship in Kingston, could see the misery in the eyes of the slaves and could hear the terrible cry. She could taste Josiah's bitterness and guilt and feel the sensation of the sea moving ceaselessly under her feet. It had all been entirely real for her.

She shook her head. She hadn't been expecting Cianna's visit when she had prepared for bed that evening. Cianna had awoken her and told her to listen to the following story in silence and then she could talk. So now she talked.

'Cianna, oh, how horrific it all is. So that explains this illness and why we have no record of it here. And is this virus wreaking havoc in Jamaica now too? Are they hushing it all up?'

'No, Gracie. There is no similar epidemic ravaging its way through Jamaica. Mandeville was an effective system in terms of contagion and, although no one could know this, the Jamaican diet is conducive to fighting the effects of this virus anyway.'

'I see. What about in Africa? I presume that's where it originated.'

'Yes. It has killed in Africa but many of the people in various regions there have built up immunity against it.'

'But why is this happening now? I have never seen this virus before.'

'You have. In your life as Gracie Abbot you are aware of it in a different form. It evolved over the years.'

Cianna was being reticent again, as if she had certain things to say but was not going to give everything away. But, no, Gracie had to repeat her question as to why this was happening in this past and hadn't happened in the past that Gracie Abbot knew.

'Something happened to change the order of events. Someone was given the opportunity to change something in the past, and that choice led to Josiah's living when originally, in the eighteenth century you were aware of, he died. He lived to go to Jamaica and return with this deadly virus.'

Gracie breathed deeply. 'Why are you here now, Cianna, telling me all of this?'

'Your moment to choose whether to remain here or return to being Gracie Abbot is precisely now.'

Panic filled every part of Gracie's being. She grasped her hands behind her head.

'But why now?'

'You stand poised to change the course of history.'

Gracie covered her mouth with her hands to stop herself from screaming aloud. *Change history! How?*

Cianna, who had been sitting on a chair before her, came and sat beside Gracie on the foot of her bed. 'Listen to me, Gracie. Here, let me hold your hands. This change has happened now in the eighteenth century, so your twenty-first century, should you decide to live there again, will have altered. It will not have changed on the outside in any way you might readily recognise. People will still work, shop and live in the same way. But in other, perhaps more important, ways, it will change a great deal. For instance, many prominent and renowned British citizens will no longer be born as a result of this virus. Their ancestors die from it. And there are those who previously did great things in this age who will also be killed by the virus before they have their opportunity. There will be a knock-on effect, as I know you'll understand, upon the future course of events, for good and bad. Britain will no longer be the country it was when you knew it in the twenty-first century. It will no longer have its powerful history. However, it and many of its people will survive, and some answer to the virus will eventually be found. Your life is many years after the events of 1803, and a sense of normality will have long since returned. Humans are naturally resilient. It is one of the things I most admire in them.'

Cianna paused and brushed some hair from Gracie's face. 'You notice that I have used the word "will" as opposed to "has". The future is poised at the moment, and only you have the opportunity to decide how it will all turn out. Never forget that you have a choice in this matter. The only correct decision is the one that comes purely from your own instincts. Did doing that not bring you here? You have something to say now?'

Gracie, who had been listening quietly, weakly nodded her head.

'Yes, Cianna. I don't understand how if all of this change is taking place in the nineteenth century then why, when I lived in the twenty-first century, did I not see the effects of this virus?'

Cianna immediately responded. 'The person who changed something in the past came from this age originally. Before he changed his event he first went to live in the twenty-first century. He lived during the same period as you. Then he returned, while you were already living in the eighteenth century, and changed events here. Therefore, you have never lived in a twenty-first century which has been affected by this virus.'

Gracie struggled to make sense of what she'd been told; it was bewildering.

'Cianna, are you hearing all of this for the first time too? You really knew nothing about a new virus, or about how I would meet Tom and begin to work on it?'

'I knew nothing. It is all a surprise to me. You will recall that I trusted there would be a reason for your being given your opportunity. And here you are. You could well provide the answer to this virus. If that is your purpose, you will restore balance to that which has been disrupted. The future will be uncertain until you make your decision. I have told you how life will have changed if you become Gracie Abbot again. If you stay here as Gracie Arundel, you hold the power to change that future, although you will never see it again.'

Gracie considered this and then asked, 'This person who changed things, did he have a Pondera too?'

'Yes, he did.'

'He had a Pondera originally in the eighteenth century?'

'Yes.'

'I see. And then he went to the twenty-first century?'

'Yes.'

'But all those years in between. When you came to know me, it was hundreds of years ago that this man and his Pondera were first together. Did you not meet this Pondera at some point? And what about—'

Cianna interrupted Gracie's frantic questioning. 'You remember when you saw Angelus's corridor? There were doors in either direction, weren't there? Everyone thinks of the time in which she lives as being the furthest point that has so far existed, until the next second passes away. We Pondera move freely within time when and where we are needed. Thus, it happens that we exist in different centuries, but that does not mean that something one of us does for someone in the thirteenth century was really carried out, in Pondera time, hundreds of years before I did something for you in the twenty-first century. In your world it does mean that, but not in ours. Time is not static to us; neither is it flat, inflexible nor unique.'

'I think I understand what you mean,' Gracie said quietly. 'But—'

'You do not need to understand—you cannot fully understand—so just accept, my dear Gracie.'

'But what is it all for? Why was this person *allowed* to change something that has brought such dire consequences to Britain?

Some force—I remember you used the term "Creator" before—well, this Creator obviously knows everything, more than you Pondera even. It gives you your instructions and you make things happen. To have me slotted into place here, it seems it foresaw that this other choice would result in this horrible virus, so why? I just don't understand, why?'

Cianna spoke passionately. 'Remember, Gracie, that above all else we Pondera thrive on bringing balance. My dear friend Magnus assisted on bringing balance to an individual's life. This was of benefit to the world generally as well as to this individual. Why? Because this man, as a part of the world, is important. We cannot make everything well and happy. That is not balance. It is also not the case that it is a good thing for the majority of people to be happy when a minority are miserable. If, as you say, the Creator foresaw how it would all turn out, it was still deemed worthwhile to give this man what he craved. Your world is far from perfect, but that is what makes it so vital and exciting. I do not know whether you will succeed in bringing an end to this virus should you choose to stay here. Your being here might not really be about that anyway. But you are happier here in many ways than you were in your life as Gracie Abbot. So, in a smaller way too, balance has been restored to your life. You have a family you love and admire and a lover you cherish and respect. These things have made it easier for you to blossom here. I trust in what will be. That is all.'

Cianna smiled and embraced Gracie. 'My dear, gifted Gracie, you must choose. You can stay here and try to fight this virus. I can give you no answers as to whether you shall succeed. Indeed, I can give you no answers to anything. Your life will be as open to possibility here as anyone else's. If you choose to stay then you will remain here until your natural death. Or you can return to being Gracie Abbot. You will exist in a somewhat altered twenty-first-century Britain. Everything would become clear to you, as it did when you arrived here. You will arrive in your old bedroom with your Renaissance machine, and everything will be as it was. I have informed you that your machine does indeed work. To answer the question you now have in your head, you have no need to worry about no longer existing in the twenty-first century as a result of the virus. You can indeed be there.'

Gracie swallowed hard and shook her head.

'I was so impatient before. I demanded the right to choose and settle down here permanently. But now . . . I'm so frightened of doing the wrong thing. I have the chance to save lives here, but remember, in the future, with my Renaissance, I *know* I can do the same.'

'Yes, Gracie. You are in the enviable position of having the chance to affect greatly either the past or the future.'

'Enviable! Oh, it doesn't feel enviable. I just want to live. I don't want to change things.'

Cianna laughed then, so much so that Gracie looked up at her in amazement.

'I do apologise, Gracie, but *you* do not want to change things? You always want to change things! That is who you are. So if you truly feel that you no longer wish to change anything, and you want simply to live, then is that not significant?'

Gracie understood exactly what Cianna was telling her, and she squeezed her friend's hand. She was not a pawn. She was an individual who had an important decision to make; she needed to use her instincts again. But whatever she did, she had a choice in the matter.

'Nothing is written. You said that to me once, Cianna, a long time ago now.'

'Yes, and it is true.'

'But it seems that everything happens for a reason. My unhappiness in the twenty-first century led me here.'

'The two are not the same, Gracie. Do you see?'

Gracie thought for a moment and then nodded, a little sadly.

'I have something further to relate to you, Gracie. You may come with me back to the future. The world will be as it was when you lived there, without the effects of the virus. Gracie Abbot does not exist though. You can see anyone you choose to again, although they won't know you. It can be either a final goodbye or a reacquaintance. What do you say? We must depart now if you want to do this. You can then decide whether to stay there or return here.'

'I don't need to go there to decide anything, Cianna. I love Tom and I'm staying here with him, but not because of any virus.'

'I see. Do you wish for the chance to say a final farewell to the future then?'

Why not? Gracie thought. Everything was so strange anyway. It seemed she should continue accepting every strange opportunity that came her way. This would be her last chance and then she would be here forever.

'Yes, I'll go.'

Cianna nodded. 'Gracie, I have heard all you have said, but you may still change your mind about going or staying after you have been to the future.'

'Thank you for telling me that, Cianna, but nothing could make me change my mind.'

16.

Interlude

Cianna continued. 'Gather your thoughts now for in a short time I shall return.'

In the semi-light of her room, Cianna walked over toward Gracie's bureau and, in an instant, vanished. After Cianna had gone, Gracie remained seated on her bed and wondered what one did to prepare for visiting the future, especially when it was also one's own past. She was still in her nightdress and dishevelled from sleep. It was almost 4:30 am. Nobody would miss her here for a few hours yet. But perhaps it would be arranged that she wouldn't be missed at all?

She made her bed and then brushed her hair. *Should I get dressed?* There seemed little point in that as she guessed she would be wearing twenty-first-century clothing for her last jaunt around London. How strange it would be to wear those clothes again!

Gracie's hands trembled as she poured herself a small glass of water. She spilt some of it against the front of her nightdress as she drank.

'Are you ready, Gracie?'

Cianna had returned, and spoke softly from the corner of the room. Gracie smiled nervously and nodded.

'When you return it will be as if you have gone for a walk alone before breakfast. You can explain your absence easily, can you not?'

'Yes, that is no problem.'

'Come then. We shall return to the same day you left. Everything will be as it was, with neither impact of virus nor Gracie Abbot. You will be allowed to go where you choose and will appear to those who see you as an ordinary and real woman. Do you know where you want to go and whom you want to see? Yes, you have it all resolved.'

Cianna unfolded a piece of paper in her hand. 'This has all the details you shall need.'

Gracie walked toward Cianna and accepted the cream-coloured paper that felt thick and expensive. Elegant black handwriting spelled the names of people from her past, and it felt bizarre to see them here. She'd kept her two worlds so separate in her head. Her legs shook. She was really going to see them again! Alongside the names were times and exact locations. Cianna then handed her a purse of crushed green velvet that, she explained, contained correct currency.

'Now for your clothing. Do you wish to wear the outfit you wore when you travelled through the corridor to arrive here?'

Gracie remembered perfectly that she had worn a smartly tailored suit.

'No, it will be a Saturday and I don't want to be dressed in that.'

How should I look? How do I want to look?

'May I make a suggestion, Gracie?'

Gracie nodded helplessly. In the next moment, before she even had time to look, she felt that she was dressed. She walked to her full-length mirror and gazed at her reflection. She looked lovely. She was wearing a long, wonderful-feeling, soft, aubergine-coloured skirt, a white drawstring top and a green vintage-looking jacket. Her shoes were quite heeled, pointed and very pretty, and she held a cloth handbag with brightly coloured flowers stitched onto its front. Yes, she felt supremely comfortable now. She had much more freedom of movement and it felt liberating. She turned to Cianna and smiled.

'Thank you. This is it, this was how I wanted to be dressed, but I couldn't verbally describe it to you. I'm so pleased you could make such good sense of my thoughts! I never dressed or looked as nicely as this before. I didn't have the taste to choose these clothes.'

'Gracie, these are all your clothes, from your old life. You did choose them.'

Gracie was stunned. Her clothes? She examined them more closely. Yes, perhaps they were familiar? But she'd never looked like this!

'Yes, Gracie, you did. You appreciate yourself more now, that is all.'

Gracie felt the threat of hot tears sting the back of her throat, and she looked at herself once more. Then her downcast eyes focussed on her dressing table, and specifically on the shell that Tom had thrown her way on the beach at Ramsgate when they met. She brought it to her lips, kissed it softly and whispered, *Soon. I'll be back soon, my love.* She slipped the shell into her jacket pocket.

'I'm ready now, Cianna.'

Holding Gracie's hand, Cianna pulled open the door of a full-length cupboard with a fancy brass doorknob, and they stepped from the bedroom into darkness. They were back in the corridor of time. The smell, as before, was quite overwhelming.

Gracie covered her nose with her hand instinctively as the door shut behind them.

'Angelus comes,' Cianna whispered.

Gracie turned to her left and could discern dots of light making their way towards her. They were regular and fixed to either side of the walls of the narrow walkway, just as before. She now knew that Angelus was progressing through the past towards them. From how far away the dots of light appeared, she estimated that Angelus was more than a hundred years away. Soon, she could also see the outlines of objects against the doors on the left-hand side of the passageway for those travelling to the past. *I'll be walking in the other direction this time*, Gracie thought. She took her hand away from her face, fearful of offending Angelus, though why he would be offended by her dislike of the corridor's smell she didn't know—she just suspected he would. And then he was before her again.

'Ah, dear Dr Abbot. How lovely to see you, though I have just popped you through a door, it seems.'

Gracie had not been called Dr Abbot for a long time, and it felt odd. She'd forgotten how strong Angelus's Italian accent was, but he looked just as she remembered him, no older. And he was still so energetic and impatient! They embraced after he bowed to Cianna. As Gracie pulled back from him, she noticed that on his feet were a pair of the pointiest and shiniest leather shoes she'd ever seen, at least since the last time she'd seen Angelus. Ah, yes, Angelus's pride was his feet!

'We go now, I think?' he said to Cianna.

Cianna nodded, and they turned to face the future. Angelus moved into position in front of them with Gracie nearest the doors. As Angelus began to advance, more candles lit up their path and Gracie saw the next door. She knew that she had just arrived in the corridor through the 1800s door, and that the one she had exited through originally was the one for the 1790s. The one in front of her was therefore the 1810s. So by simply having lived she was already a little advanced in the corridor toward her destination. It was important to her to get her bearings—she didn't want to miss a thing. She squared her shoulders and faced the future looking straight ahead.

Gracie took sure steps, and the group immediately fell into a steady rhythm; ten steps for every decade. Angelus was their orchestrator, and this was the only beat he would allow in his soundtrack to the years. Gracie took care to look at each door and examine whether it matched her understanding of history and events. Everything was seemingly as it should be although, like before, she did not recognise some faces. Approaching the beginning of the twentieth century, Gracie drew her focus away from the doors and instead concentrated on the sound their feet made against the stone floor. No, after all, she found she really needed to see nothing. A while later, she suddenly remembered that an image of her grandmother's face belonged on the door to the 1950s. She turned hastily and realised they'd already reached the 1970s. Here so fast! It wouldn't be long until she walked through a door herself. Indeed, here was the Berlin Wall, a computer whose brand she didn't recognise ... Next door: Princess Diana's death, a mobile phone, British prime minister Tony Blair. And then another door, this one showing an American newspaper with a terrible headline, Katharine Hepburn's death, an iPod ...

Angelus stopped. They'd reached the door to the 2000s.

'You remember everything I have said to you, Gracie?' Cianna asked. 'You understand nobody will recognise you? And of course, you know what you can and cannot reveal.'

Cianna leaned in close and repeated that she could change her mind if she desired. Gracie nodded.

'What do I do when I want to come back? How long can I spend in London?'

'It will be around the middle of the day when you step through that door. You may stay for as long as three or four hours, if it suits you.'

Angelus was hopping from foot to foot impatiently, but Cianna continued.

'When you wish to return, go back to the place in which you arrive. You do not have to be exact, but ensure it is the same location. Open a door and we will be with you.'

Cianna then handed Gracie her glass bell in its little red box.

'Cianna! I thought that was hidden under my floorboard!'

'Yes, it was, but I took it out while you were sleeping last night, before I woke you to tell you about Josiah and the virus. Take it once more, and if you want to stay here, find somewhere quiet and ring for me. I shall be with you directly. Make the most of your time, Gracie, and find those you want to by checking with your piece of paper.'

'Thank you, Cianna. I'll be okay. This is really just for my own curiosity as much as anything else. I know there will be no great upset or revelation. I'll be fine.'

Cianna hugged Gracie briefly as Angelus, who had been fiddling with his keys since they stopped, selected one and slotted it into the keyhole. He opened the door a little and Gracie could smell something which seemed very familiar but which she could not quite place. She could hear what seemed to be an engine, and sensed motion.

Angelus swung open the door wide and Gracie stepped into the future.

She was on a train in the London Underground. Immediately the automatic door opened, and blindly, she filed out alongside everyone else. Nobody paid her the least bit of attention. She made her way to the nearest exit and tried to look as nonchalant as she could. Gracie had used the Underground often but was out of practice with busy London life now, and couldn't react quickly enough to the pushy and jostling crowds. She bumped into a man who was walking and reading a book at the same time. He sighed impatiently while barely raising his eyes to look at her. It seemed he did not even want to take the time to reproach; she was not important enough for him to do so.

As she ascended the stairs out of the station, she took her first breath of modern London air. It felt good. It was raining. She looked up and let the rain wash over her. Why, she was near Trafalgar Square. The traffic, the smell—everything was so vivid. What a contrast to the virus-ridden England she had just left, where people were living in mortal fear, surrounding themselves with every medicinal lotion and potion they could discover and so making smells connected with illness permeate everywhere.

She fell into step with a crowd moving in the direction of the square. Nobody was looking at her oddly, that was clear. She observed more closely some of the people around her—a woman dragging a small child along the pavement, two teenage boys exchanging swap cards, a dark-skinned man eating a slice of pizza from a takeaway box. She hadn't seen a black person in years; now she was surrounded by varying shades of skin. Gracie felt truly exhilarated as she walked. She was a true Londoner and had always loved the city of her birth. Bourton was lovely, it was true, but always very quiet—too quiet for Gracie at times. She could have continued in this state for longer, just enjoying the feeling of how strange but familiar everything around her seemed. But she didn't have all day. She took her paper from her pocket and saw that her first destination was a bistro in Covent Garden. She would go there to see her original parents.

Gracie found she remembered the route to Covent Garden from Trafalgar Square perfectly. She wandered around the area and tried to find the bistro. Her parents were supposed to be there at 1 pm and it was near that time now. She gave up looking and asked a policeman for directions. He was the first modern person to whom she had spoken, and it felt a little strange to be addressed by a man in such an offhand manner. Gracie didn't mind it though; she could do very well without men tipping their hats and bowing at her.

Before she entered the bistro, which seemed very expensive, she pulled her purse out of her pocket and opened it. There was no need to worry—it was crammed full of notes and coins. The bistro was busy but the waiter showed her to a table, although not before he gave her a funny look when she said she would be dining alone. Some things never changed, it seemed.

She scanned the moderately-sized restaurant and spotted her parents almost immediately. They were seated only a few tables away from her. On seeing them again, Gracie felt a tight ball of tension knot in her stomach. She pretended to examine her menu while studying them. Even without speaking to them or seeing them for very long, Gracie was able to confirm things she had long suspected. Her parents had each independently told her that they'd remained together because of her, despite the fact that doing so had ruined their lives. Well, here was no Gracie, and her parents had clearly not divorced. Did they seem to be getting on better than they used to? No, they looked as bored with each other and as unloving as ever. Gracie suspected they clung to each other for reasons mostly connected with their colossal egos. They each alone remembered the other when they were young and still desirable. This was clearly a lot for them to renounce.

The waiter arrived, and Gracie ordered a large cola and soup. Her parents were at that moment tucking into some lobster. Expensive wine also stood on their table. Gracie smiled and shook her head; they were certainly still as extravagant as ever. Her mother then raised her eyes and looked directly at her. Gracie's heart pounded. Would she be recognised after all? Mrs Abbot stared at Gracie darkly, almost scowled, in fact. She ran her eyes over her daughter's face, person and clothing without in the least trying to hide the fact she was doing so. Gracie remembered this look well, and it was one reserved for females. What a thoroughly unpleasant woman this was. Seeing her mother jealously scrutinise her and other women in this way had bothered her before, but now Gracie found she almost couldn't help laughing. Mrs Abbot looked, for all the world, like the goblin in one of Polly's old storybooks! Her mother had once aspired to be a great actress but, of course, the arrival of Kenneth and Gracie had "ruined all of that". Gracie in particularly had been blamed for her mother's less than sylphlike figure, but Mrs Abbot was actually fatter now than ever.

Gracie's order arrived, and she took a sip of her cola with pleasure. This she had missed! As she ate her soup, she considered whether her parents might have had any children other than Kenneth, but decided this was improbable. They'd most likely been telling the truth when they'd said Gracie was an accident, discovered too late to do anything about.

She looked more closely at her father. His was a sad and pathetic case. Now in his fifties, he had lived all his days vicariously through his mother's fame. He tried acting when he was younger, but it never amounted to anything much. His mother had left him very wealthy, and he revelled in attending functions and events held in her honour. Fans, getting carried away with themselves, often treated him as if he were a sort of celebrity just by his being Grace Abbot's son. Gracie remembered cringing at her father's benevolent smiles when he signed autographs. He looked no different, still just as tanned and flashy. Gracie finished her soup, drained her glass of cola and raised her hand to draw the waiter's attention. She had seen enough.

Outside the bistro, Gracie looked at her paper again. Kenneth. She'd never stopped missing her dear brother Kenneth. He had previously worked as a banker in the City and lived with his wife and children in Wimbledon. Surely there was no reason to think any of this might be different simply because she'd not been born. The address on the paper beside his name was in Greenwich. Gracie couldn't recall any particular linkage between her brother and Greenwich. Perhaps he was just on a day out with his family. She hailed the first cab she saw. Her driver was uninterested in chatting with her and was instead talking energetically on a hands-free phone. Good, that left her room to think.

She gazed out at the familiar landmarks and remembered walking down many of these very same streets with Polly just a few years ago. How different they had looked then. Polly and Kenneth were very unlike each other. Polly was every inch the younger sibling and Kenneth every inch the elder. Through them, Gracie had been both a big and little sister, and the experience of being the elder child had certainly had an effect upon her behaviour. Should she expect to find Kenneth changed because he was now an only child? Perhaps, but it was difficult to imagine Kenneth being different—he was always so dependable, straightforward and unaffected by the things which meant so much to Gracie. They were on the Old Kent Road now. The driver had finished his telephone conversation.

'Up to anything nice in Greenwich today, love?' the driver asked. 'Weather's not too great, is it?'

'No, I suppose it is a little rainy. I've not been to Greenwich for a while. I'm off to meet my brother. I haven't seen him in a while either.'

'Oh, bit of a family reunion, is it?'

The driver then proceeded to regale Gracie with details of a barbecue he had recently attended with his family. Gracie smiled and nodded at all the right times, and got out of the cab near the National Maritime Museum. The driver wished her all the best with her brother and waved cheerily as he three-point-turned his way back down the road.

Gracie knew Greenwich pretty well. She had lunched here with Adam often and had spent many of her teenage Saturdays browsing around the second-hand bookstores. Many of the buildings in Greenwich were Georgian in design, and Gracie looked at them with pride as she made her way to the address on her paper. Written beside Kenneth's name and address was "until 5 pm", which was hours away yet. Was Kenneth going to be at this place, whatever it was, all day? The streets were busy despite the falling rain, and Gracie turned into the street she was looking for with relief. She didn't want to spend her last moments in modern London dodging tourists who stopped to take photographs of everything. It was a number 56 she was looking for, and Gracie saw that it was a shop. Why, it was one of those model shops. Kenneth had always loved building model planes and cars when he was young, that was true, but was he going to be spending his whole day here? Gracie nervously opened the door, causing its bell to ring.

It was quite a large and very nice shop, well-stocked and orderly. Gracie's gaze darted about the browsing customers but she couldn't see Kenneth anywhere. She looked at the items for sale instead and trusted that Kenneth would shortly appear. The store sold all kinds of toys, in fact, not just models, though it seemed to specialise in them. Gracie determined that it was an upmarket shop that focussed upon things from the past, classic toys and so forth. There were, mercifully, no computer games or cheap mass-produced tat here.

A man beside her was examining with interest an expensive model of James Bond's car, and he carried it in the direction of the counter. Gracie's gaze followed the man. Whoever was serving was kneeling behind the cash desk doing something, as he had been when Gracie entered the shop. This same person rose, and Gracie gasped aloud when she realised it was her brother. He worked in this shop? But what about his job in the City?

She pretended to be wholly absorbed in a colourful jack-in-the-box and concentrated on every word that Kenneth spoke.

He owned this shop. The customer was leaving his name and address to be contacted about another item he wanted, and Kenneth was saying he would try to order it in and would give the man a ring when he had it. He knew all about the James Bond cars, as well as lots of other things. Gracie scanned her memory but couldn't connect this Kenneth with the Kenneth she had known. He looked different too. Younger, less tired and careworn. He looked happier. Gracie pondered what all this meant. Kenneth was happier not being her brother, it seemed.

Was he married still? He wasn't wearing a wedding ring. Gracie hadn't cared a great deal for her sister-in-law, who was too pushy and bourgeois. She had loved her little nieces though, and she felt terrible as she realised they might no longer exist.

Kenneth put the customer's car into a bag and said goodbye. How confident he appeared. It was now obvious what he'd been doing beneath the counter. He had brought up glue and bits of wood, and he was making an incredibly intricate-looking wooden plane, perhaps for the window display. Such an activity required some skill and patience, and although she connected these things with Kenneth, the creative aspects of the task were not things she would have aligned with him. He had always looked after her and she had always depended on him. Had this somehow strangled part of his own personality, making him more uptight and sensible than he really ought to have been? This seemed to be a plausible assumption.

Gracie moved closer to the counter and Kenneth. He smiled at her and asked if she needed help with anything.

'No, I'm fine, thanks, only looking around.' She paused, and then continued. 'This is really a lovely shop. Have you been here long?'

'Yes, around ten years or so. I do pretty well here, always lots of tourists.'

He smiled at her again and continued with his model airplane.

Gracie was relieved beyond words when she spotted a photograph taped to the wall behind Kenneth's counter. It was a snap of her nieces, Alice and Rose. They had been born after all! But why no wedding ring? Gracie picked up some little rag dolls that lay in a basket on the counter and tried to work out how she could ask Kenneth about his private life. The dolls were lovely and old-fashioned, simple but so much nicer than most modern dolls. They wouldn't have appeared out of place in 1803. Gracie decided she would buy one. Now, one with a yellow dress or a purple one?

She went with one of each. As Kenneth rang them up she commented, as disinterestedly as she could, upon the pretty little girls in his photo.

'Yes, they're my daughters.'

'Really? Oh, they must love visiting this place. How wonderful to have a father who owns a toy store.'

Kenneth smiled and paused before replying. 'Yes, but I don't get to see them as much as I would like to. They live with their mother down in Brighton. One of the awful things about divorce.' He shrugged sadly.

Divorce. So Kenneth was divorced now.

There was really no acceptable way for her to stay in the shop any longer. She smiled, took her change and walked out of Kenneth's door and life. He'd said goodbye to her and, through her tears, she'd said goodbye in return with a broken voice she hoped he hadn't noticed.

INTERLUDE

There was only Adam left to see now. The paper said he would shortly be in a cafe that Gracie recognised as being near Green Park. Soon she was in a taxi again and heading sadly towards the last of her destinations.

Adam.

Oh, could she bear to see him again? What if he was with another woman? His wife even? Gracie closed her eyes and inhaled deeply. If he was with another woman, what of it? She no longer cared for Adam. She had Tom now, and she loved him in a truer way than she had ever loved Adam. Moreover, Tom loved her more than Adam ever had. She mused on when she'd last seen him. It had been the day before she'd "died". She'd gone to the flat she used to share with Adam, out of which she had moved some time before. What had she gone there for? Yes, some books, that was it. They'd had another fight; they always fought, though less in the last months. *Probably because there was nothing new to say, I suppose*, Gracie thought. Plus, they'd both been so exhausted. They had tried, even after Gracie left their home, to make things right but had failed. She had become immersed in her work, in any case. *And thank God I did.* It certainly helped blot the pain out. Adam had always resented her work, had made her feel he wanted her to choose between him and it.

But there was something Gracie didn't know.

On the day of Gracie's departure from the twenty-first century, Adam woke early with a terrible feeling of presentiment in his stomach. It was a Saturday, and he didn't have to go to work, so he stayed in bed longer than usual. But he couldn't block out the feeling that the day would be somehow momentous. He thought about telephoning Gracie to see if she was okay—he could make an excuse and pretend he needed to ask her something practical. That way, he wouldn't have to lose any pride. He still felt terrible about the argument they'd had the previous day. Gracie had cried a lot and he'd wanted to comfort her, but that was impossible now. There was no comfort for Gracie from him. From his window, he had watched her walk away down the street, her arms buckling under the weight of all her books, and marvelled at how noble she seemed.

By lunchtime, Adam decided that he cared nothing for his pride; he would go around to see if Gracie was okay. He loved her, had always loved her, and he would tell her so. He ate his lunch hastily and wondered whether he should call her first and let her know he was coming. No, he would just go there. He left his house to catch the bus around 1:30 pm. Gracie lived nearby, and he'd be there in no time. But he hadn't accounted for the hold-up all the football fans would create. He sat, irate, on the back seat as they drunkenly fell onto the bus. He got off after 2:20 pm and walked the rest of the way to Gracie's flat. It was raining, and he heard children playing noisily as he moved to press Gracie's entryphone at 2:30 pm. One of her neighbours stepped out the main door before he did so, and he was able to go straight in and climb the stairs. Gracie lived on the second floor. He paused outside her door before ringing her bell. What should he say?

Just keep it simple and tell her that you love her again, tell her that you're sorry. Tell her you'll do anything to make it right. He rang the doorbell. There was no answer, and all sounded quiet inside. Perhaps she had just nipped to the shops.

He decided he would wait on her stairs, and sat down. He tried ringing her, both on her landline and her mobile. He heard both phones ringing inside the flat, so he knew she didn't have it with her. That was strange—Gracie always carried her phone.

The feeling of premonition reared inside him again, and he was suddenly stricken with panic. She had been so dreadfully sad and upset yesterday. He paced outside her door and pushed against it with his body. The door shifted a little. She was only using one lock. Should he break in? He looked around and decided he wouldn't rest easy until he discovered whether Gracie was inside or not. Tall and strong, Adam opened the door with three kicks. He closed it behind him and called her name. He went first to her living area and kitchen before deciding to check her bedroom.

There she was. She was sitting in some sort of contraption, and there were tubes and wires attached to her temples, arms, everywhere. Her eyes were closed. Adam was no doctor, but he knew Gracie was dead. Hooked up in front of her was a machine showing an audible display of her heartbeat flatlining. He threw himself down at her feet and kissed her hands, her face.

'Gracie, Gracie!' he cried. 'My love, my life, come back! Just come back. Please, please, not like this. I love you so. Come back to me.'

Their life together flashed before his eyes in an instant, and he wept for all that was gone and all that might have been. Too late, just too late.

Gracie sat waiting in the cafe. Her hands were visibly shaking. Bang on time, Adam opened the door. Gracie couldn't help it—her hands flew to her mouth. Seeing him again after all this time was like nothing she had imagined. Her heart leapt within her. He was pushing a pram. There weren't many customers inside, but a middle-aged woman immediately jumped up to help Adam through the door. He thanked her and moved to a table near the counter some way away from Gracie but directly facing her. Gracie made a point of sipping her tea and flicking through a magazine someone had left on her table. Adam gently undid the clip of the pushchair and let a little girl of around two or three years old jump out.

'Daddy, Daddy, can I have ice cream now?'

Adam smiled, swung her up in his arms and carried her to the counter, where he promptly ordered an ice cream and a coffee. He had not looked her way. Once seated again, the little girl ate her ice cream greedily, and Adam told her she would go home soon and see Mummy.

'Have you had a good day today, Lily?'

'Yes, Daddy. But I want to hold my balloon now.'

A red balloon was tied to the back of Lily's pushchair.

'You can hold it when you've finished your dessert.'

He then looked straight in Gracie's direction but only to check the large aluminium clock positioned on the wall above her. He was still so handsome. She had to get a little closer to him before he left her forever.

Gracie walked to the counter again and ordered a hot chocolate. While the woman prepared it for her, Gracie turned sheepishly around and looked at them both. Lily had finished her ice cream and was scrambling for her balloon. She ran straight into Gracie's legs.

'Sorry, sorry.' Adam rose and apologised again. 'I hope my daughter hasn't gotten ice cream all over you.'

'Oh, don't worry about it if she has.'

Adam was so close to her now that Gracie could smell his aftershave. Why, it was the one he had worn when they were together. Gracie used to tease him, saying he didn't really like it but only wore it to keep her happy, as she had bought it for him. But here he was wearing it still; he really had liked it.

He was struggling now to untie the balloon's string from the buggy, and Gracie impulsively reached forward.

'Here, let me help you. There, there it is.'

Adam thanked her and bent down to give the balloon to his now silently observant daughter.

'Come on now, miss. Let Daddy finish his coffee and then we'll go home.'

Before he resumed his seat, Adam turned to face Gracie once more. The two locked gazes for no more than a few seconds, but something passed between them that was difficult for at least one of them to either explain or define. Gracie was sure that Adam felt some kind of connection to her. She waited with bated breath to see what would happen next, but then the woman behind the counter told Gracie her hot chocolate was ready, and she reluctantly walked back to her seat.

They made awkward eye contact, off and on, for the next few minutes, and Gracie struggled to rationalise what was happening. She loved Tom, she really did. As if to prove this to herself, she pulled the shell out of her pocket and popped it onto the table in front of her. What was happening to her? Was she not over Adam? Stealing glances at him whenever she judged it safe to do so, Gracie had to concede that though she had dismissed her and Adam's relationship as being nothing of real consequence, the reality was not the case. She and Adam had loved each other deeply, and they had shared something special and unique. She'd been angry with him for so long—it was easier to believe that it had all been nothing. That way, it didn't seem so hurtful, or such a waste. But her love for Tom hadn't supplanted her love for Adam. The two coexisted, much in the way her two lives did. She had been both Gracie Abbot and Gracie Arundel for a long time, but now it was time to choose.

Lily was growing fractious and started to cry. Adam tried to soothe her.

'Yes, sweetheart, I know you want Mummy. It's raining outside though. We'll wait a few minutes until it stops and then you'll go home.'

Gracie considered that Lily's blondeness was not the result of Adam's black hair; her mother must be fair.

Could she really let Adam go? Lily, that little girl, would cease to exist if she did not. And Tom? How could she bear to never see his face again? She held her head in her hands and tried to pull herself together. She had not expected this. If she had chosen to not see Adam again, would she have spent her life with Tom believing that she was entirely over Adam? No, she knew now that a suppressed part of her had always been aware of her true feelings for Adam. And these repressed feelings had not been without effect either, for she knew they had stopped her from entirely giving herself to Tom. She had told herself she was holding back due to her fear of being hurt again, but it was more than that. Adam had wronged her, hurt her, that was true, but he had also loved her and she could see that now. Cianna had said that nobody would know her here— so why had Adam looked at her in that way? Some kind of recognition had passed in his eyes; she'd seen it.

She looked at him again. He was dressed a little differently than when she'd known him but still looked fresh and smart. Did Lily's mother help him with his clothes? Before, Gracie had taken a lot of the credit for how good Adam looked; perhaps she had taken the credit for too many things.

She gathered her bag and belongings and walked back to the counter to settle up her bill. Lily was clutching her balloon and resting her head against her father's arm. An idea suddenly occurred to Gracie, and she reached into her bag and brought out one of her dolls, the yellow one.

Bending down, she handed it to Lily. The little girl reached for it delightedly and hugged it to her chest. The balloon bounced away forlornly.

'Oh, what do you say, Lily? Isn't that nice?' Adam looked at Gracie. 'Thank you, but—'

Gracie broke in.

'It's nothing, really. Dolls are for little girls, and I had two in my bag anyway. I hope she likes it.'

'Yes, you like it, don't you, Lily?'

Lily nodded and said thank you. There seemed nothing more to say, but Gracie was keenly aware that Adam was trying to prolong their conversation, trying somehow to halt her from leaving. He also seemed confused as to why he would wish to do this.

The rain had stopped. Adam zipped up Lily's jacket and paid his bill. Then he retied the balloon to the back of the pushchair while Gracie, still crouching, chatted to his daughter. Lily giggled.

'You have a way with children. She was screaming earlier.'

Gracie stood and straightened her clothing. 'Yes, well, I . . . I work in a nursery, so I'm used to them.'

They exited the cafe together, and Adam pointed in the direction of his route and asked if she was heading that way too.

'No, no, I'm waiting for someone here.'

'Well, thank you again for the doll. It's brightened her up to no end. I . . . we live nearby, so you'll likely see her with it again if you come to this cafe regularly.'

'Oh, I'm just visiting here today. I don't live in London.'

It was too late. The flash of disappointment that Adam's face betrayed had been clear to them both, and they both knew it.

Reluctantly he moved away from her, and he and Lily said goodbye. Gracie smiled and waved to Lily, and then took one long last look at Adam's face.

'Goodbye.'

She watched them walk up the short street, Adam's long strides matched to Lily's toddling steps as she "helped" her father push the buggy. Soon he'd be home. Would he tell Lily's mother about her? Tears poured down Gracie's face as Adam, her past, disappeared around the corner and all that could be seen was Lily's red balloon billowing behind, until, eventually, that was gone too.

'Goodbye, love. Goodbye forever.'

Feeling her heart had been ripped from her chest, and unable to hinder the tears falling unchecked down her face, Gracie ran into Green Park. Nobody looked at her. It was raining so heavily that it would have been difficult to tell whether her face was wet with tears or rain anyway. She sat on a bench and wept uncontrollably. Some passersby looked at her curiously, so she moved to a quieter spot. She felt like an interloper now, as if she didn't really belong here anymore. She wanted to go back to Greenwich and seek comfort from Kenneth, but that was no longer possible. She wanted Cianna then, and Alicia. Yes, she wished she could pour out all of her troubles to her wise mother. But there was only one other person who could really help her at the moment and that was Tom, because she loved him in the same way and just as much as Adam. She held her shell in her hands again and kissed it.

Forgive me, my darling, but I'm coming home to you. She wiped her face and looked around at the hurrying crowds. Some of them might cease to be here after the virus took hold. *Can Tom and I really stop it?* She sighed heavily; Tom likely wouldn't be involved in finding a cure if she returned to the future—he would probably become a lawyer rather than a scientist. Gracie shook her head; they could only do their best. She stood and made her way back to the Underground station.

At the same moment, Adam, having dropped off his daughter at his ex-girlfriend's, was scouring the streets near the cafe for Gracie. His instincts told him that he must find her and tell her how he felt about her, even if it meant she laughed in his face or called the police. But the woman of his dreams was nowhere to be found.

Gracie's walk to the Underground took her past the National Portrait Gallery, a place she had always loved visiting, and she pondered whether she should take a last look around. She decided against it. Hadn't she seen enough portraits of long-dead people in Angelus's corridor? Besides, it was too depressing to consider that many of those portraits might eventually disappear because of the virus.

She reached the Underground station and took in a long, last breath of modern London air before the rushing mass of people behind her knocked and pushed her inside. Cianna had said she didn't need to be exact but that she should open a door in the same location. Well, she couldn't get on the same train again, but she was back in the same place. Gracie climbed down the stairs, and as a train came into sight, she stood a little apart from her fellow travellers and tried to find a door she could go through alone. Reaching one, she pushed the button and stepped onto the train. Cianna and Angelus each took one of her arms and gently pulled her towards them. She was back in the corridor.

17.

No Going Back

'Gracie, you are certain?'

Cianna held Gracie's chin in her hand and examined her tear-stained face.

'Yes, Cianna. I don't belong there now.'

She bit her bottom lip to keep from sobbing again.

'I want Tom. I need to see Tom. And my mother and father and Polly. I love more people in the past than I do in the future.' She shrugged her shoulders lamely. 'The past wins.'

Cianna nodded. 'You are resolved. Let us take you home.'

Angelus had stood by silently while Cianna and Gracie conversed. He'd even refrained from his usual hopping about, and didn't in the least seem impatient to get moving again. He reached for Gracie's sleeve and stroked it softly.

'If the opinion of an old fellow like me counts for anything, I for one am glad of your decision, Miss Arundel.'

Gracie smiled at Angelus. He had called her Miss Arundel, not Dr Abbot as he usually did. Dr Abbot was gone, and there was only Gracie to mourn her passing. She took a deep breath, and Cianna moved to stand by her. Angelus took up the lead. They began to advance, and Gracie knew she would never walk this corridor again. She would be grounded in the past. She would die there. There could be no going back. She tried to keep the memory of Adam's face from her mind, but she could still smell his aftershave so keenly. His hair, his eyes ... she hadn't even been able to kiss him goodbye ...

'Courage, Gracie.'

Cianna gripped her arm tightly, and it gave her support.

'Goodbye, Gracie Abbot,' she whispered, as they swept past the 1970s door.

This time Gracie saw her grandmother's face on the 1950s door. A glossy black-and-white studio portrait hung alongside a similar one of James Dean.

'Goodbye, grandmother Grace, except I suppose you're not really my grandmother anymore.'

The connection had been broken. As they progressed towards the early 1800s, Gracie began to feel a little better. It felt like a homecoming. When they stopped, Angelus presented the 1800s door with a flourish. Gracie reached out and touched it. Just ordinary wood, but where had the trees used for it been grown, who had constructed it, varnished it? All questions she knew there was little point in asking. Perhaps she would learn the answers one day.

'Goodbye, Angelus.'

'My dear, it has been a real pleasure. Good luck! Your Tom is a fortunate young man. If I could tell him that I would!'

'Thanks, Angelus. Well, good luck yourself, though I don't know if you'll ever need it. I can't even begin to imagine the people you've escorted up and down this corridor.'

'Ah.' He gave her a sly wink. 'My memoirs would be a good read, that might be true!'

They all laughed, even Cianna.

'You will enter in the same spot as you did originally, Gracie. It will be before 9 am in Bourton.'

'And when shall I see you again, Cianna?'

Cianna placed her hands firmly upon Gracie's shoulders.

'Gracie, I will not be coming to see you, and you may no longer call for me. My work is done.'

Gracie fell back a little, and might have fallen entirely if Cianna's steady hands hadn't been gripping her so tightly. Never see Cianna again? No, this was all too cruel. To have so many people she loved ripped away from her, all in the space of a few hours; no, no, she wouldn't stand for it.

'I love you, Cianna. You're the best friend I ever had. Don't leave me, I need you.'

She clung to Cianna's blue silken robe and wept. To never see Cianna again—why, she would just as soon lose one of her limbs.

'My darling Gracie, my little scientist, listen to me. I love you too, and I always shall. You have meant more to me than any other person I have assisted in all my long years. We share a bond that can never be broken, you and I. But your life must go on, through that door. There are no more choices left for you to make that I must present to you, nothing left for me to explain. It would not be a life properly lived if you knew you could always call for me.'

'I won't call for you then, but might you not visit me sometimes? It doesn't have to be very often. I know you'll have other people you'll be helping.'

A tear fell down Cianna's beautiful face. 'Always asking for things, never satisfied, you are my Gracie to the end. I shall come to see you one more time. We will fix nothing in advance, but once more your Cianna will come to you. Do not wait for me, live your life as fully and passionately as you can—that is all the advice I have left to give you. Now you must go.'

Gracie returned her glass bell to Cianna, but not before taking a sad last look at it. The paper and purse, she found, had already disappeared from her pockets. This was it then, no more modern clothing.

'Oh, wait, Cianna. I bought a little doll from Kenneth's shop.' Gracie patted her pocket and felt the soft little body of the doll. 'It looks old-fashioned. Might I take it with me? I'll keep it hidden away.'

'Yes, take it with you.'

Angelus, who had been sitting cross-legged on the floor, his chin resting on one hand, stood to attention as Cianna gestured it was time to open the door. Gracie intended to keep a tight hold of Cianna's hand for as long as she could. The door opened a little, and a brisk, cool breeze blew into Gracie's face and hair. When the door swung open wider she could see it was a dull-looking day, neither sunny nor rainy.

'Goodbye, Angelus. Goodbye, Cianna.'

Gracie stepped through the door and felt a light pressure as Cianna stroked her hair. The moment both her feet were on the grass, she swung around sharply but, of course, no trace of the door existed. She was really on her own.

Her walk back to Bourton from Northleach that day was sad and lonely. *What am I doing here?* she thought, suddenly panic-stricken. The enormity of the task that lay before her, to rid the country of a brutal virus before the future changed forever, sat heavily upon her already weary shoulders. At the moment, she wanted nothing more than to sleep. Yes, that's what she would do as soon as she arrived home.

She didn't see anyone on her journey. People tended to stay indoors much more now; they had even stopped working in many cases. Her own front door was ajar, and she stepped inside and brushed down her dress. As she did so she felt Kenneth's doll in the interior of her skirts. A sudden lump in her throat threatened tears.

Alicia popped her head out of the morning room into the hallway.

'Ah, it is you, Gracie. But where have you been? We were starting to worry. Oh, my dear, what is it?' Her mother rushed towards her and looked tenderly into her eyes. 'You are not ill? Not feverish?'

'No. No, Mother, I am fine. I am a little tired, probably because of all the work I have been doing of late. It is nothing of any consequence though.'

Her mother looked unconvinced, and kissed her forehead. 'Come into the morning room then. We have a surprise for you.'

Clasping her mother's hand, Gracie allowed herself to be led into the room, where she found her father, Polly, Jack and Mrs Ford waiting for her. But the latter were not expected for days yet! Gracie then saw Tom too, standing by the window. She briefly considered that he might have witnessed how sadly she had walked up the driveway. They all turned around to stare at her now.

'Gracie, where have you been, child?'

Ernest pointed his stick towards her and motioned for her to sit in front of the fire.

'Oh, just for a walk. I couldn't sleep. But what are you all doing here? Polly, Jack, Mrs Ford, hello.'

Gracie kissed all of her relatives, and Polly clutched her sister's hands as she excitedly spoke.

'We got here earlier because we heard that they might be erecting barricades between the counties soon. It cost a lot of money to get us here so quickly ... Oh, if we were poor we'd still be in London, so thank heavens we're rich. We're all exhausted because we travelled continuously from London with no breaks for sleep or meals at all. Father said you only received my letter yesterday. That's not surprising—the post cannot be delivered easily just now. There are so few willing to carry it, and coaches are being taken up with people rather than bags of mail. The roads are in a terrible confusion. Why, we saw three bags of letters just dumped out of a mail coach on our journey here, all to make room for another few passengers.'

Polly shook her head sadly. She had seemingly grown up a lot since Gracie saw her last. Tom had come to stand behind Gracie and was resting his hands on her shoulders. The close contact with him made her feel a little awkward, but she tried to appear as normal as possible.

'What a horror it must be if you have family far from you at a time like this,' Mrs Ford continued. 'Worrying whether you'll ever see them again and not even being able to send or receive a letter. It must be unbearable.'

Gracie noticed Alicia look worriedly in Tom's direction; he was in the very position detailed. Her heart broke for him, and she swung around to face him. He looked sad, but he smiled at Gracie and kissed her hand gently. She covered his hand with her own. He was her Tom and she was his Gracie—how could she ever have felt there was awkwardness between them? She loved him as much as ever, that fact was in no doubt.

'Well,' said Alicia, 'if you weary travellers have finished your breakfast, I suggest you take yourselves up to bed for some sleep. Beds have been made up for you. Now, Henrietta, have no fear, we'll send a message to your brother that you're safely here.'

Mrs Ford scuttled off behind Alicia to Polly's old room. Jack seemed content to chat to Tom and Ernest for a while longer. Polly motioned for Gracie to follow her up to the room she would be sharing with Jack.

'Where were you, Gracie?'

'I went for a walk. To Northleach, in fact.'

'You must have risen very early. When we arrived, Mother still had her curling cap on, and you know how early she gets up!'

'Yes, well, I couldn't sleep.'

'Do you feel a little better after your walk then? You look ghastly; so tired, and your face is blotchy, as if you've been crying.'

'Well, I have been crying, as it happens. I'm so worried about the virus. I haven't thought of much else for weeks. Tom and I have been working around the clock. I suppose it all just caught up with me today.'

Polly nodded but still seemed to be examining her closely. Gracie changed the subject.

'So how is marriage treating you?'

Polly grinned and said that although her married life had coincided exactly with the loathsome sickness, true love could bring happiness anywhere.

Gracie begged off working at the Rainbow that day. She simply didn't feel up to it. Instead, she and Tom stayed at her parents' home, and went for a walk together after luncheon. After a few stilted attempts at conversation, Tom stopped abruptly and pulled Gracie towards him.

'I'm not going any further until you tell me exactly what is bothering you. Have I upset you in some way?'

Gracie stared down at the grass. How she longed to confess everything. She felt so guilty about her feelings for Adam. She thought quickly.

'Indeed, there is something I need to say to you.'

Tom immediately looked worried. Gracie took his hands to assure him of her love, but as she did, the tears she had been holding back since that morning spilled over. She led Tom to some nearby tree stumps, and they sat down. He sat quietly by Gracie's side until she had finished speaking.

'I . . . I had a dream last night, Tom. In my dream was a man I have not seen for some years. Indeed, I have tried my best not to think of him over these years. Well, I have to tell you, Tom, that this dream reminded me of the truth of something which I have long suppressed. I loved this man and . . . and I still do. He was my first love, and he hurt me very badly. I have never known hurt such as he inflicted upon me. Because I was angry with him I tried to banish him from my life and even my thoughts. I thought I was doing a very good job of this. I made myself believe I had never really loved him and that he had never loved me. This became easy when I met and fell in love with you, my darling. The dream I had last evening, however, has left me in no doubt of my feelings for this man. I loved him and still do. But I also love you, Tom—every bit as much as I love him. I love you both equally. I also realise that this man loved me very much too, and I cannot deny the fact that we might have been very happy together were it not for certain circumstances.'

Gracie stopped and swallowed hard. If Tom wanted to break everything off with her now, then that was his prerogative. She waited breathlessly for his response, but he continued to sit motionless by her side. Suddenly, he rose to his feet, his hands clenched into fists in his coat pockets.

'Who is this man!' he shouted. 'Where is he? What is his name? Given that I have been his stooge all these years, I would like to at least meet him. I knew something was different about you today, as soon as I saw you walking back to your house. You could barely look at me.'

Gracie had never seen Tom behave in this way before, and she was frightened—frightened of what he might say. Should she have remained quiet and kept the pain to herself? Was it unfair of her to have burdened Tom with her feelings about Adam?

No, she knew within herself that Tom had to know as much as she was able to tell him about Adam. She would wish to be told if she were in his place. Tom demanded once again to know the name of her former lover.

'Why is it so important for you to know that? Sit down beside me and let us talk. I am so sorry for hurting you. I love you as much as I have the power to love anyone. None of my feelings towards you have changed. I would gladly lay down my life for you.'

'Yes, but I am not the only one you would do that for now, am I?' Tom resumed his seat, positioning himself as far as he was able to from Gracie. 'You'd die for him too, I suppose?'

Gracie reached out and took his arm. He flinched at her touch but allowed her hand to remain on him.

'Yes,' she continued, 'I would have died for him. Let me tell you about him. His name was Adam. I say was because he . . . he is dead.'

Tom turned to face her sharply but remained silent.

'Yes, he is dead. But let me assure you that if I were ever forced to choose between you both then I would choose to be with you. You can be certain of that.'

Tom placed his head in his hands and wept. Gracie had never seen him cry before, and her heart thundered within her chest at the strange sight. She cried frequently, but to see Tom do so felt momentous. She had hurt him deeply and he would never forget this day. As a couple, they would be changed, and this unshakeable knowledge made her long for the early, uncomplicated moments of their courtship.

'I don't understand. I don't understand. How can you love us both equally? How can you love two people? I could never love another woman while I loved you.'

'Try to think of it as my having had two separate lives. I was another person entirely when I met and fell in love with Adam. I have never, for a moment, wished you were he, and I could never regret having met you. If I were a widow and told you that I had loved and continued to love my deceased husband, I think you would have no problem accepting this. Well, this is exactly like my situation now. Two lifetimes, two loves.'

'I never suspected anything like this, but now you have told me it makes sense. He has been between us. You never were in much of a hurry to marry me, were you? But you must have been very young when you knew this Adam. What did he do to you?'

Gracie turned away from Tom and tried to remain strong and calm for his sake.

'He betrayed me in every way that a man can betray a woman who loves him. But he betrayed himself too because he loved me. That is all I can say on the matter. It is old history and I do not want to revisit it. To do so would be of no use to either me or him—or you.'

'And he's dead?'

'Yes. You are angry with him but you are fighting a ghost. There is nobody who exists here for you to quarrel with. Except me.'

Tom rose again and walked away a few steps. He returned a few minutes later and sat back down. Gracie nervously, quietly, waited for him.

'I am so hurt because I thought you had only ever, would only ever, love me. It feels awful to think that the feelings you have for me are not unique. To still love him . . . can you not let it go?'

Gracie shook her head. 'I don't know. But can you say you would ever stop loving me if I died? Can you not love someone even if you cannot see them anymore?' Then Gracie broke down and wept. 'I know how hurt you must be feeling. But I love you and I will honour you and be faithful to you all of my days if you will still have me. Please, please, Tom. I can't lose you.'

'You're not going to lose me.'

Tom pressed Gracie to his chest, and the two embraced for a long time.

Finally, quietly, but with force, Tom said, 'We won't speak of this again, if that's acceptable to you?'

Gracie nodded. 'Very well. You know, I wish you had someone in your past to tell me about now.'

'But I don't. I've only loved you.'

They sat close, holding hands, but it still felt as though a void lay between them. A ghost, Gracie had called Adam. Tom resolved to do whatever he could to ensure that spectres from the past didn't ruin his future with his beloved Gracie, but it would take time for him to come fully to terms with her revelation, and he told her so.

'I understand. I hate to see you so sad. But I'll make you smile again, I promise. He won't be between us any longer. Now I have spoken of Adam, it's funny, but I feel even closer to you.'

He kissed her head.

'We have changed now,' he said, 'but that doesn't have to mean that it is for the worse. Our love has seen many obstacles, but with each one we overcome we prove how real our feelings are.'

He thought for a few moments and then gazed at her. ' "Love is not love which alters when it alteration finds, or bends with the remover to remove. O no, it is an ever fixed mark that looks on tempests and is never shaken; it is the star to every wand'ring bark, whose worth's unknown although his height be taken. Love's not time's fool, though rosy lips and cheeks within his bending sickle's compass come; Love alters not with his brief hour and weeks, but bears it out even to the edge of doom".' He smiled at Gracie's hopeful expression. 'You see, I still possess my Shakespeare from my schooldays, and we cannot argue with his wise words. Let us return to your parents' house now.' He reached for her hand and kissed it. 'Trust me, we'll be fine.'

Gracie and Tom spent the next several weeks in an endless round of working at the Rainbow, eating and sleeping. Indeed, it seemed all anyone ever thought or spoke about was the virus, the dreaded ter syndrome. Even the off-on war between Britain and France had been hampered as a result, although fighting and antagonism were still active in various parts of the Empire as the French tried to capitalise on its great enemy's weakened position. Many British soldiers and sailors, unable to return home, were being quartered in British-controlled areas of India. Meanwhile, the virus spread throughout their homeland at a steady and alarming rate, and cases began to be reported in Scotland, as well as England and Wales. Those Europeans unfortunate enough to have come into contact with the virus and succumbed had been placed under strict quarantine in their respective countries, and thus far the sickness seemed mostly isolated within the British Isles. Many pockets of the kingdom were still untouched, however, including Bourton. Tom's parents and brother, he was relieved to hear, were still healthy too, and he continued to look out for letters from them with every postal delivery, although their occurrences grew ever less frequent.

Not so fortunate was Mrs Chesterton, the old lady from Kent who had introduced Gracie to Jane Austen all those years ago. Gracie and Polly were much aggrieved to hear of her recent death. Polly reminisced over dinner that same evening about the night in Ashford, when Gracie and Tom danced for the first time, and Mrs Chesterton and Aunt Dawson tried to pair the two girls off with every eligible bachelor in sight. Gracie wondered whether Jane Austen had died of the virus too. How dreadful if she had. How unspeakably sad and wasteful. Gracie knew that in 1803, Austen had still to find fame and publication and to write some of her best works. Thoughts such as these inspired Gracie to work even harder at finding an antidote to the virus—so much so that her parents seriously worried that their daughter would labour to the brink of illness herself. She assured everyone that she was quite all right; she knew that most people would work as hard faced with the prospect of the portraits in Angelus's corridor vanishing forever.

The signs did not look good. Thousands of people were dead by the midsummer of 1803. Gracie and Tom, along with every other exhausted scientist and medic, could find no means of either halting the spread of the virus or curing those who had already contracted it. Dr Jenner's recent breakthrough in the fight against smallpox—vaccination through the means of cowpox—was of no use with this virus, as what could one safely inoculate with here? Time was needed to study ter in greater depth, wherein a suitable strain of the virus for vaccination purposes might be discovered, but time was in short supply.

It was a terrifying environment in which to live. The people of Bourton had a wooden house assembled at the outskirts of their village, and here they intended to place any of their relatives who showed even the least signs of the sickness. Another house had been erected for the family members of those ill. Nobody would be allowed to either visit or leave these properties until it was quite certain that it was safe for an individual to do so. For the moment, both houses remained empty, and everyone prayed that they would remain as such. As with everywhere else, Bourton was a veritable ghost town. Any rare visitor was eyed suspiciously, and nobody from Bourton travelled anywhere unless it was absolutely necessary.

As it was the summer, ordinary colds and flus were less frequent so diagnosis of an early case of the virus was relatively straightforward. The doctors throughout the country who found themselves immune to the effects of ter were a blessed commodity in any town or village, as were all others who did not succumb. Research and documentation on those unaffected was already starting to filter around the country, and Gracie and Tom learned that often, people who belonged to the same family, or people of a certain age in a community, were immune. The family immunity pointed to there being something in these individuals' genetic material that was able to fight the virus, but there were also some cases of totally unrelated spouses both being immune. This could be pure coincidence, but Gracie remembered Cianna's telling her that the Jamaican diet was conducive to fighting the effects of the illness. Should she spend more time looking into this now? With each avenue she explored, she had to spend less time on other possible leads. It was so difficult to know which road to take. Due to the tools and equipment available to her, a strong element of guesswork featured in many of her reckonings and assessments, and Gracie often had the sense that she was working in the dark. But something instinctively told her to bear in mind the similarities between ter and influenza.

Unlike influenza, ter didn't seem to mutate, but Gracie knew that if it was a virus in any ordinary sense then it would likely possess mutational qualities. She and Tom frequently discussed the possibility that ter was a new variant of influenza which, once it found its way into the immune and nervous systems of an individual, developed into something capable of causing such devastating damage. At its conception, ter was no more deadly than any other type of flu, but some days after its resultant mild symptoms, it matured and became something far more sinister.

To substantiate their theory that the virus was actually a flu variant, they tried to encourage their ter samples to mutate by manipulating them in the same way they did their influenza samples. But the samples would not mutate for them—instead, the covert ter preferred to evolve only when hidden deep within the confines of a living body. So the mystery of its transformation remained secret.

Ter also had much in common with non-contagious diseases that affected the nervous system, about which not much was known in the early nineteenth century. Gracie examined the similarities between ter and motor neuron diseases, as well as the inherited Huntington's disease. The fact that a ter victim, in the second phase of the virus, could be mistaken for a stroke sufferer, as indeed Josiah had been, was something Tom felt compelled to look further into, and he read everything available regarding circulatory disorders. Gracie longed daily for some of her old twenty-first-century equipment, but Tom, having never known anything else, was able at times to take a keener and less-cluttered approach to their findings. Eventually they rejected their theory that ter was a type of influenza, but not before testing all of their possible influenza cures and vaccinations. Nothing had any effect.

Before ter came to dominate their research, Gracie and Tom, in the relatively short time they had been working together, had made great progress in their influenza studies. They had already identified, isolated and harvested specific strains of influenza. Those vaccinated with inactivated components of these strains would be suitably protected by antibodies should they ever be attacked by the real forms of these types of influenza. Although there were many other variants (and even their isolated flu strains would evolve at large), this was significant in Gracie and Tom's, indeed history's, fight against influenza.

And they had achieved much else too. In Gracie's modern life, the flu had been known as incurable—but, a short time after Mr Franklyn's visit, Gracie and Tom had found a definite cure for one strain of the flu. They had long been in the habit of taking samples from everyone with influenza they came into contact with. Many of these same people were happy to take treatment concocted by Gracie and Tom, as long as they were assured it was safe. A local woman had contracted a case that was responsive to a cocktail of carefully selected drugs, and this mixture was then used upon other willing members of the community who also came down with the same flu. To check whether these "cured" people had still produced antibodies to the banished flu, some of them were subjected to the flu again and did not become ill. Gracie and Tom should have gained recognition and respect as a result of this remarkable breakthrough, but the outbreak of ter had largely swept their findings aside.

At the end of one particularly tiring and frustrating day, Gracie and Tom rubbed their eyes and stretched before reaching for their coats. They had no idea whether any of their endless hours spent reading and examining would ever be proven to be of any use. The couple walked back to the Arundels' in virtual silence. Tom, rather than staying alone in the village, was now residing with the Arundels in one of their many spare rooms. Mrs Ford's brother, Ernest's old lawyer friend, was also staying with the Arundels.

They had made a pact not to talk of work during the evenings, but they could not immediately rid their minds of the day's toils when they departed from the Rainbow each night, so they underwent the ritual of dealing with their own thoughts and freeing themselves as best as they could until they returned to more of the same the next day. Thus, their walks home were usually fairly quiet.

They made a sombre and reflective company at dinner that night. It was not always like this—indeed, Alicia's cheerful demeanour as well as Polly's frequent high spirits kept them from growing too dull, but a heavy downpour was affecting all of their moods that evening. Everyone retired early, and Gracie fell asleep to the sound of the relentless falling of rain.

Not far away, a Bourton farmer hauled himself out of his chair by the fire and decided he ought to take himself to bed. Andrew Johnson, a widower in his forties, lived alone. It had been a tough day. He'd felt as though his back would break while chopping firewood. How tired and thirsty he was too. He slowly climbed his stairs and started to undress for bed. He glanced out of his window towards the horses in his barn. *Yes, they would be all right in spite of the rain, tucked up cosily enough with plenty of meal to keep them going.* Johnson was glad of this. He didn't like to take any unnecessary trips away from home at the moment. After purchasing desperately needed supplies from the nearby town last week, he had everything he needed, at least for the coming weeks. He washed his face in front of his mirror and ruminated again on how awful and unreal all of this was. As he drank some water he noticed that his throat was quite tender and sore when he swallowed. He examined his face in the mirror again. It looked flushed and warm, although his body felt rather chilled. Ironclad fear suddenly gripped his heart. *Did he have the dreaded ter syndrome?*

Terrified, he lay down on his bed and told himself not to panic, to try to get some sleep and see how he felt in the morning. Shivering, he pulled the blankets over his head and eventually fell into a nightmarish sleep. Early the next morning, a feverish and aching Johnson packed some belongings into a bag and made his way to the purpose-built house a short distance from his home. There he would raise the flag that would let the residents of Bourton know that the virus was potentially in their midst.

18.

If I Should Die Before I Wake

A loud chapping at the front door roused the Arundels from their morning coffee and toast. Alicia hurried off to see who was there before Jenny the maid could even lay down her coal scuttle.

Alicia opened the door to find Mrs Myers, Sophy's mother, with a blanket tied around her face, clearly in some distress.

'Why, Janette. Whatever is wrong? Come in, come in.'

Mrs Myers looked around furtively and held back from entering. Her voice was muffled but agitated.

'Oh, Alicia, Alicia . . . have you not heard? The house, the terrible house for the sick—it is occupied!'

Alicia's hands flew to her mouth.

'Oh, how did it ever get here?' Mrs Myers continued. 'Who is in the house? The men from the village are trying to find out by doing the rounds of the properties—I take it they have not yet called here? Young Bobby, the baker's lad, saw the flag was raised this morning while he was out walking his dog. Nobody has dared to go anywhere near the house. My husband has gone off with the others in the search and he bid me stay at home, but, oh, my dear, I was out of my mind with worry. I could not remain there for anything Harold said, and I have run all the way here. When I think of all the Bourton people I have met and spoken with in the last days, and any of them now might be in that ghastly place! I might have to leave my home too before the day is out!'

Mrs Myers fell down and wept, her blanket dropping in a pathetic heap beside her. Alicia instinctively reached out to comfort her old friend, but Ernest, who had appeared at her side, prevented her from doing so by keeping a tight grip on her elbow.

'My dear Mrs Myers,' he said, 'we must all be as brave as we can and face this thing squarely. You must return home immediately and we must sit tight in our own homes until we have news of who amongst us is ill. It pains me to see you leave my door without so much as a cup of tea and a seat while you are in such a sad state, but I am thinking of you and yours as well as my own family. Go home now, Mrs Myers, and I pray we might all be fortunate enough to see our way through this and meet again in happier days. Thank you for letting us know what has happened, but go safely home now and wait for word from your husband.'

Mrs Myers had raised herself up from the ground and was trying to compose herself as best as she could. Gracie, now standing behind her parents, had never seen the woman look as dignified as she did when she took her leave of them.

'Yes, you are right, of course. I wish you all the best and I hope we may meet again one day. You have been good neighbours and kind friends. Goodbye and God bless you.'

She turned and made her way down the drive. Alicia cried on Ernest's shoulder as they watched her form recede out of sight. People they were used to seeing every day might soon be gone forever. Gracie felt guilty for how often she had dismissed Mrs

Myers as an ignorant and foolish woman, and marvelled at the transformation she'd witnessed in this same figure today. The seriousness of the situation rendered the whole family silent for several seconds, but Mrs Ford, who along with the others was now also in the hallway, soon joined Alicia's quiet tears with her own loud weeping. Her brother did his best to comfort her while Polly and Jack held each other tightly and Tom rested his chin on Gracie's head, his arms around her shoulders.

Jenny interrupted the sad scene by knocking clumsily on the wall behind where they all stood.

'Excuse me,' Jenny said to Alicia, 'but can I be going home now? I want to see whether my folks are all right.'

Jenny lived with her parents in the village and had been coming in to work for Alicia a few mornings each week despite the worry concerning the virus. Jenny's parents were poor and relied upon their daughter's wages, and Alicia had not had the heart to reduce the maid's hours to nothing. Alicia spoke hesitantly to the simple young maid.

'I think you had better wait until Mr Myers and the other gentlemen get here to let us know who has taken ill. It may not be safe for you to return home, Jenny, you know.'

The girl began to cry too.

'I think if Jenny really wants to return home then we should let her,' said Ernest. 'She has long been dividing her days between us and her family and others in the village. We say it might not be safe for her to return, but we also have no way of knowing if we offer any safer a haven. If contagion is to spread amongst us then it has likely done so already. Go home, Jenny. We wish you good luck.'

'Thank you, sir, thank you.'

She pulled her thin coat from a peg by the kitchen door, and Alicia gave her some bits of food and packages that contained candles and blankets. The girl gratefully received them. Before she left, she paused at the door and looked as if she was earnestly trying to compose her thoughts into some significant, possibly last, words to say to her employers.

'May I say,' she finally said, 'that it has been my humble honour to work for you. And I liked my job—I really did.'

Jenny then raced down the drive and was soon entirely out of sight.

'Oh, brother,' Mrs Ford moaned, 'why did I come here? Why did we leave London?'

'You would have been no safer in London, I can tell you that,' her brother assured her.

Stunned, the family made their way back to the breakfast room, where their cold cups of coffee and tea were an unwelcome sight. Alicia busied herself with clearing away the dishes and encouraged Gracie and Polly to assist her. Jack seemed unwilling to let go of Polly's hand even for an instant, but his wife kissed his head gently; this reassured him enough to smile at her as she left the room with an armful of bread.

Within ten minutes, another loud knock at the door resounded through the house. Ernest opened it. Mr Myers and another local man stood there, their faces also wrapped in blankets. They nodded at Ernest, who then explained that his family knew of the situation as a result of Mrs Myers's visit.

'But do you know who is ill? Who is in the sick house?' Ernest asked.

'We're still waiting to hear back from a few men who went to visit the houses in the opposite direction, but so far we only know that Andrew Johnson has gone to the house. His farm was empty, but he left a note stating that he has all the usual influenza-like symptoms and that he went to the sick house after dawn this morning. We don't think anyone else has gone there. He lives alone, so he has no family to worry about, but we need to know who has come into contact with him in the last week.'

Ernest shook his head.

'Not I. I haven't seen Andrew in at least a few months. Alicia, girls, what about you?'

'No, no, we haven't seen him in ages.'

In a few short moments, the entire household confirmed that Andrew Johnson was a person they had neither spoken to nor even seen in a long time. Harry Myers grimaced.

'Yes, it's the same story everywhere. No offence, I know you people will be telling the truth, but it's hard to believe that nobody has seen Johnson in all this time. People may be holding back because they're scared of leaving their homes. If everyone's telling the truth, then Johnson must have been one lonely fellow.'

'Well, what's going to happen now?'

'Stay at home—that's what we're advising everyone to do. If you or any of your family gets ill then, well, you know what you have to immediately do.'

'And what about Andrew Johnson?' said Gracie. 'There's no one to tend to him or even give him food.'

'Aye, we've thought about that. We're going to put together a basket with plenty of supplies and leave it for him a little distance from the house. One of us will bellow as loud as we can so that he will hear us. That's all that we can do for the poor man. I feel for him greatly though.'

'And everyone else that you've seen is feeling quite well?' Tom asked.

'Yes, yes.'

'I wonder,' Tom continued, 'if it would be possible to include in your basket for Andrew a note from Gracie and me asking him to leave a sample for us to come and collect.'

Mr Myers and his friend looked at each other uncomfortably.

'No, no, I don't think so, Tom, lad. We'd best leave Johnson in peace. We don't want you bringing back to the village God only knows what. If you infect yourselves, you infect all of us too.'

'It will all be carried out safely, sir. Gracie and I have been working with samples of ter for months already. We can confirm today whether poor Andrew has the virus or not. Is it not worth the village knowing this either way?'

'Well, but it seems mighty irresponsible...'

Gracie interjected. 'But it's more irresponsible, surely, to not let two scientists in the vicinity help—scientists who have been working solidly for months on a counter for this. Let us help. We don't want to endanger any lives, only save them.'

Ernest spoke quietly. 'You're sure what you propose to do will be safely conducted, with no extra danger to any of us?'

'Yes. We are extremely careful with our samples—we have not passed ter to any of you in all this time yet, have we? Please, Father, it's important that Tom and I do this.'

Her father nodded. 'I say they do it then.'

The other men nodded too but still looked far from convinced that any good could come of the undertaking.

* * *

An hour and a half later, Gracie and Tom stood shivering amongst the trees and greenery in the picturesque woods that surrounded the sick-houses and waited for Mr Johnson to leave his hideaway again. They had seen him come out to collect his basket and wave at Mr Myers and the others as they made their way back to the centre of Bourton. Gracie felt so sorry for him. Although she and Tom were some distance away, it had been easy to determine that the man was unwell. He had staggered slightly out the door of his hateful new dwelling place and kept himself tightly wrapped up in thick blankets. Gracie noticed that he'd walked with his head down, as if he felt sheepish or even ashamed.

In her previous dealings with him she'd found Andrew to be a nervous but affable sort of man, and she had no worries about his not complying with their request. He had taken himself quickly here, had he not? Sure enough, the door of the wooden house opened again, and they watched the sick man walk some distance towards them and place the basket carefully onto the grass. Then he looked towards where Gracie and Tom stood, gesturing that everything had been carried out as they had requested in their letter, before slowly walking back into his house. The pair waited a few more moments and then made their way to the basket which contained Andrew's samples. Tom lifted it into his arms, and they walked as quickly as they could to the Rainbow. They saw not another person in the entirety of their short journey.

It took some time for them to be able to tell whether Andrew did indeed have the dreaded ter but, after carrying out all of the various procedures, they recognised the distinctive and unusual pattern and their hearts sank. Andrew Johnson had the fearful ter syndrome. It was important to tell the residents of Bourton as soon as possible, so they went to the village square. Tom climbed the steep steps to the paved podium and shouted a greeting as loudly as he could to gain the attention of the many people who lived nearby. Within minutes, Gracie spied twitching curtains, and then faces appeared at the windows. Tom cleared his throat and then spoke as loudly and clearly as he could.

'I am sorry to tell you all that we have examined some samples from Mr Johnson and we can confirm that he does indeed have ter syndrome. If you can tell this news to any neighbours or friends that you might see, we would be grateful. Thank you.'

Tom's words met with a combination of resigned and panicked expressions. It felt unreal to Gracie to see all of these well-known faces behind glass, almost as if they were exhibits in a museum. Gracie and Tom then made their way back to the Arundel house to inform the family of their findings. After a light dinner, they would return to the Rainbow and work into the night, for what it was worth, in the hope they might find some solution to this nightmare which had long loomed but always maintained a comfortable distance before today. Now the nightmare was here, and it was difficult to know how to react, how to feel. But if there was even a glimmer of possibility they could halt this thing, then they had to keep on toiling—for themselves, for their families, for everyone.

'So how long do you reckon poor Andrew has?' Polly asked over dinner that evening.

'Well,' Gracie said, 'judging by what I've read of the condition, and if he really was feeling newly ill when he entered the sick house, he'll be entering phase two of the virus in another week. He'll go through the usual pattern of feeling better, and this may last for two or three days, but then he'll become much worse.'

'Yes,' Polly said, 'he'll be paralysed, won't he? And his breathing will be laboured. I read all about it months ago in the newspaper, hah, when we still had newspapers. Poor man. But when shall he be out of his misery, do you think, Gracie?'

'I should think he will be dead by the time the next fortnight is up.'

It seemed madness to talk this way about a man who had been enjoying all the vigour of health such a short time ago, but there it was. Alicia packed a picnic hamper for Gracie and Tom to take with them to the Rainbow, and Ernest gave Tom strict instructions to not allow Gracie to work all night.

'Is there anything you think I could give to Mr Johnson?' Alicia asked Gracie and Tom. 'I know it sounds frivolous and stupid, perhaps, to think of making him something nice to eat, but I feel I must do something for the man.'

Gracie took hold of her mother's shaking hands and told her quietly that he could not enjoy much to eat at the moment and in a few days, he would be unable to eat anything. Alicia held her hands to her mouth.

'How awful, how awful! I knew all of this of course, but when it is someone that you know . . . Why, I remember his wedding day so clearly, and then poor Cassandra died so young. It is the thought of him being all alone that tears at my heart so. And there is nothing, nothing in the way of medicine or drugs that you two can think of to ease his suffering?'

'Nothing, Mother. We'll continue to do our best to arrive at something, but I fear we shall be too late to do anything for Mr Johnson.'

'Yes, dear. I know how hard you and Tom have been working. Your father and I are so proud of you, Gracie, and you too, Tom. I know how your parents must be feeling about you.'

Gracie hugged her mother and kissed her goodbye before departing from the bright and cosy interior of the Arundel house into the bleak and chilly afternoon. Before returning to the Rainbow, they had one awful task to undertake, which they were dreading. Amongst his samples, Andrew had left a note asking to be informed as to whether he definitely had ter syndrome. Now they were about to shout to a man the fact that he was going to die a sure and painful death. How could they show compassion or even human feeling for Andrew without being able to look him in the eyes, to touch him? Gracie was not given to outward and physical displays of emotion, but how she longed now to hug this man, to let him cry on her shoulder ... She blinked back hot tears. Life could be cruel and hard beyond endurance. Yet this same life was what they were working so hard to hold on to.

Every few days some local men would take a basket of supplies out to Andrew, and each time, they expected him to be too unwell to come out and pick up his basket. But for more than a week Andrew did so, and he seemed to be healthy. One day, he shouted to his distant visitors that he was feeling well indeed, that his initial flu-like symptoms had cleared up after four days, and though he was expecting to become ill again, the second phase had as yet not appeared. This was unaccountable to all. Nobody else in Bourton had shown any symptoms of ter, and people slowly began leaving their homes and moving out and about in the community again. The men who had seen Andrew visited Gracie and Tom at the Rainbow.

'How can it be?' they asked. 'Have you heard of any other cases where the paralysis holds off for so long?' Gracie and Tom had not, and they studied Andrew's sample again. Yes, it was ter syndrome, and yes, it matched their other samples of the virus in look and shape. They decided to visit Andrew once more and request another sample.

Seeing him again that afternoon looking so hale and fit, almost two weeks since he had entered the house, was truly amazing. They had expected him to be almost or even dead by now. With their new samples from Andrew held securely in their basket, they returned to the Rainbow and prepared their materials for examination. Neither was prepared for the sight underneath the microscopes.

The ter appeared to be gone. All they could see were healthy and entirely normal-looking cells. There was no longer any evidence that this man was sick in the slightest! It was Gracie and Tom's practice to sit side by side at their workbench and view their samples underneath their microscopes simultaneously. They both peered and magnified for a long time before raising their heads. Tom did so first, and he turned to face Gracie silently until she did so too.

'Tom,' she said at last, 'what does this mean?'

'I don't know,' he said with a laugh, 'but I feel we have to take it as promising. Before, all we had was certain death. This change can only be welcome.'

They debated every possible explanation for this apparent transformation in Andrew's luck. Perhaps he still had ter but the second phase was taking longer to develop in him. Perhaps the virus was still in his body, hidden away and preparing for attack again. No, this was not possible. They had samples from various stages in the lives of ter sufferers, and the ter remained visible and unaltered under examination even when the patient seemed healthy. Andrew had either been able to somehow fight the virus and beat it, or he hadn't had ter at all but only an ordinary case of the flu.

Gracie began to question, 'But . . .'

'Hush, my love,' said Tom. 'Let's hold all of these thoughts for the moment. We must tell the villagers and then let Andrew know that he appears to be healthy. There will be a long day of work ahead of us, so let us discharge our tasks before we begin. At least it is good news to deliver for a change!'

When Gracie and Tom assumed their former positions in the village square and delivered their news, many people cried. Some said it was a miracle and that God at last had intervened. Others looked at Tom and Gracie sceptically and questioned whether the man had even had ter at all. Mr Myers held off the questioners, saying that first things were first: Andrew needed to be informed, and they needed to decide how much longer he should be shut away in his prison. The general consensus was that if he was still healthy following Gracie and Tom's studying another sample in three days, then he should be immediately released and ready to receive all of their best regards. Tom and Gracie were charged with delivering this information to Andrew without delay.

How much happier they set off than on the day when they'd had to tell him of his impending death. And this was much more than a stay of execution—it was a real chance of future release! They called for him, still keeping a safe distance from his dwelling place. He came out at once and dropped to his knees when he received the news. He wept freely and shouted his thanks for their interest in his welfare. It was a highly charged moment, and Gracie brushed tears from her eyes and wrapped her arms around Tom's middle as the reprieved man saluted them and made his way back into his house. They stood there a few moments longer before Gracie spoke.

'Well, you said we have some work to do now, so let's get started.'

It was possible that Andrew had been able to fight off the effects of a supposedly unbeatable virus. There was no way of proving it though. Other people lucky enough to recover were categorised as having suffered only an ordinary attack of the flu. Gracie and Tom had never heard of a case where it was certain that a patient had had ter and survived.

In the face of this lack of proof, they decided to leave aside the scenario that Andrew had indeed had ter. Instead, they would work from the hypothesis that he'd been suffering from the flu—a flu that under the microscope greatly resembled ter.

They looked and looked at Andrew's original sample and contrasted it with their samples of influenza. No, it looked like ter. Could it be that their initial hypothesis—that ter was really no more than a strain of influenza, albeit a particularly nasty one—was correct? This was unlikely. Aside from the fact that it was so much more deadly, the ter samples did not react to stimuli in the way that the flu samples did, and they could not get ter to mutate. More likely, ter originated from a particular flu variant into something altogether different, or under the microscope it simply resembled Andrew Johnson's flu type. They were well aware that they had not seen all variants of the flu—how could they, given that each mutated again and again.

Gracie knew that given the limitations of their equipment, they were not granted as clear an image under the microscope as was ideal. Further, although ter samples and Andrew's sample looked to be very similar, with modern technology it may have been less so. But still she and Tom grew more excited as they debated all of these possibilities. Now they must confirm whether Andrew's sample was indeed ter or the influenza.

They prepared their sample of saliva and attempted to make it mutate in the way influenza would but not ter. Given their expertise in influenza research, they were likely alone in Britain in being able to so visibly determine a clear-cut case of influenza. The results of their test made Gracie's heart pound. Andrew's sample had mutated; it was influenza.

Tom drummed his fingers on the bench and shook his head in wonder.

'Well, if nothing else,' he said, 'this tells me never to judge on mere appearances again.'

'But, its similarity! Does ter syndrome originate from this type of flu? Or is its appearance a coincidence? Or'—Gracie sat down heavily— 'can we try it as a vaccination for ter?'

When Gracie and Tom tried to later recall the days that followed, they found that events and ideas simply merged into other events and ideas. The pace of life had sped up, Gracie thought, rather like they were on a rollercoaster. There was no time to take in what they had eaten, with whom they had spoken, what they had worn. These things flashed by and disappeared, leaving only the experiments, the tests, the ideas.

They would follow the great Dr Jenner's lead and determine whether Andrew's strain of influenza could be used as a vaccination for ter. Jenner had already shown that an individual subjected to cowpox would become immune to smallpox. With more tests, they could tell whether there were enough similarities between Andrew's flu and ter for the same idea to be practicable in this scenario. Gracie knew of ways that the Britain she had come from could try to make a vaccine for ter—through separating the two effects of disease-causing organisms to produce matter that is unable to cause the full-blown disease but that still triggers the antigens responsible for inducing the host's immune response, or through the method of attenuation whereby a live microorganism was weakened by ageing it or altering its growth conditions, or through biotechnology or genetic engineering techniques which could be used to produce subunit vaccines. But these methods were for other centuries.

Gracie thought about the string of events that had led them to identify and use Andrew's flu as a test in the first place. She needed to be here in 1803; Tom needed to be a scientist; Mr Franklyn needed to give them money to study influenza; Andrew needed to contract his specific strain of the flu at this time, in this village; and perhaps Dr Jenner needed to set the matter of immunology alight in the scientific world before any of it. Had all of this been known beforehand? Had a plan been made by someone, somewhere, to right a disturbance in the world caused by one individual's decision to change something in his or her past? Gracie had come to this period because of her love of Jane Austen novels! But had she loved these novels so much because something inside of her recognised a connection? Certainly a little bit of luck was required for all major discoveries, but this . . .

Gracie shook her head in wonderment at these thoughts in the moments following their discovery that Andrew's flu displayed strong signs of being able to be used as a vaccination. The most beautiful balance and symmetry—why question or resist? More than she ever had at any time in her two lives, Gracie felt she was an integral and important part of her world, an important part of its forward movement. She longed to see approval or recognition in Cianna's face; somehow, she felt her friend was with her still.

'I don't care,' the elderly man said. 'I'm prepared to take my chances. This is for the future: the children. I'm an old man with a long life behind me. I have no family to trouble about leaving. Let me do this. It would be an honour, anyway—the greatest achievement of my life if it all works out.' Old Amos made his case to be the first to be given Gracie and Tom's new vaccination. It had to be tested on someone. Amos was a kindly man who had lived with his mother until she died, some years before. He was a shoemaker and a proud born-and-bred Bourton man.

Yes, yes, let him do it, the villagers agreed, standing together in the village square. It was his choice, and he'd be remembered for a long time if it all worked out as the two young folks hoped. Why, people still spoke today of that little lad from across the way that Jenner treated with the cowpox. Yes, let old Amos have his chance.

Gracie and Tom were not opposed to trying out their vaccination on an elderly person. On the contrary, they wanted their vaccine to work on anybody, no matter how old the immune system, and if it worked on the ailing Amos, it would likely be a success in younger and healthier bodies as well.

So Amos, early one crisp autumnal day, was injected with Andrew's flu virus. The vaccination was carried out in the sick house Andrew had previously occupied, and Gracie and Tom left shortly after, leaving Amos alone with provisions and books to aid his seclusion. A few days later, Amos showed signs that he was developing the flu, and Gracie and Tom, maintaining their distance, collected the sample that Amos left for them and took it back to the Rainbow for examination. Under their microscopes were the now familiar and striking cell images, and their next step was to determine whether Amos's illness was a clear-cut case of the flu.

It was.

In the course of the next week he felt better again. Gracie and Tom checked another sample from Amos, and it was now clear—he had recovered from his bout of the flu. Now came the nerve-racking test of injecting the healthy man with the dreaded ter syndrome. If it didn't work, could they ever forgive themselves? But there was no time to worry about such things. If Amos was willing then who were they to argue? Sensing their tension, the old man laughed and cajoled during the procedure, and when it was over, he jokingly said he felt like a new man. They told him they would call to collect a sample from him every day for the next few weeks. He waved to them through his small paned window as they began their journey back to the village and their next job: getting as much of Andrew's flu ready as possible.

The following day they were relieved to see Amos wave cheerily to them as he deposited his throat swab sample. Upon examination, the sample was still clear. It was the same the day after and the day after that. As cautious and unwilling to prematurely celebrate as the scientists were, when Amos's two weeks were up and he was still healthy, it was evident that Gracie Arundel and Tom Blake had discovered a vaccination for ter syndrome.

Bourton erupted into celebration for their soon-to-be-famous pair, and Amos was toasted so often he became quite drunk on all the foaming ale that passed his way. But first things were first—it was arranged that everyone in the village should be vaccinated as soon as possible, including Gracie and Tom. They would then travel to London and inform the government, the king, the Royal Society—indeed everyone—that there was a ready and willing answer to the syndrome.

Certainly more people would continue to die, but the prospect of a vastly changed Britain in the future was no longer inevitable. It had been several years ago now in 1796 that Jenner had discovered that cowpox could successfully protect one from the smallpox and still not everyone had been vaccinated, or was even in favour of vaccination, the wealthy variolators for one. Things took time, yes, but surely the government and authorities would do everything they could to help push the vaccination, given how virulent and widespread the disease was. Lives would be saved, but how ironic, Gracie and Tom considered, that this would be achieved by injecting people with influenza, the very illness they were paid to prevent.

Gracie vaccinated Tom, and then as he rolled up her sleeve to inject her, he noticed and felt the mark of the tuberculosis vaccine she'd been given while at school in the twentieth century. He asked her what it was.

'Oh, I don't know. An old scar, I think.'

'Well, I'll give you your injection beside it since your skin's already marked there.'

She grimaced as the needle penetrated her skin and thought it was fitting that she should display vaccination marks from her differing centuries side by side.

A queue had developed outside the Rainbow, and Gracie spied her mother and father standing in line with everyone else. Her father looked fit to burst with pride. She wondered where Polly and Jack were but was soon so immersed in reassuring, injecting and tear wiping that she thought of nothing else until, many hours later, when the last of the villagers had left the Rainbow and Tom turned to face her.

'Why Gracie, have you seen Polly or Jack?'

On returning home, Gracie learned that Polly and Jack had gone for a walk after luncheon and had assured the family they would be at the Rainbow within the next few hours. They had not been seen since.

'Rash, rash Polly,' Alicia said, her tone uncharacteristically scolding. 'I told her not to go far until she'd been vaccinated. Ernest, where is she? Why has she not come home?'

Ernest shook his head. Alicia and Mrs Ford could barely be restrained from going out into the dark night to seek their missing offspring as Tom and Ernest left the house, lanterns in hand.

Once out of earshot of his wife, Ernest spoke quickly to his prospective son-in-law.

'You know, I have a dreadful feeling, don't ask me why, that they are at the sick house. Let us check there first.'

'The sick house? What, you mean they might have knowingly come into contact with ter today and taken themselves directly there?'

'Think of it? What else could have happened to them? Jack's a strong lad; I don't feel they've been injured. Oh no, they're at that house!'

The sick-houses were nearer to the Arundels than the centre of the village was, and Tom and Ernest reached them before long. As soon as the sick-houses came into view it was clear that someone indeed was occupying one of them. A light shone through the little window of the house where Andrew and Amos had resided.

'My little girl,' said Ernest, his voice trembling.

Tom held Ernest's arm in support, and the two men stopped a little way from the house. Tom, bellowing as loudly as he could, asked who was there. Jack popped his head out the front door.

'I knew it, I knew it!'

Ernest was all for running in the house immediately and could not understand why Tom held him back.

'Why, I've had the vaccine, haven't I?'

'Yes, sir, but only today. Until Gracie and I have seen more results I hardly think it's a good idea to come into contact with ter so soon. If indeed Polly and Jack have it, I should have said. I know how anxious you are, but think of the family back home too.'

Ernest nodded, and he and Tom listened as Jack and Polly, who had also appeared at the door, explained how they had ended up in the sick house today of all days.

Polly wanted to take a walk by the stream. It had been so long since she'd been there. She was nervous about the vaccination and whether it would hurt, and Jack didn't have the heart to prevent her from drawing comfort in a walk. The stream was not far from a road that, before the outbreak of the disease, had been a fairly busy and well-used thoroughfare. All was quiet today though, and Jack himself delighted in being away from home, in all the greenery and freshness of the countryside.

They walked hand in hand, and shortly before they were ready to turn around and head back to the village and the Rainbow, Polly spied a clump of yellow daylilies.

'I would like to pin one to my dress for good luck,' she said. The flowers were at the other side of the water, and they hurried around the pathway to a small bridge that could enable them to cross the stream to collect them. At that moment, a carriage came careering towards them, and the driver, seeing Jack and Polly at almost the last moment, swerved to avoid them. Now free of the bridge, if a tree had not prevented it from doing so, the carriage would have overturned entirely.

The occupants of the carriage had expected to see people on the road as little as Jack and Polly had expected to see a carriage, and the fault for the accident lay on both sides. Unhurt, Polly and Jack made their way to the carriage quickly to see if anyone was injured. The driver, apparently dazed, lay on the grass, and the door to the interior had swung open. Peering inside, Polly saw an elderly woman who appeared unconscious. Her clothing suggested she was wealthy, and a thick blanket was wrapped around her body. Polly reached out to touch her. Jack made to pull her hand back, but his wife, sharply, said she would never allow any illness to take away her sense of humanity and compassion. If it came to that then she would rather take ill and die.

A basket lay at the old woman's feet, and Polly opened it and pulled out a flask of water. Climbing into the carriage, she held it to the old woman's lips. 'Here, take some of this,' she said softly, as she rested the woman's head on her shoulder and rubbed her hands with her own. The old woman wakened and sipped some of the cold water offered to her. She then looked around in distress and puzzlement at the two young people who now studied her so earnestly.

'Simon? Simon! Where is my driver? What has happened?'

'It is safe,' said Polly. 'You have been involved in a little accident and Simon, if that is your driver's name, looks to be unhurt though somewhat dazed. You are not far from Bourton.'

'Bourton, but, but, we must be going . . .'

'Yes, but where are you going to? Here, you are beside yourself. Take some more water.'

Polly stroked the frightened old woman's head, and her blood chilled as she became aware of how hot and feverish the woman's skin felt to the touch.

'You must get out of this carriage, my dear. Get out now.'

At that moment, Simon stood behind them and enquired whether his mistress was injured. On seeing she was not, he made to commence driving again immediately.

'Oh my dear, go away—I pray you will not catch this dreadful thing I have for I am ill, you see. I just wanted to see my old house one last time, that was all. Forgive me, forgive me!'

Polly and Jack had heard these words shouted from the carriage even as it disappeared from sight.

'So you see, Father,' said Polly, 'I could not come home and put you all at risk before you had your injections. Is everyone in Bourton now safe?'

Ernest sighed heavily. 'Yes, we've all been done. Tom thinks we should stay apart a little longer yet just to be safe, though I want you home tonight.'

'No, Father, it is better to do as Tom says. Jack and I shall stay here tonight. We have provisions, left over from Amos's visit.'

'We'll come back tomorrow then, my dear.'

After some more conversation, mostly regarding what they would tell Alicia and Mrs Ford, Ernest and Tom left to return home.

The mothers were frantic with worry on being told the news, as were the rest of the family. Gracie shook her head in disbelief. What a cruel joke! To be only minutes from protecting the last of those she loved and have this happen!

'How long do you think they should stay at the sick house?' she asked Tom.

'Who can say? A few days? Let's just wait until the vaccine is safely in our systems. We haven't even had time to show flu symptoms yet. Perhaps we should wait until we are recovered from any little sickness we may now get.'

'Until we are well, then. I shall tell my parents that. But, to think of her being in that dark, cold house! Thank goodness she has Jack with her. But she won't get ter, will she?'

Tom kissed Gracie's head and said they could only pray now. Inside, he knew they would soon be carrying out their daily tests on samples from Gracie's sister. Would Gracie be strong enough to endure that? He resolved to do everything he could to support her during what he feared would be a horrifying few weeks.

In the course of the next few days, Tom, Gracie and her family developed mild flu symptoms but recovered quickly. Polly and Jack submitted their first tests, which they placed into baskets. They were as yet feeling quite well.

Gracie slid Polly's results under her microscope, Tom taking Jack's. After some minutes, Tom raised his head, smiling—all was clear. But Gracie sat quietly with her head bent until Tom instinctively took the microscope from her grip and peered into it. Polly's results showed the distinctive and chilling pattern. After further testing, their fears could not be denied. Polly had ter syndrome. Jack had apparently not succumbed, most likely because he'd already suffered from Andrew's flu at some point and his body was immune to the virus.

'Why, why? What more do they want? What more can I do?'

Hysterical with grief and anger, Gracie flung her microscope from her view and then threw herself weeping onto the bench before her. Tom stroked her hair and held her close.

'Hush, hush. Who can say why these things happen? Polly made a choice to help another person that day, knowing what the consequences might be, and we have to respect her for that.'

'No! No, I don't respect it! She should have kept away; the old woman should have stayed away! What more can we do, Tom?' Gracie cried desperately. 'We've tried all our flu counters on the ter countless times. The vaccination won't stop it now, will it? No, how can it?'

Gracie's elastic mind thought rapidly but came up against brick walls.

'The only thing I can think of,' she said, 'is to develop a cure for the flu which we use as a vaccine for ter.'

Tom sighed. 'Even if we could in such a short time, remember, ter is not the flu and we have no way of knowing whether it would have any effect upon—'

'Tom!' Gracie screamed. 'Polly is my sister and if there is even the slightest possibility of saving her then I will grasp it!'

'Yes, yes, you are right, my love. We'll begin at once,' he said, retrieving Gracie's microscope from the floor. He considered that this was the only course of action to see Gracie through the next days. If she did not feel she was doing everything she could it would be unbearable for her.

The residents of Bourton, on hearing of the Arundels' predicament, were heartsore for their neighbours. Any thoughts of Gracie and Tom's leaving immediately for London had been forgotten. The couple's time was now spent trying to find some solution to ter in real cure terms, its prevention having been already tackled. Gracie attacked her research with all of the pent-up fury and frustration she had ever felt. The virus was the focal point of it all now. She was determined to beat it entirely—in fact, she felt sure she was the only one who could.

Polly and Jack were back at home now, and the family were tending to Polly's every need and whim, although she would not ask for much. She had retreated into herself and sat quietly each day, apologising for all of the trouble she was causing. Jack was fraught with suppressed anguish and wished that he could have been fortunate enough to be stricken with the disease too so he could die with his beloved wife.

Gracie could not spend much time at all with Polly during these days as she was always working at the Rainbow, trying to find a way to stop the inevitable end which awaited her sister.

Many believed Gracie's efforts to be futile. The family entirely understood and accepted her need to not give up, though, and Polly would smile and nod and say if anyone could pull it off, it would be her sister. On the morning that Polly started to show the first signs of becoming ill, Gracie left for the village even earlier than usual and stayed there until Ernest and Tom had to drag her away, exhausted, from her workbench. She knew she was growing closer. If only her weak body didn't require such annoyances as sleep, food and rest.

By the time Polly recovered from the first phase and was feeling quite well again, the family had largely come to terms with the fact that she would shortly be gone. Polly herself was preparing to say goodbye to those she loved. During one of these days, the family took a picnic by the river, and Polly laughed and teased and was almost her old self again. Gracie and Tom were absent from this event, and it grieved Alicia to think that Gracie would be able to take no comfort from these days when the worst finally came.

On and on Gracie and Tom worked, and every day that passed, Gracie grew more determined than ever that the next day, yes, the next day, would bring the breakthrough she was prepared to tear the world apart to find.

The day following the picnic it was raining quite heavily, and Gracie felt glad about this. It had been so stuffy of late, and she never got enough fresh air as it was. The rain, long needed, would lighten the atmosphere and allow her to think more clearly.

Passing quickly, as each day seemed to now, Tom managed to get Gracie to take some bread and water for dinner before she resumed her work. He was on his knees by their drugs chest, measuring out droplets from one bottle into another, when Gracie suddenly stood and pushed her bench away from her so forcefully that it toppled over. Tom immediately thought that she'd fainted from tiredness or lack of food, as she'd threatened to several times already, and he rushed to her side and held her face up to his. Instead, the look he saw in her eyes assured him that either Gracie had found the cure she had been looking for or she was close to death herself. Nothing else could have caused such an expression in her face at that moment.

'Tom, Tom.' Her voice was broken though strangely calm. 'I've got it. I've got the counter for the influenza. Look, look— I've found it!'

Tom looked with amazement at Gracie's hastily scratched notes and formulas and yes, he had to agree, this cure seemed as watertight as the cures they had discovered for the other strains of influenza.

'We must go home to Polly now.' Gracie held her head in her hands. 'But no,' she continued, 'Polly should come here. All of our equipment and drugs are here. It would take too much time for us to sort through and take all of our things back home. We should leave now and have Polly brought here in the carriage— let us go now!'

'No,' Tom said, 'it will be quicker if I go alone. I will run all the way there. You sort things out here for my return with Polly.'

'Yes, yes, that makes sense. Oh, thank you, Tom, thank you for everything. I love you so.'

It had been already decided that if they did find a cure for the influenza, Polly should firstly be injected with some of the flu vaccine. A little amount, they guessed, would raise rather than further attack her weakened immune system. It would also provide an immediate receptor for the cure she would shortly receive. They had no sure way of knowing whether the ter and the influenza were so firmly connected that a cure would serve for both, but Gracie instinctively felt that it would.

Tom ran into the Arundel house and found all in pandemonium. Mrs Ford was weeping loudly and being comforted by her brother. Alicia and Ernest held each other closely and barely raised their eyes when Tom entered the room. Jack was alone and sat ashen faced; Tom averted his eyes from him almost immediately. It was too painful to witness such agony. The little maid, Jenny, was heaped in a corner of the hallway, crying into her apron. She was the only one to raise her eyes to meet Tom's.

'But ... but ... so soon,' he stammered. 'When did it happen?'

'Oh Mr Tom, not long ago. It's so sad, such a pretty and nice young lady. I did like her ever so much.'

Tom leaned upon the bannister and could think only of Gracie. What could he tell her—she, who was waiting at this moment to try to save her sister's life? How in the world could he tell her that Polly was dead?

'And poor Mr Jack,' Jenny continued, 'he has taken it ever so hard. Always at her side, you know. She sleeps now. I've made her some of her favourite soup for when she wakes, but I don't suppose she'll be able to enjoy it!'

Jenny sniffed loudly into her handkerchief, and Ernest entered the hallway and patted Tom on the shoulder.

Tom caught hold of Jenny's word. 'Polly sleeps. You mean she's not—'

'Yes,' Ernest interjected, 'my poor little girl is asleep for the moment. Oh, Tom, the paralysis has begun and it has hit us all hard, though we were prepared for it.'

Ernest held his hands to his eyes and then jumped back, startled, when Tom suddenly grasped his shoulders.

'Sir, we have the cure! Polly must be taken to the Rainbow at once. Get the carriage and horses ready!'

Tom had barely finished these words before Jack sprang to his feet and rushed up the stairs. He appeared again moments later with Polly still sleeping in his arms.

'No time for carriages and horses. I will run to the village with her.'

'How, man? How will you get her there?' Ernest shouted.

'In my arms.'

Jack raced out into the dark and rainy night, and Tom chased him as quickly as he could. The rest of the family got the carriage and horses ready to make their own way to the Rainbow. Jack had been right; by the time all was gotten in order, he would have Polly already there.

Gracie, her nerves torn to shreds, jumped in her skin when the door of the Rainbow flung open and Tom held it wide for Jack to enter with Polly held tightly to his chest. They were soaking wet and covered in mud, but Gracie took no time to query their appearance or lack of carriage and instead motioned for Polly to be carried through to Tom's sofa at the rear of the cottage.

Polly opened her eyes a little and tried to smile as Gracie knelt over her and pulled her arm from her nightdress. It felt stiff yet lifeless, Gracie quickly noticed, as if it were no longer working in conjunction with her brain. Gracie rubbed her sister's arm gently and boldly plunged the prepared injection into the thin and pale limb. She then sat back.

'We should wait ten minutes before administering the counter to the flu I just gave Polly.'

They sat in silence, each continually glancing at the clock before them. Polly's eyes remained closed. Ernest, Alicia and Mrs Ford arrived in the carriage and joined the silent vigil. The minutes ticked by. Gracie's hands shook as she picked up the next injection.

'Tom. Tom, help me.'

He moved to her side and held her hand gently as she pushed the needle into Polly's skin.

All they could do now was wait.

Gracie awoke to the sound of the birds outside. She blinked in the bright sunlight. She was resting her head against Tom's chest, and lying on the floor. Tom was still asleep. Gracie sat up and saw that everyone was fast asleep on various chairs or bits of floorspace. In retrospect, it seemed unaccountable that they had all fallen asleep, given how worried they'd been.

But Polly, how was Polly?

Gracie crawled the short distance to where Polly still lay on the sofa; Jack's head was close to hers. Reaching down to touch her sister's brow, she felt that Polly's temperature seemed more normal, at least. Polly then opened her eyes.

'I've been awake for a little while, Gracie. I take it you have given me the cure. Either that or I am in Heaven.'

Tears spilled down Gracie's cheeks.

'Polly, how do you feel? You're talking . . . How do your limbs feel?'

'I feel as if a great weight has been lifted from me, Gracie. That is the best way I can describe it. I feel much better.'

'Oh Polly, please let it be so.'

'I want to thank you, Gracie, for . . . for everything.'

'Polly, it is nothing, you would have done the same for me—'

'Yes,' Polly cut in, 'I am thankful for all that you have done to make me well, but I also want to thank you for not going.'

'For not going? Going? Going where, Polly?'

'I don't know, I really don't, but I always just had the impression that you were never really here in the way we were. That you were preparing to leave us all forever. Every time you left the room I panicked, thinking you might never come back. Remember how I always used to follow you about when we were younger?'

'Yes.' Gracie began to cry. 'I remember. Oh, don't worry anymore. I'm here for good.'

'Promise?'

'I promise.'

Gracie gripped Polly's hand. Jack then awakened and cried for joy.

It all seemed too good to be true, but when a further test was carried out upon Polly, she was found to be clear of both the ter and the influenza virus.

It was over.

Tom and Gracie would take to London not only their vaccine to stop those still healthy from contracting ter, but also their cure.

And so the legend of the celebrated Blakes began.

19.

Fulfilment

Tom and Gracie were rapturously received by a desperate London. Once they had displayed that their vaccination and cure did in fact work, by way of a highly nervous and toadyish young adviser to the prime minister, immediate steps were taken to dispatch the necessary details and samples to all parts of the kingdom. Other doctors and scientists would then prepare exactly the same combinations to be injected into those who lived locally to them.

The couple personally vaccinated those members of the royal family who had decided to remain in London and not seek refuge in Germany. The king then presented them with a carriage, as well as a newly vaccinated driver to boot, and they departed from London as quickly as they could. In Dawlish, they were received with amazement by Tom's family. They knew nothing of their son's achievements but were wild with happiness upon discovery—and Tom was just as happy to discover that they were all still alive and well.

He set quickly to work in his old town and, in the following weeks, he and Gracie vaccinated and cured hundreds of people who came to see them in Dawlish. He then bundled his parents, brother, sister-in-law and baby nephew, whom he had only just met in the last weeks, into his smart new carriage, wherein they all began the long journey to Bourton.

There were to be no more delays and no more distractions: amidst the hectic days, a few hours would be found for Gracie and Tom to marry and celebrate their happiness with their friends and family. Saint Lawrence's church would be decked with all of the flowers and greenery available to Bourton, and the neighbours were determined to ensure that their local heroes had a perfect day. Alicia and her friends made a beautiful dress for Gracie in remarkably quick time, as well as one for the fully recovered Polly. It was to be a winter wedding: seasonal dishes to suit every taste were prepared, kegs of beer were lifted from their long storage at the bottom of the tavern and local children made the most of being able to once again run up and down the main road outside of the Rainbow, now home to Tom and his family. A real feeling of festivity was palpable. The forthcoming wedding was for Gracie and Tom, of course, but the day was also a chance for the people of Bourton to celebrate their re-emergence into a world where they did not have to live in daily fear of sickness and loss. What better way to celebrate this second chance at life than with those two who had made it possible?

Gracie and Tom's wedding day was set for a Saturday, and on the Friday evening Gracie and Tom said goodbye to each other knowing that the next time they met would be in the church before they said their vows. Gracie kissed Tom's face, her hands on either side of his head, and looked serious as she met his eyes.

'You do realise,' she said, 'how much I love you? You don't think that—'

'Hush.' Tom pressed his finger to her lips. 'Enough of that. I know you love me, and why indeed should you not? I am quite a handsome fellow, you know, and my new standing in the community only renders my attractiveness more obvious to some, I have noticed.'

'Oh, it has, has it?' Gracie smiled. 'Well just you remember that I loved you when you were a bewildered young man torn between being a scientist and a lawyer. Would you appear as dashing poring over the paper's court reports?'

They laughed.

'Well, to me you would,' Gracie continued. 'I love you for all times and I'll . . . I'll refuse to vaccinate anyone who tries to take you from me! And don't you forget that I cut quite a fine figure myself!'

'Forget?' Tom caught her in his arms. 'Why, my every waking moment is filled with happiness because I met you! I'll never let you go. I can't remember my life without you.'

Gracie and Tom separated then, pulled away by their respective families. Gracie enjoyed a last dinner with her family as Miss Gracie Arundel and departed for bed earlier than usual, to ensure, as her mother remonstrated, that she be as alert as possible tomorrow in order to make the most of her most special of days.

'So no reading, mind,' her mother called to her. 'I want that candle extinguished as soon as you are in bed!'

Gracie prepared for bed quickly as it was cold, but she wasn't tired in the slightest. She was far too nervous to be tired, although she hardly knew why. What was there to be nervous about, after all? Excited, yes, but not nervous. She heard all the familiar sounds of her family's retiring for the night, and then silence descended upon the house. She wondered what Tom was doing now, at this instant, and laughed at the thought of his mother's ushering him off to bed too. How strange that this was the night before her wedding! At long last, she was to be married. Gracie considered that she had been waiting to be married longer than anyone could ever know. All of those years spent with Adam . . .

No, she was not going to think about Adam tonight. She plumped her pillows again and quickly fell asleep for she was, in fact, more tired than she knew.

In what seemed to be the middle of the night, Gracie suddenly woke. *Perhaps it was an owl?* she thought. She turned over to try to return to sleep. Then a sweet, floral smell made her sit upright immediately. Her heart pounded for joy.

And there she sat at the foot of her bed. Cianna. Although the room should have been pitch black as no candles were lit, Gracie could somehow see her perfectly.

'Oh, my dear Cianna,' Gracie whispered, flinging herself into her friend's welcoming arms. 'I did not dare think that you might come to see me before my wedding. I did not want to be disappointed. Now everything really is perfect! Oh, I've missed you so. And how wonderful you look.'

Cianna smiled and stroked Gracie's dark hair, a strong contrast to the white of her nightdress. Cianna was dressed in a long loose gown of yellow silk, and a blue ribbon tied back her own dark hair. She said nothing and allowed Gracie to continue talking.

'I wanted to see you so much, and I've always wondered when you might come to see me again. I longed for it but I dreaded it too—yes, I did, because the next visit was also going to be the last. Is it, Cianna? Is this really to be the last time I see you?'

'Yes, dear Gracie, it is. Now, no sad faces! Not on the eve of your wedding. Your Cianna has come to wish you joy.'

'Thank you. What have you been doing? Have . . . have you been assigned to anyone else yet?'

'No, not yet. I have been living with my people. I have been happy amongst all of my dear friends.'

'I see. How did you know this was the night before my wedding? Did you always know this would be the day you would visit me?'

'No, my Gracie, but I am very glad that it is. I did not know whether you and your Tom would find a cure for this ter. The outcome, as always, was a surprise to me too. I resolved to come and see you again either before the time of your own death from ter, if that was to have happened, or at this time. How much happier it is the latter! I am proud of you, Gracie. You did well; nobody could have done any better. You will long be remembered for your achievements, and it should be all the more satisfying because you so deserve all of the accolades and acclaim. Well done, my friend!'

Cianna hugged Gracie to her again, and Gracie felt it had been no time at all since she first saw Cianna, although of course it had been—a lifetime ago. But she had changed so much, become someone else entirely, whereas Cianna, she marvelled, was exactly the same.

'No, you are wrong, Gracie. I too have changed, and it is due to you. I have learned a great deal from my time spent silently watching you and during the moments we shared in conversation and friendship.'

'Learned from me? It's difficult for me to imagine what you might have learned from me.' Gracie laughed. 'But if you have been with your people, how did you know that I was about to be married?'

'I knew it,' Cianna stated enigmatically, 'and I would have felt if you were about to die. I will, one day, feel precisely the moment you are no longer alive. I knew you had beaten the virus too. I knew that you won and I felt proud of you through every moment of your success.'

'We really are connected then, even if we don't see one another. You know, I believed so strongly you were with me the moment we discovered that we'd possibly found a vaccination for the virus.'

'I knew it,' Cianna said readily. 'I felt you and knew of your success.'

'And will it always be like this? Will our connectedness last for always, until . . . until I die?'

'It will. Every momentous moment of your life, your Cianna will know of it and feel all of your happiness, all of your sadness.'

They sat close on the end of Gracie's bed for some time, speaking of all manner of things. Finally, Cianna pulled a familiar red object from the pocket of her gown.

'Your bell, Cianna. How wonderful to see it again. And have you seen Nino recently?'

Cianna smiled ruefully and admitted she had. Gracie laughed at her friend's admission of probably the only weakness she had ever possessed.

'Now,' Cianna said more seriously, 'this is my wedding gift to you. Take it, Gracie; it is yours for all time. Remember your Cianna when you look at it and remember the love she shared with the maker of this bell. May it also remind you of the love you feel for Tom, and felt for Adam. We are all of us connected though we might not know it. Here, take it. It is now yours.'

Gracie held the red silk box in her hands a moment before opening it and feeling the cold glass beneath her fingers. It was beautiful, but she could not accept it. It was Cianna's great treasure . . .

'Take it, Gracie. I want you to have it. It is right you should have it.'

Gracie understood not to resist any further and instead nodded her head and kissed her friend in thanks.

'I'll love and protect it, Cianna, but, oh, you are now leaving?'

'I am. You will soon fall into the most refreshing of sleeps, from which you will awaken as bright-eyed as a child! Enjoy your day, Gracie, and do your utmost to have a happy and purposeful life.'

Gracie felt suddenly panic-stricken. She clutched her friend's hands in anguish. Cianna spoke softly.

'Goodbye, my dear friend.'

Cianna led Gracie back into her bed and tucked the covers around her.

'Dream the most pleasant of dreams, my little doctor.'

As Cianna kissed her for the last time, Gracie breathed in her lovely fragrance as deeply as she could.

'Goodbye, Cianna. Thank you for everything.'

They smiled at each other one final time, sharing a look of comradeship as well as friendship, and then Cianna was gone.

Gracie snuggled deeper into her bed in the now dark room. Cianna's beautiful smell lingered. She held the bell in its box to her chest before opening up one of her bedside drawers and placing it safely inside. To have this bell, so long a part of Cianna, made her feel as if she were still close to her friend, and she was glad for it. Then, just as Cianna had said, she fell into a deep and untroubled sleep, from which her mother wakened her with an exquisitely prepared wedding breakfast.

Mrs Gracie Blake kept a firm hold of her tall husband's arm as they stepped out of the church. Her long dress of white silk adorned with silver and red embroidered flowers was amongst the loveliest she had owned, and she lifted her small veil higher to take a good look at those who surrounded them. Everyone looked so happy for them, and Gracie felt as happy at this moment as she knew it was possible to feel. This was it, this was a moment to savour and look back upon, a moment to make all others seem worthwhile.

That night, as she lay in Tom's arms and watched him sleep, she reached across into her drawer and grasped Cianna's unbreakable bell, the symbol of her and Cianna's love. It was well done indeed.

There was no honeymoon period for the Blakes; rather, they reverted to their task of vaccinating or curing as many members of the public as possible. A significant number of eminent individuals, including—they were gratified to hear—Dr Jenner, now possessed the necessary means to begin this work themselves. All combined, they attempted to eradicate ter from the entirety of Britain. Gracie and Tom also knew that samples and instructions had been lodged in London for shipment to Europe as and when requested. Dr Jenner and the Blakes were covering the county of Gloucestershire between them, and Britain was slowly regaining some control as the government and authorities assisted in permanently destroying ter.

The ter vaccination received a more receptive response than Jenner's smallpox vaccination for two main reasons: ter had no history of earlier treatment—and therefore there were no practitioners to upset—and, feared as the dreaded smallpox was, it was no certain killer like ter. In due course, the ter vaccination would encourage the vaccination mentality, and people would more readily embrace the notion of being treated for smallpox too. As such, the Blakes would have a direct effect on the smaller number of people to die of smallpox, although the reverse was also true, as Jenner had certainly influenced Gracie and Tom's work and findings in all manner of ways. In later years, these three scientists would come to be regarded together, and any discussion of the Blakes would invariably lead to mention of Jenner, and vice versa. Where once Jenner had stood alone as the father of immunology, he was now joined by Gracie and Tom, and this trio provided the origin of research for all future scholars and scientists of the topic.

Despite Tom's earlier misgivings at the idea of meeting an idol, he and Gracie met the amiable Dr Jenner not long after ter was successfully eradicated, and they enjoyed the friendliest of relationships with him. Indeed, in the years following those in which the old doctor became an expert in fruit cultivation, the Blakes always had a pot of preserve on their breakfast table from his own garden. As an older man, and in his capacity as president of the Royal Society, Sir Thomas Blake would take great pleasure in introducing his esteemed colleague, Jenner, as a guest speaker at one of the society's annual meetings.

As for Gracie, and her unusual historical position as a female scientist, she encountered all of the usual prejudices associated with her gender, although those who actually conversed with her usually agreed that she had not only a formidable brain for a woman, but a formidable brain generally. Her husband never allowed his name to take precedence over hers in any pamphlet or book they jointly published, and her fame and persona encouraged many young girls to enter into a field they previously would have felt themselves barred from entering. Prevented from becoming a Fellow of the Royal Society herself due to her gender, Gracie concentrated on her studies and did not let such things trouble her unduly. Nobody, not even she, could alter everything she did not like about the world.

Gracie and Tom lived within Bourton and London for the rest of their lives, possessing homes in both places. Bourton itself changed strikingly as a result of its most famous residents. It was not unusual for travellers from elsewhere in England to find their way to Bourton, where they hoped to be personally vaccinated by the Blakes. When Gracie and Tom were at the Rainbow, the queue would snake outside and down the main road. As a result, Bourton became a prominent and wealthier place as new inns and taverns sprung up to accommodate the visitors.

One day, near the beginning of Gracie and Tom's public vaccination days, a little wagon trundled its way into Bourton. It carried a man, a woman and a little boy. They left the horse and wagon tied up and took their place in the queue. A few hours later, they were admitted to the Rainbow, and the man rolled his shirtsleeves up and cheerfully submitted to Tom's injecting of his arm. Gracie dealt with the woman while the little boy, no more than five or six years old, wandered around the Rainbow, open-mouthed at all of the books, microscopes and test tubes his piercing eyes greedily took in.

'Nothing to it, Marian.'

The man stood behind his wife and placed his big, strong hands on her shoulders as she closed her eyes and turned away. Gracie pushed the needle into her skin as gently as she could.

'No, no,' his wife agreed, 'that wasn't too bad.' She continued in a whisper. 'But Ben, we must encourage the little one to think it will not hurt at all.' Then she called out. 'Gabriel! Gabriel, dear, come to mother and let the nice lady have a look at your arm, won't you?'

Gracie turned to smile at the supremely self-possessed child, who trotted over to his mother immediately and climbed onto her lap. He tried to roll his sleeve up himself, and when he could not, he let his mother help him while he, now shy in the close company of grown-up strangers, studied Gracie carefully. Gracie patted his head and asked him if he knew any nursery rhymes. He nodded and said he knew lots.

'And what is your favourite then?'

'"Ride a cock-horse to Banbury Cross". Because that's where I live.'

'Oh, you come from Banbury, do you? And do you like any others?'

'Yes, "Doctor Foster".'

'Ah, yes, I know that one too. You have very good taste. Now, if you say those rhymes for me I promise that by the time you have finished them both I will be finished having a look at your arm.'

'All right, I'll start now. "Ride a cock-horse to Banbury Cross . . ."'

As Gabriel recited, Gracie injected the child, who flinched only a little as the needle broke his skin.

'What a brave boy you are. And how nicely you recited those lovely nursery rhymes. Here, have a stick of candy as a reward.'

He took the candy and grinned as he jumped off his mother's knee and continued exploring the most wonderful place he had ever seen. To his parents, Gracie explained the influenza symptoms they would all likely develop, and that they should disappear in due course.

'Thank you, miss. Thank you.' Ben Lockhart smiled and nodded. 'I can't thank you and this good gentleman enough for all you've done, not just in finding the vaccination and the cure and all that but, well, for not charging people for your help. Not many people would do that, I'm sure, and although I could find the money to pay for me and mine to be made safe, I know there are lots that couldn't.'

Gracie and Tom smiled and said it was entirely their pleasure.

'And you hail from Banbury, then?' Gracie said.

'Yes,' Marian answered. 'We'll arrive back home late tonight. We could have gone to our own doctor for our vaccinations but we wanted to come to see you. I hope you don't mind?'

'No, not at all,' Tom said. 'Why, Banbury is only twenty-five miles away. You're almost local,' he said jokingly.

'Yes, I suppose we are,' Marian said. 'But, well, it means a lot to us to have Gabriel made as safe as possible. He's our only child and our pride and joy. I . . . I can't have any more children, you see, so it was worth our travelling this little extra.'

'We're glad to help you. But what a clever-looking little chap you have,' Tom stated.

'Aye, a farmer's son but you'd never think it.' Ben proudly held out his hand to his son. 'Always reading and puzzling things out. Would you like to grow up one day to be a scientist yourself, son?'

Gabriel thought for a few seconds and looked stuck for an answer, but then his face cleared and he pointed to Gracie and Tom and smiled.

'Is that what you are? Sci . . . What is the word? Scientists?'

'Yes.' Gracie grinned. 'We are scientists.'

'Yes, Father, then I want to be a scientist too.'

They all laughed, and then the Lockharts departed and the next people were ushered in.

Gracie and Tom were handsomely rewarded for their endeavours and success against ter. They were a famous couple in their lifetimes and arguably even more famous in the years to follow, and Angelus smiled when he saw Gracie's portrait on the very door that she had once touched and exited through. Theirs was a happy marriage and of the best kind; Gracie never regretted her decision to remain with Tom, although she would always think of Adam on certain melancholy occasions, such as his birthday or their anniversary. Polly and Jack returned to London in due course and soon raised a fine family of sons and daughters. Gracie and Tom continued to pursue science energetically and, although they achieved other significant moments in their professional lives, they would, perhaps unsurprisingly, never again reach the peaks that they did in 1803. Gracie continued to make her annual visits to Northleach on the date she originally arrived in her new world. She would take herself there alone, with Cianna's bell hidden in her pocket, and sit on the same patch she had rested upon as a young girl. As the years passed, her prior life, Cianna, Angelus and his corridor seemed almost too fantastic to be real, and for a few brief milliseconds she would consider whether it had all been a dream. Then she would smile and recall a look or a feeling or a smell and know that her life had been blessed indeed.

20.

Birth

The woman sat upright in bed and laid her Jane Austen novel by her side. Looking straight ahead at the machine before her, she smiled, shook her head and then resumed her reading. Ten minutes later she closed the book again and listened keenly to the growing sound of footsteps that she recognised as being the familiar tread of her husband climbing the stairs of their building. Soon he would be with her in this room. Sure enough, a few moments later, she heard a key enter the lock of their front door and knew that her husband would close the door as carefully as he could. The bedroom door opened gently and his head appeared.

'Hello, darling. I thought you might be asleep so I tried to be quiet.' He deposited some packages at the door and moved towards her. 'How are you feeling? Reading again?' He gave her a kiss.

'Yes, I couldn't sleep anymore. Did you get everything we needed?'

'I certainly did. Oh, but I had to go somewhere else for the onions as Mr Baxter didn't have any left.'

'No onions, how strange? Did you only go to the shops?'

'Yes.'

'And did you get your journal?'

'Yes. Looks good too. Fascinating article on early microscopes.'

His wife shook her head uninterestedly.

'And how is our little bundle?' he asked. 'Sleeping like an angel, I see.'

'All she does is sleep or cry. How tiresome babies are really.'

'No, not tiresome, just delightful.'

He turned fully around to gaze at his tiny baby daughter, who lay sleeping in a cot by the bed, and reached out a finger to stroke her soft cheek. His wife automatically scolded him, saying he might wake her, but then shrugged.

'You might as well,' she said. 'She's due her next feed in any case.'

'It does seem such a crime to disturb such beautiful repose. What on earth is she dreaming of, I wonder?'

'I don't know. I should imagine babies are too undeveloped to have dreams. But what's that other package I see amongst those bags?'

'Ah.' He smiled. 'It is a surprise. Close your eyes and I'll give it to you.'

'Oh, really! Something else? You know we're supposed to be saving.'

'But this was something that could not be resisted. We simply had to have it! Stop worrying about money, Kitty dear. I do okay and what is money for, after all, if not to make life pleasanter?'

'It is for saving, you fool! I want a good education for our girl—'

'Now don't scold me. Close your eyes like a good girl and hold out your hands.'

His wife sighed again but did as she was told, trying to hide the fact that she was excited. She felt a flat object being placed into her hands and, on opening her eyes, she knew exactly what he'd bought her before she even ripped off the brown paper. It was a record.

'Oh, Rodney, you are incorrigible, you know! You've already bought so many records for the gramophone. And it's only a week old!'

'Yes, but this record gives us the music to that beautiful Strauss waltz that we danced to when we courted. Look, it is the same one.'

'But we danced to so many tunes—are you going to buy them all?'

'If I can. Here, let me play it for you now.'

He took the record over to the shiny new gramophone player, which stood at the foot of the bed. After dusting down the varnished wood lovingly with his handkerchief, paying particular attention to the little dog image his wife found so sweet, he placed the record into position.

'You and your machines,' his wife muttered. 'But, wait, the baby—we'll disturb her.'

'But you said she was due to waken. What better way to do so than to the strains of a Viennese waltz?'

The music began to play, and Rodney joined his wife on the bed and asked her again if she liked the gift he had purchased for her in celebration of the birth of their first baby a week ago.

'I love the gramophone, yes. But I think it is a gift to suit your interests more than mine, if truth be told.'

'Well, let it be seen as a gift for the whole family then. A wonderful piece of machinery, brand new 1921 model,' he enthused. 'The little one will get pleasure from it too, in due course.'

'The little one! We really need to think of a name for her, Rodney.'

'I know, I know. Let's finally do so then, before the day is out.'

He lay with his head on his wife's lap and thought for a few moments.

'What about Gracie?' he said.

'Gracie? Why . . . Oh I see, after the scientist, Gracie Blake?'

'Just so. It's a nice name, isn't it?' he asked plaintively.

'Was it her real name?'

'She was christened Grace Arundel, but she was always known as Gracie. In fact, I've never known of her being referred to as Grace.'

'Mmmh. I would not want my child to be known as Gracie. It's not a real name to me. But Grace is rather nice.'

'I like Grace,' her husband agreed. 'And what better start to life can we give our baby than to name her after the mother of modern science? A noble pedigree, worthy of a child of yours, my pet.'

'And you promise she will always be known as Grace, not Gracie?'

'Certainly. Are we agreed then?'

'Grace. Grace. Yes, I like it more and more. It even sits well with our surname, which not every name would.'

The baby began to move in her cot as the bars of the waltz drew to a close.

Rodney jumped from the bed to switch the machine off and picked the now crying baby up on his return. He held her to his chest for a moment before handing her to her mother for her next feed.

'There you are, sweetheart, go to your mother, little Grace.'

Kitty took hold of her crying child and smoothed down her fine hair with her hand.

'Hush now, Grace. Yes, that is your name and you must become acquainted with it.'

The baby stopped crying and began to gurgle. It was sealed. The future movie star, Grace Abbot, seemed satisfied with her name. One day, in the years to follow, she would win the Academy Award for playing her namesake, Gracie Blake, on the silver screen. The look of pride on her father's face as she placed the award into his hands would render the moment a memorable one in Grace's long and spectacular life.

Postscript, 2043

The Science Museum in London was busy. The family paid for their special exhibition tickets and squeezed past hordes of tourists being asked by harassed security staff to put away their talking key-ring cameras. The main exhibition featured the Blakes, as 2043 marked the 200th anniversary of the death of one of them.

It was the school summer holidays, and Lily had liked the idea of spending one Sunday doing something educational with her children. She'd brought her elderly but active father along with her husband and two young boys, as the family usually spent Sundays with him. None of them really knew much about either science or the Blakes although obviously they knew the main facts—that they'd been married and were mostly remembered for ridding Britain of a deadly virus.

They made their way round the displays slowly. Indeed, it was so busy they had to wait their turn to view the various objects held behind glass. The white lab coat worn by Thomas Blake in his later years was attracting a lot of attention, and Lily randomly thought that, to be so old, it still looked very white and clean. She shouted to her eldest boy, Charlie, to come and look at a detailed illustration of the effects of the ter syndrome, thinking that words such as *paralysis*, *mute* and *death* would act as a hook to capture his attention and encourage him to inadvertently learn something. Her youngest, Billy, was already staring aghast at a portrait of a smallpox sufferer.

Lily was enjoying the exhibition, although most of the science went over her head. She preferred to read and learn about the more human and ordinary side of the Blakes—what they looked like, what their families were like, what they liked and disliked, etc. No photographs of the Blakes existed, but there were several paintings to examine, and Lily thought them an extremely handsome couple.

Handsome, yes, but you can somehow tell that their faces belong in the past, she thought. *People don't look like that anymore.* There were some photographs of family members and friends, including a photo of Gracie Blake's sister, Polly, when she was an old woman. Lily couldn't make up her mind as to whether there was any family resemblance. She looked around and ordered her two children to keep firmly by her side. Where was Phil? Ah, there, looking at the microscopes in more detail than she cared to. And Dad, where was he? Lily saw her father closely examining the painting of the young Blakes.

'Yes, Billy, I know you've got money to spend in the shop afterwards.' Her attention was immediately drawn back to her children.

Adam stared at the painting of Gracie Blake, commissioned when she was newly married, not long after the discovery of the cure and vaccination for ter syndrome. He had seen some images of her before, of course—there were the statues of the Blakes in Green Park, but never this painting. He guessed it was very lifelike as everything seemed so in proportion and realistic.

The eyes, they seemed to pierce straight into his consciousness. He looked around and attempted to quell his excited and fiercely beating heart. Young Gracie Blake was exactly like the woman he had met in a cafe on a rainy Saturday many, many years before. The woman he had taken some pains to find but had never discovered. The woman he had never been able to forget. And now here she was before him!

Adam frowned. Was he losing his mind? He examined the portrait again. Her smile, her hair, the lines of her face and body—all seemed to scream recognition.

Feeling unendurably sad, he resolved to look in the shop later to see if they had a postcard of this painting. Reluctantly, he moved on and examined a display case that contained objects found in a locked trunk belonging to Gracie Blake. He sighed so deeply on viewing one of the exhibits that the glass before him became steamed from his breath and another visitor glanced at him disapprovingly. Adam saw nothing but the little rag doll with the purple dress that was numbered exhibit nine and detailed to have held sentimental value for the scientist, perhaps belonging originally to one of her nieces. The woman in the cafe, she had given Lily a doll that looked *exactly* like this one save for the fact it had a yellow dress. He still had it at home. The woman had told him she had two dolls in her bag, he remembered.

Some minutes later, Lily found her father still standing in front of the portrait of the young Blakes. She placed her hand on one of his shoulders and asked him if he was ready to leave. When he didn't respond, she took a closer look at him and saw that he was white and trembling, and his eyes were filled with tears.

'Dad? Dad, what is it?'

He shook his head and was about to speak but instead sighed and pointed towards the painting.

'That was love,' he said. 'That was love.'

Lily hugged her father and, thinking that he was referring to the love the Blakes evidently shared, she wondered at this strange proof that her father could be so romantic.

On a much quieter day, a woman wearing a long dark velvet coat, the hood up over her face, swept into the same museum and looked around the Blake exhibition. Moving from display case to display case, she appeared to be paying due attention to every word and item. She kept her head down mostly but an observant bystander, should he or she have chosen to, could have at certain moments caught a clear side view of the woman's impossibly perfect features.

Coming to stand before the portrait that had so captivated Adam, she gazed at it for a long time and recognised it as being the one now hanging on one of Angelus's doors. She moved on and arrived at the section containing the items found in a trunk after Gracie's death—objects apparently of some value or importance to Gracie, although even the most knowledgeable Blake biographer could find no connection between them and their owner's life. They wondered why, for example, Gracie had kept a violet drawstring purse full of shells? Or a complete set of works by Jane Austen? Had this novelist meant so much to her? A topaz cross, pretty and very much of the period—a gift from Tom, perhaps? A rag doll that once probably belonged to a niece. But the item they all wondered most about was an exquisitely made glass bell dating back to the Italian Renaissance period. How on earth had she come to possess this? Nobody had arrived at a satisfactory explanation, and the reason was lost, they sadly surmised, in the midst of time though doubtless, there lay an interesting story behind it.

Cianna's pulse quickened as her bell lay in her sights again. She closed her eyes and breathed in the moment for a long time. Then she turned and made her way out of the museum knowing precisely where she was going.

Finis